A FABLEHAVEN ADVENTURE

DRAGONWATCH
WRATH OF THE DRAGON KING

BRANDON MULL

ILLUSTRATED BY
BRANDON DORMAN

ALADDIN

NEW YORK   LONDON   TORONTO   SYD.

D0062096

This book is a work of fiction. Any references to historical events, real people, or real places are used fictitiously. Other names, characters, places, and events are products of the author's imagination, and any resemblance to actual events or places or persons, living or dead, is entirely coincidental.

ALADDIN
An imprint of Simon & Schuster Children's Publishing Division
1230 Avenue of the Americas, New York, New York 10020
First Aladdin paperback edition September 2019
Text copyright © 2018 by Brandon Mull
Illustrations copyright © 2018 by Brandon Dorman
All rights reserved, including the right of reproduction in whole or in part in any form.
ALADDIN and related logo are registered trademarks of Simon & Schuster, Inc.
For information about special discounts for bulk purchases, please contact
Simon & Schuster Special Sales at 1-866-506-1949 or business@simonandschuster.com.
The Simon & Schuster Speakers Bureau can bring authors to your live event.
For more information or to book an event contact the Simon & Schuster Speakers Bureau
at 1-866-248-3049 or visit our website at www.simonspeakers.com.
The text of this book was set in Goudy Old Style.
Manufactured in the United States of America 0820 OFF
2 4 6 8 10 9 7 5 3
This book has been cataloged with the Library of Congress.
ISBN 978-1-4814-8505-0 (pbk)

WRATH OF THE DRAGON KING

Contents

CONTENTS

CHAPTER ONE

Old Friends

The red-maned dragon coiled in the courtyard, rippling scales flashing in the sunlight, tail swishing lazily. Prowling forward, the lengthy body unfurled, several sets of legs working to bring the leonine head ever closer to the lone boy. Yawning, the dragon displayed a jagged array of yellowed fangs surrounding a fat tongue.

"What's the matter?" the dragon inquired in a slightly mocking tone. "Speak. Move."

Large nostrils approached the boy's face and flared, sniffing. The nearby mouth was probably big enough to swallow him whole. Or at least to bite off the top half of his body.

Seth willed himself to lean away. To lift an arm. To murmur a reply.

His body refused to respond. He could not twitch a

finger. He could not glance away. He was utterly paralyzed by dragon fear.

"Nothing?" the dragon asked. "You're not really in any danger."

I know, Seth wanted to say. *You're my assistant.* Marat usually stayed in human form, but he had made an exception today after Seth had requested a chance to test his ability to resist dragon fear. If his sister, Kendra, could do it, there had to be a way!

"Come on, Seth," chimed a little voice from his pocket. Calvin, champion of the nipsies, could keep his composure in the presence of a dragon, and he was only a couple of inches tall. "Try smiling. When I was just a boy, I remember my papa could smile his way out of anything."

Seth could hear Calvin but couldn't turn his head to see him. Seth could breathe. He could feel his heart beating. But his mouth refused to form words. His muscles would not budge, not even to pull his lips into a smile. He was a dragon tamer while holding Kendra's hand. But now he was speechless and immovable. This wasn't fair. She could maintain her composure while confronting a dragon alone—even in the presence of Celebrant, the Dragon King.

What made all this even more humiliating was that this encounter was staged! Seth knew the dragon was a friend and meant him no harm. There was no rational reason to fear. Why couldn't his intellect overpower his instincts? Was he really this spineless?

The long body reeled in as the dragon shrank into a

mild Asian man in elaborate silken robes. The climate of fear evaporated and Seth could move.

"I wasn't scared," Seth insisted.

"Very few can resist dragon terror," Marat said.

"Sure, I was frozen," Seth admitted, "but I wasn't afraid."

"Your mind was free?" Marat asked. "That is something. But I still could have killed you at my leisure."

"Am I just not desperate enough?" Seth asked.

"Petrified people are routinely devoured by dragons," Marat said. "They remain immobilized throughout the process. Trust me, all of them are plenty desperate."

"What made the difference for Kendra?" Seth wondered.

"She is fairykind," Marat said. "She found a way to bring her power to bear. As a shadow charmer, you might in time do likewise."

"Any tips?" Seth asked. "I need to master this. The dragons are madder than ever, especially at me after we got the scepter."

"I'm no shadow charmer," Marat said. "And I don't feel dragon terror. You need a different tutor. Have you asked your sister?"

"No way," Seth said. "Her power is different from mine. What's she going to teach me? How to befriend fairies?"

"Kendra could teach anyone a great many things," Marat said. "Perhaps your reluctance relates to her being your sister?"

"Of course it does!" Seth said. "Who wants their sister to teach them anything?"

"My sister helped me learn arithmetic," Calvin piped up from Seth's pocket.

"Big deal," Seth said. "That's just math. Kendra can talk to dragons alone! And I can't."

"Your nipsie might have ideas," Marat said.

"I'm not sure I can help much," Calvin said. "I don't have techniques like holding my breath or crossing my fingers. My only advice is not to get scared."

"You don't get scared of dragons?" Seth asked.

"Not to where it freezes me," Calvin said. "I can't explain how or why except I don't really get scared of anything."

"Really?" Seth asked.

"I know dragons could kill me," Calvin clarified. "I don't want to die or get maimed. The danger makes me alert, not scared."

"Marat, I want to try again," Seth said. "Get ready for alertness."

"Could you perhaps pause your exercises for a moment?" a voice asked from behind Seth.

He turned to find Agad emerging from a door into the courtyard. The wizard, dressed in traveling clothes and a cloak, was followed by Newel, Doren, and Tanu.

The arrival caught Seth so off guard that he hardly knew where to look first. It had been longest since he had seen Tanu, so his eyes settled there. The Samoan potion master wore a large pack, and several pouches dangled from his belt. Still broad and thick, he looked a tad leaner than when Seth had last seen him.

"Tanu!" Seth cried. "Have you lost weight?"

"Not on purpose," he replied with a pained smile. "I have been swimming in choppy waters. Things are messy out there."

"We're here too," Newel said with a wave.

"Been eating well," Doren added, patting his belly.

Seth had seen both satyrs just a couple of days before when he had gone back to Fablehaven through the teleportation barrel. "What are you guys doing here?"

"Things were getting dull without you around," Newel said.

"We like to be where the action is," Doren said.

"Since when?" Seth challenged. "You guys run from everything."

Newel squinted one eye. "We like to be *in the vicinity* of the action. Not necessarily getting our hands dirty."

"Or chopped off," Doren added.

"Life can be like television from the proper distance," Newel explained.

"Bringing the satyrs was my idea," Agad said. "Seth, I thought you would find value in their companionship during these troubled times."

"You told us there were acres of food," Doren accused.

"The storerooms beneath this keep are all I promised," Agad mumbled.

"Remember our road trip to see the Singing Sisters?" Newel asked Seth. "You introduced us to fast food! And convenience stores! Any time we get permission to leave our designated preserve is a thrill."

"Especially if the food is good," Doren said. "And the company."

"Any news about Bracken?" Seth asked.

Agad exchanged a glance with Tanu. "No glad tidings,"

the wizard said. "He had been captured, and we found where he was being held, but he was already gone by the time we arrived. We have no idea who took him."

Seth hated to hear Bracken was lost, and he knew the news would devastate his sister. "Do you think he's alive?"

"I suspect so," Agad said. "A quick examination of the horn he left with Kendra will confirm."

Seth walked up to Tanu. "Did you help find him?"

"I helped find his empty cell," Tanu said. "We were trying. Soaring Cliffs has become a perdition of rampaging dragons. We were lucky to get out alive."

"Sounds like the kind of adventure best viewed from a distance," Doren commented.

"That's one way to put it," Tanu said. "The world is turning upside down. I understand there has been commotion here as well."

"The dragons tested our defenses," Seth said. "It looked bad for a while. Kendra and I recovered a scepter that strengthened the keep's protections."

"And you made a firmer enemy of Celebrant in the process," Marat said.

"The Dragon King's enmity was inevitable," Agad said. "We are facing a global rebellion."

"Wait a minute," Newel said. "You told us there was unrest. Not a worldwide rebellion."

"Unrest here," Agad said. "A global rebellion is under way. We're laboring to stop it. By no means is the uprising complete."

"You can tell because we're not all dead yet," Tanu said.

"But Blackwell Keep is secure," Doren checked. "And the storerooms."

"Locked up tight," Agad said.

A long, low note was blown on a horn, the hollow sound gradually growing deeper before fading.

"What was that?" Doren asked.

"Start of the satyr hunt," Tanu said with a grin.

"The proudhorn," Marat said, turning his gaze toward the sky. "An unexpected dragon approaches."

"I think I may have left a scarf back at Fablehaven," Newel said, edging back toward the door. "A real important one. Striped."

"I'll lend a hand," Doren offered.

"The dragon can't harm us," Agad said. "I told you the keep is protected."

"Which dragon?" Seth asked.

"Let's find out," Marat said.

CHAPTER TWO

Invitation

When the proudhorn blew, Kendra was sitting cross-legged atop the keep's outer wall, her back to the battlements, facing a semicircle of nine fairies. All but one had dragonfly wings. The other was the stockiest, with wings like a beetle. They all seemed generally hardier than the Fablehaven fairies, still lithe and lovely, but somewhat more muscular and noticeably warier.

Most of the fairies took flight at the sound of the horn, wings becoming a blur. The others were on their feet, ready to spring. Kendra stood and looked outward to find a gleaming dragon, smaller than most, gliding toward the Perch—a tower at the edge of the keep, designated for conversing with dragons.

"It's just Raxtus," one of the fairies chirped.

"He's acting strange lately," another remarked.

"Almost like a dragon," a third said with a giggle. The other fairies tittered.

"I should go," Kendra said. "He must have come to talk."

"I thought *we* were talking," one of the fairies complained.

"It could be an emergency," Kendra said. "Thank you for attending. We'll meet again tomorrow. You have your assignments. Spread the word to the other fairies—I want to know about any suspicious dragon activity."

Kendra turned and started trotting toward the Perch. Behind her, she heard fairies murmuring about how bossy she was but decided to ignore them. Fairies were hard to manage, but they could move around Wyrmroost with relative freedom and were small enough to be practically invisible to dragons. Because of Kendra's fairykind status, they had to obey her, and so they could make excellent spies.

The situation with the dragons had become critical. Kendra had openly defied Celebrant, and it was only a matter of time before the Dragon King struck back. Where and how the dragons would retaliate seemed impossible to predict, but Kendra suspected that when it came, it would potentially be catastrophic. It really didn't matter if the fairies complained about her, as long as they helped monitor the dragons.

Henrick the alcetaur, gamekeeper of Wyrmroost, came loping along the top of the wall to Kendra. He had the shaggy body of a moose, but from where the neck would normally be, there sprouted the torso of a man with broad shoulders, strong arms, and a stern face. Kendra had grown to trust Henrick after he had helped her and Seth retrieve the scepter and return it to Blackwell Keep.

Reaching down, Henrick scooped up Kendra and deposited her astride his back. "This is the dragon you know?" he asked.

"Raxtus, yes," Kendra said. Normally she would have been thrilled to see her old friend, but during their last conversation, she had found he tended to side with Celebrant, his father, on the subject of the dragon rebellion. "I wonder what he wants to tell us."

Air rushed past Kendra as Henrick zoomed along the wall. He clattered to a halt at the Perch just as Raxtus was about to land. The original Perch had recently been demolished by Celebrant, but Seth had used a portable tower obtained from the giant Thronis to replace it. Kendra slid off the alcetaur.

Quiet as a whisper, Raxtus landed with a graceful swoop. Kendra knew firsthand that the dragon was a talented aerialist. Unusually small for a dragon, his body was comparable to the dimensions of a large horse, though his wings, neck, and tail added to his size. His glittering armor of silvery white scales reflected a prismatic sheen that hinted at his unusual origin—Raxtus had been hatched by fairies.

"Hi, Kendra," Raxtus said without his usual enthusiasm, his voice like a group of teenage boys speaking in unison. "Can the moose guy go? I can speak more freely if we're alone."

"Could be a trick," Henrick warned, one hand straying to his bow.

"I'll take that risk," Kendra said. "Can we have some space? What's an arrow supposed to do? I'm not sure any dragon has tougher scales than Raxtus."

Henrick gave a humph and clomped away.

Raxtus brought his head close to Kendra, the stream-lined surface gleaming brighter than chrome. "Thanks for the compliment, but I know my dad has harder scales, and I suspect several other—"

"Stop being humble," Kendra said.

"Are you doing all right?" Raxtus asked.

"I'm not hurt," Kendra said. "Dragons all over the world are rebelling. Bracken went missing when Soaring Cliffs fell." She clenched her fists at the mention of Bracken, will-ing away her tears and the sudden clogged feeling in her throat.

"Sorry to hear that," Raxtus said. "I tried to warn you."

"I remember," Kendra said.

"You could still get away," Raxtus said. "This is just get-ting started. It will only get worse."

"That means somebody has to stop it," Kendra said. "It's my job now. I'm the caretaker of Wyrmroost."

"Find a replacement," Raxtus said.

Kendra sighed. "Do you think they would be using chil-dren as caretakers if they had replacements?"

"What they are doing is criminal," Raxtus said. "Humans were never meant to run these big sanctuaries. Let alone young humans. Aren't there laws against endangering human children?"

"Probably," Kendra said. "But people do what they must

in emergencies. We can't let dragons take over the world. There would be no going back."

"It's too late," Raxtus said. "Soaring Cliffs already got things started. More sanctuaries will follow. The dragons have waited a long time for this. They will not give up. People had their turn running the planet. Things are about to change."

"People allowed dragons to live in peace on sanctuaries," Kendra said. "Will dragons do the same for people?"

"We don't know what dragons will do," Raxtus said. "They have been imprisoned in these giant cages you call sanctuaries for too long."

"Dragons used to roam free," Kendra said. "What did they do then?"

Raxtus looked away and spoke sulkily. "They killed just about everybody they met."

"And then?" Kendra asked.

"Dragons fought to take over the world," Raxtus said. "But that was after people started hunting them."

"People hunted dragons because dragons were already hunting people," Kendra replied.

Raxtus bowed his head. "True."

"Dragons can't be let loose," Kendra said. "They were placed inside sanctuaries for a reason."

Raxtus brought his head near again. "Maybe dragons wouldn't be the best caretakers of the world," he admitted quietly. "But do we deserve to live out our existence trapped like prisoners? And more importantly—it's too late to stop us."

"Then why is Celebrant still here?"

"It's only a matter of time, Kendra. We will be free."

"*You're* already free, because we trusted you. The other dragons are the prisoners."

Raxtus drew himself up straight. "My father has asked me to stand with him and our kind."

"I know," Kendra said. "He assigned you to his personal guard."

"I've never fit in, Kendra," Raxtus said, almost pleading.

"The timing is interesting," Kendra said.

"I knew you would say that," Raxtus said, wounded. "This is a crucial time. Father is mustering all who will answer the call. But it's also because I did well at Zzyzx. I finally proved myself."

"And you're scared to risk what you gained," Kendra said.

"Sure, we're friends, Kendra. But am I asking you to turn against your family? Your people? What would you say?"

"Did my family start including me for the first time a couple of months ago?"

Raxtus stretched his wings and shook his head. "I know it might not be real. I'm starved for acceptance, but I'm not stupid. I know Father sent me today because he thinks it will help convince you."

"Convince me of what?" Kendra asked.

"I have a message at the base of my neck," Raxtus said. Only then did Kendra really notice a small cylinder attached to a strap. "You'll need to unclasp the chain."

Kendra approached, pulled the delicate chain until she

found the clasp, and unhooked it. She started trying to open the cylinder.

"Don't bother," Raxtus said. "You can read it later. It's an invitation to the Feast of Welcome."

"What? Where?"

"Skyhold—my father's castle. Not his private lair at Moonfang. This is where he interacts with other dragons. Where he rules."

Kendra laughed in disbelief. "We can't go there."

"I agree," Raxtus said. "And you can't turn down the invitation. So you should leave."

"We can't leave," Kendra said. "Seth and I are the care-takers. We have to hold back the dragon uprising. And why can't we turn down the invitation?"

"Because no caretaker ever has," Raxtus said. "The dragons have the right to hold a feast once each year for the leaders of Wyrmroost. It would be an enormous insult to refuse."

"It was a bigger insult when Celebrant tore down the Perch and attacked this keep," Kendra said.

"Father can be a bit extreme . . . ," Raxtus muttered.

"That seems like enough reason to revoke his privileges as caretaker," Kendra asserted.

"Keep dreaming," Raxtus said. "You're brave, Kendra. I watched you strike down the Demon King. And you stood up to my father. Your defiance did more than enrage and embarrass him. It hurt his credibility. Already he has been challenged twice for his crown."

"By other dragons?"

Raxtus nodded. "For the first time in hundreds of years."

"What happened?"

Raxtus snorted. "They got destroyed. Wasn't even close. They are resting in pieces."

"Can any dragon take him?"

"Probably not for hundreds of years more. He is still in his prime. The dragons who tried were a couple of the most ambitious, but not the strongest. Father has been the undisputed king of dragons for so long for a reason. You shook that up. He wants you in pieces too."

"Hey, Raxtus," Seth called, running up to the Perch.

"Hi, Seth," the dragon replied.

Seth leaped over the parapet and dropped to the Perch. He adjusted his caretaker's medallion around his neck. "At least you're one dragon who doesn't freeze me with fear."

Raxtus gave a chuckle. "Most dragons can increase the fear effect with willpower. When I try, people tend to relax."

"Really?" Seth asked. "Do it!"

Raxtus looked around, then spread his wings wide and gazed intently at Seth. The surfaces of his scales shimmered like sequins.

Kendra took a deep, refreshing breath and felt tension ease from her body. She wanted to sit down. Or maybe lie down. Seth slumped a bit and started to look drowsy.

Raxtus folded his wings and assumed a regular posture. The shimmering ceased.

"Not bad," Seth said. "Perfect around nap time."

"And another way I don't fit in," Raxtus said.

"Not all dragons are the same," Kendra reminded him.

"Glommus was powerful enough to guard the Dragon Temple, and his breath put people to sleep."

"Glommus was huge," Raxtus said. "He put large groups and powerful creatures to sleep so he could devour them. But I see your point. Thanks."

"Are you still on the wrong team?" Seth asked. "Kendra told me last time you were siding with the dragons."

Raxtus gave a nervous laugh. "I want you guys safe. I really do. I'm not sure the dragons can be stopped."

"But you'll help us," Seth said.

"The best help I can give is advice," Raxtus said. "Don't fight this battle. Leave Wyrmroost. Lie low."

"You really got fooled by them," Seth said.

"They are my kind," Raxtus said. "Celebrant is my father."

"The Dragon King just invited us to a feast," Kendra told Seth, holding up the cylindrical container.

"Are we the meal or the dessert?" Seth asked.

"You will be honored guests," Raxtus said. "Your safety is guaranteed."

"Guaranteed by the dragon who wants us dead?" Seth asked.

"Guaranteed by the hospitality laws of the preserve and of all magical folk," Raxtus said. "Including dragonkind."

"It has to be a trap," Seth said. "He doesn't want to honor us."

"All of Wyrmroost is a trap," Raxtus said. "You should leave. I tell you because I care."

"Do you get a promotion if you scare us off?" Seth pressed.

Raxtus shifted his forelegs uncomfortably and swished his tail. "I'm helping you as best I can."

"We're trying to help your father," Kendra said. "And the dragons. We didn't come here to hurt them or to insult them. We are here to take care of them. Celebrant attacked us. He is supposed to be a caretaker. He is supposed to help, not work against us."

"Dragons aren't meant to laze around in cages like some shabby old declawed circus lion," Raxtus said. "You can't give a Dragon King a menial position and expect him to act like a human."

"You don't think he can be a real caretaker?" Kendra asked. "His duty is to watch over the sanctuary and take care of the creatures here. Is he unfit?"

"You're twisting my words," Raxtus said.

"You're backing the aggressors," Kendra said.

"Is the lion in the cage the aggressor?" Raxtus asked. "Or is it the prisoner?"

"Maybe not the lion," Kendra said. "But the convict is an aggressor. The convict goes to prison for a reason. Dragons were placed here for trying to destroy the world. They are the original aggressors. They live comfortably here. And now they want to fight."

"Actually, at the moment, they want you to feast," Raxtus said. "You have your invitation. Agad has attended in the past. Go ahead and ask him. You will give great offense if you refuse to attend. My father will use it against you. And remember, your safety is guaranteed. And if you think nothing about it is safe, you're right. I better go."

"Yeah," Seth said. "Before I throw up. You used to be our friend."

"I love you too," Raxtus said. "I'm still trying to help. Leave Wyrmroost."

Raxtus sprang into the air, wings heaving down, making air rush over Kendra and Seth. Sparkling in the sunlight, the dragon swiftly rose into the sky.

CHAPTER THREE

Suspicions

Knox peered around the edge of the floral hedge, watching as butterflies, dragonflies, and fat bumblebees flocked around Tess. His younger sister sat cross-legged on the lawn, her pretend fairy wings in place, plastic wand in hand, as she held court for the insects, smiling and nodding.

He leaned back behind the hedge, disgusted with himself. Was this what he had been reduced to? Spying on his boring sister? It was like secretly watching grass grow. Who cared?

And yet, there were a lot of insects swirling around her. As usual. That didn't happen anywhere else. Were they attracted to her scent? Her glittery wings?

So much about this place didn't add up.

His parents had dumped him and his sister with his

grandparents while they went driving around New England with his aunt and uncle. For the first little while, his cousins Kendra and Seth had been here, until they mysteriously "went off to camp." Before Seth left, they had been attacked by a crazed bear that was finally fended off by a whirlwind.

Then the weirdest thing had happened.

Seth had appeared one day and urged him to climb inside a barrel. Knox had emerged a moment later at a castle full of people in a mountainous region. Surrounded by strange weather, Knox had retrieved a scepter from outside the castle walls. Not long after he succeeded, he had come back through the barrel to where Grandma and Grandpa Larsen lived.

Supposedly it had all been some kind of virtual-reality simulation that somehow wired directly into his senses.

He knew there was no such technology, but he had half believed Seth's VR story at the time because a barrel that could teleport him to a castle seemed even less plausible. But the more he thought about it, the surer he became that there had to be another explanation.

Before he could examine the barrel in the living room, it had been moved by Grandpa Larsen and Dale down into the basement. Later in the day he had tried to enter the basement to investigate but was stopped by a locked iron door. He felt positive Grandpa Larsen was hiding something.

Knox peeked around the hedge again.

A large butterfly balanced on Tess's finger. She spoke to it animatedly. A dragonfly rested on her shoulder.

Tess had a big imagination. She had tea parties with her

stuffed animals, drew colorful pictures with crayons, and loved to pretend fairies were real. Though ten years old, she looked and acted younger.

She normally had zero attention span, hopping from idea to idea. He had never seen her as dedicated as she was to this game of the insects being fairies. She spent hours with them. Was it the novelty of the insects gathering around her? When would that excitement wear off? And did insects ever gather like this?

Knox came out of hiding and stalked over to his younger sister. "Playing with the fairies?" he asked.

"They saw you behind the hedge," Tess said.

"Is that a fairy on your finger?"

"Her name is Nora."

"Tell her to fly in a circle around your head," Knox suggested.

"She doesn't want to," Tess said.

"Because she is just a butterfly."

Tess giggled. "She has butterfly wings."

"Since she is a butterfly."

"They used to look like butterflies to me at first," Tess said. "Look hard."

Knox folded his arms. This was absurd. But something was going on. He got down on his hands and knees and stared closely at the butterfly on her finger. The violet wings had dark markings and seemed slightly translucent. He saw thin antennae, bulbous eyes, and a curled proboscis. It was definitely a butterfly.

"Not a fairy," Knox said.

"They told me the milk would help me see them," Tess said.

"What milk?"

"At first I just saw and heard them a little," Tess said. "Mostly they still looked like bugs. But I heard them sometimes. They tried to help me by telling me about the milk in the pans around the yard."

"You drank it?" Knox asked.

Tess made a disgusted face. "It was outside. And it was warm. I only like milk from the fridge."

"You started seeing them better anyhow?" Knox guessed.

"All the time now," Tess said. "It got easy."

"But you're just pretending," Knox said.

Tess giggled.

"Right?" he asked.

"No," Tess said. "It's funny because they are so obvious and you think they're just bugs."

"Because they *are* just bugs."

Tess looked at the insects and giggled. "He can't see you at all," she said.

Knox scowled. Something weird was going on here. What about running from a bear through the woods with goats? And going to an inexplicable castle? The bugs were weirdly calm. They had settled on the grass all around them, as if interested in the conversation. Knox waved a hand and several took flight, but none strayed far.

"Don't make them mad," Tess warned. "They have magic."

Knox felt a reflex to scoff, but resisted. "Where is the milk?"

"I don't know," Tess said. "Around the yard." She stared at a dragonfly hovering near her, then looked back at her brother. "The closest one is under a bush over there." She pointed.

"Where exactly?" Knox asked.

Tess got up and followed the dragonfly. The other insects stayed with them, loosely orbiting Tess. The dragonfly led them to a neatly trimmed bush. Beneath it Knox found a tin saucer with milk in it.

Some of the butterflies and dragonflies splashed in the milk.

"The fairies like it," Tess said.

"I don't want milk with bug germs in it," Knox said.

"Fairies, not bugs," Tess said. "But gross, right? Warm milk under a bush? Can't you just see the fairies? They're everywhere. Look hard."

Knox looked around again, but it was ridiculous. They were just insects.

Including a dragonfly that could lead them to milk when instructed.

Something out of the ordinary was going on. Had been from day one. What if the milk could help unlock the answer? Was it crazy to try? Or crazy not to try?

Knox knelt down and pulled the saucer of milk out from under the bush. The insects cleared away and the milk sloshed gently, not spilling. Knox lowered his face and sniffed. It didn't smell rotten.

"Are you going to taste it?" Tess asked.

"Are you daring me?" Knox replied.

"Sure," Tess said.

Knox lowered his face to the saucer, felt his puckered lips brush the creamy surface, and gently slurped. The inrush of air carried a milky spray into his lungs, and he coughed a little, but he also swallowed some.

And suddenly there were fairies everywhere.

Small, slender beautiful women with butterfly wings, dragonfly wings, and bumblebee wings fluttered around him. Several waved. High-pitched voices called, "He sees us! He sees us!"

"There really are fairies," Knox said, staring in amazement, afraid to move.

Tinkling laughter surrounded him.

"Aren't they beautiful?" Tess asked.

"They are," Knox admitted in amazement. The colors of their wings were brighter than they had been as butterflies. Even under the afternoon sun, the fairies had a glow to them, especially if they flitted into shadows.

"Now you can play with us," Tess said.

Knox looked at his sister. "This is impossible. Fairies aren't real."

"Not just fairies," Tess said. "Little people in the house. A big dirt man. Goat guys."

Knox remembered Seth asking what he would think if he heard there were fairies around. Or monsters. He had brushed off the questions as silly. They *were* silly! Except . . . for all the fairies he now saw.

He held out a hand. "Come here. Land on me."

No fairies approached.

"They don't like to be bossed around," Tess said.

"Please," Knox tried, deciding to lay it on thick. "You're so pretty, I just want to look."

Three fairies vied for a spot on his palm. A shimmering silver fairy won, her hair short and stylish, the little dress she wore revealing lithe limbs. Knox could feel her tiny bare feet against his skin. He carefully reached out and stroked a wing. The fairy giggled shyly.

She was real. He could feel her, see her, the details all perfect. Fairies were real, and he had one in his hand.

"You like my sister?" he asked.

"They don't talk much," Tess said. "I don't know if they all speak English."

"I hear you talking to them," Knox said.

"A few speak more than others," Tess said.

"We all enjoy your sister," a fairy said off to Knox's right, hovering not far from his head. "And we all laugh at you."

The rest of the fairies tittered. The one on his palm leaped into the air. Knox tried to grasp her, but she darted away.

"Now he knows," a few fairies exclaimed.

"Now you know," Tess said.

"Why were they laughing at me?" Knox asked.

"Because you didn't believe," Tess said.

"Well," Knox said, "it seemed impossible. But now I get it. What else is real?"

"I told you," Tess said. "The goat guys. The dirt man. The little people in the house."

"Do you talk to them?" Knox asked.

"Not yet," Tess said.

"Do the goat guys normally look like goats?" Knox wondered, thinking about his adventure in the woods with Seth.

"How should I know?" Tess said. "They look like guys with goat legs to me."

"Thanks, Tess," Knox said. "See you fairies later. I need some answers."

Knox dashed to the house. Grandma and Grandpa Larsen had to know what was going on here. Seth did. Even Tess sort of did.

Knox found Grandpa Larsen in the kitchen, making a sandwich. He looked up as Knox entered. "Are you all right, Knox? You look flustered."

Knox paused. They stood in the kitchen, with no evidence of magic anywhere. What if Grandpa Larsen didn't know? He would look so foolish. But he could prove it! He knew where to find the milk.

"You have fairies," Knox blurted.

Grandpa Larsen wiped mayo on a paper towel and set down the butter knife. "I was beginning to wonder if you would figure it out. Some never do. I thought you would be full of questions after Blackwell Keep."

"You know about that?" Knox asked.

"Stan filled me in."

"Tess knows," Knox said.

"She plays with them a lot," Grandpa Larsen said. "I wasn't sure yet how much was her own make-believe."

"She doesn't need the milk to see them," Knox said.

Grandpa Larsen raised his eyebrows. "Are you sure?"

"She's never tried it," Knox said. "She sees them and talks to them. She led me to the milk."

"Incredible," Grandpa Larsen said. "Unheard of."

"What is going on here?" Knox asked.

"Have a seat, my boy," Grandpa Larsen said. "Allow me to introduce you to a larger, weirder world than you ever suspected."

Decisions

Grandpa Sorenson removed his glasses and looked up from the invitation in his hand. "A feast? At Skyhold? You have got to be kidding me."

"This is no joke," Agad said. "The consequences of snubbing the dragons could be serious."

Seth stood beside Kendra in Marat's private study. Agad, Grandpa Sorenson, Grandma Sorenson, Tanu, and Marat shared the room. Grandpa considered Newel and Doren too frivolous to participate in private councils. Calvin remained in Seth's pocket.

The chamber smelled of old books, spent candles, and wood polish, with a faint undercurrent of burnt hair. Seth stared at the various oddments assembled on desks and shelves, including several carved wooden boxes, an abacus, and a collection of animal teeth. He wondered if the large hourglass with blue sand really would last an hour if over-turned. And why blue sand? Was it magical?

"More serious than our caretakers falling into enemy hands?" Grandma Sorenson asked.

"Potentially," Marat said. "Unless we provide a legitimate excuse and quickly offer to fulfill the request on an alternate date, Celebrant could claim Kendra and Seth have abandoned their post as caretakers."

"Celebrant was so mad the last time I saw him," Kendra said. "I know he wants revenge for us stopping his attack."

"You and Seth would be protected by hospitality law," Agad said. "Those protections are not only a matter of honor. If he violated them, Celebrant would lose his status as care-taker, magical punishments would be brought to bear, and his good name would be ruined in the magical community."

"No dragon would violate a hospitality code, simply as a matter of dignity," Marat said. "A dragon of Celebrant's status would not consider it."

"Raxtus warned it wasn't safe," Seth said.

"Of course it isn't safe," Agad said swiftly. "The dragons will seek every advantage they can through the interaction. Other leaders of Wyrmroost will no doubt be present. Celebrant will want to make you look foolish and incompetent. He will try to compromise your integrity. He will seek to intimidate you. And who knows what other motives he may have."

"But they won't eat us," Kendra said.

"Not at the feast," Marat said. "They will not physically harm you there."

"Should I go alone?" Kendra asked.

"Both caretakers were invited," Grandpa said. "At least the two of you should attend."

"I'll go too," Calvin offered from Seth's pocket.

"Who could come with us?" Kendra asked.

"Only those who can resist dragon fear," Grandpa said.

"Marat?" Seth asked.

"None of dragonkind who have sided against their own should cross into Skyhold," Marat said. "Unless explicitly invited, we would be considered traitors, not visitors."

"That includes me and every true wizard," Agad said.

"Because you're all former dragons," Kendra mused.

"I could probably brew up a potion that would let me temporarily resist dragon fear," Tanu said.

"A courage potion?" Seth asked.

"A specific type of courage potion," Tanu said. "Tuned for dragons."

"Would it work on me?" Seth asked.

"Worth a try," Tanu said.

"I'd rather not hold hands the whole night," Seth said.

"Might be awkward while eating," Kendra said.

"And during every other second," Seth said.

"Could anyone else come?" Kendra asked.

"Skyhold is high in the Ragged Mountains," Agad said. "The only practical way to arrive is by griffin, and none could carry Henrick."

"Nobody else here can withstand dragon fear," Marat said.

"There is a road," Grandpa said.

"The road to Skyhold is long and winding," Agad said. "I'm not sure Henrick could get there by tomorrow."

"With Tanu there they will have trusted supervision," Grandma said.

"I'll supervise too!" Calvin volunteered.

"I'm not sure whether our numbers at the feast will have much bearing on their safety," Marat said. "They will not face direct physical danger. A possible pitfall I foresee is Celebrant wanting to strike deals or alter the official relationship he has with you. That should be avoided."

"This all presupposes Kendra and Seth will choose to attend," Agad said.

"Sounds like we better," Seth said.

"Celebrant is up to something," Kendra murmured.

"I know," Seth said. "But Agad already explained that Celebrant can't attack us there. Don't you trust Agad?"

"Yes, of course," Kendra said. "We'll just need to be extra smart." She eyed her brother.

"I'm always smart," Seth said.

"He's smarter with me," Calvin said.

"Okay, I'm in," Kendra said. "We can't abandon our duty. With all the unrest, we need to strengthen our position as caretakers, not weaken it."

"What can we do there to help our cause?" Seth asked. "Spy?"

"Keep all eyes and ears open," Agad said. "Most important, you must go and return without weakening your position. At present, with the scepter in our possession, the dragons simply cannot invade Blackwell Keep, no matter their numbers. We need to keep it that way. Enter no agreements with Celebrant, regardless of how enticing they may seem. Just coming home will be a victory."

"How many feasts can they throw?" Kendra asked.

"If you attend this one, we should be in the clear for at least a year," Marat said.

"Other leaders of the various factions at Wyrmroost will be present," Agad said.

"Like who?" Seth asked.

"The leaders of the protected territories," Agad said. "Lord Dalgorel of Terrabelle, Raj Faranah of the Zowali Protectorate, Grand Imperator Karzal of Gundertun, Amulon of the Herdlands, and Lowly Vatka of the Sludgeholes."

"I know Dalgorel," Seth said. "None of the rest."

"The Zowali Protectorate are the talking animals," Kendra said. "What was the name of their leader again?"

"Raj Faranah is a mighty tiger," Marat said. "His territory has long been allies of the caretakers."

"They send you the mute Luvians," Kendra said.

"Yes, very good," Agad said. "Fascinating to watch those horses read. I find it calming. Gundertun is the gnome kingdom, run by Karzal."

"The Grand Impersonator," Seth said.

"Imperator," Grandpa corrected. "You'll want to master that word. Gnomes can be bristly."

"Amulon rules the taurans here," Marat said. "That includes the alcetaurs, like Henrick; the cervitaurs, who are half deer; the rumitaurs, who are half elk; and some centaurs."

"What type is Amulon?" Seth asked.

"Rumitaur," Agad said. "With a grand rack of antlers projecting from his head."

"A human head with antlers?" Seth checked.

"Yes," Agad said.

"Sweet," Seth said, holding his hands up to his forehead, fingers splayed.

"What about the last one?" Kendra asked.

"Lowly Vatka might be the least likely to attend," Marat said. "She speaks for the inhabitants of a marshy region called the Sludgeholes."

"She has the best name," Seth said.

"Vatka is a fairly powerful hag," Agad said. "Her philosophy is that a leader should be the servant of all, hence the 'lowly' title. She has managed to unite several races under her influence."

"Will it be good for us to meet these people?" Kendra asked.

"The dragons will be working hard against us," Marat said. "We need all the allies we can muster."

"None of the leaders of the free territories want the dragons to overthrow Wyrmroost," Agad said. "But some may expect it is inevitable and align themselves accordingly. We want as many leaders as possible to believe you can hold control of the sanctuary. It would not hurt to make friends."

"Aren't the Fair Folk always neutral?" Seth asked.

"Generally, yes," Marat said. "But they will quietly assist one side or the other when it suits them. All members of the free territories have magical protections that would hold even if the preserve fell—but they would all prefer for it to survive."

"If the sanctuary falls, they lose their outermost defenses," Agad said. "And they no longer have caretakers watching over their interests. If the preserve falls, and the dragons so choose, the territories will not last."

"Which is why some might hope to align themselves with Celebrant," Marat said. "The dragons are a big enough threat. We'd rather not have the whole preserve turn against us."

"Isn't a festival night coming up in a few days?" Tanu asked. "The summer solstice?"

"Another problem," Grandpa said with a sigh.

"I imagine a festival night is especially violent here," Grandma said.

Agad and Marat exchanged a tense glance.

"We avoid meddling in the festival nights," Marat said.

"It is pandemonium from dusk till dawn," Agad agreed. "We hide behind our defenses until the night ends."

Seth had lived through some festival nights at Fablehaven, when many of the ordinary boundaries at the preserve fell and the inhabitants could run wild for a night. His first festival night was the most memorable, when he had made the house vulnerable by opening a window and almost getting his grandparents killed. Wyrmroost was a much larger sanctuary than Fablehaven—he could only imagine how dangerous Midsummer Eve might be with dragons involved.

"The feast is tomorrow," Kendra said. "Let's survive that first."

"The solstice comes two days later," Grandma said.

"You would depart early tomorrow evening," Agad said. "Then return that same night."

"Can I take Tempest?" Seth asked.

"Her wild nature served you well dodging and outrunning dragons," Marat said. "But for this outing, steady, experienced griffins would be the wise choice. You want the evening to go smoothly."

"Kendra, Seth," Grandpa said. "If you, Calvin, and Tanu are doing this, we have logistics to manage. You are determined to attend?"

Kendra nodded.

"A whole castle full of dragons," Seth said reverently. "I wouldn't miss it."

🐾 🐾 🐾

After the meeting, Kendra wandered over to the churchyard, picking her way through the gravestones until she found the one marking her ancestor, Patton Burgess. Most of the headstones around it were broken or tilted. Some were worn smooth. Patton's sturdy marker still bore a clear inscription:

PATTON BURGESS
WORD TO THE WISE
TREAD LIGHTLY AMONG DRAGONS

Kendra knew there was no body in the grave. The headstone was a fake to appease some dragons who had been disgruntled at Patton. She also knew that the headstone extended far beneath the ground and contained a secret message that had helped her find one of the keys to Zzyzx, the demon prison.

But reading his name still helped her feel close to Patton. This was a monument to someone she knew and loved. Someone who had helped her in times of need. Though he had died long before she was born, Kendra had met him, thanks to a time-travel device called the Chronometer. She wished he were here now. There never seemed to be a problem he couldn't handle.

"Everyone is depending on me," Kendra said quietly. "I'm worried this feast with dragons is just the beginning. One of the dragon sanctuaries has already fallen. Bracken is lost. The whole world is falling apart. And I'm supposed to hold it together."

The headstone had no reply.

"Maybe you're the lucky one," Kendra said. "You already lived your life. How did you last so long, through so much danger? The stress alone feels like enough to crack me up sometimes."

She tried to imagine Patton, calm and confident. How would he have answered her question? One day at a time? One crisis at a time? Doing what had to be done? Wishing on a lucky star? Eating her vitamins? Her imagination felt insufficient.

Kendra looked at the fortress around her. It was so big to have a staff of roughly twenty—a misfit skeleton crew of people and magical folk. Blackwell Keep could easily have housed hundreds. Most walls and towers looked abandoned. She felt less like the commander of a fort and more like the watchperson of a derelict castle.

Would hundreds of defenders matter against a dragon? Couldn't a geyser of flame roast a hundred soldiers as easily as five? The real protection came from the treaty that had founded Wyrmroost and the magical defenses that kept enemies out. Not even Celebrant could huff and puff his way past the invisible barriers shielding the keep.

And if the Dragon King ever breached the walls with his followers? Well, nobody inside the keep would survive for very long.

This invitation to the feast had to be part of Celebrant's revenge plan. There might not be a way for the Dragon King to directly harm her or Seth at the feast, but it had to be part of a larger strategy. Maybe if she stayed aware, she could use the feast to get a sense for what the dragons were planning.

Kendra took out the horn Bracken had left her. Unicorns shed their first two horns before the third and final one. This was his first. Squeezing it tightly, Kendra tried to send words to Bracken, asking if he was all right, asking him to speak. Sometimes she could sense his words in her mind. Not right now.

Where was he? Wounded? Alone? In need of rescue? The thought of him in danger somewhere was almost too much to bear. She felt so useless.

An extremely fit fairy with grayish skin, a green shift, and dragonfly wings bobbed in front of Kendra before alighting atop Patton's headstone. She looked up at Kendra expectantly.

"Hello," Kendra said. "Do you have news?"

The fairy stamped a foot and splayed her arms. "I wouldn't seek out a human for fun."

"Doesn't get much more fun than a graveyard," Kendra said. "What happened?"

"A dragon got into a brawl with a bunch of hill giants," the fairy said.

"Does that happen often?" Kendra said.

"Hill giants will fight just about anything," the fairy said. "That level of ugly doesn't worry about injuries. Most look better after losing a scuffle or two."

"Thanks for the info," Kendra said.

"I'm not to the important part yet," the fairy scolded, stomping both feet.

"Go on."

"The fight was up by Wolfbane Reservoir," the fairy said. "They broke the dam."

"Will it flood down here?" Kendra asked, looking toward the outer wall of the keep.

"No, the water washed down Thirsty Gulch," the fairy said.

"So the dragons broke a dam?" Kendra asked.

"The giants fighting the dragon broke the dam," the fairy said. "And the flood took out the bridge at Thirsty Gulch."

"What bridge?" Kendra asked.

"Where the High Road crosses Thirsty Gulch," the fairy said. "That's your news." She flitted away.

"Thank you," Kendra said. "Keep reporting on any unusual dragon activity."

The fairy did not look back.

Kendra leaned against Patton's grave and folded her arms.

A dragon and some giants had gotten into a fight and caused serious damage. Was this an isolated incident? Did such brawls occur often? Or was this a hint of worse problems to come?

It wasn't even Midsummer Eve yet.

How bad were things going to get?

CHAPTER FIVE

Stingy

"We're getting gear?" Newel asked, biting into an apple as he walked along the corridor beside Seth.

"So he can feast with dragons," Doren said from the other side, untangling the string of a yo-yo as he strolled along.

"You should bathe in a nice marinade," Newel suggested.

"Maybe a curry?" Doren asked. "Do dragons fancy curry?"

"They're more into hot sauce," Seth played along. "I'll make a necklace of jalapeños."

"Use ghost peppers," Doren suggested. "Or Carolina Reapers."

"What kind of gear?" Newel asked.

"From the storerooms," Seth said.

"We have a key to some storerooms," Doren said. "Agad gave it to us."

"That's food storage," Seth said.

"Ham, sausages, jerky, flour, oats, barley, honey, molasses, jams, cheeses, and so forth," Doren recited. "Enough to feed an army for a year."

"Or two satyrs for a month," Newel said.

"These are different storerooms," Seth said. "Grippa the ridge troll watches over them. I guess he can be tough to deal with. Henrick offered to come."

"Who needs a moose guy when you have goat guys?" Newell asked.

"He has more legs," Doren pointed out.

"With two of us it's a tie," Newell said. "Besides, the taurans look ridiculous. Six limbs is overkill! They hardly look like people."

"He's pretty muscly," Doren said. "Probably handles himself well in a fight."

"Are we fighting the troll now?" Newell asked.

"Maybe arguing," Seth said. "He is stingy with the gear."

"You're a caretaker!" Newell said. "It's your gear!"

"That's why I didn't want Henrick along," Seth said. "I can make my own arguments. I don't want to look weak."

"Nobody would call you weak," Doren said. "A little gangly maybe, but that's your age."

"I'll just keep quiet," Calvin said from Seth's pocket. "Not everyone at the keep knows about me yet."

"Not many would notice you either way," Newel said. He took another bite from his apple and swatted Seth's arm. "What kind of gear do you want?"

"Just some magical stuff in case things turn ugly," Seth said.

"They have items that can protect against a castle full of dragons?" Doren asked.

"Not weapons to slay dragons," Seth said. "Just gear. It's good to be ready." He slapped the satchel that served as his survival kit.

"You'll have Tanu," Doren said. "That means potions."

"And his special courage potion works against dragons," Seth said. "We tested it facing Marat last night. Tanu and I could both still walk and talk."

"That would be embarrassing to freeze up at the feast," Newel said.

"Kendra could always hold my hand," Seth said. "But that's embarrassing too."

They reached a door bisected into top and bottom halves. "This should be it," Seth said, knocking.

"One minute," called an unseen, accented voice.

Seth paused, then knocked again.

"I'm coming," the muffled voice assured him.

The top half of the door swung open. Grippa had small, snug blue scales with black markings. Three fins projected from his reptilian head, and bony spikes bristled at his joints. He had narrow, orange eyes with slit pupils and a wide mouth full of sharp, pointy teeth.

"Ah, the young caretaker," Grippa greeted in unctuous tones. He glanced at Newel and Doren. "And a pair of satyrs." His eyes returned to Seth. "Should I summon help? Are you a hostage? What is the ransom? Flutes?"

"Not all satyrs play the pipes," Doren said.

"How about you two?" Grippa asked.

Newel shifted uncomfortably. "Well, sure, on occasion."

"I've never heard you play a flute," Seth said.

"We're not showboaters," Doren said.

"It lends itself to stereotypes," Newel said.

"I've also played some accordion," Doren said.

The troll slapped his hands down on the bottom half of the door. "How may I be of service?"

"I need gear," Seth said.

Grippa stared. "A vague request."

"I'm going to a feast at Skyhold," Seth said. "I need some equipment to help me stay safe."

"You'll be protected by hospitality rights," Grippa said.

"And the dragons want to kill us," Seth said. "So I want to be prepared. Henrick told me you have an amazing knowledge of the items here."

"I'm deaf to flattery," Grippa said. "The reason we have items of value in our stores is because my predecessors and I have protected them."

"If we never use them, they serve no purpose," Seth said.

"If we use them indiscriminately, they will not be here when most needed," Grippa replied. "What exactly do you want?"

"See if he has an accordion," Doren whispered.

Seth stifled a laugh. "Do you have a weapon that could come in handy if a dragon gets grumpy?"

"Fresh out of accordions," Grippa said. "Perhaps the brownies could rig something for you?"

"I asked about a weapon," Seth said.

"I assumed that an accordion would qualify," Grippa said. "We do have some pipes."

"I'll take a set of bagpipes," Newel said. "And the hours when you retire for bed."

"We have two sets of bagpipes," Grippa said, "and many rules against playing them."

"I really need a good weapon," Seth said. "You must have something."

"We have more than twenty thousand weapons in our care," Grippa said. "Roughly one-third of them would be too heavy for a lad your size to employ effectively."

"So give me the best of what would work," Seth said.

"The best?" Grippa asked incredulously. "The best, you say? Why would you deserve our best weapon? Why take it to a feast? How would you even determine which weapon is best? The rarest? The most costly? The most powerful?"

"The most powerful that I could handle," Seth said.

Grippa leaned forward. "Powerful in what way? Capable of killing the most people the fastest? Most threatening to a dragon? Able to cause the most structural damage to a building?"

"Those three sound good," Seth said.

Grippa covered his eyes with one hand, the hornlike nails on his fingertips yellowed almost to brown. "You can't have any of them, let alone all of them!"

"Why?" Seth said. "I'm a caretaker."

"I'm the property master," Grippa replied.

"I'm in charge of you," Seth reminded him.

"He said it," Newel muttered.

"Sure did," Doren murmured in reply.

Grippa grinned. "Is that how it works? You're going to bully me? My job is to guard the armaments and other property of interest belonging to this garrison. I decide what goes and what stays."

"What if I fire you and take what I want?" Seth asked.

Newel and Doren subtly sidled away from him.

The grin was gone. "Have you ever dealt with a troll before?"

"Once or twice," Seth said.

Grippa drummed his fingers on the lower half of the door. "I'm going to cut you a break because you're young, you're in over your head, and you'll probably be dead soon. Trolls don't appreciate threats. We have long memories. We don't give something for nothing. Trolls bargain."

"And you work for me," Seth said.

Doren made a choking sound that may have started as a laugh. Newel patted his back firmly.

"I was not employed by you," Grippa said. "I have a contract. It has been in my clan for generations. I suppose there are protocols you could engage to relieve me of my position, forms to fill out, covenants to break, deposits to relinquish. Are you sure you can replace me? Do you know where the hidden rooms are and how to access them? You're familiar with the hundreds of secret stashes that contain the most valuable items? You have the expertise to distinguish a phantom knife from a dagger of despair?"

"You lost me at forms," Seth said. "Is a phantom knife good? Does it cut ghosts?"

"The blade of a phantom knife can pass through solid matter," Grippa said, "but the tip can be made tangible at any moment. It is primarily used by skilled assassins to kill without an entry wound."

"So, a couple of those," Seth said. "What does the dagger do?"

Grippa balled his hands into fists. "We have one phantom knife. It would be nearly impossible to replace. And it would serve almost no purpose among dragons."

"What would be most useful where I'm going?" Seth asked. "What would you bring?"

"Am I to deduce I am keeping my job?" Grippa asked.

"If you give me some good stuff," Seth said.

"That's a threat again," Doren offered helpfully.

"Can I speak with our friend for a moment?" Newel asked, putting an arm around Seth's shoulders.

"What are you, his attorney?" Grippa asked.

"'Attorney' is such an ugly word," Newel said. "How about 'adviser'?"

"This will only take a moment," Doren assured.

Newel guided Seth several paces down the hall and leaned in close. "Trolls are hoarders. This clown doesn't want to part with any gear. He doesn't want to let you know what gear he has. He thinks of it as his. I have a feeling Henrick or Marat or Agad could twist his arm and get him to move, but better for your reputation if you do it yourself."

"I'm trying," Seth said.

"Trolls like a good bargain," Newel said.

"Why should I bargain?" Seth complained. "He works for me!"

"And he can work against you," Calvin said quietly from Seth's pocket.

"True," Newel agreed. "Listen, you don't want to bargain

with an employee. It seems weak. But maybe it's actually smart. Do you want good gear or not?"

"I want it," Seth said.

"Then be clever," Newel said. "Trolls are notoriously selfish. If it works to his advantage to give you good gear, he'll be much more willing."

Seth nodded. "I get it."

Newel patted his back, and Seth returned to the doorway. The troll watched him smugly.

"Sorry, I've been under a lot of pressure, and I was being hasty," Seth said.

"A common flaw of youth," Grippa said.

"Useful in a race, though," Seth added.

The troll barely chuckled.

"You've heard Soaring Cliffs fell?" Seth asked. "The dragon sanctuary?"

"Everyone knows," Grippa said.

"Dragons are in rebellion around the world," Seth said. "Celebrant has threatened us. Kendra and I might not be perfect caretakers. Everyone knows we're too young. But we're what you've got right now. At least for a year."

"Celebrant can veto any potential replacements for twelve months," the troll recited.

"And he will," Seth said. "He knows we're inexperienced. He thinks appointing us was a bad move. Maybe it was."

The troll shrugged. "You got the scepter. It showed toughness and leadership."

"And we're really young," Seth said. "We might fail. We could be the last caretakers Wyrmroost ever has."

Grippa squinted pensively. "You against the dragons for a year? Even with the protections inherent to the keep, I put my money on the dragons. At least three to one. That's assuming you have better advisers than these fauns."

"What would the odds be with us as the advisers?" Doren asked.

"I'd pack my bags," Grippa said. His eyes returned to Seth. "What's your point? Trying to scare me off?"

"I do have good advisers," Seth said. "I mean to hold off the dragons. You want me to survive."

"If you and your sister die, Celebrant becomes the sole caretaker," Grippa said. "Same if you flee the sanctuary. The dragons rule Wyrmroost. Yeah, I want you to live."

"If we die, you lose all this stuff," Seth said. "No Blackwell Keep—no items to protect."

"I hear you," Grippa said. He paused, twisting his neck to the side until it clicked. "I don't want you to lose anything I lend you."

"Seth has some experience with magical items," Newel inserted.

"Quiet down, Bagpipes," Grippa said. He gazed at Seth. "Do you?"

"I used to have Vasilis," Seth said.

The troll's eyes lit up. "One of the five legendary swords?"

They had been conversing in English. With a small effort, Seth switched to Duggish, the language of trolls. "I used it to kill Graulas and Nagi Luna. Then my sister took out the Demon King with it."

"I suppose I knew that," Grippa said. "You speak Duggish like a native."

"Part of being a shadow charmer," Seth said.

"Where is the blade of legend now?" Grippa asked. "Perhaps I could keep it safe?"

Seth smiled. "I have to keep that a secret. But I have used powerful items from time to time, including the Sands of Sanctity and the Chronometer. As we get to know each other, I may store items with you."

The troll rubbed his hands together. "You need gear for the feast. In case something goes wrong."

"What do you recommend?" Seth asked.

"You'll take care of these items?" Grippa asked.

"I will," Seth said. "And I won't let Blackwell Keep fall."

"Fair enough," Grippa said. "You'll want a weapon."

"Yes," Seth said.

"I have the sword of Tregain, former prince of Stormguard Castle," Grippa said. "It's a short sword; he used it as a boy. But no edge in our arsenal is as durable or as keen. The blade was created by master smiths with the help of the wizard Egar. It tends to push attention away from itself when unsheathed, and the effect increases with the size of the attacking creature. Also, in great need, and at the price of the blade, with the phrase 'sharpness begone,' the blade will become a bolt of lightning. Using the sword that way would leave you with only a hilt. I advise against it, except in greatest need. The keenness of the blade and the distracter component are more valuable."

"And you have it?" Seth checked.

"Hidden, yes, but of course I have it," Grippa said.

Seth tried to maintain his calm. He needed to keep a good poker face. "Would a bolt of lightning kill a dragon?"

"Depends," Grippa said. "Probably not, under most circumstances. But a dragon would surely notice. And most beings would stand no chance."

"The sword will do," Seth said. "What else?"

Grippa stared for a moment. "I have a pair of fleet boots."

"For wearing on ships?"

"Fleet as in fast. They help whenever you're in motion. Feels strange at first. They assist with every step. Wearing them, you will increase your top speed, and you can keep a quick pace much longer than ordinary. They're also unusually quiet."

"All right," Seth said, at war against a smile. "Anything else?"

"I hesitate," Grippa said. "The last item I suggest is dangerous to all. Under ordinary circumstances it would be foolish to use, but if desperately cornered, you might be glad to have it."

"What is it?"

"The vial of horrors," Grippa said. "It will work only once. Unstopper it and every being present will see some of their worst fears come to pass. Including you. The effect is all illusion, but incredibly vivid. Lasts only a few minutes, but that might be long enough to escape a tight spot, if you keep your wits."

"Sounds good," Seth said.

"If I were going among dragons, I would want it," Grippa said.

"What about my sister?" Seth asked.

"I figured you would mention her," Grippa said. "She might appreciate our rare and wonderful bow of plenty."

"Tell me about it," Seth said.

"Nock an arrow and it is an ordinary bow," Grippa said. "But pull back the bow without an arrow and one will appear. Up to three hundred per day."

"Cool," Seth said.

"That is not all," Grippa continued with a grin. "Once the arrow has appeared, name any number of arrows remaining for the day, and that many will simultaneously fire."

"A hundred at once?" Seth asked, unable to contain his excitement.

"Up to three hundred in one shot," Grippa said. "If you want to use them up that way."

"They spread out?" Seth asked. "If you shoot a bunch at once?"

"Yes," Grippa confirmed. "With a tendency to seek targets."

"Maybe I should have that too," Seth said.

Grippa shook his head. "Up to you, I suppose, but that will leave Kendra without a significant weapon. Our stores are not limitless. I see the value in protecting the keep. I am offering those that could serve you best."

"All right," Seth said. "Anything else for Kendra?"

Grippa sighed. "I hesitate again."

"What?"

"It can be quite effective against dragons under the right circumstances."

"Sounds like what we need."

"It would be nice to keep in the arsenal just in case," Grippa said.

"We'll try to bring everything back," Seth said.

Grippa shrugged. "It would not hold off dragons forever."

"I'm so curious," Seth said.

"A sack of gales," Grippa said.

"A bag of wind?" Seth asked. "Are we back to bagpipes?"

"To loose the drawstring of the sack is to unleash a mighty wind," Grippa said. "With a dragon on the ground, the sack would do little. But it could cause real problems for dragons in flight."

"How much wind?" Seth asked.

"When full, a fierce gale for at least a minute," Grippa said.

"Is it full?" Seth asked.

"Currently, yes."

"How long to refill?"

"It varies," Grippa said. "The sack is fed remotely by wind collectors in several strategic locations around the globe. Under ideal conditions, the bag can refill in hours. Or it can also take days."

Seth scrunched his brow. "If the sack can blow a dragon off course, won't the person holding it go flying?"

"The bag is magically stabilized," Grippa said. "Otherwise the holder would blow around like an untied balloon."

"What else?" Seth said.

"You don't know when to quit," Grippa said. "I have

offered all the most sensible options. If the feast goes according to plan, you will need none of them."

"I've learned the hard way that life doesn't always follow a plan," Seth said. "I like to be ready."

"I cannot fault you," Grippa said. "Sometimes good preparation helps prevent trouble from starting."

"I hope so."

"Shall I fetch the items?" Grippa asked.

"Sure, thanks," Seth said.

Grippa gave a little bow and withdrew.

Newel sidled close. "What did you say?"

"It sounded like you were gargling mud," Doren added.

Seth had almost forgotten he had switched to Duggish. "We reached an agreement. He's getting some magical weapons and items for me and Kendra."

"Any mention of those bagpipes?" Newel asked casually.

"I think we better quit while we're ahead," Seth said.

CHAPTER SIX

Feast

Kendra sat rigidly in her griffin saddle as Didger the dwarf buckled her legs in. The creature shifted beneath her, saddle creaking, plumage ruffling near the neck. She patted the feathery shoulders, powerful muscles rolling beneath her palm.

Didger went to the head of the griffin and took the reins. "Steady, Sheba, the girl is already nervous." He handed the reins to Kendra.

"Should you tell her that?" Kendra asked.

"She can smell your fear much better than I can see it," Didger said. "Fortunately, with Sheba, your worry makes her gentler. She's our oldest griffin, and the most considerate of her rider. Gave her to you for a reason."

Kendra looked over at Tanu and Seth on their own griffins. "And the others?"

"Sage for Seth, since she is faster and more maneuverable than some but still obedient," Didger said. "He wanted Tempest, but her temperament is too volatile for a peaceful mission when she will be stabled by strangers. And Tanu rides Titan, our strongest griffin, since the potion master is, well, larger than some."

Tanu caught Kendra staring and gave a little salute. She smiled back, then jiggling the reins, glanced down at Didger. "How do I steer?"

"Hold the reins loosely," Didger advised. "The griffins know the way. When you leave the feast, Tanu will assist you into the saddle. Just tell Sheba 'home.' She'll do the rest."

"All right," Kendra said.

"Straps feel snug?" Didger asked. "Can't pull your legs out, can you?"

Kendra squirmed, but her legs were immobilized. "I'm stuck."

"Perfect," the dwarf replied, his smile showing a couple of gaps in his teeth. "When you're ready to dismount, pull the release down, right, and away like I showed you."

"Got it," Kendra said.

Somebody patted her leg, and Kendra turned to find Grandpa and Grandma Sorenson on the opposite side of the griffin from Didger. "You take care and watch out for your brother," Grandma said.

"I will," Kendra promised.

"Be polite, and make no agreements with Celebrant," Grandpa reminded her.

"But don't take any of his sass," Grandma said.

"I'll do my best," Kendra assured.

"You come home safe," Grandpa said. "Stay near Tanu."

"I will," Kendra said.

Grandpa and Grandma moved on to Seth, who was drinking a potion. Kendra knew the courage effects would let Seth and Tanu interact with dragons for about eight hours. They each carried two extra doses just in case. Once the doses were gone, that was it; Tanu lacked some of the ingredients required to make more.

"Come on, Mendigo," Kendra called. "Time to meet the dragons."

A featureless wooden humanoid with hooks for joints, Mendigo stood his ground, which was peculiar. He always obeyed direct orders. Kendra had brought the animated puppet to Wyrmroost after Agad had restored him to her, and he had generally stood guard over her ever since.

"Mendigo, come," Kendra said.

The limberjack held up both palms and shook his head.

"Agad," Kendra called. "Can Mendigo be afraid?"

The wizard approached Mendigo. "What is the problem?" he asked.

"Mendigo doesn't want to come with me," Kendra said.

"That doesn't seem right," Agad said. "He is an automaton. He follows commands. Mendigo, go to Skyhold with Kendra."

The puppet shook his wooden head again.

"I've never seen him scared," Kendra said. "When Seth and I fought Siletta, her poison nearly destroyed him. Only his hooks remained. Do you think he remembers?"

"Perhaps on some level he does," Agad said. "Animating objects is a peculiar form of magic. As you bestow enough intelligence to follow commands and make simple choices, you risk bestowing some degree of individuality. Mendigo was created once by the witch Muriel, and then the wizard Vernaz helped me reanimate him from his meager remains."

"Won't you come protect me?" Kendra asked Mendigo.

The puppet folded his arms and turned away.

"There could be some residual trauma from his previous demise," Agad said. "He could be starting to develop a modest will of his own."

"It happened to Hugo when the fairies resurrected him," Kendra said. "He started developing free will. But that came from their magic, I think."

"This new quirk was not deliberate," Agad said. "But a fear of dragons seems to have taken hold. Best to leave him behind on this venture."

"Watch out for Grandma and Grandpa," Kendra said.

The limberjack immediately headed toward her grandparents, lingering nearby. Apparently he had not stopped obeying orders altogether.

Although the sun had just gone down, Kendra felt too warm in her heavy coat and gloves. Didger had warned that it would get colder at higher altitudes.

Didger snapped his fingers, and Sheba followed him to the center of the courtyard. Agad joined them there. As the other griffins drew near, the wizard raised both hands, addressing all three riders. "Sadly, by the time you return,

I will be gone. There are other crises to deal with."

"You'll keep looking for Bracken?" Kendra asked, squeezing the reins, her throat constricting with grief.

"He is alive," Agad said. "The horn of his you carry confirms that."

Kendra reached down and touched the horn strapped to her side in a sheath, like a knife. "You can take it if it would help you find him."

"Alas, I already tried," Agad said. "Through the connection the horn has to his lifeforce, I could sense he is alive. But I could derive no guess of where he is being held. I do not expect that will change. He wanted you to have it. If by chance he gets an opportunity to reach out, he may try to link his mind to yours using the horn. It should stay with you."

"All right," Kendra said.

"Good luck at the feast," Agad said. "You are doing an extraordinary job here. Tanu, I will miss your company."

"See you soon," the potion master said.

"Seth, stay out of trouble," Agad said, "and far from the Blackwell."

"I will," Seth promised.

Kendra knew there was a deep pit full of the undead beneath the keep. Agad had warned Seth on multiple occasions to stay away from it, out of worry that her brother might try to communicate with some of the undead denizens and somehow unleash them.

"We will see you later tonight," Marat said. "Fly safely."

"Griffins away!" Didger cried, waving his arms.

"Griffins away!" two other dwarfs called out.

Wings sweeping downward, Sheba leaped into the air. The griffin continued to rise, wings heaving to gain altitude as Kendra wobbled in the creaking saddle. Seth ascended off to the right, Tanu to the left. The three griffins climbed steadily, turning Blackwell Keep into a toy model behind them. The sunset gradually reversed until Kendra was squinting in the sunlight.

"It's still day up here," Seth yelled.

Kendra waved to show she heard him, but quickly dropped her hand back to the saddle because letting go made her feel unsteady. Meanwhile Seth had both arms raised like he was riding a roller coaster. Kendra tried to enjoy the cool air in her face and the spectacular view, but when she looked down at the tiny trees beneath her, she couldn't help shivering at the thought of the enormous fall.

She knew she was strapped to the saddle. But what if some of the straps broke? How old was the saddle? And how competent were the dwarfs who had cinched it on? What if it came loose? Didger had mentioned that Sheba was the eldest griffin. Still gaining altitude, her wings worked hard. What if the griffin had a heart attack? Did that ever happen?

Kendra tried to stay calm. This was going to be fine. The worst-case scenarios in her mind were far-fetched. She would arrive without incident. To panic about imagined hypotheticals was silly.

Under most circumstances she would have also worried about running into dragons. But the invitation to the feast included a promise of safe passage through the skies if she chose to arrive by griffin. Was it possible for the dragons to break their word? Or for one of them to go rogue? Or for some other creature to bother them?

She checked the bow Seth had acquired for her, secured to the saddle. If something did choose to attack, at least she could give it three hundred arrows in the face. The sack of wind could come in handy as well. Henrick had been impressed with the items Seth had gotten from the storerooms, so Kendra knew they must be effective.

As they flew higher than some of the nearest peaks, the chill intensified from cool to cold. Kendra became grateful for the heavy coat and gloves, and she ducked her chin to better hide her face from the wind. As different scenery flowed by beneath her, Kendra gained a greater appreciation for the sheer size of Wyrmroost. She knew the sanctuary was protected from detection by a distracter spell, but it still amazed her that such a large piece of land could go unnoticed by the outside world.

Kendra hunched forward, head down, letting her hood block the wind as her cheeks became numb. Jagged mountains and ridges scrolled by below. After soaring over a high pass between a pair of particularly tall peaks, she saw an enormous mountain, the entire top half of which was carved into a gigantic castle.

Heedless of the frigid air in her face, Kendra stared at Skyhold in astonishment. Several dragons circled around the rugged towers of the gargantuan stronghold. The closer she flew, the more she realized that the vast castle was meant to house dragons, not humans. Huge entrances yawned behind oversized balconies. Dragons roamed spacious terraces open to the sky and perched on long ridges; one waded in a wide, shallow pool. Though the castle had walls and towers, she saw no brickwork or mortared stones— everything seemed to have been shaped by shaving away portions of the mountain. She assumed the top of the highest tower had once been the peak.

A large dragon with bright red scales glided toward them, then wheeled around to guide them. Kendra watched the last of the direct sunlight disappear from the top of the highest tower. Sheba descended to a great open-ing at the base of the castle. The griffin landed smoothly on a rocky shelf, and hardy goblins in clean livery and powdered wigs hurried to help Kendra down from the saddle. They unbuckled her so quickly that Kendra didn't have to work the release on her own, and as soon as her feet hit the ground, the attendants were leading the griffin away.

"Wait," Kendra called, following Sheba.

The goblins pulled the griffin to a halt.

"I need my bow," Kendra said, loosening a strap and pulling the bow from where it had been secured. She also grabbed the small quiver of eight arrows meant to disguise the ability of the bow to produce arrows spontaneously.

"This place is big," Seth said, coming alongside Kendra.

"Has to be," Tanu said. "Think how huge our castles are, and they only house people."

"The fancy goblins crack me up," Seth said. "See the wigs?"

Kendra hushed him. "We don't want to offend anyone."

"We're protected, aren't we?" Seth asked with a smile. "Might be fun to ruffle some feathers."

"These are dragons, not chickens," Kendra reminded him.

"Remember what I told you," Tanu said. "Err on the side of caution tonight. The potion will protect you from dragon fear, but it could also impair your judgment, make you over-confident. Don't say and do everything you think."

Seth shrugged. "I can be as dull as we need."

"Where are they taking the griffins?" Kendra asked.

"I saw stables over that way as we were landing," Tanu said.

A large raven swooped toward them, hovered near the ground, and expanded into a gaunt old woman with moss and slime in her tangled hair. Prominent veins snaked around her thin, bare arms like leafless ivy. Bedraggled clothing hung like becalmed sails on her spare frame. Her lips had shriveled almost out of existence, and her small eyes failed to look directly at Kendra or Seth as she spoke.

"The new caretakers," she said abruptly. "Puppies in a weighted sack."

"Excuse me?" Kendra asked.

"Lobbed into a river," the old woman said. "Never had a chance."

"Are you Vatka?" Seth asked.

"Lowly Vatka, at your service," she said, inclining her head.

"You can turn into a raven," Seth said. "What else can you become?"

"This and that, at need," Vatka replied. "Sad to see innocence abused. Funny too. The sludgefolk wish you well. Not that wishes can help."

"Do you know something?" Kendra asked.

Shuffling away, the woman cackled, then spoke in a higher voice. "Yelp, yelp! We're drowning! Yelp, yelp, yelp." She gave a strangled little howl that dissolved into laughter.

"She's cracked," Tanu said. "Remind me to never become queen of the Sludgeholes."

"She thinks we're doomed," Seth said.

"Then she may not be very crazy," Kendra said. "Come on."

Kendra led the way to the large opening in the wall of the castle. No door covered the cavernous entrance. A goblin guard in a furry hat stepped forward and croaked a single word: "Invitations."

Tanu produced the invitation, and the guard looked it over. He touched the sword hanging at Seth's side and ran a hand along Kendra's bow. Seth spoke in a garbled language, and the guard spoke back, waving them through.

Beyond the entrance, Kendra found a vast hall that took up a lot of the space inside the mountain with a single room. The immensity of the cavern seemed to shrink her enough that she wondered if she was having an experience similar to that of an ant entering a sports arena.

Gold dust glittered on the walls and ceiling, giving the entire room a metallic shimmer. Complex grooves carved into the walls were either decorative patterns or perhaps some elaborate form of writing known to dragons. No furnishings interrupted the tremendous space except for a pair of long tables toward the center, sized for humans, set for dinner, with goblin attendants standing ready, white wigs in place, white gloves on their hands, brass buttons polished. Many guests were already seated in the high-backed chairs.

An impressive assortment of dragons prowled the room: an oily purple dragon with a face like a mass of squirming tentacles; a bulky dragon with scales like armored plating, huge horns like a bull's, and a clubbed tail; a sleek white dragon with crystal-blue eyes; a dark-gray dragon with two heads; a golden-brown dragon with long quills bristling atop the head, down the neck and tail, and all over the bulky body. Kendra counted sixteen of the giant reptiles in total, which probably spoke more to the enormity of the room than any other detail.

At the far end of the room awaited Celebrant on a raised platform. Only his head and neck had been visible when Kendra had interacted with him on the Perch. She had never really had a chance to appreciate the grand scale of his entire form. A flawless armor of gleaming platinum scales adorned every visible inch of his anatomy. From the majestic horns on his head to the tips of his razor-like claws, the Dragon King was glorious and lethal. Kendra could not help noticing the shining crown circling his head at the base of his horns, made from some metal more intensely bright than silver, and studded with scarlet gems.

A goblin with exceedingly fleshy cheeks stepped forward and blew a bugle. The brassy notes reverberated across the otherwise quiet hall. "Kendra and Seth Sorenson have arrived, with their manservant," he announced. "Also Lowly Vatka of the Sludgeholes."

Celebrant raised his head. "The guests of honor," he said, his voice as resonant as a men's chorus speaking in unison. "Welcome, my fellow caretakers. Mingle with the other humanoids and please enjoy the food. We'll get to the more formal portion of the evening after you are fed and settled."

"Does the manservant get to eat?" Tanu mumbled with a small smile.

With a surprising rush of wind, Raxtus landed beside them. "Greetings, Seth and Kendra. We'll talk more later. For now, just follow instructions." He sprang away before Kendra could reply, gliding to the side of the room.

A squat, plump goblin with a deeply indented face led them to the table and pulled back a chair for Kendra. Lord Dalgorel of the Fair Folk rose to greet her, impossibly handsome in his dressy uniform, complete with a sash, epaulets, and several polished medals.

"Greetings, Kendra Sorenson," Dalgorel said. "And Seth, of course."

"Are those medals of neutrality?" Seth asked.

"Charming as ever," Dalgorel replied. "Not all great deeds occur on a battlefield, though some of mine did, long ago. You remember my daughter, Eve."

Kendra noticed Seth staring at Eve in her simple but gorgeous gown. She was about his age and as exquisite as any of the Fair Folk.

Seth walked up to her, took her hand, and kissed it.

Kendra gaped in astonishment. She glanced at Tanu,

who watched with wide eyes. She knew it must be the courage potion.

"How did you get to come?" Seth asked.

Eve waved an arm at the rest of the room. "I've always wanted to see dragons. Father needed a companion, and Mother hates journeys."

"It's amazing," Seth said. "I've only seen more dragons than this a couple of times. Never so many so close. Some are so weird."

"The porcupine one!" she whispered loudly.

"And the one with a noggin like a hammerhead shark," Seth replied. "The fear doesn't bother you?"

"Father tested me," Eve said. "I passed. I've always been brave."

"We should sit," Dalgorel suggested, motioning Seth away from his daughter to the seat on the far side of Kendra. Seth followed the recommendation reluctantly, and Tanu sat just beyond him.

Kendra took her seat beside Dalgorel and spread the silky napkin on her lap. Across from her sat a little man with a bulbous nose and a gray beard that ran along the underside of his chin. "Well met, caretaker," he said, his voice rather high.

"The Grand Imperator Karzal," Dalgorel introduced.

"Good to meet you," Kendra replied in Gnomish.

Karzal's eyes widened and his eyebrows raised. "It has been many cycles since a caretaker bothered to learn our tongue," he said in Gnomish.

"I'm honored to meet you," Kendra said, pleased by

the good impression she was making. She reached for the nearby goblet of water.

"Wait a moment," boomed a deep voice powerful enough to vibrate the glassware. It was the bulky dragon with the bull horns. "Before everyone gets too comfortable, I formally challenge Celebrant the Just for the kingship."

CHAPTER SEVEN

Challenge

The vast room inside Skyhold became utterly silent. All eyes turned to Celebrant.

Seth failed to suppress his grin. How was he this lucky?

"Madrigus, my faithful servant," the Dragon King said smoothly, a hint of warning behind the words. "This is a poor occasion for rude humor."

"Bah," Madrigus replied harshly, stomping his heavy feet and shaking his wings. "I'm no jester. Prepare to surrender your crown."

Celebrant shook his head. "You are a member of my personal guard. Second in seniority. This verges on treason. And it is a matter for dragons. We do not handle such affairs before company. If you insist on a challenge, issue it after our visitors depart."

"Afraid to fall in front of your fellow caretakers?"

Madrigus asked. "Adjourn to the proving ground with me now or face your puny guests as a coward."

Celebrant's eyes narrowed, his gaze intensifying. "Very well. But for this insult I will disperse your bones without honor."

"You'll have to win first, small one," Madrigus said.

Seth pumped a fist. "Yes. Dragon fight."

Beside him, Kendra looked shocked. Most people appeared astonished. Lord Dalgorel's mouth hung open. Seth looked down the table to Eve and finally saw his joy reflected.

Tugging on a pair of white gloves, Dalgorel stood. "This spectacle is a rarity indeed."

"How rare?" Seth asked.

"I've lived a very long time," Dalgorel said. "I've never seen it. Nor met anyone who has."

"Will it be dangerous?" Kendra asked.

"Two of the most powerful dragons alive are about to fight to the death," Dalgorel said. "We are here by invitation and are not to be harmed. But I will not be pressing for a close seat."

"There are close seats?" Seth asked.

Raxtus approached. "Sorry about this. You don't have to watch."

"I wouldn't miss it," Seth said. "Where is the proving ground?"

"Right here in the castle," Raxtus said. "It's basically a big courtyard. Father wants me to escort you and see to your safety."

"How do you know?" Seth asked.

"He can speak directly to my mind," Raxtus said. "How would you like that? Unfair amount of parental supervision, if you ask me. Come on."

Raxtus led them up a wide, slowly winding corridor. Tanu walked between Seth and Kendra. Seth realized there were no doors in this castle, or small hallways—only spaces that could accommodate dragons.

"Can Madrigus beat your dad?" Kendra asked.

"Madrigus is tough," Raxtus said. "He has killed more than a few dragons over the years. He has thick, strong scales and seems built to shred dragon hides. His whole body is like a can opener. But no dragon has ever scratched my father. Not a single scale has even been damaged."

"What would it mean to have a new Dragon King?" Seth asked.

Raxtus chuckled. "Not going to happen. Here we are— the royal vantage."

They emerged onto a high balcony above a huge, open-air arena. Below, dragons gathered on all sides to watch the contest. The sleek white dragon with crystal-blue eyes already rested in the balcony, gazing below.

"Hello, Mother," Raxtus said. "This is Kendra, Seth, and Tanu, along with Lord Dalgorel and his daughter, Eve."

"I am Raina," the dragon said with a mesmerizing voice. "I'm sorry Madrigus interrupted your feast. Waste of a strong dragon."

Down below, Celebrant entered one side of the arena; Madrigus, the other. The sunset was fading, but magical globes of light flared to life around the arena, bathing it in sterile, white radiance.

Seth studied the challenger. Madrigus had a relatively short, thick neck supporting a large head and wide horns. The huge plates of his scales armored him like a tank, and spikes protruded everywhere—some straight, some barbed, some hooked—all sharp. The swollen lump at the end of his tail bristled like a pineapple.

"To honor your centuries of service, I offer you one last chance to yield," Celebrant said loudly. "Choose banishment and live."

"I return the same offer," Madrigus replied. "Leave the crown and go into exile."

"Madrigus is so dead," Raxtus murmured. "I think he's hoping to rattle Father by challenging him in front of guests and by being rude. It's going to backfire. He's just making him angry."

"This is conduct unbefitting a member of my personal guard," Celebrant said. "I strip you of all rank and honors. You die a rogue and a traitor."

"The honor of your guard was disgraced the moment you added your son," Madrigus said. "You expelled Obregon for Raxtus? Being a member of your guard was once a rare privilege. Your nepotism turned it into a disgrace."

Seth glanced at Raxtus, who stared into the arena in silence, still as a statue.

"It is not your place to question your king," Celebrant said. "I have reasons for all I do. Obregon can fill the vacancy you have created. Two other dragons have challenged me of late. How many of our own must perish?"

"They were weak," Madrigus said.

"No dragon living has a chance against me, but they had less chance than most," Celebrant said. "Now that I consider it, both of them knew you well. Podenholm and Rondet. Did you put them up to it?"

"I may have helped the fools toward their folly," Madrigus said. "Fanned the flames of stupidity."

"You were testing me," Celebrant said. "Studying me. To prepare for today."

Madrigus gave a roar that could have rivaled volcanoes. Hands over his ears, Seth felt the air trembling and stared at the many rows of serrated teeth made visible, as if multiple mouths were nested within one another.

"Very well," Celebrant replied as the last echoes faded.

Lowering his horns, Madrigus charged forward with astonishing speed. Celebrant twisted out of the way at the last moment, ducking a swipe from the clubbed tail and trading sides of the arena.

"Dull," Celebrant remarked.

"Are you going to run from me all night?" Madrigus asked.

For the first time, Celebrant snarled.

The dragons rushed toward each other, crashing together with a sound like colliding locomotives. After the initial impact, they thrashed and rolled and snapped and slashed, accompanied by the jarring shrieks of sharp objects grating across impenetrable surfaces. After the ferocious flurry of engagement, the dragons parted, prowling in a loose circle, eyes fixed on each other. Both were enormous, but Celebrant was longer from snout to tail, while Madrigus possessed more overall bulk.

Seth saw no damage to either dragon. He glanced at Eve, who gazed transfixed. Kendra had her head partly turned away. Raxtus watched intently.

Celebrant darted at Madrigus, coming in low but finishing high, claws raking at the other dragon's face before his teeth clamped down near the base of the neck. Madrigus retracted his head almost like a turtle and bashed Celebrant in the side with his club tail. The impact made Seth think of a wrecking ball.

Again the dragons separated. Celebrant had no mark from the mighty blow, but on the shoulder of Madrigus, part of a plate had been torn aside.

"Nobody finds the seams like Dad," Raxtus whispered.

Rising up straight, Madrigus inhaled deeply. Celebrant laughed, puffing out his chest at the other dragon and baring his teeth.

"What is Madrigus doing?" Raxtus wondered. "No breath weapon can touch my father."

Madrigus exhaled a concentrated stream of darkness. Celebrant pivoted away from the black column at the last moment, but the exhalation struck the side of his chest before he spun to the ground. Platinum scales sprayed into the air like coins.

"What?" Raxtus exclaimed.

Now Madrigus was laughing.

"How?" Celebrant demanded. "Not a single dragon has

mastered the seething night since Grugnar of old."

"My ancestor," Madrigus boasted.

"He kept that breath weapon a secret," Raxtus said, worry in his voice. "No wonder he thought he had a chance against Father—seething night can eat away any material."

Madrigus charged forward, and Celebrant turned, offering his back to his enemy. The resounding collision knocked Celebrant flat on his belly, while Madrigus raked and stabbed at his back.

"Father has to protect his chest," Raxtus muttered. "He's never been in this position before. He's never been wounded. His other scales won't hold out forever. Not against Madrigus."

Seth wondered what it would mean if Celebrant died. Would Madrigus inherit the position of caretaker along with the kingship? Or would the position perish with Celebrant? Though he felt bad for Raxtus, Seth wondered if the death of the Dragon King would benefit them.

Without fully rolling over, Celebrant arched his head up and back, and his jaws found the flesh beneath the other dragon's damaged plate. Roaring, Madrigus tore away, and gore fountained into the air. Celebrant tried to rise, but Madrigus charged back in, shoveling with his horns in an attempt to flip the Dragon King and expose his chest. In a flash, Celebrant whirled around, outstretched claws ripping the wound at the base of his enemy's neck, tearing away more scales. Madrigus lunged for Celebrant's damaged chest, but the Dragon King vaulted the attack and created space.

Squaring up to face the Dragon King, Madrigus inhaled

again, but as he prepared to open his mouth, Celebrant blasted him in the snout with a bolt of white lightning. Stunned, Madrigus staggered back and started to inhale again. Celebrant raced forward and slashed into his mouth as it opened, severing part of his tongue.

"Dad won't let him use seething night again," Raxtus said. "It takes Madrigus too long to muster it. It was foolish to keep trying. Now he's really hurt."

Celebrant now ran quick circles around Madrigus, twisting away from attacks and occasionally hacking at his wounded opponent. Madrigus continuously coughed dark fluid from his mouth, and gore streamed down his front from the wound beside his neck. A patch on the side of Celebrant's chest lacked scales and looked charred, but that didn't seem to hinder him.

"Madrigus is slowing down," Raxtus said. "This is over."

Like a striking snake, Celebrant streaked forward, clamping his jaws around the top of the other dragon's throat, just below the head. Seth winced at the crunch. Without releasing his grip, Celebrant inhaled deeply, then exhaled powerfully. White flames erupted from the eyes of Madrigus as well as from his nostrils, mouth, earholes, and the wound at the base of his neck. Celebrant released his grip, and Madrigus collapsed into a lifeless heap, smoke rising from his roasted head.

"Yikes," Raxtus murmured. "Father is angry."

Celebrant looked fiercely at the crowd. "This fight was wasteful. But now I'm in the mood. He wounded me. Who wants to try next?"

Silence prevailed after his question as his gaze swept the crowd.

"Who is your king?" Celebrant cried.

"Celebrant the Just," the dragons answered as one.

Celebrant gave a nod. "I am true to my word. We will deal with the corpse after the feast. His bones will be scattered across Wyrmroost."

After stretching his wings wide, Celebrant folded them and went back into the castle. The light globes dimmed, and the other dragons followed. Raina withdrew from the overlook, and Raxtus started leading the others back toward the feast. Seth noticed Tanu lingering, staring down at the proving ground, then followed his gaze to the corpse of Madrigus.

Seth approached Tanu and whispered, "Ingredients?"

Tanu gave a slight nod, eyes misty. "A treasure trove."

"You could make some amazing potions," Seth said.

"Celebrant means to disrespect the body," Tanu said. "A fresh kill—blood, glands, tissues, organs—a male in his prime. It will all go to waste."

"Some of it probably got fried when Celebrant filled him with fire," Seth said.

"The eyes got cooked," Tanu said. "A lot of the tissues and fluids in the head and neck might be toast. But there is plenty left. Dragons are very durable. And who knows? Maybe a baked tonsil has interesting properties."

The globes dimmed further.

"Want me to sneak down there?" Seth whispered.

Tanu looked at him sharply. "Don't even think about it."

"Give me a container," Seth said. "I can at least collect some blood. Don't forget I can shadow walk. I'm almost invisible in the dark. And I have stealthy boots on."

Tanu hesitated, taking a couple of deep breaths. "And if you get caught, relations with the dragons get even worse. They might even have an excuse to harm you."

"They're going to scatter the bones," Seth said. "Is there a chance Celebrant would give you permission?"

Tanu shook his head. "No way. He knows what those ingredients could become in the hands of a potion master. And we're his enemies."

"Can Celebrant make potions out of Madrigus?" Seth asked.

"I don't think so," Tanu said. "I've never heard of dragons using potions. Most potions only work on mortals."

The light globes went out. The sunset dwindled against the mountaintops. Deep shadow engulfed the proving grounds.

"It's abandoned," Seth said. "They all went back to the feast. Let me go down there quickly."

"You'll be missed," Tanu said.

"Let me go," piped a small voice.

Seth had nearly forgotten about Calvin.

"I'm small," the nipsie said. "Nobody will notice."

"It's also really far for you," Tanu said. "And you can't carry much."

"Far never bothered me," Calvin said. "And something is better than nothing."

"I'd rather you stay with Seth," Tanu said. "Go on. I'm going to loiter here for a few minutes."

"You're going to try to swipe something, aren't you?" Seth asked.

"Don't be absurd. Only a maniac would take such a risk." Tanu bent close, his lips almost touching Seth's ear. "But if your manservant gets caught doing something unacceptable, swear to me you will disavow me."

"Maybe you shouldn't—" Seth began.

"This is a never-in-a-lifetime opportunity," Tanu whispered. "Won't happen again. And war is brewing. I'll just dawdle for a minute or two. Maybe take a closer look. Pay my respects. You are needed inside. You're not sure what that manservant of yours is doing."

"Don't get caught," Seth whispered.

"Swear you will disavow me or I can't do it," Tanu said.

"Do what?" Seth asked.

"Good boy."

"Let me join you," Calvin said quietly. "What's the harm? I may be able to access otherwise unreachable cavities."

Tanu paused.

"Take him," Seth said, removing Calvin from a pocket and passing him to the potion master. Tanu accepted the nipsie and turned away.

Seth hustled back to his table.

CHAPTER EIGHT

Declaration

Kendra watched Seth return to his seat beside her. "What took you so long?"

He shrugged. "I didn't want that to end. Now I can die happy."

"Where is Tanu?" Kendra asked.

"I think he's trying to find a restroom," Seth said.

Celebrant stood once again at the front of the room, the dark wound on the side of his chest now interrupting his platinum perfection. "I apologize for the unplanned diversion. Please enjoy your meal."

Seth cupped his hands around his mouth and shouted, "Are you all right?"

"I am just fine," Celebrant assured him. "Don't let me distract you from the meal. The wound is ugly but shallow."

Kendra turned her attention to the food. She had not

been sure what to expect at a dragon feast, but to her relief the fare on the table was not an assortment of bugs or bizarre unmentionables but rather beef, chicken, potatoes, cheese, bread, squash, and soup. She sampled most of it—the meats and vegetables were heavily seasoned but still tasty, the cheese was a little too sharp, the bread was warm and delicious, and the soup tasted like some kind of gooey, creamy punishment.

She was taking a bite of bread when a bugle blared.

"Creya the Eagle, standing in for Raj Faranah of the Zowali Protectorate," the goblin announcer called.

A large golden eagle glided to a halt beside Kendra, perching on the back of Lord Dalgorel's chair. "Hello, Dalgorel," the eagle said in a female voice. "Raj sends his regards." The bird looked down at Kendra. "You must be one of the new caretakers."

"I'm Kendra, and this is my brother, Seth," Kendra said.

"You're wearing the medallion, Kendra," Creya said.

"My turn today," Kendra said. "We switch off."

"She's a proper caretaker," Karzal said from across the table. "Speaks Gnomish."

"Did I miss anything?" Creya asked.

Dalgorel chuckled. "Take a look at Celebrant."

"Sweet mercy!" Creya exclaimed. "What happened to him?"

"Madrigus," Dalgorel said.

"No—he's one of their top dragons. He's part of his guard."

"Challenged him tonight," Dalgorel said. "In front of us."

"I missed it?" Creya complained. "Events like this tend to be dry."

"Not to a discerning eye," Dalgorel said. "The currents of politics are always swirling. Tonight certainly had some extra thrills."

"Somebody finally injured Celebrant," Creya said.

"It's the beginning of the end for him," Dalgorel said.

"Really?" Kendra asked.

"No time soon, mind you," Dalgorel clarified. "But now he has been challenged by a real contender, and he has been hurt. The scales will grow back, but the memory is forever. Kendra started it all by standing up to him. Authority can be fragile."

"Have you met the other leaders of the protected territories?" Creya asked Kendra.

"All but Amulon," Kendra said.

"He's down at the end of the table," Dalgorel said. "I believe he arrived during the challenge. He's speaking with Bag Zou, chief of the western cyclopses."

Kendra saw the rumitaur standing beside the table, gnawing on a hunk of cheese, large antlers projecting from his head and forking to many points. His light-brown skin nearly matched the hide of his elk body. Beside him on a low, wide stool sat a hulking man dressed in a primitive tunic, with shaggy hair and a single prominent eye above his nose.

"Are there eastern cyclopses too?" Kendra asked.

"Not here at Wyrmroost," Dalgorel explained. "There are different breeds of cyclopses—eastern, western, and Mediterranean."

"And Himalayan," Eve piped up.

"I'm talking about the major groupings," Dalgorel said.

"The Himalayan cyclopses are the most fascinating," Eve said. "Their one eye is a third eye."

"They are physically blind," Dalgorel said. "Or so the story goes."

"They see with their minds," Eve said.

"You should go meet Amulon," Creya encouraged. "You need all the support you can get."

Kendra glanced at Seth, who was busy talking to Karzal. It might be best not to disturb her brother. In his current mood, he might provoke a war with the rumitaurs.

Kendra rose and walked along the table until she reached Amulon. He stood at least as tall as Henrick, and the looming antlers made him extra imposing. His neck and shoulders were particularly muscular.

"Excuse me," Kendra said. "I'm Kendra Sorenson."

The rumitaur looked down at her. "The child caretaker," he said. "A bizarre novelty."

Bag Zou twisted on his stool to view her. If he stood, Kendra estimated he would be twice her height. He patted his broad belly. "I've eaten mouthfuls larger than you tonight," he said in a voice so deep it made the words hard to understand.

"I don't mind being underestimated," Kendra said, offended by their condescension. "Celebrant did that, and now he's missing scales."

"Madrigus broke the scales," Bag Zou said, huge hand resting on his knee. Kendra noticed how tiny his fingernails were, the ends ragged as if he chewed them.

"If you say so," Kendra replied.

"The girl is not wrong," Amulon said. "She defied Celebrant on the walls of Blackwell Keep. Undermined him."

Bag Zou blinked. Winked? "I could squish her on a whim."

"Not tonight," a new voice said. "You would die before your fist could fall."

Kendra turned and found a handsome young man behind her, maybe a couple of years older than her. He had thick black hair, intense dark eyes, and a strong jawline. His dressy black robe of Asian design fit snugly and had subtle touches of embroidery at the neck, near the wrists, and around the fancy buttons. Was he one of the Fair Folk? He didn't look quite as perfect as them—his nose was a bit crooked, as if it had been broken once or twice, and he had a faint scar through one eyebrow. The little flaws almost made him even more attractive.

"Who's going to stop me?" Bag Zou asked. "You?"

"Dragons," he replied simply. "Kendra is under the care of dragons tonight. And she runs this sanctuary. You ought to show her more respect. It was generous of her to introduce herself."

"Kendra, I am Amulon," the rumitaur said. "Good luck surviving your assignment."

The cyclops turned back to the table.

"Bag Zou," the young man said. "Where is your introduction? You're being rude."

The cyclops turned. "Am I supposed to know you?"

"You are supposed to know Kendra," the young man said with a grin. "She oversees everyone and everything here."

The cyclops rolled his eye. "Celebrant leads the dragons because he vanquishes all who challenge him. I am chief of my tribe through victories in combat. Kendra is a child nominated by a wizard."

"She could teach you plenty," the young man said. "Beginning with depth perception."

Kendra managed to stifle her laugh.

The cyclops stood menacingly. He was easily twice as tall as Kendra. "Are you under protection from the dragons, little man?"

"I am not," the young man said. His grin did not falter. "Would you like to step outside with me?"

"You read my mind," Bag Zou said.

Amulon placed a staying hand on Bag Zou's chest. "Do you know who you are addressing?"

Bag Zou glanced at Amulon. "Does it matter?"

"How many humans are at Wyrmroost?" Amulon asked.

"Very few," Bag Zou said.

"When did this one arrive?" Amulon asked.

"I did not notice his arrival," Bad Zou said.

"Some dragons can take human shape," Amulon said.

The cyclops paled.

"An introduction is owed," the young man said.

"I am Bag Zou of the western cyclopses," Bag Zou said. "Stay off our land or we will stomp you into wine."

"Not polite," the young man said. "But you are a cyclops. Manners are not to be expected. Shall we lighten the mood? What does a cyclops call an eye patch?"

"What?" Bag Zou asked.

"A blindfold."

"I'm here to eat," Bag Zou said, turning back to the table and sitting. Before his backside reached his stool, the young man nimbly slid it out of the way, and the cyclops fell flat on his back. The brute sat up, huge fists balled tight, face reddening. "You try my patience."

The young man leaned toward him and flicked his nose. "Manners."

The cyclops ground his teeth. "I have protection from dragons here tonight."

"Who says I'm a dragon?" the young man asked.

"Amulon," the cyclops said.

"Want to go outside and find out?" the young man asked.

The cyclops took a deep breath, huge chest rising and falling. "Off with you, pest. The meat is calling." The cyclops situated his stool and kept a hand on it as he sat.

The young man nodded at Amulon and led Kendra back toward her seat.

"Are you a dragon?" Kendra whispered nervously.

"Absolutely not," the young man said. "Don't be absurd."

"Then who are you?"

The young man stopped. "I insisted on introductions and failed to provide my own." He bowed. "I am Ronodin, known to some as the dark unicorn."

Kendra stared at him in shock. Bracken had been looking for Ronodin!

"You look surprised," Ronodin said. "You've heard of me?"

"Kind of," Kendra said, not wanting to give anything away. Was he like Bracken? Could he see her mind?

"I know plenty about you," he said. "I captured your boyfriend."

Shock gave way to anger. "Where is he?"

"There is some fire," Ronodin said. "Yes, I see it now. Bracken is alive and well."

"Where?"

"It would be clumsy to tell you," Ronodin said. "He is my prisoner, and you wish to rescue him."

"Why are you here?"

"We all have secrets. And reasons. And many of us have earlobes."

"Are you trying to be funny?"

"No," Ronodin said. "I am succeeding."

"I'm disappointed," Kendra said. "You were nice back there. You were gallant."

Ronodin shrugged. "I was trying for rude. Cyclopses are the worst."

"I thought you were sticking up for me."

"I was, I suppose; no use pretending otherwise."

"And you took Bracken."

"I do whatever I want."

"You sound like a child," Kendra said.

"I am unshackled."

"What do you want from me?"

"He was right about you," Ronodin said. "You shine bright. I've never shone as bright as you."

"Some people say that. I don't see it."

"How charming. You have his first horn."

"What?"

"Is anything more tedious than when people pretend? You have it with you right now. I am not guessing. Will you give it to me?"

"Are you kidding?" Kendra asked.

"I'd trade a lot for it," Ronodin said.

"Give me Bracken," Kendra said.

"No, I need Bracken. But I would give so much for that horn."

"I wouldn't trade it to you for anything."

"Don't be hasty. I may not look like much, but I have a lot to offer. I can turn into a horse. With a horn." He scowled. "Oh, no."

"What?"

"One horn. Does that mean I have something in common with cyclopses? Did I mention they are the worst?"

"I'm pretty sure you're the worst."

Ronodin smiled. "In some ways, maybe. Yes, in some ways I am worse than any cyclops would dare to dream. I'll take your insult as a compliment."

"It's not a compliment," Kendra said.

"Looking at me now, doesn't it seem absurd that I can turn into a horse? Not just any horse—a unicorn. Ridiculous, if you ask me. But when I'm a unicorn, taking a human shape seems equally absurd. No, more absurd. Tottering around on two legs."

"Why are you here?" Kendra asked. "Just to bother me?"

"You have little to do with why I'm here," Ronodin said. "Bothering you is a happy accident. Life can be generous some days. But watch out—the price of living is pain. Same price as loving."

"You don't live at Wyrmroost?" Kendra asked.

Ronodin made a disgusted face. "Absolutely not. I go wherever I want, do whatever I want."

"What are you doing here?"

"Since you keep asking, I'll answer as a courtesy. I told Celebrant how to defeat you."

Kendra was worried he was serious. "How?"

"No," Ronodin said. "Nothing more on that subject. Not if you ask a hundred times. Unless you choose to give me the horn."

"I'm keeping the horn," Kendra said.

"Then I'm keeping my secrets," Ronodin said. "You better get back to your seat. Looks like Celebrant has a big announcement to make."

Kendra gave him one last stare. Why did he have to be so handsome? It seemed incongruent. She returned to her seat.

"Who was that guy?" Seth asked. "He's still watching you. Now he's watching me."

"He's Ronodin, the dark unicorn," Kendra said.

"How do dark sparkles work?" Seth asked.

"It's no joke," Kendra said. "He has Bracken."

"Should we beat him up?" Seth asked.

"Maybe," Kendra said. "Where is Tanu?"

"How am I supposed to know?" Seth said.

"My guests," Celebrant began, standing tall on his platform. "I hope you enjoyed your meal. We now begin the more solemn portion of the gathering. As you know, I am a co-caretaker of Wyrmroost, along with Kendra and Seth Sorenson. We have reached an impasse about how to jointly run this sanctuary. And so, as king of all dragons, and as a co-caretaker of Wyrmroost, I find my human counterparts out of line, and I formally declare war on them and on all who support them."

Murmuring broke out along the table. Kendra glanced at Seth, finding her own shock and worry echoed in his features. She looked back at Ronodin, who smiled and nodded, then pointed at Celebrant.

"This war has been centuries in the making," Celebrant continued. "Magical creatures have been repressed and abused by humanity for far too long. The hour has come for us to govern ourselves. All of the creatures of Wyrmroost are invited to unite with our cause. Any who do so will be rewarded. Those who resist will be crushed. We invite our human overlords, if they so choose, to depart in peace and leave us to govern ourselves. Otherwise they will be destroyed."

Kendra glanced at Dalgorel, who frowned deeply, eyes on Celebrant. Did his long-established policy of neutrality mean he would continue to avoid choosing sides?

"I give the citizens of Wyrmroost until noon tomorrow to sort out their allegiances," Celebrant went on. "I give my enemies until midday tomorrow to prepare. And then it is open war until a victor emerges. Make no mistake. The dragons will prevail. Soaring Cliffs has already fallen to the dragons, and I learned earlier tonight that Crescent Lagoon, the island sanctuary, has fallen as well."

There was another stir as those present reacted to the news. Kendra noticed the dragons around the room studying them, somewhat like hungry cats watching mice.

"Thank you for your attention," Celebrant said. "You are welcome to depart. Unfortunately, some hill giants broke into our stables tonight during the festivities. Several mounts were killed, including the griffins from Blackwell Keep. The giants have paid for their effrontery with their lives. I apologize for any inconvenience their senseless attack has caused. Of course, the road remains available to all who must make their way home."

CHAPTER NINE

Homeward Bound

Seth left his seat and went to Dalgorel. "What does war mean?" he asked. "What can they do?"

"It's without precedent here at Wyrmroost," Dalgorel said. "The protective barriers should continue to hold. I believe Celebrant is trying to justify uniting your enemies against you and attacking anyone who opposes him."

"The griffins," Kendra mourned. "Sheba. Sage. Titan."

"Treacherous and shrewd," Dalgorel said. "Your mounts were in the care of the dragons without being under their direct protection. The dragons needed to defend you from any enemies, but they only needed to take reasonable precautions with your mounts. They can blame the hill giants for the slayings."

"Celebrant must have set it up," Seth said.

"No question," Dalgorel said.

"Can we get home safely?" Kendra asked. "Do protected roads go all the way?"

"There are protected roads," Dalgorel said. "You could possibly make it."

Seth glanced over at the dark unicorn, who continued to watch them from a distance. "What is Ronodin doing here?" Seth asked.

"He supposedly told Celebrant how to defeat us," Kendra said.

"The gnomes will stand with the girl who speaks Gnomish," Karzal said, stepping over the top of the table on short legs and extending a hand to Kendra. She shook it. "Many dragons consider gnomes a delicacy. They eat us like candy."

"What about the Fair Folk?" Seth asked.

"You know our policy, Seth," Dalgorel said. "Neutrality in all outside matters."

"Nobody is ever really neutral," Seth said.

"In most practical ways we come close," Dalgorel said. "Neutrality is a choice. It has dangers. A big risk is that neutrality leaves us without allies. And that is our choice."

"What about the animals?" Kendra asked the eagle.

"I cannot speak for Raj in this," Creya said. "But the Zowali Protectorate has always sided with the caretakers of Blackwell Keep."

"The territories will not openly fight you," Dalgorel said. "Amulon will probably remain neutral, unless he should desperately need help, and Vatka is tough to read."

Seth caught Ronodin staring at them again. "One moment," Seth said.

He crossed to Ronodin, who calmly watched him approach, arms folded, wearing a small smirk.

"Did you set this trap?" Seth asked.

"The hill giants killing your griffins so you have to walk home?" Ronodin asked.

"Yeah," Seth said.

"No, the dragons are handling all of the tactics," Ronodin said. "I simply gave Celebrant a key piece of information that will enable him to win his war."

"Can we stop him?" Seth asked.

"You could try, if you knew enough," Ronodin said. "Look how dark you are—almost as dark as your sister is light. It's like I'm talking to the Sphinx."

"You know him?"

"Back when he was interesting."

"He got boring?"

"Doesn't everyone?"

"What do we need to know to stop Celebrant?" Seth asked.

"See, you're already boring me," Ronodin said. "I used to be extremely bright, you know, but the shadows suit me better. They look good on you."

"I'm not evil," Seth said.

"Give it time," Ronodin replied.

"Dark doesn't have to be evil," Seth said.

"Evil can be so relative," Ronodin said. "Do you have any evil relatives?"

"I have a cousin I don't always like," Seth said.

"Why not?"

"He thinks he's awesome."

Ronodin smiled. "We're destined to be friends. I have a cousin like that too! I recently captured him."

"Bracken?"

"Yes. Some free advice? Capture your cousin. It helps."

"Where is Bracken?"

Ronodin's eyes became droopy, and his head sagged. He started snoring.

"Did I bore you again?"

His eyes opened. "You're catching on! What would you say if I asked how I could get into Blackwell Keep and kill everyone?"

"Probably nothing," Seth admitted.

"And so I don't bore you by asking," Ronodin said.

"I could also misinform you," Seth said.

"Which would make me lose respect for you," Ronodin said. "I'm hard to fool. I seldom lie. The truth, artfully handled, usually suffices."

"Am I wasting my time talking to you?" Seth asked.

"Depends on what you want," Ronodin said. "I could help you develop your powers. You bought the product but lost the owner's manual. You could do more than you realize."

"I don't want you as a teacher," Seth said.

"We could relate," Ronodin said. "I used to be shiny. Had a shiny sister. An annoying cousin. We could be quite a pair. I don't offer mentorship often or lightly."

"I'm on a home-study course," Seth said.

"Tell you what—get that unicorn horn from your sister, give it to me, and I'll not only tell you how to defeat Celebrant, I'll help you get back to Blackwell Keep."

"I have a map," Seth said. "We can get back to Blackwell Keep on the road."

"Theoretically," Ronodin said.

"What's the catch?" Seth asked.

"No more hints."

"What would Celebrant do if you told me how to defeat him?"

Ronodin shrugged. "I owe loyalty to no one."

"Then why help Celebrant?" Seth asked.

"I have my own reasons."

"Big fan of dragons? Okay, I'll admit, me too. Who can resist? But not if they're going to kill everyone."

"Have a pleasant walk home," Ronodin said, turning and striding away.

Seth returned to Kendra, who stood talking to Lowly Vatka.

"But will you support us?" Kendra asked.

"You may as well try your question on the reeds or the puddles," the hag said. "The servant cannot respond for the master."

"Come with me," Dalgorel said. "Eve and I arrived on griffins as well. I must inquire after their health. If all is well, Kendra, you and Seth could borrow one for a return flight to Blackwell Keep, and the other could bear Eve and me home."

Seth fell in next to Kendra, and they followed Dalgorel toward the platform at the opposite end of the room from the entrance. Several of the guests at the tables were already departing.

"What did you think of Ronodin?" Kendra asked.

"I think you should consider sending a hundred arrows his way," Seth said.

"No violence here," Dalgorel said over his shoulder. "Engage in hostilities against anyone present and you open the door for retaliation. The dragons would love an excuse to pounce on the two of you."

"They might capture us and not kill us," Seth said.

"To avoid another mortal caretaker taking your place?" Dalgorel asked. "Perhaps. But if Celebrant were sole caretaker, he could still veto possible replacements for a time. I'm not sure the Dragon King would weep if harm came to you."

"There's Tanu," Seth said, relieved. Hopefully Calvin was with him.

The potion master was walking straight to Ronodin.

"Think he knows who he is?" Kendra asked.

"Looks like it," Seth said.

"King Celebrant," Dalgorel called as they drew near to the platform. "Thank you for the excellent feast. I must inquire after the griffins from Terrabelle."

"One survived, one perished," Celebrant said. "Thankfully, I believe the remaining griffin should be able to carry you and your daughter."

"I trust you are correct," Dalgorel said.

"Am I to assume your territory will remain neutral throughout the upcoming conflict?" Celebrant asked.

"Yes," Dalgorel said. "True to our long-standing policy."

"You didn't protect our griffins," Kendra said to the Dragon King. "You should replace them."

"Alas, such is not our arrangement," Celebrant said. "And I'm not sure if you would have much luck taking up your complaint with the hill giants. You are welcome to try."

"It's not right," Seth said.

"If you want a chance to settle your grievance with me, challenge me to a duel," Celebrant offered.

Seth glanced at the blackened patch on the side of Celebrant's chest. He fingered his sword. What might a blast of lightning do to that vulnerable spot?

"Don't even think about it," Kendra muttered through clenched teeth.

Seth had no idea how strong a lightning bolt the sword would release. And he didn't know if even a serious lightning bolt would be enough to kill a big dragon like Celebrant, vulnerable spot or not. "No, thanks," Seth said. "You've had a rough night."

"You are welcome to tarry here," Celebrant said. "Or else the road awaits. Deliberate wisely. At noon tomorrow, your experience at Wyrmroost will change drastically."

"You already attacked us," Seth said.

"Is that what you think we did?" Celebrant asked. "Attack? Wait until you see what is coming."

"Come on, Seth," Kendra said.

"We're not afraid of you," Seth said.

Celebrant stared unblinkingly.

Seth stared back.

Kendra grabbed his elbow and gave a tug. Following her lead, Seth walked away from the platform alongside Dalgorel.

"I'm sorry that I won't be able to aid you in your journey home," Dalgorel said. "The road will be tedious but should provide safe passage. The magical protections along the main roads are reliable."

Raxtus approached from one side. "Sorry about the griffins," he said.

"Sheba was gentle and strong," Kendra said, her voice quivering. "They were all good creatures. Your friends and family are murderers. And so are you."

"It was the giants," Raxtus said.

Kendra stopped walking. "Get lots of giant attacks around here?"

"Well, no," Raxtus said.

"Are you dragons too weak to defend your own stables inside your own castle?" Kendra asked.

"The giants were killed," Raxtus said.

"Don't play dumb," Seth said. "Have a great war."

Raxtus moved away. Seth, Kendra, and Dalgorel continued toward the door.

"There was another issue with hill giants," Kendra said. "They fought with a dragon and took out a bridge."

"Yes," Dalgorel said. "At Thirsty Gulch."

"Let me guess," Kendra said. "It's on our way home."

Dalgorel nodded. "Yes, that bridge is part of your most

direct route home. Without it, you would have to work around the gulch by leaving the road for quite a while. Or you would have to avoid the gulch entirely by taking the road the long way around."

"Which would be more than three times farther," Tanu said, approaching. "Most likely a week on foot. And right past Stormguard Castle."

"You met Ronodin?" Kendra asked.

"I've met him once before," Tanu said. "Smug as they come. It's rough we lost the griffins."

"The hill giants were pawns," Seth said.

"Most creatures are pawns compared to a dragon," Dalgorel said.

"We need to get a message to Blackwell Keep," Tanu said, "so they can send help."

"How?" Seth asked.

"Maybe Creya," Tanu said, looking around. "Creya!"

The golden eagle flew over and landed near them. "I was about to depart. How may I be of service?"

"Can you fly to Blackwell Keep and explain what happened to our griffins?" Kendra asked. "Tell them we're taking the road home."

"It would be my pleasure," Creya said. "Anything else?"

"We'll probably try the long way," Tanu added. "It would be madness to leave the road under these conditions."

"Tell them about the war," Seth said.

"Will do," the eagle replied. "Away I go."

She flew ahead of them and out the door.

Eve rejoined her father, and Seth stared at her with a smile. In all the commotion he had almost forgotten she was here. He had never met a girl he liked so well.

"How are our griffins?" Eve asked.

"One perished," Dalgorel said. "The other survived."

Eve looked downcast. "Filthy dragons. Well, I'm walking back to Terrabelle."

"No you're not," Dalgorel said. "War is on the immediate horizon. The bridge at Thirsty Gulch is out. You will return with me on whichever griffin remains."

"It'll be Lady," Eve said. "Starfire would have attacked the giants. He never would have let harm come to Lady."

"Whichever remains, we will ride home together," Dalgorel said.

"I refuse," Eve said.

Dalgorel looked at Seth, Kendra, and Tanu. "Excuse us for a moment." Dalgorel led his daughter away. Seth watched him talking to her animatedly.

"Somebody is in trouble," Seth said under his breath.

"We are," Kendra said. "We're really far from the keep."

Seth waved a dismissive arm. "We'll be on a protected road! No big deal. This will be a chance to see more of our sanctuary."

"The dragons won't make it easy," Kendra said.

"Let's put some distance between us and this castle before we discuss more," Tanu suggested.

"Should we wait for Eve?" Seth asked, looking back.

"I'm not sure her father would appreciate it," Kendra said.

"We should get going," Tanu said.

Seth glanced at the potion master's pouches. "How did it go?" he whispered.

Tanu gave him a hard stare. "Let's leave, Seth."

"Is the Tiny Hero all right?" Seth asked.

Tanu stuck up his thumb.

Kendra grabbed one of Seth's arms. Tanu grabbed the other. Together they marched out of the castle, found where the road began, and started down the chilly mountain.

CHAPTER TEN

Barrel

Knox nudged the door open, the faint light from the hall spilling into the dimness of Dale's room. The lanky man rested on his side, head on his pillow, snoring softly. His room seemed to smell more like him than he did.

Since discovering the true nature of Fablehaven, Knox had become even more interested in the barrel that had transported him to Wyrmroost. Unfortunately, he hadn't been able to get through the locked basement door to examine it again.

This morning Knox had seen Dale use a key on his key ring to enter the basement. So he had stayed up late in his bed, waiting until the house grew silent. All was now still. And Dale was snoring.

Knox needed to find that key without waking the handyman.

Knox crept into the room, nearly closing the door behind him, stepping lightly, breathing softly. He knew it would look bad if Dale awoke to find him sneaking around. A floorboard creaked, and though to Knox it sounded almost like he had stepped on a land mine, Dale kept snoring smoothly.

In the meager light, Knox scanned the walls, wondering if there might be a peg. Coming up empty, he checked the nightstand beside the bed, but no keys were there, either. Where else? In a drawer?

Then he noticed the pants draped over the back of a chair. Knox was pretty sure they were the pants Dale had worn today. He tiptoed over to the brown corduroys and slipped a hand into one of the front pockets. Nothing. But he heard a slight jingle as he took his hand out, and in the other front pocket he found the key ring. As he eased it out of the pocket, some of the keys jangled, and Dale snorted, sitting up.

Knox lunged to the foot of the bed and lay flat, heart hammering. He heard Dale smack his lips. "Somebody there?" he mumbled in a blurry voice.

Cheek against the floor, Knox held his breath. What would happen if he got caught? Did Fablehaven have holding cells for delinquents? At best it would be so embarrassing.

He heard Dale flop back onto his pillow, smacking his lips some more as he arranged his covers. Knox waited. A hasty move now would be costly.

There were seven or eight keys on the ring, and he held them pressed together so they couldn't rattle. Knox waited as long as he could bear. Then he silently counted to a hundred, resisting the urge to rush. Dale began lightly snoring again.

Knox crept out of the room and softly closed the door. As he moved down the hall, relief and excitement replaced his fear of getting caught. Now he just needed to make his way to the basement and locate the barrel.

He quietly descended the stairs to the main level. The house looked different in night shadow, the furniture reduced to shapes in the gloom. At least there was a glow coming from the kitchen.

Knox walked carefully toward it, in case the light meant somebody was grabbing a midnight snack. When he peered around the corner, he found little men and women scurrying around on the countertop. Some were rolling out dough, others were cutting it into fanciful shapes, and others were placing the shapes onto cookie sheets.

Grandma Larsen had told him that she would sometimes leave out ingredients that brownies would combine into treats. Even though he had seen plenty of fairies in the yard, Knox still wasn't used to running into magical creatures yet. He quietly spied, enthralled by their speed and precision.

When fingers touched his hand, Knox jerked away and almost cried out. He found Tess looking up at him with wide eyes, wearing an oversized T-shirt and shorts. She pointed excitedly at the brownies.

He took her by the elbow and led her out of sight from the kitchen. "What are you doing up?" he whispered.

"I like to try to see the brownies," Tess said. "I've only spotted them once before."

"You get up in the night looking for brownies?"

"Sometimes," Tess said. "They don't like to talk, though. They run away so fast when I try."

Knox peeked back into the kitchen. No brownies were in sight now. "They're gone."

"Grandma told me they're really hard to see," Tess said. "They have really good hearing and are very shy."

"Speedy little guys. The cookies they were making are still on the counter."

"They'll finish up later," Tess said. "Where are you going?"

"What do you mean?" Knox asked, trying to act innocent.

"You have keys," Tess said.

Knox looked at the keys in his hand. "I found them. I'm not sure what they open."

"Let's try things," Tess said.

"No," Knox replied. "You should be in bed."

"It's too exciting here to sleep much," Tess said.

"Go back to bed," Knox said. "I have some things to do."

"I'll do them with you."

Knox folded his arms, the keys still in one hand. "You're going to get in trouble."

"So are you."

"You can't tell anybody you saw me down here," Knox said.

"Sure I can," Tess replied.

"You have to keep it a secret," Knox said.

Tess stared at him. "Make me part of the secret and I'll keep it."

"What do you mean?"

"Let me do what you're doing and I won't tell anyone," she said, pantomiming as if zipping her lips closed.

"You won't like it," Knox said. "I'm going down in the basement."

"There's a basement?" Tess asked, quietly clapping her hands. "I want to come!"

"It will probably be scary," Knox said.

"Why would a basement be scary?"

"It could be all dirty and moldy."

"Who cares?" Tess said.

"There might be monsters."

"Hopefully nice ones."

"Go to bed or you're going to get in trouble," Knox warned again.

"Let me come or I'm telling," Tess said.

Knox winced. "You really don't want to come. I'm going to a dangerous place called Wyrmroost."

"Why do you want to see worms?"

"It's not a place for worms," Knox said. "It's a place like this. Only better."

"What makes it better?"

"It's all top secret," Knox said.

"How do you know it's better?"

"I went there once."

"What's it like?"

"Dangerous. There's a castle there. And dragons."

Tess looked at him in astonishment. "A castle? I want to see it!"

"It's not like a fairy princess castle," Knox said. "It's more like a fort."

"Forts are cool! And so are dragons. I want to meet one."

"I'm not sure you do. Grandpa didn't explain much, but they sound dangerous."

"Grandpa told you about Wormplace?" Tess asked.

"Wyrmroost. I asked him about it after I saw the fairies and learned what is really going on here. When I went to Wyrmroost before, I hadn't ever tried the milk. Grandpa only told me a little about it. He avoids the topic."

"How did you get there?" Tess asked.

"I've already shared too much."

"The more you tell me, the less I tell Grandma."

"You're becoming a con artist."

"I want to see the castle," Tess insisted.

"I went through a barrel," Knox said.

"How dumb do I look?"

"I'm serious," Knox said. "A magic barrel. Grandpa stored it in the basement."

"Now I *have* to come with you. I've got to see this."

"If you come, you'll get in huge trouble. You could also get hurt or killed."

"Then why do you want to go?"

Knox looked at his sister. "Because I think Kendra and Seth are there. And it's a preserve like Fablehaven, but better. I think we're at the petting zoo. Wyrmroost is the real deal."

"I have to see it," Tess said. "I miss our cousins. It seemed like we hardly saw them before they went away."

"There's no reason they should get to see the cool place and not us," Knox said.

"Right," Tess said. "*Us*. I'm coming."

"You'll be a pest, though."

"I won't."

"I don't think you can help it. Being a pest is in your DNA. It's who you are."

"It'll be less fun for you alone," Tess said. "Plus, I can see the creatures without the milk. You might need me."

"All right, come on, then, before I change my mind," Knox said.

"We're going to find the magic barrel?" Tess asked.

"If we can," Knox said.

He led the way through the still kitchen to the door granting access to the basement. As when he had previously explored, the door at the top of the stairway was not locked, but the iron door beyond the bottom of the staircase refused to budge when Knox tried it. With only the light from the kitchen, it was dim.

"I don't see a light switch," Tess said.

"We don't want it too bright. Somebody might notice us."

"If we had a light, we could shut the door to the rest of the house," Tess said. "That might hide us better."

"Right," Knox said.

"Should I look for a flashlight?" Tess asked.

"Maybe later." Squinting, Knox checked which keys looked to be the right size for the keyhole in the iron door.

The first two he tried would not quite go in. The third slid in perfectly and turned with little effort.

He opened the door to reveal a long hallway. It was too dark to see how far it extended, but the cool draft hinted that it might go a long way.

"That's dark," Tess said at his side. "Light switch!"

Naked light bulbs illuminated at intervals down the long corridor. The barrel stood not ten paces away. Just beyond the barrel, a scrawny, greenish, humanoid creature with bat-wing ears sat on a short three-legged stool. He sprang to his feet and shook a fist.

"Why the light?" the creature asked with a snarl. "Is this an emergency?"

Knox slapped off the light and stood frozen. What had he just seen? Some kind of monster!

A match flared to life, and then a lantern was glowing. As the scowling creature marched toward them, one hand on the lantern, the other on his hip, Tess slipped behind Knox.

"What's your business down here?"

Knox wondered if he should bolt. Maybe the door was made of iron for good reason. But though the creature looked fearsome, he wasn't very big, and he seemed more disgruntled than enraged. Some kind of guard? Protecting the barrel, probably. If Knox wanted to get into the barrel, it was now or never.

"We're supposed to go to Wyrmroost," Knox said.

The creature stopped a pace or two away and held out the lantern toward him. "Human kids. Not the ones I normally see, though it's hard to tell—you all look so much alike. Why is the little one hiding?"

"I'm not really hiding," Tess said, looking around Knox. "You just look kind of scary."

The creature puffed out his chest. "You bet I do." He snorted and spat. "First lick of good sense I've heard all day. Not much is more intimidating than a goblin in his prime."

"What's your name?" Tess asked.

"You've never heard of Slaggo?" the goblin asked. "You must be new around these parts."

"We're just passing through on our way to Wyrmroost," Knox said.

"I had no knowledge of that," Slaggo said. "I'm supposed to watch this barrel. Nobody comes out except the Sorensons. Nobody goes in without word from Hank or Gloria."

"Hank and Gloria are our grandparents," Knox said. "Who do you think gave us the keys? We're supposed to catch up with Seth and Kendra."

"I just need word from Hank," Slaggo said.

"He's sleeping," Knox said. "He had a hard day."

"Gloria sleeping too?" Slaggo asked.

"Everybody," Knox said.

"Why are you still up, then?" Slaggo asked.

"Because this is when we were supposed to go to Wyrmroost," Knox replied.

"To see the castle," Tess chimed in.

Slaggo rubbed his bony chin. "Well, I suppose if you don't belong, they won't let you through on the other side.

I don't see what harm a couple of kids could do. I'll need to hold those keys, though. Can't have those going off to some other preserve."

"Sure," Knox said, handing over Dale's key ring. "Can we get going?"

"I suppose," Slaggo said, stepping aside. "I get sick of speaking English. Twists my mouth up in terrible ways."

"You do a good job," Tess said.

"'Course I do," Slaggo said. "Been practicing. Who knows why, though? Hideous language. Come along."

Knox hoped the guards on the far side would let him through. With some luck, whoever greeted him would recognize him from his previous visit. "I better go first," Knox said.

"Suit yourself," Slaggo said, waving a dismissive hand. "I'll be relieved to douse the lantern."

"How will you see?" Tess asked.

"Goblins see best in the dark," Slaggo said. "It varies with other amounts of light. Who needs it?"

"I do," Tess said.

Knox climbed into the barrel. "Tess, after I disappear, get into the barrel and squat down." He squatted down. "Wyrmroost," he said, like he had when he had crossed over with Seth.

A hand grabbed his shoulder and stood him up. It was another goblin, this one taller, beefier, and more apelike. Knox was in a new room, the same place he had arrived on his previous visit. "You again?" the goblin asked. "I don't have word about visitors."

"I'm supposed to see the Sorensons," Knox said. "I'm just following instructions."

The goblin helped him step from the barrel. "That was incredible you got the scepter. We might have been roasted without it."

"My little sister is coming too," Knox said.

The goblin looked into the barrel. "So she is." He lifted her out. Tess stared at the goblin with wide eyes.

"Thanks," Knox said.

"I need to report your arrival," the goblin said. "It's my neck on the line if this is some kind of mischief."

"Sure," Knox said. At least he had made it here. And this time he could see the goblin for what he was. On his previous visit, the occupants of the castle had all looked like people. What a difference the milk made.

"Brunwin!" the goblin cried. "We have visitors!"

CHAPTER ELEVEN

On the Road

As Kendra made her way along the dirt road winding down from Skyhold, dragons circled high above, shadowy forms with moonlit highlights. Tanu had a flashlight, but suggested that the moon provided enough light. He kept refusing to converse, so they walked quickly, using the downhill slope to stay at a brisk pace. The air was chilly but not insufferable, and between the exertion and her coat, Kendra stayed warm.

What she most wanted right now was distance from the dragons. They had overtly declared war! No more pretending. How were she and her brother and their few allies supposed to fight dragons? Kendra wanted to be within the walls and barriers of Blackwell Keep. Would simply hiding behind protections be enough to win a war? She supposed it was better than nothing. She felt so exposed.

Would standing on the road really shield her from dragon fire?

When they heard a clatter behind them, Kendra was so startled she nearly jumped off the road. She, Seth, and Tanu moved to one side to allow the gnome leader, Karzal, to approach in his little chariot pulled by five large dogs. "Whoa," the gnome called, tugging his reins to pull the wolfish canines to a halt.

"Nice ride," Seth said.

"Not a bad way to travel," Karzal conceded in English. "I'm sorry about your griffins. It can be a dirty business dealing with dragons."

"Is your kingdom far?" Kendra asked.

"A fair distance," Karzal said, staring out into the night. "Getting to Skyhold takes considerable planning. I left my kingdom as soon as the invitation arrived to get here on time."

"Why not fly?" Seth asked.

Karzal winced. "Gnomes were never meant for the skies. Close to the earth for me. I'm sorry this vehicle is insufficient for big folk or I would gladly offer a ride."

"I'm not sure the dragons would smile at that," Kendra said, glancing skyward.

"Why should I care?" Karzal asked. "Dragons only smile about gnomes if they are hungry."

"Do gnomes use the roads a lot?" Kendra asked.

"Now and again," Karzal said. "These roads provide valued protection for the inhabitants of the five territories, particularly when we need to travel beyond our borders."

"So nothing can bother us on the road," Kendra said, hoping it was true.

"Not until Midsummer Eve," Karzal said. "On the festival night the defenses on the roads fall. Only the defenses around the territories and the keep remain. And, in a pinch, the occasional roadhouse. With only two days left, you'll want to hurry."

"Unfortunately, we can't use the shorter way to the keep," Kendra said. "The bridge is out at Thirsty Gulch."

"Really?" Karzal asked. "Then you're heading the same way as me. Careful when the road nears Stormguard Castle. I prefer to pass by there at full speed under broad daylight."

"Why?" Seth asked.

"You don't know the legend of the cursed castle?" Karzal asked.

"No," Seth said, glancing at Tanu. "You?"

The potion master shrugged. "No details."

"Nobody has the full story," Karzal said. "And nobody is likely to learn it. Not often does a thriving castle go silent overnight. Those who investigate either don't get close enough to learn anything or never return."

"This longer road goes by there?" Kendra asked.

"'Course it does," Karzal said. "Used to be the heart of Wyrmroost. The castle predates the sanctuary."

"Did the dragons curse it?" Seth asked.

"Hard to know for sure," Karzal said. "Not likely, though. The castle isn't scorched or damaged. There was no obvious attack. It just fell silent."

"How recently?" Kendra asked.

"Centuries ago," Karzal said. "Before my time." He looked back up the mountain. "I had best be off. You as well. Try to make the nearest roadhouse tonight. They're spaced regularly. At least you'll have beds. Best of luck. I need to inform my people of the latest developments. The gnomes are with you!" He shook his reins. "Yah!"

The dogs scampered quickly to a run, and the little chariot clattered out of view. Kendra, Seth, and Tanu started walking again.

"Think the gnomes can help much?" Kendra asked.

"Maybe if the dragons get hungry," Seth said. "Snacks can be distracting."

"What are we going to do about Midsummer Eve?" Kendra asked. "If we're still on the road, we're in trouble."

"We'll hope Creya delivers our message and Blackwell Keep sends aid," Tanu said. "If not, it sounds as though these roadhouses might work like safe huts."

"I have a map," Seth said.

"Me too," Tanu said. "We'll check them when we have more light."

"What if the dragons try to block us from the safe huts?" Kendra asked.

"We'll fight our way past them," Seth said, patting his sword.

"I wouldn't get too cocky," Kendra said.

"It's the potion talking," Tanu reminded them.

"I wish we had dog carts," Seth said. "Those dogs were fast!"

"Griffins would be faster," Kendra said.

A few minutes later they heard hoofbeats approaching from behind. They moved to the side of the road again, and Amulon raced by. The rumitaur did not pause or acknowledge them.

"Too bad elk boy won't give us a lift," Seth said. "He seems really fast."

"I'm not sure he likes us much," Kendra said.

"'Course not," Seth said. "He isn't shorter than my waist. We need taller allies."

"Hey!" Calvin complained from his pocket.

"We'll take what we can get," Seth amended.

"For now, let's get down the mountain," Tanu said.

"Want to tell us about raiding Madrigus?" Seth asked.

"I want to be farther from Skyhold," Tanu said. Lowering his voice, he continued. "It was beautiful, though. The only problem was my limited carrying capacity. I emptied all I could from my pack. Still, imagine being in the richest treasure room in the world—tons of gold, heaps of jewels—and only your two hands and a pack to carry stuff out. One trip." He shook his head. "So much was left behind."

"Not that cooked tear duct," Calvin said. His tiny fist knocked against Seth. "There can be advantages to short allies."

"I was glad to have our little helper," Tanu said. "He went places I could not have reached with so little time."

"You got good stuff, though?" Seth asked.

"What I left behind may haunt me forever," Tanu said. "Riches a potion master can only dream about. But I got so much. My pack is stuffed with abundant ingredients I never imagined obtaining. It has been decades since anyone brewed with jellied dragon pancreas."

"Can you do much with it now?" Kendra asked.

"A little, perhaps," Tanu said. "Much more if I set up a proper brewing environment. I wish I could get some of my haul on ice!"

Kendra led the way as they continued down the road, walking faster than before. What would it look like when the war officially began? What preparations were necessary? They needed more time. The night got slightly warmer as they descended, but the air remained chilly. Moonlit dragons continued to glide above them against a backdrop of bright stars.

The road finally leveled out and then ended at an intersection. "Right or left?" Kendra asked.

"This is the Outer Road," Tanu said.

"One of the five main roadways," Seth added.

"Right is the quicker way back to the keep," Tanu said. "With the bridge out, I think we need left."

"You need help," a voice called from behind.

Kendra turned to find Eve approaching out of the night, trotting quietly.

"What are you doing here?" Kendra asked.

"I gave my father the slip," Eve said. "Listened to his lecture. Acted compliant. Then ran off while he was making preparations at the stable."

"Lord Dalgorel will be furious," Tanu said.

"Isn't he looking for you?" Seth asked.

Eve smiled and looked at the sky. "He keeps swooping

around up there. I just duck off the road when he gets near."

"Unwise to leave the road," Tanu said.

"I've never had a real adventure," Eve said. "I read about so many. Always wanted one."

"We're in real trouble," Kendra said.

"Exactly," Eve replied. "Not just sneaking pastries from the kitchen or exploring a creaky old windmill. Actual danger!"

"I understand the itch," Seth said.

Kendra swatted her brother on the shoulder. "You're not helping."

"Good to see you," greeted Calvin from Seth's pocket, his head poking out and one arm waving.

"Is that Calvin?" Eve asked, leaning forward. "How are you?"

"A little soaked in dragon guts," Calvin said. "Are you sure you should run away?"

"I can help," Eve said. "You're all new here. Are you really going left? Past Stormguard Castle?"

"Until we get aid from Blackwell Keep," Tanu said.

Eve clapped her hands. "How thrilling!"

"What do you know about it?" Seth asked.

"So many rumors," Eve said.

"The castle was here before Wyrmroost," Kendra said.

"Long before," Eve said. "It was originally a secret domain of the Fair Folk. That's why so many Fair Folk still reside here. Good King Weldon, ruler of the Fair Folk in this part of the world, allowed the founders of Wyrmroost to create the sanctuary around his ancestral home, and the territory of Terrabelle was reserved for the Fair Folk not of the castle."

"But the castle was cursed," Kendra said.

"King Hollorix was the last ruler of Stormguard Castle," Eve said. "He had three sons—Tregain, Heath, and Lockland. There used to be regular interactions between the citizens of Terrabelle and the castle folk. One day the castle went silent. We don't know what happened. We only know that nobody ever came out, and none who have ventured inside ever returned."

"Maybe we can ring the doorbell and run," Seth teased.

Kendra wanted to pinch him for never being serious.

"I wouldn't risk it," Eve said. "Those who do a close examination of the castle do not return."

"Sometimes little people can slip in and out of places unnoticed," Calvin suggested.

"Not a bad idea," Eve murmured.

"Are there any guesses what happened?" Kendra asked.

"Nothing that really fits," Eve said. "There was no visible damage. From one day to the next, the whole castle went quiet."

"Maybe a plague?" Seth asked.

"If so, it acts fast enough that nobody ever returns with information about it," Eve said.

"I don't know of any plague that incapacitates so quickly," Tanu said. "Some kind of magical curse is the more likely culprit. Which means we should stay far away."

"How do you beat a curse?" Seth asked.

"Depends on the curse," Tanu said. "A curse that paralyzed or destroyed an entire castle? You don't ask how to beat it. You figure out how to avoid it."

"We have enough problems without chasing after curses," Kendra said.

"This road will take us right by Stormguard Castle, though," Eve said. "We'll get closer than we probably should."

A griffin whooshed by not more than ten feet above their heads. Eve froze and held a finger to her lips as the creature soared up the road. After a moment it passed out of view.

"Your dad?" Seth asked.

Eve nodded.

"How did he miss us?" Seth asked.

"He should know he won't find me," Eve said.

"Did he go blind?" Seth asked. "And the griffin too?"

"I have a talent," Eve said quietly.

"What do you mean?" Kendra asked.

"All the Fair Folk have a gift," Eve said. "At least one. A magical talent."

"You can make people blind?" Seth asked.

Eve giggled. "Almost, sometimes. I can help others see what I want them to see."

"What did you make your dad see?" Seth asked.

"I wasn't focusing on him specifically," Eve said. "I was covering us so we would blend in with the road to any onlookers. Worked on both my father and the griffin."

"You never hid off the side of the road to avoid your dad," Seth accused.

"No," Eve said. "Griffins are too fast and quiet. How would I have known when he was coming?"

"How long can you hide us?" Kendra asked.

"For a while," Eve said. "I get fatigued. It's like running

a long distance. The longer you go, the more tired you get. After long enough, I get worn out. And the more appearances I try to alter, the quicker I tire."

"Can you make me look like a bear?" Seth asked.

"Yes," Eve said. "Until somebody studied you closely. My gift works best when the things I disguise are only half noticed, blending in with the background. A bear might not be a smart choice, because if somebody glimpses a bear, they will probably focus on the bear."

"And if they focus on the bear, your illusion fails," Kendra said.

"Exactly," Eve said. "I try not to explain my gift very often. It is less effective when people know what I can do. But since we're adventuring together—"

"And since we caught you using it," Seth interjected. "What did we look like to your dad?"

"I made us match the color and texture of the road," Eve said. "Like chameleons. I'm still doing it, because eventually he will come back. There are limits to how far you could have traveled since leaving the feast. When he fails to find you on the road, Father will suspect I am concealing you. He'll keep after us."

"Is it wise for you to come with us?" Tanu asked. "We may well get caught on the road for Midsummer Eve."

"If it comes to that, we'll take cover in a roadhouse," Eve said.

"Will a roadhouse stand against a festival night?" Tanu asked.

"It should hold if travelers are inside," Eve said.

"Against dragons?" Kendra asked.

"In theory," Eve said. "The road defenses will go down, but the roadhouses should stay protected."

"Hopefully we'll receive aid before then," Tanu said.

"How often will we find roadhouses?" Seth asked.

"There is roughly a day's walk between them," Eve replied.

They marched forward in silence for a time. Kendra watched the moon sinking toward the mountaintops. The ghostly forms of dragons continued to drift high above, distant enough to feel almost irrelevant.

After some time, the griffin came zooming up the road again, straight toward them, flying not more than fifteen feet off the ground. Kendra and the others held still as the creature whooshed by not far overhead. Before long it was gone again.

"Your dad is persistent," Seth said.

"So am I," Eve replied.

"I'll vouch for that," Calvin said. "In Terrabelle, she was relentless until I waded in that custard."

Unsettling sounds issued from the darkness at either side of the road—foliage rustling, branches snapping, along with occasional growls or strange cries. Kendra kept walking, trying to trust the protective barrier that isolated the road from the rest of Wyrmroost. In the distance, a chorus of distant howling rose to frantic shrieks and cackles.

"What was that?" Kendra whispered.

"Best not to think about it," Tanu said.

"What?" Seth pressed.

"I know that sound," Tanu said. "Werewolves."

"People who turn into wolves?" Seth asked.

"Many werewolves end up surrendering their humanity," Tanu said. "Human form becomes a rare state, and even in human shape, they behave like beasts."

"There is a problem with these creatures at Wyrmroost," Eve said. "Especially in the backcountry—wereboars, werelynxes, werewolves."

"Were they making a kill?" Seth asked.

"Sounded like it," Tanu said. "Notice how they have gone quiet now?"

"Are they eating?" Seth asked.

The calm suddenly seemed more sinister than the noise.

"Can we change the topic?" Kendra asked.

"Sorry," Tanu said, eyes searching heavenward. "Beautiful stars tonight."

"Hard to look up without seeing dragons," Kendra said. "Can they see us while we're camouflaged?"

"If they have been following you since Skyhold, my deceptions won't work," Eve said. "If they stop watching, though, it may be a little tricky for them to find us again. I'll do my best."

Seth leaned closer to Kendra and lowered his voice. "You have to admit, she could be handy."

"We don't want the Fair Folk to hate us, though," Kendra said. "They clearly don't want her involved with us."

"Don't worry," Seth said brightly. "They're always neutral."

The moon had set behind the mountains by the time

the roadhouse came into view. A squat building made of fitted stones with a slate roof slanting down from a single chimney, it wasn't much more than a cottage. Although it wasn't their final destination, Kendra felt a sense of relief wash over her. The solid front door was unlocked, and after Tanu lit a little lamp, Kendra was surprised by how tidy it looked inside. The wood floor was clean, if not polished, the glass-paned windows had curtains, and a full wood box awaited by the fireplace. She observed no cobwebs and no dust, and she counted six cots, two rocking chairs, and a table with four chairs.

"Should we light a fire?" Tanu asked. "I don't think our presence is a big secret."

"Not to my father," Eve said, picking up a note from the table and waving it.

"What does it say?" Seth asked.

"That he will come for me in the morning," Eve said. "I bet he went to deliver news to Terrabelle. He'll be back."

Tanu started positioning logs in the fireplace. "We need to get some sleep. Lots of ground to cover in the next couple of days."

"I won't leave you," Eve said resolutely, setting the paper down.

Seth flopped onto a cot. "Can he drag you onto a griffin?"

"I guess we'll find out," Eve said, bolting the door. "Want me to take the first watch?"

"We should be safe here," Tanu said. "Let's all sleep."

He poured some powder on the logs in the fireplace and struck a match, and a fire blazed to life. Kendra took off her shoes, peeled back some covers, and stretched out on a cot. The war against the dragons would start tomorrow. What might that look like? Two nights from now would be Midsummer Eve. That would be pandemonium—a total nightmare. The dragons supposedly had a way to win the war. Kendra and her friends had a lot to figure out. Was it too much to hope that somebody besides her would uncover the solution? So many uncertainties. And it was late. Kendra was exhausted. Now that she was at rest, she seemed to be melting away. Her fatigue gave way to dreamless sleep.

CHAPTER TWELVE

Stranded

As Brunwin led Knox and Tess through Blackwell Keep, Knox tried to look in all directions at once. There were dwarfs, and a snake lady with six arms, and torches and oil lamps instead of electric lights, and towers, and battlements, not to mention that he was following a big, shaggy minotaur.

"Are there really dragons here?" Tess asked breathlessly.

"You don't want to see any of them," Brunwin said. "They'll freeze you right to the bone."

"You're Brunwin," Knox said. "The same person who helped me out of the barrel last time?"

"Correct," the minotaur said.

"You look cooler now," Knox said.

"I looked human to you before?" Brunwin asked.

"Yes," Knox said.

"Then of course I look better now," Brunwin said with a sniff.

"I never met a cow man," Tess said.

Knox did not manage to completely stifle his laugh.

"Bull man," Brunwin said, miffed. "Minotaur, preferably. The women are cow women, I suppose, but I would avoid that language."

Knox followed Brunwin down a hall and into a room, where they found Stan and Ruth Sorenson talking to an elderly Asian man. A large bird of prey perched on the headboard of the bed in the room.

Stan turned to Knox in astonishment. "Am I dreaming? What are you doing here? And Tess?"

"We came to see the dragons," Tess said.

"And how did you know to do that?" Ruth asked.

"She can see the fairies," Knox said. "Without the milk. She can see all of it. I finally drank some."

"Drinking milk does not get you to Wyrmroost," Stan said.

"It takes a barrel," Knox said. "You know I came here before."

"Does your grandma Larsen know you're here?" Ruth asked.

"Nobody knows," Knox said. "Where are Seth and Kendra?"

"That was our present topic," the large bird said.

"This is Creya the eagle," Ruth said. "And Marat, former caretaker of Wyrmroost."

Marat gave a small bow.

"The eagle can talk," Tess said.

"Creya is a representative from a territory of talking animals," Ruth explained.

"Kendra and Seth have found themselves in danger before," Stan said. "But this time they're at a dragon sanctuary where anarchy may soon reign."

"Why don't they just come home?" Tess inquired innocently.

"They can't, at least not the same way they left," Stan said. "They had a meeting with the dragons, and their rides were slain. The roads offer protection from dragons, but those protections fail in less than two days, when the sun goes down on Midsummer Eve."

"The roadhouses would provide refuge," Marat inserted.

"I don't like it," Stan said, folding his arms. "We need to get them home before the solstice."

"We can release griffins," Marat said. "But under the circumstances, the dragons may not permit the griffins to arrive. We could also release some of the Luvians on the road."

"Luvians?" Tess asked.

"Really smart horses," Ruth explained. "Fast and strong, too."

"What if the griffins flew low?" Stan asked. "Followed the road?"

"The protection only fully holds if they stay on the road," Marat said. "If dragons chose to harass them, the griffins would have to run to Kendra and Seth. Over long distances, they would probably be slower than the Luvians."

"Can I help?" Knox asked. "Last time none of the dragons could attack me."

"Now you have drunk the milk," Stan said, "and you know what is really going on here. It was your complete obliviousness that protected you last time."

"Are there really dragons?" Knox asked.

"You have no idea," Stan said, sober eyes meeting Knox's gaze.

"He's a dragon," Ruth said, indicating Marat.

"In human form," Marat explained.

"You can turn into a dragon?" Knox asked incredulously.

Marat gave a nod that included a partial bow.

"Do it," Tess said, clapping her hands and bouncing.

"Enough!" Stan interrupted, closer to a yell than Knox had ever heard from him. "Kendra and Seth may not make it back alive. This is not a game. The dragons have declared war!"

The room was silent. Taking a step closer to Knox, Tess grabbed Knox's hand. "Start the Luvians running," Stan said. "The ones that carried Kendra and Seth before. And maybe two others."

"Shall we dispatch Henrick as well?" Marat asked.

"Tell him to follow his best judgment," Stan said. Marat exited the room. Stan turned his attention to Knox. His expression was grim.

"How did you kids get here without anyone noticing?" Stan asked. "I thought Hank put the barrel in the dungeon."

"I may have swiped Dale's key," Knox said.

Stan blanched. "Nobody knew you went to the dungeon? How did you lock the door?"

Suddenly Knox felt worried he might have done something very wrong. "I left the key with Slaggo."

Stan closed his eyes. Knox saw him struggle against anger. "The goblins are not given keys. The goblins are not trustworthy."

"We need to get to the barrel," Ruth said, urgency in her tone.

"Yes, we should," Stan said, hustling out the door.

"Brunwin, with us," Ruth said to the minotaur waiting outside the room.

Knox and Tess followed Brunwin back through halls and down stairs until they reached the room with the barrel. Stan and Ruth stood in shock. The barrel was gone. The apelike goblin lay sprawled on the floor in a pool of dark blood.

Tess shrieked.

Ruth quickly walked her out of the room, talking soothingly.

Bovine nostrils flaring, Brunwin knelt and checked the body. "Dead."

Stan was quivering, lips pressed tightly, hands balled into fists. He glanced at Knox.

"I'm sorry," Knox blurted. "What happened?"

"Hard to be sure," Stan said curtly. "Brunwin, we need to find that barrel. Until we do, our security is compromised."

Brandishing a huge ax, the minotaur rushed away.

"Did Slaggo come through?" Knox asked.

"Almost certainly not Slaggo," Stan said. "He would be no match for this goblin. But Slaggo had Dale's keys. And a dungeon full of options. Many things could have come through."

"I'm sorry," Knox said, a sick feeling stewing in his gut.

"You didn't know," Stan said. "I'm sure nobody explained the stakes to you. We're in the middle of a war against the dragons. If they win, it could mean the end of the world."

"Not the whole world," Knox said. "We have guns, tanks, bombs."

"Humanity would put up a fight," Stan said, "but the dragons have magic. Think we should chance it?"

"No," Knox said.

"There are people who want the sanctuaries to fall," Stan said. "People and beings who want to destroy this fortress. And now they may have a way in."

"What should I do?" Knox asked, trying to keep his voice steady. He almost wished Stan would spank him. Hard. It would match how he felt inside.

"You can't go back to Fablehaven," Stan said. "Not until we find that barrel and make sure the other end is uncompromised as well."

"I'm stuck here?"

"For now. We'll need to somehow get word to your Grandma and Grandpa Larsen. They will be worried. And we need to place the keep on high alert. Come with me."

Knox followed Stan into the hall, where Ruth stood hugging Tess. Stan patted Tess on the back. She looked up at him. "Who hurt the monster?" she asked.

"We need to figure that out," Stan said. "Probably something showed up in the barrel, and the goblin made the mistake of touching it. Ruth, take the kids to the satyrs, then help me alert everyone."

"The satyrs?" Ruth questioned.

"Do you have a better idea?" Stan asked. "We know Newell and Doren are on our side. They're clever enough to sense danger and typically stay far away from it."

Ruth nodded. "I agree. But mostly because I can't think of anyone else."

Stan patted her arm. "Keep an eye out for intruders."

Stan hurried away. Ruth walked Knox and Tess through an archway and across a courtyard. They entered a hall, and Ruth knocked on a door.

A satyr answered—horns on his head, wearing a loose vest over a bare chest, his bottom half supported by two goat legs. "Ruth, good evening. Knox? What's he doing here?"

"Are you one of the goats that came with us in the woods?" Knox asked.

"You finally drank the milk," the satyr said. "I'm Newel. My friend Doren was the other goat."

Doren came to the door. "Hello."

"We have a problem," Ruth said.

"We know about Kendra and Seth," Newel said. "We were at the stables when Marat came to get the Luvians."

"That was recent," Ruth said. "You came straight back here?"

"We wanted to gear up," Doren said. "See if we can help."

"Did you see anyone strange?" Ruth asked. "Anyone with a barrel?"

"Did something happen to the barrel?" Newel asked.

"It's gone," Ruth said. "The goblin who was guarding it is . . ."

"I know already," Tess said with a shiver. "He looked pretty dead to me."

"This is serious," Newel said.

"Dire," Ruth said. "If access to the keep is open, we could all be in major trouble. And the dragons just declared war."

"What can we do?" Doren asked.

"Watch the kids," Ruth said. "Keep them safe. And keep an eye out for anyone who does not belong."

Newel saluted. "We're on the job."

"You kids be good," Ruth said, and she bustled away.

"You guys are part goat?" Tess asked.

"Only the best parts," Doren said.

"You know what 'goat' stands for, right?" Newel asked. "Greatest Of All Time!"

"Can I pet you?" Tess asked.

"Ordinarily, no," Doren said. "For you, I'll make an exception." He stuck out a leg, and Tess ruffled the fur on his outer thigh.

"Not very soft," Tess said.

"We're part goat, not part llama," Newel replied.

"So you looked like this the whole time we went to the bear?" Knox asked.

"Yes," Newel said. "Goat guys. And the bear was an ogre. Welcome to a stranger world than the one you knew."

"Strange is right," Knox said. He looked around. "What now?"

"Come inside," Newel said, stepping back from the door. "We can get you some snacks."

Knox entered, followed by Tess. Newel shut the door.

"Do you like cheese fondue?" Doren asked. "I improvised some. Not bad."

"Melted cheese sounds good," Knox said.

"We don't have television," Newel said. "We found some books, but they're thick ones, and we haven't gotten that desperate yet."

"Do you think Kendra and Seth will be all right?" Knox asked.

"They have survived their share of scrapes," Doren said. "This one could be a doozy, though."

"Doren and I were just scheming about how we might help," Newel said. "We were getting ready to go see somebody."

"You go," Doren said. "I'll watch the young ones. Stuff them full of cheese."

Tess yawned. "I'm sleepy."

"You can rest," Doren said. "Take my bed."

"Cheese first," Tess said.

"She has her priorities straight," Newel said. "See you soon." He exited the room, closing the door behind him.

Doren went and locked it. "Just in case," he said.

"Is somebody going to attack us?" Tess asked.

"Probably not," Doren said, his smile a bit forced. "Still a good habit, though." He winked at Knox.

Knox was not very comforted.

CHAPTER THIRTEEN

Roadblock

Seth awoke to find a little mouse doing push-ups on the floor beside his bed. Seth squeezed some magical walrus butter from the tube he kept with him and took a taste. The mouse became a tiny figure. Seth watched as Calvin leaped to his feet, dashed across the floor to touch one of Seth's shoes, then sprinted to the other shoe, slapped it, and raced back to a midpoint between the footwear to drop for more push-ups.

"You're up early," Seth said quietly.

Calvin sprang to his feet and saluted. "You're up last! The others just stepped outside."

Seth looked around. The other cots were made up and the roadhouse was empty. Charred logs fumed in the fireplace.

"Did Lord Dalgorel show up?" Seth asked.

"No," Calvin said. "Eve sounded a little worried."

Seth paused at the mention of Eve. He had been a little goofy last night. Had he kissed her hand? What had he been thinking? They were both kids! Nonsense like that was only for the most embarrassing of adults. Must have been the potion. Hopefully she thought he was joking around. His attention returned to Calvin. "Do you exercise every morning?"

"You don't become a champion by relaxing," Calvin said. "I spent a lot of yesterday in pockets."

"Sorry," Seth said. "That must get old."

"Are you kidding? I went to a dragon castle! I saw dragons duel!"

"Always good to count our blessings," Seth said. He got out of bed and put on his shoes. "Lots of walking today. Can you keep up on the ground?"

"I bet I could," Calvin said. "I'm fast. But I'd rather stay close to you."

Seth placed him in a pocket and walked out the door. Tanu, Kendra, and Eve stood together eating cookies.

"Who brought cookies?" Seth exclaimed.

They turned to him. "The roadhouse had a stash," Tanu said.

"Trying to gobble them down without me?" Seth asked.

"There are plenty," Kendra said. "They're probably not what you're picturing."

"What do you mean?" Seth asked.

"They taste healthy," Eve said.

Seth groaned. "Let me try one." Kendra handed him a

cookie, and he studied it. The treat looked suspiciously earthy. He could see little grains and nuts. "Are those weeds in it?"

"Just try it," Kendra said.

Seth took a bite. It tasted bland and mealy. He chewed dutifully. "Gross. I need water."

Tanu passed him a flask. Seth guzzled some down.

"It's like concentrated oatmeal," Seth said. "I feel it expanding inside of me."

"Can I try a bite?" Calvin asked.

"You can have all of it," Seth said, sliding the rest of the cookie into his pocket.

"You should eat," Tanu said. "We have a long way to go. All I have are raw dragon parts. I dumped all the rest I could dump."

Seth glanced at the pack. He could see where wetness was seeping through the material in places. "How are the parts holding up?"

"Getting squishy," Tanu said. "Dragon parts spoil slowly. Still, I'd love to get them on ice."

"Not bad," Calvin said, munching the cookie. "Nutritious, with a hint of honey."

"A very subtle hint that only you noticed," Seth said.

"Functional food," Calvin said. "It will keep us energized and alive."

"Who wants to survive if life tastes like that?" Seth asked.

"Spoken like a kid who has never truly starved," Tanu said. He handed Seth another cookie. "Finish that one."

"Then give me more water," Seth said. "I won't have any spit left after two bites."

"I snuck some food from the feast," Eve said. "I was planning to come with you once I heard what happened. Made a few sandwiches out of bread and meat."

"Yes, please," Seth said, handing the cookie back to Tanu. Eve gave him a sandwich.

"Now that Seth is awake, we should walk as we eat," Tanu said.

"Do we have any chance of making it to Blackwell Keep by Midsummer Eve on foot?" Seth asked.

Tanu scowled. "Not as we are. Maybe if I brewed a fleetness potion."

"Can you?" Kendra asked.

"Improvising with dragon parts, probably," Tanu said. "But without some of my gear, it would likely take most of the day. And I can't guarantee it will work."

"Should I take a courage potion?" Seth asked, fingering a little bottle.

"We have a long way to go," Tanu said. "Save it for when we encounter a dragon."

"Midsummer Eve will be here in less than two days," Kendra said.

"Let's make it to the next roadhouse," Tanu said. "I want to get farther away from Skyhold."

Seth looked back. The mountain castle remained in plain view. Multiple dragons glided high overhead.

"Can you cloak us?" Seth asked Eve.

"I could try," Eve said. "If we walk back inside and then come out already disguised, that gives us the best chance to slip away."

They reentered the roadhouse and waited for a moment.

"Seth, you didn't make your cot," Kendra scolded.

"I'm keeping the brownies employed," Seth said.

"Does this place have brownies?" Kendra asked.

"Probably a skeleton crew," Tanu said. "At least part-time. It is too remote to be so tidy otherwise."

"Let's go," Eve said, leading the way out the door.

"I don't see any difference in us," Seth said.

"I'm not wasting my energy concealing us from one another," Eve said. "Only from external bystanders. Come on."

It was a bright morning, the sun already having crested the eastern peaks. The road wound along the base of forbidding mountains. Several large dragonflies hovered and darted near the road, their spindly bodies glossed in iridescent greens, blues, and purples. "Think you could ride one of those, Tiny Hero?" Seth asked.

"I might be a little heavy for them," Calvin said. "Maybe I could use one to glide from a high place to a low place."

"I bet the big ones could take you anywhere you wanted to go," Seth said.

"Dragonflies are really hard to catch and not very smart," Calvin said. "I work better with animal brains."

"Still no sign of your dad," Kendra said to Eve.

"I'm worried about him," Eve said.

"I bet the dragons don't want anyone near us," Tanu said. "It might explain why we haven't seen any griffins from Blackwell Keep, either."

"They need to send Tempest," Seth said. "She could make it through."

"Maybe they will," Kendra said.

"Maybe they have," Tanu added. "We need to plan like there will be no rescue. We may have to save ourselves."

"At least no dragons are right above us anymore," Kendra observed. "Our camouflage might be working."

"It's not a coincidence," Eve said. "I'll hold our disguise as long as I can."

The sun climbed. The day grew warm. Seth tied the sleeves of his coat around his waist. His fleet boots that Grippa the troll had recommended kept his feet incredibly comfortable. Walking at the current pace felt like no trouble at all, even though Tanu was gently panting. Seth could not help wondering what top speed he could reach in them and what pace he could sustain.

"We have company," Tanu said.

Glancing to his right, Seth saw a trio of two-headed wolves come running out of the trees toward the road. He instinctively flinched away as one of the wolves collided with the unseen barrier at the edge of the trail. After some barks and snarls, the wolves contented themselves with running alongside the travelers, sometimes racing ahead or behind. Their heads were as high as Seth's chest. Soon a fourth and fifth wolf joined them.

"Dreadwolves," Tanu said. "Stay toward the center of the road, and be glad for the magical barrier. Those two heads coordinate well, attacking very effectively. While one is distracting, the other is drawing blood. Occasionally I've seen some with three heads."

Seth heard them making little growls and barks as they

dashed along the roadside. Now and then one would snarl, showing vicious teeth.

"I guess our disguises don't work on them," Kendra said.

"No," Eve said. "It is hardest for me to confuse creatures that hunt by smell."

"Looks like a couple of dragons are flying above us again," Tanu said. "The dreadwolves led them back to us."

"Then I'm dropping our disguises," Eve said. "I'm already overtaxed. I'll save my talent for an emergency."

The sun climbed higher, and the dreadwolves eventually stopped accompanying them. Seth studied the surrounding trees and rocks, wondering how far away the canines had actually gone.

When the sun was directly overhead, Tanu paused and looked up, shielding his eyes. "Midday," he said. "Somewhere, the war has begun."

"I think this war has been under way for a while," Kendra said. "Celebrant just made it official."

"Sure felt like a war at Soaring Cliffs," Tanu said.

"Won't be a war for the Fair Folk," Seth said, glancing at Eve.

"War is always war," Eve said. "We'll interact with it differently. It could still lead to our destruction."

"Then why not fight?" Seth asked.

"I'm not in charge," Eve said.

"Would you fight if you were in charge?" Seth asked.

"Would I send my whole people to war?" Eve asked. "That's a big choice. I'd have to make sure I fully understood the whole story, all aspects. Would I go to war personally? I'm here, aren't I? I'm not supposed to be."

"Could you get your people in trouble?" Kendra asked.

"Father warned he might have to disavow me if I helped you guys," Eve said. "I can live with that."

"Can you?" Tanu asked. "They are your people."

"They live in one little territory on a closed sanctuary," Eve said. "If exile means I get to explore the world, give me exile."

"You're brave," Seth said.

"Are you just barely picking up on that?" Eve asked.

"Sometimes leaving your people to explore new lands is necessary," Calvin said.

"You're brave too, Calvin," Seth assured him.

"Are there Fair Folk elsewhere?" Kendra asked.

"There are a few other populations around the globe," Eve said. "The group of us here at Wyrmroost is not the largest."

"Where are they?" Seth asked.

"That is not my secret to tell," Eve said.

They continued along the dusty road for another hour. As they came around a bend, they found several rumitaurs waiting, Amulon at the front, his impressive antlers reaching high above his head. Most of the other rumitaurs had no horns; a couple of them were women. A few alcetaurs were also with them, reminding Seth of Hendrick, as well as some smaller cervitaurs and a centaur. In total at least twenty taurans confronted them, blocking the width of the road several ranks deep. All bore weapons, ranging from spears to bows to clubs to axes, and they had large shields. Amulon carried a mighty mace.

"Greetings, caretakers," Amulon said. "This road leads to the Herdlands and is closed to you. Kindly leave at once."

"We're not anywhere near the Herdlands," Eve complained.

"Nevertheless, you are no longer permitted on this part of the road," Amulon said. "Please do not compel us to use force."

An alcetaur led several taurans off the trail. They loped past Seth and his companions and lined up behind them, blocking any retreat along the road.

"You sided with the dragons," Kendra accused.

"I sided against interference from humans on our preserve," Amulon said. "Being watched over by novice children was the final insult."

"Friend," Tanu began with a smile, "if you run us off the road, we will be killed."

"Dragon sanctuaries are perilous," Amulon said grimly. "Those who cannot survive here should not visit. Let alone pretend to lead."

"You're giving us a death penalty," Kendra said.

"I'm closing the road to you," Amulon said. "What happens beyond that is none of my affair. I wish you good fortune."

"What did the dragons offer you?" Eve asked.

"Does it matter?" Amulon said. "I struck a bargain with the caretaker I most respect."

"My father will not be pleased about this," Eve said.

"Who fears the displeasure of Dalgorel the Undecided?" Amulon asked. "It's time for this sanctuary to service beings savvy enough to survive here. You were foolish to leave home, daughter of Dalgorel. Another overindulged child with delusions of grandeur."

"This is an act of war," Tanu said.

"This is a time of war," Amulon replied.

"War between you and the caretakers," Tanu said. "You will lose your territory."

"War between the taurans and the *human* caretakers," Amulon said. "I stand with Celebrant and the dragons."

"Then get off our road," Kendra ordered.

"We have as much right to this road as you do," Amulon said. "By tradition, by proximity to the Herdlands, and by Celebrant's authority."

Seth drew his sword. Nobody seemed to notice. He wondered how Amulon would handle a bolt of lightning. Would it electrocute some of the other nearby taurans? The rest would surely attack.

"Off the road," Amulon said, stepping forward, leading with his shield.

"What gives us the best chance?" Seth asked. "Taurans or leaving the road?"

The back row of taurans nocked arrows.

"What about your bow, Kendra?" Seth asked.

"They have bows too," Kendra replied. "And big shields. And they are ahead and behind. And we have no armor."

"Forward!" Amulon called, increasing his pace and swinging his mace. Hoofbeats rumbled from ahead and behind.

Almost involuntarily, Seth scampered off the road, away from the charge. The others moved with him. Seth studied the foliage. What if the dreadwolves were nearby? Or some dragons? Kendra looked panicked. The fear made sense! They were exposed.

Amulon and the taurans lined up along the near edge of the path. "You are no longer welcome on the road. We will defend it to the death. Find your own way." He raised his mace high. "Warning shots!"

As Amulon lowered his weapon, arrows hissed from bows, thudding into the ground in front of Seth and the others. One landed hardly a step away from Seth's foot.

"Begone," Amulon commanded.

"They're all facing the same direction now," Kendra said, unslinging her bow and pulling back the empty string.

Seth looked from her bow to the taurans. Did she have the guts to let the arrows fly? Was it the wisest choice?

"One hundred," Kendra muttered, releasing the string.

A cloud of arrows zipped through the air, spreading wide as taurans ducked behind their shields. Dozens of arrows thunked against shields. Amulon's looked like a pincushion. One of the rumitaurs and one of the cervitaurs staggered, arrows having pierced their legs. An alcetaur had an arrow in his meaty shoulder.

And then Seth found he could not move. He could see and think, but his muscles refused to respond. A shadow fell across him as a huge green dragon plopped down behind him, crushing bushes and undergrowth beneath its bulk. What was he supposed to do? He couldn't budge! From the corner of his eye, he saw the head whip forward and the huge jaws clamp shut around Kendra, totally engulfing her.

Seth tried to scream. He tried to reach for his sister. The dragon fear held him utterly paralyzed.

Then Seth tipped and felt himself being dragged. Though aware of the hands supporting him, he could make no motion to help.

The green dragon sprang upward, taking flight, wind ruffling the surrounding vegetation as enormous wings heaved. Two other dragons—a black one with large spikes down the neck and the one from the feast with a face full of tentacles—dropped from the sky and landed nearby, the ground quaking at the impact.

Seth could not blink. He could not bend his legs or his waist. Eve was dragging him, stiff as a board, diagonally away from the road, into the cover of heavy bushes. She dropped him flat on his back and rummaged through his satchel. A flask came to his lips, and she was pouring fluid into his mouth.

For a terrifying moment Seth worried the liquid would drown him. But suddenly he could swallow, and he gulped down the rest. It was the courage potion! Control over his body returned. He sat up, furious.

"That dragon ate Kendra," he said, staring up at the green dragon rising higher into the sky. What was the range of his lightning sword?

"Not here," Eve whispered, dragging him to his feet. "Not now. Run!"

The other two dragons were both biting at something. Tanu, perhaps? There was no time to think. Seth followed Eve. Her pace felt slow. The boots were helping him.

Seth was in shock over Kendra. He could barely process

what he had seen! Kendra had been gulped down before she had any chance to react. And now Tanu was perhaps getting killed too.

There was no time to absorb it. He had to survive. For the good of the sanctuary, and for the hope of any payback, his first job was to escape. Was that even possible? If the dragons were going to get him, shouldn't he turn and give them a fight to remember?

"Dragons are great hunters," Eve said breathlessly. "I'll only be able to cloak us for so long. Right now we look like fleeing deer. You should hide."

"Let's stick together," Seth said.

"We're both more likely to die if we're together," Eve said. "Do it for me. Do it for you."

Seth knew he could run faster without her. But how much did that matter against dragons? Wasn't her ability to disguise them more important? Was she trying to use him as bait to lure the dragons away from her? If she was, he would do it, and kill both dragons singlehandedly if he had to.

"Where do I go?" Seth asked.

"Try the cave in that hillside," she said. "They might pass it by. Or it might run narrow and deep. Maybe you can escape."

He saw the dark cavity in the steep, rocky slope. It might go back only a few feet. At least it would provide some cover, and the opening was much too small for a dragon to enter.

"Do it," Calvin advised from his pocket. "Splitting up is smart."

Seth broke off from Eve toward the hillside, upping his

pace to a full sprint. Amazed at the length and speed of his strides, Seth doubted he had ever run half this fast.

Behind him, dragons roared. As he slipped into the little cave, his last glance back showed the dragon with the tentacled face rising into the sky. Seth rushed deeper into the cave. It was more than an indentation, but it narrowed to a dead end after about twenty feet. At least the space looked empty.

Seth kept still, holding his breath.

"Come out," a slithery voice called, like many voices speaking at once, all of them with too much saliva in their mouths. "I saw you enter, caretaker. Surrender."

Holding his breath, Seth pressed back against the rear of the cave. Hopefully Eve was escaping while this dragon was distracted. Of course, there had been two.

What were his assets? The sword in his hand could shoot a bolt of lightning. He also had the vial of horrors. Was now an effective time to try the vial, cornered in a cave? Against a single dragon? Who would be more scared? Would the courage potion help protect him?

A head snaked into the cave, mostly filling the tunnel, and a mass of squirmy tentacles writhed toward him. Seth felt fear but was not overpowered. He slashed his sword through the grasping appendages, severing at least four, the blade passing through them cleanly. Ichor fountained and the head withdrew.

"Good one," Calvin encouraged.

"For Kendra," Seth muttered.

"You'll pay for that," the dragon threatened. "Out you come or I roast you."

"Too scared to fight me face-to-face?" Seth cried.

"You dare insult my courage?"

"I always heard Wormface was the most cowardly dragon," Seth yelled. "Fights human children from a distance."

"Orders or not, you die now," the dragon declared. The head wriggled back into the cave, and Seth held his sword ready. Suddenly the head flopped to the floor and stopped advancing, tangled tentacles squishy and limp, the severed ones still oozing juices.

Seth stared, wondering if it might be a ruse. The dragon seemed weirdly still considering how angry it had sounded.

"Hurry, boy, come quick," a deep voice boomed.

"Who's there?" Seth asked.

"Your dragon slayer," the voice replied.

Now Seth recognized the voice! It was the Somber Knight! Stepping on mushy tentacles, Seth scrambled around the dragon's head and past the somewhat narrower neck until he exited the cave. The huge knight had to be at least ten feet tall, and he stood beside the spot where the scaly neck had been cleaved in two. The gigantic body of the dragon lay lifeless. The knight clutched a sword with a blade longer than Seth from head to foot.

"Eve," Seth said, anxiously looking for her.

"We must aid her," the Somber Knight said. "And your sister."

"A dragon ate Kendra," Seth said, mildly surprised he could spit out the dreadful words.

"No," the Somber Knight said. "Your sister lives."

CHAPTER FOURTEEN

Captive

In the moist, humid enclosure, Kendra sat on a damp, muscular tongue surrounded by meaty walls. She could only faintly see the cruel fangs and the mucosal surfaces, which meant there was little light. Mysterious fumes and gurgles issued from the clenching tunnel at the rear of her prison. The environment gently rocked, bobbed, and swayed, evidence that they were flying, but also that her captor was trying to keep her level. The sour air reeked of half digested kills.

Covering her nose, Kendra attempted to ignore when the tongue rippled beneath her. She tried not to get saliva on her bare skin, because it burned and tingled. What was going to happen to her? If the dragon meant to swallow her, why not get on with it?

Her captor was obviously taking her somewhere. What

if it intended to feed her to baby dragons? The image came too vividly to her mind. Or maybe she would be dropped from a great height? Or tortured?

She still had all her gear. The sack of gales was an option. But did she want a windstorm inside of a dragon mouth? Not when flying through the air. Anything that might make the dragon spit her out would not end well for her.

And so she sat as still as possible in the uncomfortably warm, rank air, trying very hard not to overanalyze what might come next. She paid attention to acceleration tugging on her as they turned or sped up or descended.

Suddenly Kendra felt like she was inside a plunging elevator, followed by a rush of forward movement. And then she came to a halt. A moment later, her enclosure tipped forward and opened, dumping her onto a rocky floor.

Her hair had spilled over her face, temporarily screening her view. Knees and elbows smarting from the tumble, Kendra pushed her hair back and stared up at Celebrant, he on his dais in his cavernous hall, she on the floor like a mess coughed up by a giant cat.

"That did not take long," the Dragon King said contentedly. "Hardly an hour past midday."

Having seen only the inside of the mouth of her captor, Kendra looked back at the dragon behind her. Emerald-green scales covered a creature nearly as immense as Celebrant.

"She offered no trouble," said a voice that sounded like dozens of women speaking together. A pair of fins just behind her head fanned out and then retracted.

"Excellent, Jaleesa," Celebrant said. "And her brother?"

"Numrum and Chiro should be behind me," Jaleesa said.

"And the manservant who desecrated the corpse of Madrigus?" Celebrant asked.

"He was with the boy," Jaleesa said. "They had no chance for escape."

"Were Numrum and Chiro following you here?" Celebrant asked.

"Not that I could see," Jaleesa said.

"Berzog, Luria, go investigate," Celebrant ordered.

An amber dragon and a dragon covered in quills took flight, exiting the vast room.

"Jaleesa, congratulations on delivering the girl unharmed," Celebrant said. "You are dismissed."

The green dragon moved away. Kendra got to her feet, her clothes gooey with dragon spit.

"Don't hurt Tanu," Kendra said.

"Your manservant is already dead," Celebrant said. "I want your brother alive for now."

"You won't get away with this," Kendra said.

"I will accomplish so much more than this, you ridiculous girl," Celebrant said. "I'm just barely getting started. You can make things easier on yourself and your brother—and on all your allies at Blackwell Keep."

"How?" Kendra asked.

"Unconditional surrender," Celebrant said. "Relinquish the caretaker's medallion. Name me sole caretaker of Wyrmroost. In return, I vow to see you safely delivered to the borders of the sanctuary to depart with any of your compatriots who care to join you."

Kendra clutched the medallion. "You are no caretaker. You care only about yourself, and maybe the dragons. This sanctuary is meant for all who live here. And it is meant to protect the world from you. I won't give it up."

"I can slay you at my leisure," Celebrant said casually.

"I guess you can," Kendra said.

"Foolish girl," Celebrant said. "Do not tempt me."

"Was this the plan Ronodin gave you?" Kendra asked.

Celebrant narrowed his eyes. "What did he tell you?"

"He told you how to win the war," Kendra said.

"The dark unicorn did bring some information that will aid our cause," Celebrant said. "I lay my own traps. Catching you took less effort than a yawn."

"What did he tell you?" Kendra wondered.

"You will know soon enough," Celebrant said. "If you live to see it. I will give you some time to think. Perhaps once I have your brother, you will be more persuadable."

"Don't count on it," Kendra said, secretly worried she might do anything to save Seth's life.

"She's alive?" Seth asked. "You're sure?"

The Somber Knight gave a nod. "First, we have another dragon to punish." He waved an arm, and a huge bull came plodding up to him. The animal was made of tar, with horns carved out of stone, and the tall knight had to reach up to pat the neck. Pulling with one arm, the Somber Knight leaped astride the bull—a feat that should have been impossible in his heavy armor. The bull turned and charged in the direction of the black dragon with spikes down the neck.

"Chiro!" the Somber Knight called, his voice booming. "Come face your doom!"

The black dragon had been moving away from Seth and the knight, presumably still hunting Eve. But now the dragon turned, eyes flashing. Chiro sprang into the air and glided low toward the Somber Knight.

"Butcher!" Chiro called out, her voice a soprano choir. "Today your atrocities end."

Seth considered ducking back into the cave in case the dragon sprayed fire or worse. The Somber Knight stood up on the back of the bull, still racing straight for the dragon, and started twirling a chain with a grapnel at the end. As the dragon's mouth opened, the Somber Knight hurled the grappling hook, which caught hold of Chiro's lower jaw.

The dragon tried to swerve away, but the Somber Knight leaped from the back of the bull, chain tautening in one hand, sword gripped in the other, and began a wide swing. His weight jerked Chiro's head down, and the Somber Knight curved swiftly into the air. Crashing into the dragon's side, he plunged the sword up to the hilt.

With a shriek, Chiro lost altitude and plowed into the ground, tumbling and tearing up huge chunks of earth. Sword in hand after it ripped free from the dragon in the landing, the Somber Knight rolled to his feet and began hacking at a wing as he dashed along the body. Wheeling around, the bull of tar lowered its horns and rammed the far side of the dragon.

As the Somber Knight sprinted toward the base of the neck, Chiro arched her head around and exhaled bubbling dark-blue liquid all over him. The fluid sizzled on the ground, acrid fumes rising, and though the knight was drenched, he charged forward and slashed the base of the neck.

Chiro tried to bite the Somber Knight, but he bashed her head aside with his shield and plunged his sword into her eye. Tail flailing, wings spasming, the dragon withdrew her head, and the Somber Knight opened the base of the neck wider with a mighty swipe of his sword. Dark-blue fluid fizzed from the wound as Chiro slumped to the ground, twitching but no longer trying to rise. The Somber Knight stomped over and chopped off the head.

"You got her," Seth said, drawing closer.

"Stay back, lad," the Somber Knight said. "Her corrosive bile could eat right through your boots." He removed the grapnel from the dragon's mouth and started winding the chain.

"It didn't ruin your armor," Seth said.

"Not much can harm this armor," the Somber Knight said, coming to Seth.

"That was amazing," Seth said. "You killed two dragons."

"It's my job," the Somber Knight said. "You made the first one easy. Dreadwolves sometimes shelter in that cave. Lucky for you it was empty today. The second dragon took some effort."

"You cut off her head," Seth said.

"Best way to be sure," the Somber Knight said. "Dragons can be resilient."

The Somber Knight whistled, and his bull came plodding over.

"Is it made of tar?" Seth asked.

"Mostly," the Somber Knight said. "I have ridden to battle on Umbro many times. He's a dullion, kind of like a golem. He's fast and tireless."

"I got attacked by a dullion once," Seth said. "It was shaped like a big person."

"They come in many forms," the Somber Knight said. "No real life in them. No personality. Umbro just follows orders. Which makes him much more useful than many people I have met."

"How did you find me?" Seth asked.

"I had a tip from Lord Dalgorel," the Somber Knight said. "I sensed when the dragons declared war. I'm in tune with the treaties and boundaries of Wyrmroost. As I was preparing to depart, Dalgorel came and told me where you, Kendra, Eve, and your manservant were heading."

"We need to find Eve," Seth said.

"Right here," she said, seeming to appear at his side out of some wisps of steam.

"You were still hiding," Seth said.

"Can't be too careful," Eve said. "Nice work, Ryland."

"Few have bothered to learn my name," the Somber Knight said.

"I like the old stories," Eve said.

"What about Tanu?" Seth asked.

"I noticed your manservant over yonder," Ryland said.

Seth peered in the direction the Somber Knight had

indicated and noticed a cloud of gas shaped exactly like Tanu. "He must have seen the dragons coming just in time to take a gaseous potion," Seth said.

"Where to now?" Eve asked.

"More dragons will be on their way," Ryland said. "Not all are as foolhardy and incompetent as Chiro, or as careless as Numrum. First we should get back on the road."

"What about the taurans?" Seth asked.

"Explain," Ryland said.

"Amulon and the taurans forced us off the road," Seth said bitterly. "They basically handed us over to the dragons."

"I arrived too late to witness that," Ryland said. "Yet your words reverberate with truth. Amulon has committed treason."

"He isn't alone," Seth said.

"Amulon!" Ryland shouted in a voice that rivaled dragon roars. "Come face your judgment."

The Somber Knight mounted Umbro, then extended a gauntleted hand down to Eve. After hoisting her aboard, he hauled Seth up as well. The back of the bull was too wide for Seth or Eve to straddle without doing the splits, so they knelt behind Ryland. The bull did not run smoothly, and Seth found it took all of his concentration to maintain his balance.

In a few moments they were back on the road, confronting Amulon and about twenty other taurans, who huddled together, weapons ready. They looked distrustful and angry.

"Amulon," Ryland said, his voice more grave than Seth had ever heard it. "You forced the active caretakers of Wyrmroost off the road and into mortal peril. How plead you?"

For the first time since Seth had met Amulon, the rumitaur appeared uncertain. "Celebrant is also a caretaker. I was acting under his orders."

"Celebrant was a lesser caretaker who has declared war against the rightful caretakers of Wyrmroost," Ryland said. "You side with the dragons in this conflict?"

Amulon straightened. "We do."

"And you are guilty of forcing the caretakers off the road?" Ryland asked.

Amulon thrust his powerful chest forward. "I am proud."

"Then I find you guilty of treason," Ryland said. "As no lives have been lost yet, resulting from your actions, Seth can choose between death and exile for you."

"Wait, I choose?" Seth asked.

"Yes," Ryland said. "Shall I claim his head or banish him?"

Seth frowned. "Kendra is alive?"

"For now, yes," Ryland said.

"I need no mercy from a whelp," Amulon said. "If you want my head, you clattering relic from days long gone, come try to take it."

"I await your command," Ryland said to Seth.

"Exile," Seth said. "Not fair to kill him if we all lived."

"Very well," Ryland said, raising his sword above his head. "Amulon, son of Warrow, seeing as you speak for the taurans, and a score of your fellows aided your crime, I, the Somber Knight, Dragonslayer of Wyrmroost, hereby revoke your claim to your territory, along with access to the thoroughfares reserved for the friends of Blackwell Keep."

"Celebrant will reinstate us," Amulon said.

"Your new domain will encompass the barrows, lackluster wood, and the adjoining meadows," Ryland continued.

"That is a domain of haunts and shades," Amulon scoffed.

"And now of the taurans as well," Ryland said. "Sleep lightly. Get to your new domain promptly. Anywhere else on this preserve, you are in extreme violation of trespass, with prejudice." He slashed his sword twice in their direction.

"This cannot be," Amulon said, beginning to look panicked.

"They'll be hunted anywhere else they go," Eve said. "Fair game to any creature."

"Those taurans still at the Herdlands are also trespassing," Ryland said. "Warn them if you can. Should they linger longer than a day, their lives are forfeit. Once they have departed, reentry is of course barred. And you will be rejected by the protections of this road the moment my sword touches the ground."

Amulon and the taurans all scattered to the left side of the road—all except one rumitaur, who glared at Ryland until the tip of his sword touched the dirt. Brilliant streaks of energy enveloped the stubborn rumitaur, hurling him off the road to land on his side, fur badly singed. One of the cervitaurs shot an arrow at the Somber Knight, but it failed to cross the edge of the trail, deflected with a flash.

"Begone, taurans," Ryland called. "I will consider your lingering an invitation to combat. Do not forget, I am among the predators who can hunt you outside the barrows."

"All this for bothering children?" Amulon cried.

"This is for siding with the dragons against the caretakers," Ryland declared. "Let it be a warning to all."

The taurans ran away.

"You have some serious power," Seth said.

"In this instance, my power derives from the treaty they violated," Ryland said.

"The dragons violated the treaty too," Seth said.

"Which freed me to attack them," Ryland said. "But the territories are tied to direct treaties with the caretakers. I could banish the taurans from their homes for treason. There is no equivalent for the dragons—except I can revoke Celebrant's status as a caretaker."

"You can?" Seth asked.

"He declared war," Ryland said. "I can and will revoke his status. I will approach in my capacity as a herald. And I will endeavor to rescue your sister. I will likely perish."

Seth didn't want the knight to die. How did he speak so calmly of taking action that could end him? Could he die and still save Kendra?

"Celebrant has her?" Seth asked.

"I strongly suspect so," Ryland said.

"How is she all right?" Seth said. "I saw the dragon eat her."

"You saw Jaleesa scoop her up," Ryland said. "I saw too,

from a distance. The dragon did not swallow, but rather flew off toward Skyhold. If your sister had been killed, I would feel the crime. Such an act would reverberate across all the treaties of Wyrmroost."

"You don't think you can survive rescuing Kendra?" Seth asked.

"If I go as a herald in a time of war, the dragons cannot attack me," Ryland said. "But stripping Celebrant of his caretakership constitutes an act of aggression, and that invites retaliation. A herald brings a message. Executing justice changes the nature of my visit. But the Dragon King's status must be eliminated. The downgrade will weaken the dragon rebellion. Reduce their options. The dragons will kill me for it. I don't know how I could get away. So I will do my best to save your sister before I expire."

"I'll come help," Seth said.

"No," Ryland said. "You cannot be jeopardized. Wyrmroost is in plenty of danger without handing both caretakers to the dragons."

"Then what am I supposed to do?" Seth asked.

"Stay alive," Ryland said. "Find shelter for the festival night in a roadhouse if need be. Then get back to Blackwell Keep alive and resist the dragons."

"We'll have to go by Stormguard Castle," Seth said. "You don't know the story, do you?"

"Stormguard Castle was never under my purview," Ryland said. "It predates Wyrmroost. Old, powerful magic resides there. You would be wise to get no closer than necessary."

The translucent, gassy form of Tanu drifted onto the road.

"Hey, Tanu," Seth said. "More dead dragons over there."

Tanu covered his ears and shook his head, a pained expression on his wispy face.

"I bet you want their guts," Seth said. "You probably can't carry much more anyhow. Even if you weren't made of smoke."

Tanu slumped theatrically.

"Kendra is alive," Seth informed him. "The Somber Knight is going to try to rescue her."

Tanu brightened and gave a thumbs-up.

"I will most likely fail," Ryland said. "If I fall, I will instruct Umbro to come find you, Seth, and to help you get home. If I live, I will come help you myself. You will probably get no assistance. The dragons will most likely destroy both of us."

"You are not very positive," Eve said.

"I am positive we will all eventually die," Ryland said. "Only the timing remains in question. Soon, by realistic forecasts."

"He's not the Cheerful Knight," Seth said.

The Somber Knight looked skyward. "Berzog and Luria are circling up there. Keeping their distance while we are on the road, I imagine. Wait, what is this?"

Seth saw a griffin approaching in the distance, flying low, with three other dragons in pursuit. The griffin dove really low, disappearing into some trees, then popped out, going a different direction.

"That's Tempest," Seth said. He waved his arms and shouted. "Come on, Tempest! You can make it."

Tempest gained a little altitude, then plunged directly toward Seth and the road. The two circling dragons moved to intercept, but they were too slow, and the three in pursuit trailed by too far. All the dragons veered away as Tempest landed on the road.

Seth ran to the griffin and hugged her neck. Her feathers were damp with perspiration, and flecks of lather stood out on her fur.

"We might have a faster way home," Seth said.

"You want to risk the dragons?" Ryland asked.

"She got here, didn't she?" Seth replied.

"She will not be as maneuverable with riders," Ryland said.

"What if one of the riders can disguise her?" Eve asked innocently.

The Somber Knight rapped his helmet twice and pointed at her. "That thought has potential. Indeed it does."

CHAPTER FIFTEEN

Rescuers

I have bad news, and I have worse news," Doren announced the day after Knox and Tess had arrived at Blackwell Keep. "And a bit of minor good news. And some random news."

Knox, Tess, and Doren stood in the nearest courtyard to the rooms where the satyrs were living. Several dragons patrolled up high, in the distance.

"You're starting to lose me," Knox said. "What is the bad news?"

"The griffins that we're sending to rescue Seth and Kendra are no longer just getting turned back," Doren said. "They're getting killed by dragons. We've lost two so far."

"What is the good news?" Tess asked.

"I finally learned how to make my yo-yo sleep," Doren said. "You know, when it reaches the end of the string and just hangs there spinning? But a flick of the wrist will make it wind up again? It takes the right touch. I think I've got it."

"What's the worse news?" Knox asked.

"Still no sign of the barrel or the person who, um, did harm to the goblin," Doren said. "The whole keep is on alert, and there are no leads." He gave Tess a tentative smile. "But I'm sure we can all sleep tight and have happy dreams."

"I know the goblin is dead," Tess said. "This is a scary place. What is the random news?"

"I swiped a pie from the kitchen and ate it," Doren said. "The whole pie. By myself. That could have been good news, but I saved none to share. I have selfish moments. Peach pie—never trust me around peaches."

"I'm sick of waiting," Knox said. "What can we do?"

"We really haven't been waiting very long," Doren said. "You just arrived last night."

"I want to help Seth and Kendra," Knox said. "They're in real danger. And I wouldn't mind seeing some dragons up close."

Doren's eyes widened. He gestured at the sky. "Those dragons are the perfect distance. Most people see dragons up close only one time. The experience does not last long."

"But the magic walls will keep them out," Knox said. "Can't you lure some down? Leave out a dead deer or some-thing?"

Doren put a hand to his forehead. "Where are we supposed to hunt deer? And why would a dragon want our shabby meal? These are apex predators. They eat whatever they want, pretty much whenever they want."

"It would be fun to see one closer," Tess said. "But not if it eats us."

"You have seen dragons flying around all day," Doren said. "Few ever see a dragon and live to tell the tale."

"But they're so far away," Knox said. "They almost look like kites."

"And where are the fairies?" Tess asked. "I thought this place was supposed to be so magical."

"The fairies are probably hiding like everything else with a brain," Doren said. "The dragons declared war."

"Kind of a boring war," Knox said with a sigh.

Doren raised his hands. "That's the best kind of war. Trust me."

"Have you been in a war?" Knox asked.

Doren folded his arms. "I've seen plenty on TV. And I lent a hand against some demons once. Not a comfortable day."

Newel came trotting over, a shimmery length of fabric folded under one arm. He looked pleased.

"How did it go this time?" Knox asked.

"He finally gave me something," Newel said.

"Not bagpipes?" Tess asked.

"Grippa is pretending he never mentioned bagpipes," Newel said. "I keep pestering him to let us recover his investment for him by helping Kendra and Seth. That troll is stubborn. I was as frustrated as a lumberjack in a petrified forest. But he finally gave me this." He unfolded the fabric with a flourish. It was a hooded cape. "Behold—the cloak of innocence."

"That sounds weak," Knox said.

"Shows what you know," Newel said with a huff. "If somebody is new to a preserve, has caused no harm, and intends no harm, this creates a powerful shield around them and any traveling with them. Even if the companions are scoundrels."

"How much protection?" Knox asked.

"It makes you invulnerable," Newel said. "It was crafted by the wizards who first designed the preserves to provide complete protection to neutral visitors. It draws on the power of the treaty that founded the preserve. The whole sanctuary would have to fall in order for the cloak to fail."

"What's the catch?" Doren asked. "These things always have a catch."

"Don't interrupt," Newel said. "I was getting to it. If anyone under the protection of the cloak harms a creature or steals something, the protection is ruined for all."

"So the companions shouldn't be scoundrels," Knox said.

"Or go near peach pie," Tess added with a smile.

"Why peach pie?" Newel asked. "I love peach pie!"

"Kids," Doren said with a vague shrug. "You never know what arbitrary examples they'll mention next."

Newel looked betrayed. "You didn't all share a peach pie without me?"

"Who would share peach pie?" Doren asked, absently wiping the corner of his mouth.

"The cloak," Knox prompted.

"Yes, the cloak," Newel said, shaking it slightly. "This

might grant you the freedom you had last time, Knox. We can use your innocence to rescue Kendra and Seth."

"I want to help them," Knox said. "I feel terrible I messed up security here when I came through the barrel. Would the cloak protect against dragons?"

"It should," Newel said.

"How will we know it's working?" Knox asked.

"It will kind of gleam," Newel said, putting the cloak around Knox's shoulders. The entire piece of clothing turned black.

"Oh, dear," Doren said.

"What have you been up to?" Newel asked.

"Nothing," Knox said. "I've been with you guys."

Newel hit himself in the forehead with the heel of his hand. "You took the scepter. After you brought it here, that must have counted as stealing something."

"Am I innocent?" Tess asked.

All eyes slowly turned to her.

"She doesn't even drink the milk," Doren murmured.

"No," Newel said. "We couldn't. She's so little."

"I'm not little," Tess said. "I'm ten. Two digits. Same as most people."

"Most humans," Newel corrected.

"Worth a try," Knox said, taking off the cloak and putting it over his little sister's shoulders. It shrank a little to fit her and turned a gleaming white, with faint hints of other colors.

"Looks like we have a winner," Doren said.

"Take it off," Newel said, removing the cloak. The fabric

returned to a shimmery gray. "You'll draw attention."

"I have magic," Tess said. "I knew I was really a fairy."

Knox rolled his eyes. Newel glared at him.

"There is definitely a certain magic to innocence," Doren said. "Why don't you go play with my yo-yo for a little bit?" He handed it over.

Tess accepted the toy with a dubious look. "This is hard. It gets tangled."

"Up and down," Doren said. "Pop your wrist a little. It takes practice. Try it over by the wall. Stiller air there."

"You want to talk without me," Tess said. She skipped over to the wall.

"We can't really take advantage of an innocent little girl?" Newel asked.

"You took advantage of me," Knox complained. "With the bear that was actually a troll."

"An ogre," Newel corrected.

"And with the dragons," Knox said.

"That was primarily Seth taking advantage," Newel said.

"We were definitely accomplices," Doren confessed.

"It's the same," Knox said. "She'll be safe."

"Were you safe?" Newel asked.

"I think so," Knox said. "More or less."

"Probably less," Doren said. "But you survived."

"What would Stan and Ruth do to us if we even suggested it?" Newel asked.

"Stan and Ruth are not our grandparents," Knox said. "The Larsens are. Seth and Kendra are my cousins."

"That doesn't make you disposable," Doren said.

"How safe are we here?" Knox asked. "There's a murderer loose. Didn't they say the road is protected? We might be safer if we go. And we might actually be useful, too."

Newel stroked his chin. "Not a bad argument. Let's face it. The girl will be safe with the cloak on. And Kendra and Seth need help."

"And I'm sick of being stuck in this boring fort with a killer," Knox said. "I want to do something."

"This could all go terribly wrong," Doren said. "We could get eaten. And by 'we' I mean you and your sister. Newel and I have a knack for escape."

"Especially when we're with somebody slower who can serve as bait," Newel said.

Doren elbowed him.

"As long as we don't steal anything or harm anybody, the cloak protects all of us," Doren summarized.

"But it turned black for me," Knox said.

"Under the protection of Tess, we get to start fresh," Newel said.

"If one of us under the protection breaks the spell, we are all exposed," Doren reminded him.

"Then we don't break the spell," Knox said, "and we'll be fine. Easy."

Newel cringed. "Don't label any endeavor as 'easy'! No matter how much you think it. Is this your first day on Earth? Avoid saying 'nothing can go wrong,' 'all our trouble is behind us,' and 'this ship can never sink.'"

"Common knowledge," Doren said. "Even among the least superstitious."

"I'm not superstitious," Knox said. "It doesn't matter if I think something will be easy or hard. It will be what it is going to be."

"This guy might become a philosopher," Doren said.

Newel put his fists on his wooly hips. "A really unlucky philosopher."

"We have what we need," Knox said. "Let's go."

"I doubt we can get permission," Newel said. "And we can't just march off down the road. We'll be spotted."

"I've been scouting," Doren said. "There's a secret way out of the fort. One below a wall without guards."

"Could we make it to cover?" Newel asked.

"Maybe thirty yards to cover," Doren said. "Then we can stay under trees until we join up with the road out of sight."

"Why the road if we have the cloak?" Knox asked.

"We want as much safety as possible," Newel said. "With Tess wearing the cloak, we can venture off the road as needed."

"I'm excited to learn the lay of the land here," Doren said.

"Dragon sanctuaries are legendary," Newel agreed. "And of course we want to find Seth and Kendra."

"Stan and Ruth will flip when they find us missing," Knox said.

"I'll leave a note in our room," Doren said. "I'll explain we want to help with Kendra and Seth, and we felt like a fort with a murderer loose was not a safe environment for children."

"That's good," Newel said. "Sounds responsible."

"More responsible than they deserve," Doren said. "Who trusts satyrs to babysit?"

"Very distracted people," Newel said. "Should we pack up and go?"

"No sense waiting," Doren said.

"How did you find the secret door?" Knox asked.

"When I get bored, I follow people," Doren said. "From a distance. A certain minotaur who normally works in the dungeon has used this passage once or twice when he thought he was unobserved."

"That's shady," Newel said. "Could he be the murderer?"

"I don't think so," Doren said. "I had suspicions too, and watched him carefully. He went to relieve his bladder in the woods and walked under the trees for a short time. Smelled some flowers. I think he just likes to get away from the dungeon from time to time."

"Good detective work," Newel said. "Knox, grab your sister. Doren, write the note. I'll gather supplies."

Tess wandered back over to them and held up a knotted mass of string connected to a yo-yo. "See, I told you it gets tangled."

CHAPTER SIXTEEN

Traitor

Kendra sat on the floor in the same room where the dragons had held the feast. Her back was against the wall, and a chain connected an iron shackle on one ankle to a spike in the floor. She had expected a dungeon, but instead she remained in the same vast room with Celebrant and several other dragons. After some goblins had chained her to the spike, she had received no further attention.

Seth had not yet appeared, which she considered a good sign. Celebrant had mentioned that he meant to take her brother alive. Hopefully his absence meant he had somehow given the dragons the slip. She tried not to think about him possibly being dead.

Watching the dragons was interesting. They were so large, so foreign, so powerful. The way they stretched their necks or flexed their wings. The way their sides billowed as they breathed. The scrape of their claws over the rocky floor of the room. Kendra felt like she was at an exotic zoo, except inside the cage.

Even all together in this huge chamber, the dragons did not socialize much. Most curled up and appeared to sleep. A few paced about. They struck her as basically solitary creatures enduring a social environment.

"Want a drink?" someone asked.

Kendra looked up and found that Ronodin had approached. "You're still here?"

"You're back," Ronodin said, sitting down beside her and handing her a cup. "Just water. Nothing gross. I brought some berries, too." He set a bowl between them. "Lots of good leftovers from the feast still."

"Why are you being nice to me?" Kendra asked. "What do you want?"

"I believe in courtesy," Ronodin said. "We want a civilized world."

"Are you after Bracken's horn?" she asked.

"Always," Ronodin said. "Nobody could take it from you if they tried. They didn't bother to confiscate any of your gear. Careless. Never underestimate an enemy."

"You think I can cause trouble chained up here?" Kendra asked.

"Many of our worst choices are made due to overconfidence," Ronodin said.

"You seem confident," Kendra said.

Ronodin smiled. "I'm in touch with reality, so of course

I'm confident. But overconfidence is sloppy. Have some berries. I selected only the ripest."

Kendra eyed the bowl. What if they were poisoned? Or sabotaged somehow.

"If I wanted to harm you, there are easier ways," Ronodin said.

"I'm not supposed to underestimate an enemy," Kendra said.

"I captured Bracken and helped the dragons," Ronodin bragged. "I guess that looks bad. The berries are fine."

Kendra took out Bracken's horn and used it to stir the berries.

"You're teasing me," Ronodin said.

"I'm purifying your offering," Kendra replied. She put the horn away and tried a raspberry. Ronodin was right. It was perfect. "Thanks."

"Festival night tomorrow," Ronodin said. "That will probably be the night you lose the war."

"Feels like I already lost," Kendra said.

Ronodin laughed lightly. "You personally may have already lost. But this is just the start. Your whole side probably loses tomorrow. The dragons win."

"This is because of your advice?" Kendra asked.

"It's impolite to brag," Ronodin said.

"You shouldn't be proud," Kendra said. "What did you tell them?"

He popped a berry into his mouth. "I'm almost tempted to tell you. Here you are, chained up and helpless. If we're going to have a war, a connoisseur wants it at least to be interesting. Do you like sports?"

"Generally, yes," Kendra said.

"How about basketball?"

"Sure."

"Right now the Dragons are ahead of the Children by at least seventy points," Ronodin said. "Their players are seasoned pros, spectacular athletes, most of them over seven feet tall. The Children are a team of young novices, still trying to learn to dribble, and none have reached the five-foot mark. How much fun is it to watch that lopsided game?"

"Fun if you like the Dragons," Kendra said.

Ronodin winced. "Is it? Even if you adore the Dragons, you want them to be tested a little. A discerning fan hopes for some excitement. A chance for talent to be displayed. An opportunity for some heroism."

"What can you tell me?" Kendra asked.

"Nothing," Ronodin said. "I'm Team Dragons all the way. I was just explaining why giving you a hint is tempting."

"I think it's kind of funny that you're scared to give me a tip," Kendra said. She shook her leg, jangling her chain.

"Not scared, just careful," Ronodin said. "No need to take unnecessary risks. Especially with nothing in return." He leaned close, and his voice dropped to a whisper. Kendra tried to ignore the sincere intensity in his eyes. How crazy was she to find anything about him charming under these conditions? "Now, if you give me Bracken's horn, I will tell you the secret—and break you out of here tonight."

Kendra paused. What good was the horn if the dragons

won? What would happen to the horn if the dragons killed her? Could Ronodin just take it anyway?

"I'm sorry," Kendra said. "The Children want to win on their own."

"You hesitated," Ronodin said. "It's a good deal."

"Why do you want the horn?" Kendra asked.

"Too many questions," Ronodin said. "It's creating a toxic atmosphere." He stood up. "You want a guaranteed loss instead of a chance. Interesting strategy. I'll leave you to it. Enjoy the berries."

He walked away. Kendra tugged on the chain. It was secure.

She needed a plan! But what could she do? They had not confiscated her bow, but if she shot any arrows, they probably would. And what good were arrows against dragons? She could use her sack to make wind, but again, they would just take it from her when it ran out.

She was chained up. She was stuck.

And Ronodin was gone. If he came back, should she consider his offer? Not if it might make Bracken vulnerable to him. It wasn't worth it. She would rather die. Bracken had trusted her with the horn. She had to hold true to that.

A goblin blew a trumpet.

"Announcing the Somber Knight," the goblin declared.

Kendra stood, her chain rattling.

The Somber Knight came striding into the room, an imposing figure encased in full armor that left no flesh visible. He held an enormous sword, with another smaller one across his back, a slender chain looped at his side, and

WRATH OF THE DRAGON KING

several knives in various sheaths. It looked like he had seen some fighting recently—his armor was scuffed, with grassy clods of earth stuck here and there. A huge bull made of tar trailed behind him.

"You are unwelcome, Sir Knight," Celebrant said from his platform at the far end of the great hall.

"If I were welcome here, I would be doing my job poorly," the Somber Knight said, still walking.

"You recently slew two of my subjects," Celebrant said.

"You recently declared war," the Somber Knight replied.

"I am a caretaker," Celebrant said. "You serve me."

"I am here to remedy that," the Somber Knight said, coming to a standstill. "The dragons I dispatched were attacking a caretaker." He gestured at Kendra. "You have the other caretaker chained up here. And you have declared war."

"Mind your tongue," Celebrant said. "Soon I will be the sole overseer of Wyrmroost."

"Not so," the Somber Knight said, raising his sword. "As Dragon Slayer of Wyrmroost, enforcer of the treaty, I find you in violation of your caretaker's oath."

"Nonsense," Celebrant said. "The other caretakers were out of order."

"You were only ever a junior caretaker to them," the Somber Knight said. "I hereby revoke your title, including all rights and privileges as a caretaker of Wyrmroost." He planted the tip of the sword against the stone floor. A small shock wave radiated outward from that point, accompanied by a sound like breaking glass.

Kendra smiled. Stripping Celebrant of his role as caretaker was a step in the right direction.

"Very well," Celebrant said, anger in his tone. "Who needs to be a lowly caretaker when he is king! Stripping my title is an act of aggression. You no longer have heraldic immunity."

"Your move," the Somber Knight said.

"Attack him," Celebrant called. "Destroy him!"

Kendra gasped as dragons swept in from all directions, blocking the Somber Knight from view. His bull charged one of the dragons from behind.

Grabbing her sack of gales, Kendra pointed the mouth toward the knight and loosed the drawstring. With the howl of a raging typhoon, wind gushed from the mouth of the bag. The dragons who were airborne immediately twisted in crooked ways, three of them slamming brusquely against the far wall. Only those on the ground could resist the gale, keeping low, wings tucked. The wind did not seem to bother the Somber Knight, who was busy carving deep gashes into the base of an orange dragon's neck.

Kendra felt a rush of air from one side and found Raxtus had landed beside her. She had not seen the fairy dragon since Jaleesa had taken her captive. Should she turn the sack on him? Was he attacking? Before she could determine his intent, Raxtus quickly bit through the chain near her ankle, leaving only a few links connected to the manacle.

"Come on," Raxtus said, grabbing Kendra with his front claws and springing into the air. Kendra yanked the drawstring closed.

"Raxtus!" Celebrant thundered. "Don't do this! Traitor! Stop him!"

Raxtus zoomed toward the exit as other dragons closed on him. He spiraled and weaved to avoid swiping claws and gnashing teeth. A large black dragon blocked the exit, but Raxtus swooped up and shot out through an opening high in the wall.

The speed left Kendra breathless as they whistled through the afternoon air. Roars sounded from all directions as dragons joined the pursuit. Kendra noticed that Raxtus was shimmering brighter than usual—certain magical creatures drew power from her upon physical contact, and Raxtus was one of them.

"The Somber Knight," Kendra said.

"He's on his own," Raxtus replied. "Doesn't stand much of a chance. Most dragons have wanted a piece of him for a long time. He has killed a lot of us over the years."

"What's your plan?" Kendra asked as Raxtus steeply ascended. Below and behind them, many dragons followed.

"I'm getting you out of here," Raxtus said. "Hopefully back to Blackwell Keep. I just needed a diversion. The Somber Knight gave me the opportunity I've been waiting for."

They flew into a cloud. Kendra closed her eyes against the stinging mist. Raxtus tucked her close against himself, sheltering her as much as possible, but at high speed through moist air, there was no keeping Kendra dry.

They burst through the top of the cloud into the sunlight, and suddenly the world looked pillowy and safe— no dragons in sight. Clutched by Raxtus, Kendra felt more secure than in the griffin saddle. She had traveled like this before and felt confident he would not drop her. "What will happen to you?" Kendra asked.

"My father will disown me," Raxtus said. "I'll be wanted for treason."

"Death penalty?" Kendra asked.

"A traitor's death," Raxtus said. "Bones scattered."

"I thought you intended to side with your father," Kendra said.

"I did," Raxtus replied. "I wanted to live up to all his expectations. I wanted to make him proud. Even if he was just using me. I knew I could surprise him. Surprise everyone. Rise to the occasion."

Dragons began to emerge from the tops of the clouds. Raxtus tucked his wings and dove. Cool vapor doused Kendra as they knifed through foggy air. Kendra's stomach flip-flopped as they plunged and swerved. Dragons bellowed.

Back in view of the ground, Kendra saw that not only were the dragons on their tail, but distant dragons were converging on them as well. They could not flee forever.

"And now you're being hunted," Kendra said.

"Once you showed up as a prisoner, I knew I had to help you," Raxtus said. "I've killed in battle, or hunting. I've never killed a captive, let alone a friend. If I had let them harm you, the most important part of me would have died. Probably forever. It was a point of no return. I could feel it. I wanted to be accepted by my father and my fellow dragons. But not at the cost of who I am. I thought for a time I could do both—be myself and have my father's respect. I thought maybe I could help the dragons be more reasonable. Improve the system from the inside. I influenced them very little, but they were changing me a lot. In the end, it was one or the other—be myself, or please my father. I chose me. And loyalty to my real friends."

"Thank you, Raxtus," Kendra said, tears in her eyes.

"This feels good," Raxtus said. "I'd rather die this way than live that way. This is the best I've felt in a long time."

Raxtus began changing directions erratically. Sometimes he rose, other times he plummeted down. The pursuing dragons continued to adjust, constricting the hunt ever tighter.

"They are cutting off Blackwell Keep," Raxtus said. "Keeping us away from there is clearly their top priority. Second priority is keeping dragons between us and the edge of the sanctuary. They don't want us fleeing Wyrmroost."

"What does that leave us?" Kendra asked, watching forests and rivers below, miniaturized by their altitude.

"I think our best bet is the Zowali Protectorate," Raxtus said. "I could probably make it to the Sludgeholes as well, but the protectorate contains your firmest allies."

"All right," Kendra said.

The wind washing over her cloud-dampened clothes felt chilling. Kendra gritted her teeth to stop them from chattering and tried to be brave. The speed was exhilarating, and the fear of capture helped her partially ignore the cold.

"I'm trying not to be obvious, but they're catching on where I'm heading," Raxtus said. "They're trying to adjust while still keeping lots of dragons between us and Blackwell

Keep. I think we can make it to the Zowali Protectorate."

"Your father has a plan for Midsummer Eve," Kendra said.

"I have heard rumors," Raxtus said. "I don't know specifics. Supposedly it will help the dragons win the war."

"Do you know anything that can help us?" Kendra asked.

"For a member of his personal guard, I was kept largely in the dark," Raxtus said. "I don't think Father ever really trusted me. But I'm not sure he realized I would defy him this openly."

Kendra scanned the horizon in all directions, counting so many dragons. Dozens. Maybe a hundred. "None of the dragons behind us are gaining," she said.

"I'm small but fast," Raxtus replied. "We're nearing the border of the Zowali Protectorate. I can't go inside."

"Why not?" Kendra asked.

"The protective barrier will keep me out," Raxtus said.

"But I'm the caretaker," Kendra replied.

"And the animals manage their own barrier," Raxtus said. "It would take a lot of negotiating and effort for any dragon to pass. I'm not sure the animals would agree to it even with you vouching for me. And if they did agree, by the time they figured it out, the dragons would have torn me to ribbons."

"I'm not leaving you," Kendra said.

"I'm leaving you," Raxtus said. "Nothing you can do about it. Don't worry—without you, I'm faster and can fully use my camouflaging abilities. I'll get away."

"Be careful," Kendra said.

"I can't promise that," Raxtus replied. "Fast and stealthy is more the goal."

Ahead, behind, and off to the sides, dragons were closing in. Raxtus dove low. Kendra could feel her toes skimming the top of the tall grass.

"There is a creek ahead," Raxtus said. "It marks the border here. I'll let you down, and you run across."

"The other dragons are too close," Kendra said, as the creek rapidly drew near. "After you drop me, lie low."

There was no time for a response. They had reached the creek, and other dragons were converging from multiple directions. Raxtus set Kendra on her feet at the edge of the water and then fell flat.

As dragons dove toward them, she loosed the drawstring on the sack of gales. Wind screamed from the bag, and she aimed it from one oncoming dragon to another. The targeted dragons spun out of control, some thrust away haphazardly, others tucking their wings and crashing to the ground.

Kendra backed into the creek, the water up to her shins, still letting the furious wind gush freely. "The sky is clear nearby!" Kendra shouted, closing the bag.

Raxtus sprang into the air, wings flapping furiously as he turned invisible. "Thanks!" he called.

"Help Seth and Tanu if you can!" Kendra cried.

"You got it," the unseen dragon answered, his voice more distant.

Kendra reached the far side of the creek and exited the water. Her shoes were not much wetter than the rest of her.

Dragons charged toward her over the ground, wings folded, keeping low profiles. Fire, acid, frost, and lightning blasted in her direction, coming to a halt against the unseen barrier above the middle of the creek. Roaring in fury, raging dragons lined up on the far side of the unimpressive stream.

But none could cross.

Kendra walked away.

CHAPTER SEVENTEEN

Incarcerated

The dragons are all flying away," Seth said. "This is our chance."

"Could it be a trick?" Eve asked. "What would make them leave like that?"

Seth had been walking along the road with Eve, Tanu, and Tempest, heading toward the next roadhouse, waiting for the right opportunity. Despite her wild reputation, Tempest had remained calm since arriving. Dragons had circled above during the entire walk, but suddenly they were soaring away in a similar direction.

"Must be the Somber Knight," Seth said.

"They're not going toward Skyhold," Calvin observed.

"Whatever they're doing, while they're not watching us, Eve can cloak us," Seth said. "I don't think we'll get a better chance."

The gaseous form of Tanu waved for them to go. Seth helped Eve into the saddle and, with frequent glances at the sky, hastily strapped her in. Then he sat on the saddle in front of her, unsecured. "Still all clear. Can you disguise us?"

"Done," Eve said. "Let's go."

"Home, Tempest," Seth said, flicking the reins.

The griffin leaped into the air. Seth gripped with his legs and held on tightly. Since he wasn't strapped in, the risk of falling was very real. The dragons in sight were all flying away from them.

"Oh no," Eve said. "We're not alone."

Seth looked back and saw a huge green dragon rising from some trees not far from the road. It looked like the same dragon who had taken Kendra, and it was coming right at them.

"Dragon, Tempest," Seth said.

The griffin turned evasively. Seth hung on with all his might. The dragon followed.

"It must have been watching us," Eve said. "We need to get out of sight to lose it."

"Go into the trees," Seth suggested.

Tempest dove into the nearest stand of tall trees. Seth hunched down as branches whipped by. As the griffin weaved through trunks, tilting and swerving, Seth held tightly to the saddle, trying to lean in harmony with the movements of his flying mount.

They burst into a clearing in the middle of the woods where a large herd of winged deer were grazing. "Startle the perytons," Eve said. "They'll provide cover."

Shrieking, the griffin streaked toward the deer. Roaring clamorously, the herd took flight. Tempest ascended with the herd.

"We'll look like one of many perytons to the dragon," Eve said.

Sure enough, after considering the herd, the dragon continued to fly low over the trees, looking downward, moving away from them. Seth held his breath as they climbed higher. The herd did not continue ascending, and the dragon continued to scour the trees.

Tempest gained altitude, and Seth tried to appreciate the afternoon sunlight and the beautiful view. In the distance, a lot of the dragons were flying up into a cloud.

"I think we lost the green one," Eve said.

"You're amazing, Tempest," Seth said, patting the griffin.

"Hey," Eve complained.

"You too," Seth offered.

For a long while they flew without interruption. Seth watched their shadow far below, sliding over fields and forests. The skies were mostly empty.

That changed as Blackwell Keep came into view in the distance. Dozens of dragons patrolled the sky near the keep. Whatever had drawn away the other dragons had not diverted these.

"Think we can dodge them?" Seth asked.

"I'll try to hide us," Eve said.

As they drew nearer to the keep, a couple of dragons roared and flew in their direction. Others followed.

"I'm sorry," Eve said. "They spotted us."

It was still a long way to the keep. "What do we do?" Seth asked.

"We could go to Terrabelle," Eve said. "We'll be safe from the dragons there, and I don't see dragons that way."

"Terrabelle," Seth ordered.

Tempest banked into a long turn and set off on a new course. The dragons who had given chase fell away. Seth figured their primary duty was to guard Blackwell Keep.

Terrabelle came into view before too long—a lush valley dotted with farmhouses and windmills. Tempest flew to the walled city at the heart of the valley, built around a stately castle, the buildings old but clean and tidy. Eve gave some instructions to Tempest as they got closer, and they landed in a courtyard.

"It's Eve," some of the guards called. "Summon Lord Dalgorel!"

Seth dismounted and helped Eve out of the saddle. He patted Tempest. "Good girl. You saved us."

A worried guard approached Eve. "Are you all right?"

"I'm fine," Eve said. "Thanks to my friend Seth."

"He visited not long ago," the guard said.

"Yes," Eve replied.

Dalgorel came running into the courtyard, followed by guards and other underlings. Seth marveled at how tall and attractive all of the Fair Folk were. Dalgorel lifted Eve into a hug and spun her around. Then he set her down.

"I am so relieved you are safe," he said. "That was terribly foolish of you to run off."

"I thought you would come back for me," Eve said.

"You saw the note," Dalgorel said. "I tried to return. Once you snuck away and I couldn't find you, I returned to Terrabelle to warn them about the upcoming war. When I tried to fly back toward Skyhold, dragons barred the way. I barely made it back to Terrabelle with my life. You're unhurt?"

"I'm fine," Eve said. "I was with Seth."

"We tried for Blackwell Keep first," Seth said. "Too many dragons were guarding it."

Lord Dalgorel placed a hand on Seth's shoulder. "Thank you for seeing my daughter safely home."

"You're welcome," Seth said.

"Unfortunately, you have placed me in a quandary," Dalgorel said. "The dragons have declared war against you, and our position is one of neutrality. The dragons could raise legitimate grievances if we give you safe harbor here."

"Are you kicking me out?" Seth asked.

Dalgorel smiled. "I have a better alternative. Caretaker or not, you are under arrest for trespassing."

When the guards left Seth in his cell, they did not bother shutting the door. Was "cell" even the right word? Brightly lit by multiple lamps, the room had two sofas, a padded rocking chair, a writing desk, a loaded bookshelf, rugs on the floor, paintings on the walls, and a large four-poster bed.

"The Fair Folk need better punishments," Calvin said. "This room is great."

"Dalgorel was grateful," Seth said. "I think he'll let us go if that's what we want."

"Might as well get some rest while you can," Calvin suggested.

"I'm too wound up," Seth said. "I'm worried about Kendra. And the Somber Knight."

"Me too," Calvin said.

Eve had promised to visit him soon, but for now he and Calvin were alone. Seth sat down in the rocking chair and, pushing off with his feet, tipped it back so far it felt like the chair might flip over. But it didn't. He rocked back harder, and the chair hovered at the brink of overturning, then tilted forward again. Pushing off hard and heaving his body back, Seth tipped the chair over backward and rolled from his seat in an awkward reverse somersault.

"I never knew how dangerous those chairs could be," commented a man in the doorway.

Seth scrambled to his feet. Lean and tall, the handsome, well-dressed man in the doorway had a dark complexion and a creatively trimmed goatee. "I was horsing around," Seth confessed.

"May I come in?" the man asked.

"Who are you?"

The man gave a swift bow. "A fellow prisoner. Lomo, son of Targon, outcast of the Fair Folk."

"I've heard of you," Seth said. "You're like the only other prisoner here. You're the guy who didn't want the neutrality policy. You went out and fought anyhow."

"There is one other permanent prisoner here, a giant

named Pugwig," Lomo said. "He's not good company. And a wereboar comes in a few days each month, still trying to resist his feral side."

"I heard you could leave if you would pledge to stay neutral," Seth said.

"True," Lomo said. "I'm accused of no crime other than violating our neutrality policy. If I vowed to follow the policy, I would be released on probation."

"Why not get out?" Seth asked.

"Neutrality is selfish and unacceptable," Lomo said. "Neutrality is a refusal to live. For me, no crime outweighs neutrality in a time of crisis."

"I like how you think," Seth said.

"Then you join a very small club here in Terrabelle," Lomo said. "In fact, if you were willing to go public with your support, you would stand alone."

"The others who agree with you won't speak up?" Seth asked.

"Nothing more than a grumble," Lomo said. "I believe our leaders have good intentions. They want to preserve our way of life. They want to protect us as a people. But they have succumbed to the slow, insidious evil of passivity. To be part of the world, we must participate. Otherwise we may as well be extinct."

"Celebrant declared war," Seth said.

"I heard," Lomo replied. "Word of that sort travels fast. I knew it was coming. And still our leaders insist on neutrality."

"Could the Fair Folk fight dragons?" Seth asked.

"We have in ages past," Lomo said. "Could the citizens

of Terrabelle defeat the dragons of Wyrmroost in open combat? Not likely. We would be exterminated. But one does not engage dragons in open combat. You fight dragons intelligently or you perish. Of course, we currently do neither. We let children fight for us."

"The Somber Knight took out some dragons," Seth said.

"He is your greatest weapon in this war," Lomo said.

"He went to Skyhold alone to demote Celebrant from being a caretaker," Seth said.

Lomo grimaced. "He may not return from that mission."

"The dragons have my sister," Seth said.

"I'm sorry, young caretaker," Lomo said. "By coming to Wyrmroost, you inherited calamitous trouble. And look what you do!"

"Flip over my rocking chair?"

"You stand and fight! While a nation of ancient adults cowers behind policies of appeasement."

"Ronodin is here," Seth said.

Lomo reached for his sword but did not draw it. "The dark unicorn?"

"You have a sword?" Seth asked. "What kind of prison is this?"

"The most relaxed dungeon you will ever inhabit," Lomo said. "Wherever Ronodin roams, tragedy follows."

"He told us he taught the dragons a sure way to win the war," Seth said.

"I'm surprised he revealed so much," Lomo said. "Do not underestimate his words. I have not known him to make empty threats."

"Do you know him?" Seth asked.

"I have had the displeasure of encountering him before," Lomo said. "Ronodin is an agent of chaos, formally aligned to nobody, but routinely on the fringe of the great disasters in the magical world. Did he give any clue as to what he told the dragons?"

"Nothing," Seth said. "He wanted Bracken's first horn from Kendra."

"Bracken entrusted his horn to your sister?" Lomo asked. "She must be an impressive girl."

"I guess so," Seth said. "She killed the Demon King."

Lomo rubbed the whiskers on his chin. "That was the day the real trouble with the dragons began. The day the demons failed. You were there. And here you are now. Perhaps we still have hope."

"We're going to try," Seth said.

"You came here alone?" Lomo asked.

"I flew here with Eve on a griffin named Tempest," Seth said. "Kendra was captured by the dragons. My friend Tanu turned into a gaseous state to survive a dragon attack. He's a potion master, but since he was gassy, we had to leave him on the road. And I have my secret friend."

"Secret friend?"

"Calvin the nipsie."

"I wondered if you would let me speak," Calvin said. "Sometimes he keeps me a secret. I like your thoughts on neutrality, Lomo. Good job following your heart."

"Can I see him?" Lomo asked, coming closer.

"Sure," Seth said.

Calvin climbed from Seth's pocket onto Lomo's palm. "Hello," Calvin called.

"Amazing," Lomo said. "So small and well formed. A perfect little man. I have beheld only one other of your kind."

"He would have been smaller," Calvin said. "I am under a spell that turned me into a giant. Well, a giant compared to my people."

"The other I met was a female," Lomo said. "And she was your size."

"Do you remember her name?" Calvin asked urgently.

"I believe it was Serena," Lomo said.

Calvin looked up at Seth. "That's her! My true love!"

"You know Serena?" Lomo asked.

"I adore her," Calvin said. "I would swim oceans for her. Scale mountains. Cross deserts. Where did you see her? When?"

"Perhaps five years ago," Lomo said. "I was part of an organization dedicated to resisting the Society of the Evening Star."

"The Knights of the Dawn," Seth said.

"Yes, I almost forgot you are affiliated," Lomo said. "By habit I mention it carefully."

"Do you know where Serena went?" Calvin asked.

"She was with a woman of human size," Lomo said. "I never got her name. They were investigating demonic curses, if I recall."

"That fits," Calvin said.

"I believe they were going to the Titan Valley sanctuary," Lomo said. "I was to investigate rumors at Soaring

Cliffs. Back then we thought the demons would be the end of us. We did not anticipate the dragons becoming our main threat so quickly."

"Titan Valley," Calvin said reverently. "A dragon sanctuary as well."

"One of the three with a temple," Lomo said.

"Thank you for the news," Calvin said.

"How did you end up back here?" Seth asked.

"I have the Sphinx to thank," Lomo said.

"I have him to thank for plenty too," Seth said.

"The Sphinx wrote a letter to Dalgorel complaining that my involvement against the demons violated the Fair Folk's policy of neutrality. He threatened that if Dalgorel did nothing, he would call the neutrality policy into question. So Dalgorel dispatched some talented agents who found me and brought me in. I tried to evade them but was unwilling to fight them."

"How long ago?" Seth asked.

"Nearly three years," Lomo said.

"Have you tried to escape from here?" Seth asked.

"Not in earnest," Lomo said. "My incarceration is a way to protest. My countrymen know I am here and why. It promotes thought and discussion that might not happen otherwise."

"I can't stay here long," Seth said. "There's a war."

"Dalgorel placed you here mostly for your safety," Lomo said. "It enables him to shelter you temporarily without being accused of playing favorites. You will not be held long."

"If you got out, would you help us?" Seth asked.

"Until I am apprehended," Lomo said. "Dalgorel would have to try to catch me to preserve his claims of neutrality. For now, let me introduce you to the food here. It is outstanding."

CHAPTER EIGHTEEN

Stingbulb

Kendra stood frozen, staring at a hulking brown bear. She had not yet traveled far from the creek where she had separated from Raxtus. Stepping out from a grove of aspens, she had found herself less than thirty feet away from the golden-brown beast. Humps of muscle rolling, the bear stood up on two legs and faced her direction.

What if she had survived dragons to get mauled to death by a bear? What was she supposed to do? Play dead? Where had she heard that? Was it reliable advice? Or would the bear just come pounce on her? Had somebody once told her to run in a zigzag? Or that bears did not do well running downhill? There were no hills nearby.

She had her bow. But would arrows stop something so massive? It was half again as tall as her, with shaggy fur and a thick body. Could arrows penetrate deep enough to matter?

Then again, she was supposedly in the kingdom of talking animals. Raxtus thought they were her firmest allies.

"Hello?" Kendra tried.

Staring in silence, the bear dropped down to all fours and started coming her way. The creature seemed to be in no hurry.

"Is this the Zowali Protectorate?" Kendra asked. "I need help."

"And you hope I can talk," the bear said in a deep, serious voice.

"Yes!" Kendra exclaimed with relief.

"What if talking bears still attack people?" the bear asked.

"Do you?" Kendra asked.

The bear stopped near her and sat on his haunches. "Not ordinarily." He scratched his side. "Almost none of us would eat another talking animal. Including a human. But watch out for the crocodiles. They have been known to bend the rules."

"What do you like to eat?" Kendra asked.

"Fish—especially salmon and trout," the bear said. "I can also do beehives, ants, moths, berries, fruit, acorns, worms, roots, carrion, voles, turkey sandwiches, waffles, quiche, crème brulée, and so forth."

"Do you have a name?" Kendra asked.

"Gorban," the bear said. "And you must be Kendra Sorenson, one of our new caretakers."

"That's right," Kendra said. "Hardly a week on the job and already at war with the dragons."

"War started brewing as soon as Celebrant became a

caretaker," Gorban said. "You're bold to come here alone, and not by any road I know. I see no griffin."

"A dragon dropped me off," Kendra explained. "We were on the run."

"You have a manacle on your ankle," Gorban said.

"He bit through the chain."

"What dragon carried you here?"

"Have you heard of Raxtus?"

"Sure, the little one. Helped you, did he?"

"He risked everything for me," Kendra said, checking the sky. She could see a few dragons in the distance. None looked like Raxtus.

"I'm glad he did you a good turn," Gorban said.

"Are there lots of talking animals here?" Kendra asked.

"Many species, yes," Gorban said. "Some more social than others."

"Are only the crocodiles dangerous?"

"I'm dangerous," Gorban said. "Especially if you're a squirrel's nut cache hidden within reach of the ground."

"You seem nice," Kendra said.

"Watch out if the crocodiles seem nice," Gorban said. "They're only nice when they're hungry. Who should you really avoid? The snakes are seldom up to any good. The vultures want you to die. Coyotes can be punks. Most of the animals are amiable enough."

"I should try to find your leader," Kendra said. "There is a war coming."

"We have a large territory," Gorban said. "It's a fair distance to Shelter, where Raj lives."

"Can I ride you?" Kendra asked.

Plopping forward to all fours, Gorban shook from side to side, loose hide sloshing. "I don't get that request often. Ever, really. But hop on. Let's give it a try. We'll get word out and maybe get you a proper mount."

Coming to the side of the bear, Kendra could not figure out where to grab to mount up. "How do I do this?"

"Don't be shy," Gorban said. "Take hold of my fur. Scramble up. I'm not fragile."

Reaching up and over his broad, furry back, Kendra grabbed hold and pulled while swinging a leg up. With a little grunting and struggling, she managed to lie across the powerful back. After some shifting, she straddled him. Gorban started walking at a reasonable pace.

"I can't believe I'm riding a bear," Kendra said.

"I don't recommend trying this without permission," Gorban said.

"I hear you," Kendra said. "Where else are there talking animals?"

"A few of the other preserves and sanctuaries," Gorban said. "We're the largest, most organized population. Some of our kind are still out in the wild playing dumb. A talking dog can pass for a normal dog just fine as long as he stays quiet. A few of us are even in zoos, living the easy life. I know of a pretty famous panda who can secretly speak—mostly in Chinese, but she is working on her English."

"How do you get your news?" Kendra asked.

Gorban huffed a chuckle. "A little bird told me."

Kendra laughed. "Really?"

"Yeah. Most birds are gossips."

"Giving rides now?" a chipper voice called from off to one side. "Can I climb aboard?"

"Nice try," Gorban said.

Looking down, Kendra discovered that the newcomer was a fox. "Hello, I'm Kendra."

"Sherman," the fox said. "We wondered if you would pay us a visit. You have your work cut out for you, sister."

"Dragon war," Kendra said. "Are there other types of magical creatures in your territory? Besides talking animals?"

"We allow a few types," Sherman said.

"Fairies, of course," Gorban said. "Good for the flora."

"We might get more if Azalar stopped trying to eat them," Sherman said.

"An owl," Gorban clarified.

"Gnomes sometimes," Sherman said. "The occasional nymph. Usually it's just us fleabags."

"Can the fleas talk?" Kendra asked.

"Not the insects," Gorban said.

"Can you imagine?" Sherman asked. He imitated a little voice. "Stop scratching, we're trying to bite you."

"I've heard of talking tarantulas but never met one," Gorban said. "Those are arachnids, of course."

"I met a talking cricket once," Sherman said.

"Don't make up stories," Gorban said.

"I really did," Sherman said. "Nervous little guy."

"The talking animals are seldom smaller than mice," Gorban said.

"And we tend to be bigger than others of our species,"

Sherman said. "Better looking, too. And we live a lot longer. You've noticed my sleek fur?"

Kendra had to admit he was a large, attractive fox with glossy orange fur and a bushy tail. "You could win a fox contest."

"She has a keen eye," Sherman said. "Sharp for a human. You're right—I'm a good fox. We have hens here, you know. Talking ones. These are prime hens, plump and juicy, straight out of a greedy daydream. How many hens go missing on my watch? Tell her, Gorban."

"None so far," the bear said.

"That's right," Sherman said. "I guard them like a brother. Hunt other game. Meanwhile these fat, slow hens wander about, pecking at the ground; almost no survival instincts whatsoever."

"You watch them a lot," Gorban said.

"Don't misunderstand him, Kendra," Sherman said. "I watch *over* them."

"A lot," Gorban said. "You talk about them a lot, too."

"Everybody talks about hens," Sherman said. "They're a great topic."

"Sherman, can you do us a favor?" Gorban asked. "Run ahead and spread the word that Kendra is coming. We're heading to Shelter. Tell some birds if you can. She could use a proper mount."

"Is she too heavy for you?" Sherman teased.

"I'm not very fast," Gorban said. "And she could be more comfortable."

"I love your fur," Kendra said.

"I'll run ahead," Sherman said. "You'll have help in a jiffy."

The fox darted away across the meadow.

"Now we might be able to listen to nature," Gorban said. "Enjoy our surroundings."

"Does Sherman talk a lot?" Kendra asked.

Gorban chuckled. "He talks like words are on sale and the sale ends soon."

"He's not the only flashy animal," Kendra said. "You're a very good-looking bear. Big and strong. Thick fur."

"I suppose that goes without saying," Gorban replied.

They continued for a good while before a horse came galloping their way, sleek and white, groups of muscles bulging. "I'm Captain," he said, coming to a stop near Gorban. The bear stopped as well. "You must be Kendra. Heading for Shelter? I can take you from here, if you like."

"Makes more sense," Gorban said. "Pleasure to meet you, Kendra. Don't take any nonsense from those dragons."

Kendra slid off the bear to the ground. "Thanks for the ride. And the company. Will I see you again?"

"I'll keep heading the way we were going," Gorban said. "You have me curious. I'll be quite a bit faster without worrying about making you fall."

"Okay, see you later," Kendra said, turning to Captain. "You're a big horse."

"Sorry, no saddle," Captain said. "We don't often give rides around here. But I run smoothly."

"I can help," Gorban said, sliding his head between Kendra's legs from behind and boosting her up.

"Thank you," Kendra said as she got situated on Captain.

"You want to see Raj?" Captain asked.

"Yes, please," Kendra said.

"Have you ridden anything besides a bear?" Captain asked.

"Yes," Kendra said. "In fact, I rode one of the Luvians from Blackwell Keep quite a bit."

"Which horse?" Captain asked.

"Glory."

"That's my sister," Captain said. "One of the smartest horses I know. Just couldn't talk. What a shame."

"She likes Jane Austen," Kendra said.

"I'm more of a Hemingway fan," Captain said, beginning to trot. "Or Rambugwa."

"Who is Rambugwa?" Kendra asked.

"He's a baboon," Captain said. "Literally. Excellent novelist. Adventures, mostly. Twisted sense of humor."

"Bye, Gorban," Kendra called over her shoulder.

"Is that a hint?" Captain asked, advancing to a canter. "Are you all right?"

Even without a saddle or reins, Kendra felt secure and balanced. And what a novelty to be able to talk to her horse! "I feel great."

Captain increased his pace to a full gallop. The gait remained smooth. As the afternoon light waned, Kendra passed through woodlands and fields. They slowed to cross streams, water splashing up against her calves, or to traverse uneven ground. Even through thick forests, Captain tended to find paths, so the gait seldom dropped below a canter.

Kendra found herself enjoying the peaceful journey. This was a beautiful part of Wyrmroost. From time to time she saw animals at a distance—deer, pheasants, squirrels, a buffalo. She wondered if all of them could talk.

Despite the pleasant scenery, her mind kept returning to the problem of the dragons. She could not guess what they were planning. Celebrant seemed unstoppable *without* help from Ronodin. What could the dark unicorn have told him to make it worse?

Kendra worried about Seth and Tanu. She fretted about her grandparents back at Blackwell Keep. She hoped Raxtus had made it away from the dragons all right.

The sun was nearing the horizon when Kendra and Captain came into view of what looked like a hybrid between a lodge and a giant stable. Captain ran to the building, then slowed as he entered through a door large enough to accommodate just about any animal Kendra could imagine.

Inside they found a spacious room with a wooden floor and sturdy logs and beams forming the rest. Stalls ran along two sides of the room, with another large entrance on the far side. Stairs led up to unseen lofts. Logs blazed in the hearth dominating the center of the room, the smoke escaping through a hole in the ceiling. There was little furniture, but several perches offered places for birds to roost, and many feeding troughs could be seen around the room.

Kendra felt surprised by the assemblage of animals visible, including gazelles, monkeys, elk, panthers, owls, wolves, camels, beavers, bison, otters, hippos, and ostriches.

Near the fire, resting on a pile of cushions, awaited a huge tiger, licking a broad paw with a plump, coarse tongue.

The animals had been speaking, but all conversation came to a halt as Kendra slid off Captain to address the tiger. She assumed he could talk, but it was still intimidating to realize this deadly predator was only a short pounce away. "Raj Faranah?" Kendra asked.

The tiger stopped licking his paw and gazed intensely at Kendra. She felt like food. "You have found him, Kendra Sorenson," Raj said, his voice calm, rich, and educated. "I trust Captain has been good company?"

"Yes," Kendra said. "Gorban too. Thank you for letting me shelter here."

"I wish we could do more," Raj said. "Some of us are fierce, but we are no match for dragons in combat. I can offer safe harbor for as long as you need it. And I have a gift." The tiger turned his head. "Come forward."

A handsome man came into view from behind the hearth. He wore a mustache, had a sturdy build, and was dressed like he was a century behind in his fashion.

"Patton?" Kendra asked. "No. Impossible. He's dead. You're dead!"

"You got that right," Patton said.

"Are you a ghost?" Kendra asked.

"Don't I seem solid?" He stepped forward and gave her a hug. It felt good to press her head to his strong chest. This was her ancestor!

She backed out of the hug. "You seem perfect. But how can it be you? Chronometer?"

"No," Patton said. "But we had our adventure with the Chronometer at Fablehaven not too long ago, from my point of view. This isn't really me, Kendra. I'm a knockoff. A copy."

"You're a stingbulb," Kendra realized. Stingbulbs were rare fruit that could replicate anybody they stung. When planted, the bulb would grow into an imitation of the person in roughly ninety minutes.

"You got it." Hooking his thumbs in his pockets, he looked at Raj Faranah. "Told you she was a sharp kid."

"You won't last long," Kendra said.

"A few days at best," Patton agreed. "I stung myself and put the stingbulb in a null box. Left it with the animals in case of emergency. Raj was around back then, but not in charge. It was an elephant."

"Hinto the Great," Raj said. "One of our finest leaders."

"What's a null box?" Kendra asked.

"You know how a Quiet Box keeps a person in stasis?" Patton asked.

"Yes," Kendra said.

"A null box is smaller and even more intense," Patton said. "Time and entropy basically stop in there. I would sometimes store my avocados in this one when they were just right. It also keeps toast warm."

"And keeps a stingbulb from growing," Kendra said.

"Until some friendly critters plant it," Patton said.

"We had the stingbulb for years in case of an extreme emergency," Raj said. "When we heard you had reached our territory, Kendra, we planted it and told Patton to serve you when you arrived."

Kendra remembered that stingbulbs were very impressionable and would unquestioningly obey the orders of their first master. "You have Patton's memories?" Kendra checked.

"I am not really Patton," the stingbulb said. "I am a replica of who Patton was in a certain moment. I have the personality he had then, the vocabulary, the memories, the aptitudes. I feel like him. And I know I am not him. I know it would be very hard for me to become much more or less than who I am right now. I can't learn as he learned, but I can perform as he performed."

"Maybe you can give me some advice," Kendra said.

"I hope so," Patton replied.

"The dragons have declared war," Kendra said.

Patton gave a little nod. "Seems like a good time to rouse me."

Kendra explained about how the dragons had helped at Zzyzx and how Celebrant had become a caretaker in return. She told about how she and Seth had become caretakers and recovered the scepter. She described going to the feast. She related what she had learned from Ronodin, and told about the Somber Knight revoking Celebrant's caretaker status, as well as her escape with Raxtus and her fears about the fate of her brother and Tanu.

Patton gave a soft whistle. "You're in a quandary, no doubt about it. Of all you told me, Ronodin concerns me most. He promotes chaos like nobody I know. He said he told the dragons how to win the war?"

"And that it would happen on Midsummer Eve," Kendra said. "Tomorrow night."

Patton turned and looked somberly into the fire. "Without Ronodin, the advice is simpler. Stay behind boundaries. Enforce whatever penalties you can on aggressors. Offer them no footholds. Wait it out. Eventually the dragons will tire of beating against walls that don't break. But what you heard from Ronodin, well, that changes everything."

"Do you know what he's talking about?" Kendra asked.

"I have a strong suspicion," Patton said, glancing at the surrounding animals. "I hope I'm wrong, but I'm afraid I'm not. Ordinarily I would not speak about it to anyone, let alone in front of a group. I'm a curious fellow, sometimes too curious, and sometimes I learn things that are better left unknown. Best to leave certain monsters buried deep, undisturbed. But if the dragons have learned what I know—and I believe they have, because it all fits too cleanly—then it might be best for many to know."

"What is it?" Kendra asked.

"The Wizenstone is hidden here at Wyrmroost," Patton said.

Nobody responded.

"I gather that none of you knows what that means," Patton said. "But the wisest of wizards knows, the five monarchs know, those who study the rarest and most powerful relics know. The Wizenstone is a source of powerful magic. The Wizenstone can also undo magic. For example, it could erase all boundaries at this or any preserve. It could disenchant a magical item. Or it could strip a wizard of his powers." Patton stepped close to Kendra. His voice dropped to a whisper. "And the Wizenstone could force dragons into human form. Permanently. Without making them wizards."

"The dragons would win the war in hours if they got it," Kendra said.

"No magical boundaries," Patton said. "The sanctuaries would fall almost immediately."

"We could win the war if we had it," Kendra said.

"If you were up against a bunch of powerless humans instead of dragons, the war would be a snap," Patton agreed. "The mere threat of forcing dragons into human shape would be a powerful deterrent."

"Where is the stone?" Kendra asked.

"That's where this gets upsetting," Patton said. "The Wizenstone is hidden inside Stormguard Castle."

CHAPTER NINETEEN

Reunions

Calvin drew his sword, raised it above his head, and brought it down in a vicious arc, cleaving open a cream puff. "You want half?" he asked Seth.

Seth looked across the table at Lomo. "I want ten more, but I think I might actually explode."

Calvin wiped his sword on a napkin and scooped out a handful of creamy filling. "This stuff is heaven."

"I ate too much during my first few days here," Lomo said. "Pace yourself. Everything is this good."

"But this dinner had so much variety," Seth said. "Bacon-wrapped figs? Crab legs with melted butter? Chilled banana soup? Like half of the food was brand-new to me. And so good. Not to mention three desserts."

"It's like that every meal," Lomo said. "The Fair Folk go out of their way to eat in the dungeon. Some commit minor crimes. One day a week, law-abiding citizens can make reservations. It gets booked up six months in advance. Best food in town."

"I'm so full," Seth said, patting his stomach. "But I want more of those tastes."

"Take nothing for granted," Calvin said. "One day you'll be starving and thankful for all you had here. You'll feast in your memories."

The door opened and Tanu entered, accompanied by a pair of guards. He looked dusty and scratched up, but alive and tangible.

Seth sprang to his feet. "Tanu! You made it!"

The big Samoan smiled.

"Lomo, can you show him where he can wash up?" one of the guards, a lovely redhead, asked.

"I'd be happy to," Lomo said, rising and motioning Tanu toward a sink in the corner. "You look like you've had a rough day."

"Not a vacation," Tanu said, scabbed lips caked with dirt. He scrubbed his hands and forearms under the running water, then scooped handfuls of it up to his face. As he dried himself off with a soft, white towel, his eyes went to Seth. "I heard you were all right. I'm so happy you made it here."

"How did you get here so fast?" Seth asked. "Did you find a way to fly?"

Tanu indicated some of his scratches. "If I had been flying, I got dropped a lot. I was kind of dragged." His eyes strayed to the table. "Look at that spread."

"All for you," Lomo said. "We've had our fill."

"Almost," Calvin called from the table, chewing on a hunk of fig.

Tanu looked down at himself, patting his torn, dirty clothes. "I'm not sure I've ever felt underdressed to eat in a dungeon."

"Welcome to Terrabelle," Lomo said cheerfully. He glanced at the guards. "We can take it from here."

The guards withdrew and closed the door.

"The hot stuff might be a little cool," Seth apologized. "And the cold stuff might be a little warm."

Tanu was already popping bacon-wrapped figs into his mouth. "These are good! Remind me to trespass in Terrabelle more often."

"You said you got dragged here?" Seth asked. "What do you mean?"

"The Somber Knight survived," Tanu said. "Just barely. I found him on the road, clinging to what remained of his bull."

"What was left?" Seth asked.

"Most of the head, one horn, the front legs, and about half the body," Tanu said. "The Somber Knight was not in much better shape. He had hooked the damaged bull with his grapnel and managed to get dragged back to the road where the dragons couldn't keep attacking."

"He's all right?" Seth asked.

"He thinks he'll live," Tanu said. "He lost a leg up to the hip and an arm just above the elbow. His armor looked shredded."

"Why didn't he bleed to death?" Seth asked.

"I don't think he bleeds," Tanu said.

"What?" Seth asked.

"My guess is he must be undead," Tanu said.

"Like a zombie?" Seth asked.

Tanu shook his head, blotting his lips with a napkin. "No, something well beyond a zombie or a wraith. More powerful and evolved. It's just a guess."

"We have similar guesses among the Fair Folk," Lomo said. "The Somber Knight is no ordinary being."

"Does that mean he'll be all right?" Seth asked.

"He wanted to get back to his lair beneath the city," Tanu said. "Who knows how much he can regenerate? Time will tell."

"Speaking of regenerating, I take it you weren't gassy when he found you?" Seth asked.

"The potion had just worn off," Tanu said, expertly snapping crab legs and removing the meat with his fingers. "He offered me a lift to Terrabelle. We had to leave the road at Thirsty Gulch to get here. Almost got killed by dragons. Even with just the two front legs, that bull is fast. The Somber Knight and I clung to what was left of the body, rode it like a sled. Dullion or not, that bull deserves a medal."

Seth braced himself before asking his next question, worried about the possible answer. "What about Kendra?"

"She got away!" Tanu said. "The Somber Knight saw Raxtus rescue her after she was delivered to Celebrant."

"That must be who the dragons were chasing," Calvin said, "when we came here on Tempest."

"Probably," Tanu said. "She's the only quarry who would have drawn that much attention."

Seth was smiling. "Raxtus did the right thing. I was worried we had lost him."

"It was brave," Tanu said. "He'll be hunted by his own kind for the rest of his days."

"At least until we win the dragon war," Seth said.

Tanu gave a chuckle as he spooned gnocchi onto a plate. "I like your optimism. Even if we win, Raxtus will forever be hated for what he has done. It was noble."

"A dragon rescuing a human," Lomo said. "Just when I thought the times could not get stranger."

Calvin flopped down onto the table on his back, his arms and legs spread wide. "I can't eat another bite. Why do I do this to myself?"

"Don't take this food for granted," Seth teased. "How about some more cobbler?"

Calvin hugged his stomach and rolled from side to side. "I think I'm full to the top of my throat. Anything I try to swallow will stay in my mouth."

"There's always room for peach cobbler," Seth encouraged.

Calvin closed his eyes and puffed out his cheeks. "I went beyond my limits."

"Maybe we could fill in the cracks with some milk," Seth suggested.

"You're going to make me puke!" Calvin said. "It would be a lot of puke. Let me suffer in peace."

The door opened again, and two guards admitted Creya

the eagle. "You have a visitor," the red-haired guard announced.

Creya flew from the guard's forearm to the table and perched on the back of a chair. "I have a message from Kendra," the eagle announced.

"You do?" Seth exclaimed, relief flooding over him. "That means she and Raxtus must have outrun the dragons!"

"Yes," Creya said. The large bird glanced from Seth to Lomo. "The message is secret."

"That will be enough for now," Lomo told the guards. They exited.

"I can leave if you wish," Lomo said. "But I am still a Knight of the Dawn in full fellowship. Inner circle. I'm incarcerated for violating our neutrality policy. That is all."

Seth felt in his gut he could trust Lomo. Of course, he had once placed some trust in the demon Graulus as well.

"Inner circle?" Tanu asked. He walked around the table and whispered something. Lomo whispered something back. They had a few more quiet exchanges.

"He knows the right code phrases from his time," Tanu said. "He should be safe."

"Stay," Seth invited.

The potion master gave a slight nod as he returned to his chair and served himself some cobbler. He took a bite and closed his eyes. "Almost worth getting dragged through dragon-infested briars."

"Go ahead," Seth urged Creya.

"Kendra made it safely to the Zowali Protectorate," Creya said.

"That's a relief," Tanu murmured gratefully.

"She has learned how the dragons intend to win the war," the eagle announced.

"How did she do that?" Seth asked.

"She met with a stingbulb of Patton Burgess brought to fruition by Raj Faranah," the eagle said. "After hearing what she knew from Ronodin, he understood the plan."

"What's the plan?" Calvin asked.

"You know he's here?" the eagle checked, looking at the nipsie.

"Don't mind me," Calvin said. "I have a food hernia."

"He's loyal," Seth said.

"And on my deathbed," Calvin said, "tell my mother I love her."

"An object called the Wizenstone is hidden here at Wyrmroost," Creya said.

Tanu started coughing up cobbler and wiped his face with a napkin. "Did you say the Wizenstone?"

"Yes," Creya said.

"That should be long gone," Tanu said, shifting uncomfortably. "The stuff of legend. Too powerful to really exist."

"Not according to Patton," Creya said. "It's inside Stormguard Castle."

Tanu bowed his head. "Of course it is." He looked up. "The dragons know this? Why not just leave it there? How are they ever supposed to get it? Nobody has been inside Stormguard Castle since it was cursed."

"Patton has," Creya corrected. "Briefly."

"What does he know?" Tanu asked.

"Lethal defensive barriers protect Stormguard Castle all but four nights each year," Creya said.

"The festival nights," Seth guessed.

The eagle stretched her wings and ruffled her feathers. "Yes. On the solstices and equinoxes each year, the castle can be accessed by certain individuals."

"Who?" Seth asked.

"Let me guess," Tanu said bleakly. "Scraped-up potion masters full of cobbler."

"Mortals," Creya said. "Fair Folk. And magical creatures with a human avatar."

"So dragons can enter," Seth said.

"Only in human form," Creya said. "Magic is stripped from those who enter. The dragons would have to remain in human form. The Fair Folk would lose any magical talents."

"What about nipsies?" Calvin asked.

"Any other magical creatures cannot enter," Creya said. "Only those who can take mortal shape."

"But I'm really small," Calvin said. "These kinds of spells often don't take the especially tiny into account."

"I know only what the stingbulb told us," Creya said. "Apparently, if the dragons get the Wizenstone, they will win the war easily."

"And they are going after the Wizenstone tomorrow?" Seth said.

"We assume," Creya said.

"Tomorrow is Midsummer Eve," Lomo noted.

"What if we get it instead?" Seth asked.

"Patton thinks we could use it to win the war," Creya said.

"This is huge," Seth said. "We were in trouble. We didn't know what the dragons were planning. We didn't know how to approach this fight. Now we have a chance."

"It's better than nothing," Tanu said. "Does Kendra have a plan?"

"To go after the stone tomorrow night," Creya said. "She hopes you and Seth can help."

"The Zowali Protectorate is a good distance from Stormguard Castle," Tanu said. "How do they hope to arrive?"

"They are currently devising a plan," Creya said. "Access to the castle does not begin until an hour after sundown."

Tanu scowled. "That makes it really difficult. We will be unprotected for up to an hour before entering the castle."

"I can't imagine there will be anywhere near the castle to hide for that hour," Calvin said. "Maybe we can time our arrival perfectly, though that means traveling on a festival night."

"We have to attempt it," Seth said. "If the war depends on this, how do we not try?"

Tanu rubbed his eyes and then ran both hands through his thick hair. "We must. Meanwhile, I think I know a way to get us to Kendra."

The prison door opened. Two guards entered, followed by two satyrs and two children. "This is our busiest night in ages," the red-haired guard announced.

"There you are!" Knox exclaimed to Seth. "Eating dinner? Any left for us?"

Seth leaped to his feet. "Knox? Tess? Newel? Doren? What the heck are you all doing here?"

"We were trusted to watch the little ones," Newel said.

"So naturally we've been cast into a foreign dungeon."

"The road from Blackwell Keep runs straight to here," Doren added.

"We saw some dragons," Knox said. "A few came really close to the road."

"You drank the milk?" Seth asked.

"I knew all your VR nonsense had to be a lie," Knox said.

"It was the best I could do on short notice," Seth said. "How do you like my sanctuary?"

"*Your* sanctuary?" Knox asked.

"Well, I'm one of the caretakers," Seth said. "The guy in charge. Me and Kendra."

Knox gave a scoffing laugh. "Right. That's why you're in a dungeon."

"I really am a caretaker," Seth said, looking to the others.

"True," Tanu said.

"He is," Newel affirmed. "We could have told you that."

"Seth and Kendra are the caretakers," Creya said.

"The talking bird!" Tess said.

"Nice to see you again," Creya said. "I'm a golden eagle."

"You must be the worst caretaker ever," Knox said.

"That's possible," Seth replied. "I haven't been on the job very long, and the dragons have already declared war. And I guess I did end up in a dungeon. Wait, why are you even at Wyrmroost?"

"We came through the barrel," Tess said.

"Do Grandma and Grandpa Sorenson know you're here?" Seth asked.

"They know we're at Wyrmroost," Knox said. "I came without permission. Tess tagged along."

"I'm surprised they let you leave the keep," Seth stated. "Do they know you came to Terrabelle?"

"We came to save you," Doren said.

"You brought *Knox* and *Tess* to save me?" Seth asked. "They are so new here! They have no clue!"

"There were reasons," Doren said. "There is a murderer loose at the keep. The barrel to Fablehaven is missing and possibly sabotaged. And Tess is our key to roaming free at Wyrmroost."

Tess pivoted at the waist, swinging her cloak from side to side. "I have my fairy queen robe."

"It's actually a cloak of innocence," Newel said. "It offers enormous protection if worn by someone new to the sanctuaries who has broken no rules and means no harm."

"And you came here without permission," Seth said. "Grandma and Grandpa are going to skin you alive."

"We had the cloak, and we stayed on the road," Knox said.

"We had help from the lion bird," Tess said.

"We ran into a griffin on the road," Newel said. "One of the ones that went looking for you but was forced out of the sky by dragons. He was heading back to the keep, but he agreed to carry Knox and Tess here. On foot, of course. Paws and claws, not wings. Doren and I ran."

"We're good runners in a pinch," Doren said.

"I don't want to do that again soon," Newel said. "My sides got sore."

"I'm not sure I've ever sweated so much," Doren said. "Not even when Newel and I play tennis."

"I'm glad you got here safely," Tanu said. "These are very foolish times to explore the sanctuary."

"We weren't exploring," Knox said. "We were on a rescue mission." He looked around. "Where is Kendra?"

"She's with the talking animals," Seth said.

"The eagle can talk," Knox said.

"They have a whole territory," Seth said. "Kendra is there. And we need to get there. Or *I* need to get there."

"You want to leave this city?" Knox asked. "Have you seen the girls? They're almost as pretty as the ones in Texas."

"Almost?" Seth asked.

"Yeah, pretty close," Knox said.

Seth rolled his eyes. "You should stay, then. I bet a bunch of them want a thirteen-year-old boyfriend with a basketball full of fake signatures."

"That's okay," Knox said. "I want to help get Kendra. My job is only half done."

"You're not saving me," Seth said. "I'm fine."

"In a dungeon is not fine," Knox said. "You were lost, and we found you."

"And we rode a lion bird," Tess said. "It's been a good day."

Seth looked at Tanu. "What do we do?"

"I have an idea that could get us to the Zowali Protectorate," Tanu said.

"How many of us?" Seth asked.

"As many as want to come," Tanu said.

"I'm interested," Lomo said, "if we can break out."

"Are any of the doors here locked?" Seth asked.

"The outermost one," Lomo said. "Security is lax."

"This whole dungeon is weak," Knox said, looking around the comfortably appointed dining area. "The Fablehaven one looked more legit."

"The food is excellent, though," Tanu said, patting his belly.

"I'll talk to the chef," Lomo said, rising. "He'll prepare some sustenance for you newcomers."

"I like how this guy thinks," Newel said.

"Get him on the team," Doren advised. "Are these cream puffs?"

"Where has this dungeon been all my life?" Newel asked, smelling the cobbler.

"Shall I take a message back?" Creya asked.

"No," Tanu said. "We'll need you. I must have words with the chef as well. I have a potion to brew."

CHAPTER TWENTY

Shrunken Chances

S eth, wake up."

Jolted out of sleep, Seth sat upright with his fists clenched to find a goat standing by his bed. Seth relaxed and stared at the animal through squinty eyes. A quick taste of walrus butter revealed the goat to be Newel.

"Scary dream?" the satyr asked.

"Tough week," Seth said. "Lots of running for my life."

"Ready for more?" Newel asked. "Come on."

The satyr left the room. Seth slid out of bed and slipped on his boots. Returning to the dining area, he found Tanu, Lomo, Newel, Doren, Calvin, Creya, and Knox already there. Knox looked newly awakened, his eyes puffy. He wore his hair short on the sides and longer on top, and right now the longer part was disheveled and matted.

"What time is it?" Seth asked.

"Maybe an hour before dawn," Lomo said.

"I did the quick and dirty version," Tanu said, indicating a bowl of beige fluid on the table. "It should shrink us, though."

"To my size?" Calvin asked hopefully.

"A little bigger than you," Tanu said. "Strong stuff, though. Three or four inches."

"What if the bird just eats us?" Knox said.

"I don't eat talking creatures," Creya said. "Ask our rodents."

"We can trust Creya," Lomo said. "Her reputation precedes her."

"You're coming?" Seth asked Knox.

"Sounds like you need all the help you can get," Knox said.

"Are you an expert with cursed castles?" Seth asked.

"Are you an expert dragon fighter?" Knox countered.

"I killed one with Kendra," Seth said.

"Really?" Knox asked, surprised.

"A poison one," Seth said.

"Well, maybe you have some experience, but you had to start someplace," Knox said.

"True," Seth said. "Do you get that you might die? We all might."

"Not me and Newel," Doren said. "If magical folk can't enter the castle, no use in us tagging along. We'll watch Tess."

"Keep her safe through Midsummer Eve," Seth said.

Newel winked. "We'll hole up here. Eat dungeon chow."

"I might try for a life sentence," Doren said, patting his belly.

"You may get in some real trouble if Dalgorel determines you helped me escape," Lomo said.

"We'll play dumb," Newel said.

"It's a specialty," Doren added.

"Anyway, I'm in," Knox said to Seth. "If you can take this risk, so can I."

Seth shrugged. "Your funeral."

"The brew I made will shrink our clothes," Tanu said. "But no items. And no magical clothing. And certainly no magical items."

"My clothes didn't shrink last time I used a shrinking potion," Seth said.

"Tiny naked Seth Breath," Knox said with a smirk.

"It's more complicated to get the clothes to shrink," Tanu said. "But I had dragon parts to work with. Superior ingredients."

"My sword?" Seth asked. "It could be useful."

Tanu held up two small drawstring bags. "Creya is our ride to the Zowali Protectorate. She will carry two bags." He raised one. "This one is normal. We'll ride in it." He raised the other. "This one was just loaned to me by Lord Dalgorel. It's an extradimensional bag."

"Like the knapsack we used to have?" Seth asked.

"Yes," Tanu said. "The inside of this little bag is the size of a large trunk. We can bring anything that will fit through the mouth."

Seth retrieved his sword and the vial of horrors and put

them inside the magical bag. He removed his fleet boots and stuffed them in as well. "They're magical," he explained. Lomo added a sword.

"I already included some of my gear," Tanu said. "Lord Dalgorel reluctantly let me store many of the dragon parts I collected in an ice house here."

"Won't the bag be heavy with all that stuff inside?" Knox asked.

"Doesn't work that way," Tanu said, handing Knox the bag. "The little bag still feels empty. What the bag actually contains is a small gateway to a pocket dimension."

"This breaks the laws of nature," Knox said, reaching his arm deep inside the tiny bag.

"It enhances the laws of nature," Tanu replied. "Makes clever use of them."

Knox handed the bag back to Tanu. "The goo in that bowl will actually shrink us?"

"No time like the present to find out," Tanu said. "Might be wise to use the cover of night while it lasts."

"How much must we drink?" Lomo asked.

"You're with us?" Seth asked.

"This problem is bigger than all of us," Lomo said. "The Fair Folk won't like it, and they can disavow me if they must, but I can't withhold my help."

"This is a potent batch," Tanu said, producing a measuring cup. "A quarter cup should do it." He dipped the cup in the bowl. "Who wants first try?"

Seth intended to volunteer, but Lomo beat him to it. The man took the cup from Tanu and downed it. Over a matter of seconds, his body diminished in size until he was no bigger than Seth's pointer finger. His clothing shrank with him. The measuring cup sat on the floor beside him.

Tanu picked up the measuring cup, refilled it, and handed it to Knox, who stared suspiciously at the gooey fluid. "What's in this stuff?"

"You probably don't want to know," Tanu said.

"Camel snot," Seth said. "Oyster slime. Dragon sweat. It's sort of a chowder."

"Must be where you get your Seth breath," Knox said, drinking it down. "Not bad," he said as he started to shrink. "Not good either." His voice sounded higher as he got smaller.

Knox dropped the measuring cup, and soon he stood beside Lomo on the floor. Seth retrieved the measuring cup and handed it to Tanu. "Any word about Eve?" Seth asked.

"She is basically a prisoner in her room," Tanu said. "Lord Dalgorel was not happy with her." He gave the cup back to Seth.

"Down the hatch," Seth said, tipping the cup back. The creamy fluid tasted like a mix of sweet and salty, with a grainy texture. Seth tried to banish thoughts of camel snot as he gulped it down. He quickly set the cup on the table once he was done.

Tingles sparked through his limbs as the table went from the height of his waist, to eye-level, to a towering structure high above him. Tanu and the satyrs looked like giants.

"Let's get you on the table," Tanu said, crouching. Seth, Lomo, and Knox climbed onto his large brown hand. It felt like an amusement park ride as Tanu lifted them to the dizzying heights of the table and let them hop off his palm. At their normal sizes, Lomo was taller than Seth, and Knox was a bit shorter. Their sizes relative to one another remained the same.

"Hi, Seth," Calvin said from a little farther down the table.

"Hey, Calvin," Seth said. The nipsie ran to him, and Seth found that the young adult came up to his chest.

"We still don't quite match up," Calvin said. "But closer than before."

Tanu sat on the edge of the table and drank a quarter cup of the potion. He promptly shrank, still sitting on the edge of the table. He got up and hustled to the others. "Your turn, Newel!" Tanu called.

Newel brought the regular drawstring bag, opened it, and let them climb inside. Seth quickly discovered that it was not comfortable to sit at the bottom of a bag with four other people.

"This is how we're traveling?" Knox complained as he jostled against Seth.

"No," Tanu said. "Soon we'll be dangling from an eagle's talons hundreds of feet above the ground."

"I will carry you true," Creya said, her voice coming from somewhere above the bag. "I slip by dragons all the time. I got here just fine."

"Keep silent," Newel told the inhabitants of the bag. "I have the eagle and am heading out."

Seth could see nothing from inside the bag. The opening was closed tight. Newel carried them some

distance, then stopped as he spoke to some unseen person. "I'm bringing the eagle out," the satyr said. "Creya has to get home."

A door opened. Newel walked some more.

"We're out," Lomo whispered.

Seth sat in silence, swaying in the bag with his friends. Newel paused again. "Good luck," the satyr whispered.

Seth's stomach lurched as the bag soared upward. The acceleration drove the occupants of the sack into one another. For a brief while Seth had most of Tanu on top of him, until the Samoan shifted.

"We're away," Creya announced. "Best to keep quiet. Some predators have excellent hearing."

As they reached a steady speed, the bag leveled out, swaying gently. Sometimes the eagle ascended or dipped down or turned, making the bag swing one way or another. Invisible forces tugged at Seth in unpredictable ways. It was difficult to rest. He waited and listened, wondering if a dragon would spot them.

After some time, Knox asked in a loud whisper, "How do we get big again?"

"It'll wear off," Seth whispered back.

"What if it wears off while we're flying?" Knox asked.

"We have enough time," Tanu said. "At least ninety minutes."

Seth waited in the wobbly darkness. The air got stale and took on the slightly humid odor of multiple bodies. Seth tried to relax and let time go by. He tried to appreciate the fact that they were not being attacked by anything.

"We're over the Zowali Protectorate now," Creya finally announced. "Feel free to speak."

"Calvin, is this how you feel in my pocket?" Seth asked.

"A little," Calvin said. "But your pocket is more stable. And I'm alone. Also, I can sometimes stick my head out for air."

"I'm sorry," Seth said. "This gets old."

"You see why I sometimes want to get out and stretch my legs," Calvin said.

"The smell in here!" Knox said. "I keep trying to hold my breath. It backfires because then I breathe deeper afterward."

"Slow and steady," Tanu suggested.

"On the bright side, I may never be part of a stranger jailbreak," Lomo said.

Everyone laughed.

"Three inches tall, dangling from an eagle in a little sack?" Tanu asked.

They laughed again.

"Here we are," Creya announced. "Shelter. We beat the sunrise. Not by much."

The bag came to rest on a hard surface. Fingers pulled open the top, and Seth stared up into the face of an enormous chimpanzee before the bag slumped sideways and he crawled out. Seth found himself on the floor of a gigantic stable or barn. The air smelled fresh compared to the stuffy sack, although there were definite odors of animals and hay.

Gargantuan animals surrounded them. At his current size, Seth thought the immense animals seemed significantly larger than the dragons. The chimpanzee stood nearest. Creya had alighted on a perch high above them. Seth also saw a huge tiger, a buffalo, a pair of wolves, a camel, a horse, a vulture, some rabbits, and a bear, most looming like colossal monuments. He had never felt tinier.

"Can they all talk?" Knox asked.

"Welcome to Shelter," the tiger said. "I am Raj Faranah, guardian of the Zowali Protectorate. We expected Creya to return with information, not passengers. Most ingenious. One of you is Seth Sorenson?"

"That's me," Seth said, waving up at the gigantic tiger. It seemed unlikely that such an immense beast would hear or notice him. "Creya said my sister, Kendra, is here. Can I see her?"

"Your sister is currently resting," Raj said. "You are most welcome here."

"Does she have a plan?" Seth asked.

"We'll get to that in due time," Raj said. "The stingbulb of Patton is out doing reconnaissance. A very agreeable man."

"I'm excited to see him," Seth said.

"Nobody will eat us, right?" Knox asked.

"Humans can be so fearful of animals," the chimpanzee said in a precise accent. She scratched her head. "Do you know what predator hunts the most species in this room?"

"People," Seth said.

The chimp tapped her nose and pointed at him. "People hunt all of us for food. For decoration. For sport. Some of us are poisoned like vermin. Others are enslaved. Or used in experiments. Once, we could roam the wide world, our only limit the division between earth and sky. Now we cower where we can, our options ever shrinking, bordered by humanity on all sides. Who should be afraid of whom?"

"We're tiny," Knox said.

"I see," the chimp said. "You're currently vulnerable. You worry about vengeance. Or perhaps you realize that weaponless, even a full-grown man is no match for a tiger. Take solace that if you perish, your species will be just fine. Not many mammals number in the billions. Those who do tend to be rodents or domestic animals like cattle or sheep. Some species of animal, including tigers, are down to the thousands. Or even the dozens. Some of us are no more."

"You're in no danger, human," the bear said. "None of us eat other creatures who can speak. Is this the proper time for activism, Tasha?"

"It's always the right time for positive messages," the chimp replied.

"Remain here until you regain your size," Raj said. "The Shelter is a safe place for creatures great and small. There will be time for plans soon enough."

"Thank you for your hospitality," Tanu said with a bow.

"I won't be growing like the others," Calvin said. "Don't be disappointed. I'm a nipsie."

"You are all welcome here," Raj assured them.

Knox stretched. "I'm going to get some sleep."

Seth nodded. "We have a long night ahead of us. Wake me when Kendra gets up. Or if we're going to eat. Or if dragons attack."

CHAPTER TWENTY-ONE

Preparations

Kendra awoke to a juicy tongue sliding across her cheek. She started with a little shriek.

"Sorry," Sherman the fox said. "I wasn't sure the best way to wake you."

Sitting up, Kendra rubbed her cheek dry. "You startled me."

"I wasn't trying to be rude," Sherman said. "The licking is something foxes do. I wasn't tasting you! I promise."

"Is Patton back?" Kendra asked.

"Not yet," Sherman said. "I hear he is on his way. But you have other visitors."

Kendra exited the stall where she had been sleeping to find Tanu, Seth, Knox, and a handsome stranger sitting around a wooden counter eating scrambled eggs and drinking milk. "Seth?" Kendra cried. "Tanu? What are you doing here? Knox? Am I still sleeping?"

Seth ran to his sister and gave her a hug. "I was worried about you!"

"Just because a dragon gobbled me up?" Kendra asked.

"I thought you had been eaten," Seth said.

"There are more comfortable ways to travel," Kendra replied. "I got spat out in front of Celebrant. How did you get here?"

"Tempest found us, and Eve and I made it to Terrabelle," Seth said. "The Somber Knight helped Tanu get there with his bull."

"The Somber Knight survived?" Kendra asked.

"Barely," Seth said. "He lost limbs, and his bull got all torn up. We met Lomo in Terrabelle. Do you remember hearing about him? The rebel of the Fair Folk who wanted them to get involved."

"He was locked in the dungeon," Kendra said.

"Hello," Lomo said with a wave.

"Tanu made a shrinking potion, and we escaped with Creya," Seth said. "We know about the Wizenstone. We're here to help."

"And Knox?" Kendra asked.

"I snuck to Wyrmroost through the barrel," Knox said. He briefly explained how the murder of the goblin and loss of the barrel had caused a breach in security. "I heard you and Seth went missing, so I went exploring with Newel and Doren, and we found Seth."

"You shouldn't be here," Kendra told her cousin. "You have no idea how dangerous this is."

"I drank the milk," Knox said. "Tanu gave us some

walrus butter from his supplies this morning. Same effect."

"It's not just drinking the milk," Kendra said. "You can't know how dangerous this castle will be."

"Neither can you," Knox said.

"At least we have some experience," Kendra said.

"Did you have experience the first time?" Knox asked. "This is my second attempt to save Wyrmroost. The first time I saved it without even knowing what I was doing."

"He's determined," Seth said.

"This is life and death," Kendra said. "Emphasis on death. We've had friends die."

"I get it," Knox said. "Riding a dirt bike is life and death too. I'm in."

Kendra did not understand that mentality. Death was so final, so permanent! But she knew Seth sometimes had similar feelings. "Tasha made breakfast?" she asked.

"Yeah, the chimp," Seth said. "Talking hens still lay eggs."

"The apes are good cooks," Gorban said. "Excellent omelets."

"You made it here!" Kendra cried, walking over to give the bear a hug. "Seth, have you met Gorban? He found me when I crossed into the Zowali Protectorate and helped bring me here."

"Most of the animals don't like cooked meals," Gorban said. "I appreciate variety."

"I see you have a manacle on your ankle," Calvin said. "I'm handy at picking locks."

Kendra put her foot beside the nipsie, and he slipped

his sword into the keyhole. A moment later the manacle clicked open.

"Thanks," Kendra said.

"What are friends for?" Calvin replied, sheathing his slender blade.

"Did you see who else is here?" Seth asked, indicating some horses.

"Glory!" Kendra exclaimed. "And Noble! How did you find us?"

She rushed over to her saddled mount and hugged the horse's neck. Then she patted Noble.

"Some Luvians form a bond with their rider," a female horse said. "Glory formed one with you, Kendra. When her keepers turned her loose to find you, she was just supposed to run the road to Skyhold. But she sensed when you came here, and it was closer for her. Noble arrived with her late in the night."

"Good girl," Kendra said, petting Glory. "I'm so happy you found me."

"Come have some eggs before they get cold," Tanu called. "You need energy."

Kendra went and obediently finished off the warm, salty eggs. Then she downed a glass of creamy milk.

"Tonight is Midsummer Eve," Seth said. "Do we have a plan?"

"I think so," Kendra said. "Patton must still be out investigating. We need to get to Stormguard Castle an hour after sundown. We have to time it right or we will be stranded outside on a festival night."

"What's so terrible about a festival night?" Knox asked.

"Most of the rules and boundaries at a preserve break down on festival nights," Kendra said. "The creatures run wild. It's bad at Fablehaven, and it's supposed to be worse here."

"Better for us to arrive to the castle a little late than early," Seth said. "We don't want to be stranded in the open."

"But not too late," Kendra said, "or we miss time finding the Wizenstone."

"I could brew another shrinking potion," Tanu said. "I brought enough ingredients." He pointed to a drawstring bag on the table.

"It's tiny," Kendra said.

"It's like our old knapsack," Seth said. "Bigger inside."

"Think you could fly us there in the bag?" Tanu asked Creya.

"On Midsummer Eve?" the eagle checked. "It would be suicide. No birds fly on Midsummer Eve. The sky phantoms alone are plenty of reason to stay grounded."

A dove swooped through the Shelter entrance and alighted on a perch. "Patton is almost here," he announced.

"He'll have our plan," Kendra said.

"I can get behind whatever Patton wants," Seth said.

They heard approaching hoofbeats, and then Patton rode through the entrance on Captain. Seth ran over to him. Patton laughed as he smoothly dismounted and gave Seth a big hug. Captain and Glory touched muzzles.

Patton released the embrace and stepped back, appraising Seth. "You're getting taller."

"I guess," Seth said. "It's so good to see you."

Patton raised both hands. "Full disclosure: You are giving all this affection to a mutated piece of fruit. I'm just Patton's stingbulb. I'll degenerate into mush in a couple days."

"You're better than a photo," Seth said.

"That much is true," Patton said. He looked to the others. "Hi, Tanu. Good to see you. And Lomo, too?"

"Patton helped encourage my sentiments against neutrality," Lomo said.

"You finally went for it?" Patton asked.

"I did," Lomo said. "Escaped prison at Terrabelle to come here."

"Good man," Patton said. "Who is the new kid?"

"Our cousin Knox," Kendra said.

Patton smiled. "Bringing in more family?"

"He's on mom's side of the family," Seth clarified.

"Welcome, Knox," Patton said. "You picked one tumultuous day to meet up with this crew. Who am I missing?"

"Me!" shouted Calvin. "The tiny one!"

"What the devil are you?" Patton asked. "You're too big to be a nipsie."

"I'm a giant nipsie," Calvin said. "Under a spell. Sworn to Seth."

"Good choice, little fellow," Patton said. "Seth is one of the best. You may not be able to enter Stormguard Castle, though."

"Sometimes spells miss people smaller than fairies," Calvin said. "We get forgotten a lot."

"It's quite a curse on that castle," Patton said. "But anything is possible. Your help is welcome. I won't be able to enter either."

"You won't?" Seth asked.

"I'm vegetable, not animal," Patton said. "Not really a person. But I'll help you get there."

"You have the plan worked out?" Kendra asked.

"It's a go," Patton said. "Best I could manage on short notice."

"What are we doing?" Seth asked.

"Going to meet a fairy named Risenmay," Patton said.

"A fairy?" Knox asked.

"No typical fairy," Patton said. "One of the greater fairies. Kind of like a queen bee."

"Is she a unicorn, like the Fairy Queen?" Kendra asked.

"No, Risenmay is a true fairy," Patton said. "Larger than normal. She has powers that will help us tonight."

"What powers?" Seth asked.

"I can't say," Patton replied.

"Is it a secret?" Kendra asked.

"Well, yes," Patton said. "But I can't reveal it no matter how much I want to. My lips are sealed by magic. It is part of the price of bargaining with Risenmay."

"But she can help us get to Stormguard Castle at the right time," Tanu verified.

"Exactly," Patton said. "Literally couldn't have said it better myself."

"She lives in the Zowali Protectorate?" Seth asked.

Patton shook his head. "Outside, in the Bewilderness."

"That sounds made up," Knox said.

"It's a dangerous region," Patton said. "Mostly forested. No dragons go there."

"Does it adjoin the Zowali Protectorate?" Seth asked.

"No, but the Bewilderness is on the border of the Sentient Wood, which can be reached by a tunnel from the protectorate," Patton said. "We'll all want to bring mounts."

"The Sentient Wood can be entered only with permission," an owl said from a perch.

"I just got the permission," Patton said. "One of the wooden henchmen owed me a favor."

"Wooden henchmen?" Knox asked.

"Woodlings," Patton said. "I'll explain on the way. Everyone needs a mount," he repeated.

"I'll go with Glory," Kendra said. Glory bobbed her head, then nuzzled Kendra as she drew near.

"Noble is good for me," Seth said.

Noble stamped in agreement.

"I'll stick with Captain," Patton said. "We need three more mounts."

"I'll take the big one," a large chestnut mare said. "I'm Charlemagne." Tanu approached and introduced himself.

"I'm Rodolfo," said a gray stallion with a black mane and tail. "It would be my pleasure to carry Lomo."

"I'll take the other boy," a Bactrian camel offered.

"Whoa," Knox said. "Are you fast?"

"I'm excellent over long distances," the camel said.

"Do I sit between the humps?" Knox asked.

"Precisely," the camel said, kneeling down. "Call me Babak."

"Knox."

"Short for 'obnoxious,'" Seth said.

"And Seth is short for 'Seth Breath of Death,'" Knox said.

"Do I need a mount?" Calvin asked. "I usually just ride in Seth's pocket."

"A mount would be sensible," Patton said. "Maybe not at first, but all will become clear before the day is out."

A male rabbit cleared his throat. "I may have trouble keeping up with horses, but it would be my honor."

Calvin brightened. "I was talking with Thistleton before breakfast. He'd be great!"

"We can carry the rabbit most of the way," Patton said.

"Deal," Thistleton agreed, hopping over to Captain. "I've never ridden a horse before."

Kendra mounted Glory and patted her neck. Patton scooped up Thistleton and leaped onto Captain.

"Would you like an escort?" Raj Faranah asked.

"Just send word to the other animals to watch out for us," Patton said. "We ride for the secret tunnel to the Sentient Wood."

"Thanks for your hospitality," Kendra said.

"Thank you for your courage against the dragons," Raj replied.

"'Bye, Gorban," Kendra said. "'Bye, Sherman."

The bear and the fox bade her farewell.

"Off we go," Patton said. He and Captain led the others

out of Shelter. They rode together under the morning light.

"So what is the Sentient Wood?" Seth asked.

"Like it sounds, the trees are intelligent," Patton said. "Much more conscious than most trees. Anything made from their wood comes to life."

"Can dragons attack us there?" Tanu asked.

"There is a powerful barrier around the wood," Patton said. "Not even caretakers can enter without permission."

"But you got permission," Knox said.

"I once helped one of their henchmen out of a tight fix," Patton said. "Trees remember."

"Then the Bewilderness," Kendra said.

"Yes," Patton replied. "It will be dangerous."

"What else is new?" Seth said.

"It's a risk worth taking," Patton said. "If we can find Risenmay before sundown, our chances of making it to Stormguard Castle on time improve markedly."

"Then we should pick up the pace," Babak said.

Kendra held on as Glory increased her gait to an easy lope. The other mounts did likewise.

CHAPTER TWENTY-TWO

The Sentient Wood

The sun was almost directly overhead when Captain came to a stop in front of a large gate in the side of a hillock. Beyond the gate, a tunnel slanted downward. Seth and the others halted alongside him.

"Back already?" asked a whispery voice that startled Seth.

He turned to find a snake leaning out of a dying tree with spindly branches. The serpent was doing a good job of blending with the wooden limbs.

"I brought my friends," Patton said. "Meet Samba the boomslang."

Seth and the others greeted the snake.

Patton dismounted and opened the gate. "We're ready to leave the protectorate. No trouble today?"

"No trouble ever," the boomslang said. "A guard is not

really needed on this end. But I like the area for my own purposes, so I keep watch. The only beings with access from the other side are the woodlings and a few hamadryads."

"Are you poisonous?" Knox asked.

"My bite can kill," Samba said. "We all have our ways to survive."

"Any tips on crossing the Sentient Wood?" Patton asked.

"Show no weapons that could harm trees," Samba said. "Hide axes or hatchets for sure."

"What about beavers?" Babak asked.

"We keep the beavers and woodpeckers far from view of the Sentient Wood," Samba said. "Out of respect for our neighbors, no trees are felled in this part of the protectorate. No wood is burned."

Patton remounted Captain. "We'll treat the Sentient Wood with respect."

"Do whatever you wish," the boomslang said. "What is it to me? However, if you can scare some small game in my direction, the kind who do not speak, I would be most obliged."

"Some of us do not eat other animals," Charlemagne said.

"How you get so large eating hay is a mystery the universe may never unravel," the boomslang said. "Do not act superior for consuming weeds. What cunning does that require?"

"You know better than to cross words with a serpent," Captain said. "Don't keep arguing or we'll be here all day."

"Yes," the boomslang said. "Why think? Why engage?

Better to mindlessly trot off where your riders direct you."

"We have a purpose in—" Charlemagne began.

"Don't," Captain cut her off. "All day."

Captain led the group past the iron gate and into the large tunnel. The way was wide enough for them to ride two by two. After they were all through, Patton dismounted again and closed the gate.

"Hay is not a weed," Charlemagne grumbled. "Neither are oats. Or carrots."

Seth could sit tall in his saddle as the earthy tunnel slanted downward. Here and there Patton had to crouch a little. The soil around them smelled freshly dug, but Seth supposed that was not likely. Before they had gone far, the tunnel leveled out. Tanu switched on a flashlight. They continued underground much longer than Seth had expected.

"Camels do not belong underground," Babak said after some time.

"Neither do horses," Captain replied. "But we do what we must in emergencies. Be grateful the passage accommodates us."

"Rabbits quite like it below ground," Thistleton said. "But this tunnel is not very cozy."

Eventually the tunnel began to slant upward, and daylight came into view ahead. Tanu switched off his flashlight as the tunnel ended at a gate manned by a wooden figure exquisitely carved to resemble a bearded gentleman. The wooden man held up a hand, and they all stopped.

"Greetings," Patton said, waving. "I have returned with my friends." He gestured at the others, then motioned toward the gate and walked the fingers of one hand across the palm of the other. "You granted permission earlier for us to cross the Sentient Wood on our way to the Bewilderness."

The wooden gentleman gave a nod and opened the gate, standing aside to let them pass. Seth stared at the wooden man as he rode by, and the man appeared to stare back.

"Do they talk?" Knox asked. "The wooden people?"

"I have never heard them speak," Patton said. "Nor the trees. I'm not sure how well they hear, either. Pantomime seems to help them understand."

Seth rode forward into the noonday twilight of a forest full of tall trees, none of them crowded together but rather spaced just right for their branches to block out all but a few patches of sky. The variety of trees struck Seth: towering conifers with deep grooves in the bark; mighty oaks with twisty, sprawling branches; bushy cypresses; maples with their broad, shapely leaves; the fat trunks of banyans with rambling roots; and various tropical trees that looked like they belonged in a steamy jungle.

No undergrowth obscured the ground between the trunks. The road ahead was discernible only because it was the sole line of sight that did not end with a tree.

"I feel like we're being watched," Kendra said as they followed Patton forward.

"Maybe not watched," Patton said. "But definitely noticed."

"How can you tell the trees are smart?" Knox asked. "They just look like trees."

"Well, anything made from their wood comes to life," Patton said.

"That's where the wooden people come from?" Seth asked.

"Exactly," Patton said. "The wooden henchmen are controlled by the trees. They act on behalf of their masters."

"Who made the first wooden person?" Seth asked.

"I don't know," Patton said. "My guess would be a dryad or a hamadryad. Now, the woodlings make one another, according to the desires of the forest."

"They must have axes," Knox said.

"I suspect they have some tools," Patton said. "But let's not discuss it anymore right now. I'm getting the feeling that we're being too noisy."

"There is a hush," Charlemagne said in a quiet voice. "No animal sounds."

As they fell silent, Seth could not help sensing the unusual stillness around him. He kept wanting to glance around to see who was spying on him. He felt observed from all directions. But wherever he looked, it was just more trees.

At first, only the footfalls of their mounts disturbed the silence. As they advanced, the more Seth paid attention, the more he noticed strange creaks and groans issuing from the trees, branches shifting or swaying with no discernible wind. There was a way trees normally sounded in a breeze, and this was different. The forest seemed to murmur.

"Over there," Kendra whispered.

"Woodlings," Patton said.

Off to the right, Seth saw a huge barrel with legs walking along with two wooden figures. The figures were humanoid but not carved in detail like the bearded man at the gate. As Seth watched, the barrel paused, and one woodling turned a spigot in the side of the barrel to fill a bucket. The other figure knelt with a trowel by a knobby tree, carefully digging near a root. The figure with the bucket went and started pouring water near a tall elm.

As they progressed through the wood, Seth caught sight of other woodlings ranging between three and eight feet in height. Some appeared to be weeding. Others were caring for the trees directly.

They paused at one point as Patton looked around. "I don't want to lose the path," he muttered softly. "This appears to be a crossroads."

"How can you tell?" Knox asked.

"I see a couple of directions in which the way is devoid of trees," Patton said. "These paths do not curve much."

"What's the problem?" Knox asked.

"We have been generally heading north, which is the direction we desire," Patton said. "The pathways here appear to run only east, west, and back south, the way we came."

"Flip a coin?" Seth asked.

"West veers gently north," Patton said. "We'll try that way and hope for the best."

"I'm thirsty," Babak said.

Seth looked back at him.

"Kidding," Babak said. "Camel humor."

They went a good distance before Patton stopped again. "This time we can go directly north again."

They had not gone far before an enormous wooden figure came into view. Astride his horse, Seth came slightly higher than the waist of the wooden giant. It looked sturdily built, though the face and carved details were rather primitive. It held up a crooked hand for them to stop.

"We're here with permission," Patton said, accompanying his words with hand signals. "Just passing through. Treading lightly."

The giant pointed off to one side and motioned for them to come.

"We're going north," Patton said, indicating the way ahead.

The giant shook its head and pointed off to the side once more.

Patton looked back at the others. "It appears we're heading east for now." He gestured to the east and said, "Lead on."

The wooden giant began plodding forward. The way twisted and turned, making Seth wonder if this was a path or if the giant was simply improvising a route among the trees. Seth began to notice an increasing number of woodlings. For the first time, the woodlings were noticing them as well. As Seth and the little caravan of riders went by, the wooden figures would come in their direction and follow behind.

"They're following us," Knox quietly said out of the side of his mouth.

"Are we in trouble?" Kendra wondered.

"We'll sort it out," Patton said.

Seth kept glancing back. A dozen woodlings expanded to a score. Most were humanoid figures, but a few walking barrels joined the parade as well.

Up ahead, the giant led them into a clearing. A single enormous oak tree awaited, the trunk rivaling a sequoia, contorted branches spreading across lofty heights. A mob of woodlings surrounded it, tall and stumpy, intricate and plain, though none were as large as the giant guide.

"What is going on?" Seth mumbled.

The giant brought the group to a halt not far from the base of the tree. Woodlings crowded around them. Seth hoped that if things went bad, they could make a run for it. A fight would probably not end well.

A tall, slender woman came around from the far side of the tree, her gown an artful collage of green leaves, her shawl a masterpiece of silken spiderwebs. In her bare feet she stood almost as tall as Patton on his horse.

"Are you the hamadryad of this tree?" Kendra asked.

The woman smiled as if to confirm the guess. Then she looked at the woodlings and motioned them away. "Give our visitors some space," she said in a soothing voice.

"She should play basketball," Knox murmured.

"Seldom do visitors cross our land," the hamadryad said. "I am Eldanore, a servant of this grove. Your courtesy has been appreciated. We ask of you a favor."

"I bet she could dunk without jumping," Knox muttered.

Seth motioned for his cousin to zip it.

"How can we be of service?" Patton asked.

"Woods like ours have dwindled," Eldanore said. "Pray, take these seeds and plant them where they might thrive."

She held out to Patton a bowl made of stone. "Oak, redwood, and banyan," he said.

"Not together," she advised. "Far from here. Some of the elders worry that our enclosed populations pose a threat to ruminating forests. A single disaster could eradicate so many."

"It would be our pleasure," Patton said.

"You come from a tree," Eldanore observed.

"Indeed I do," Patton replied. "I took human form for a brief while."

"You chose an excellent human," Eldanore said. "Safe journey."

"Might I ask, what is the best route to the Bewilderness from here?" Patton inquired.

"Yimo will show you the most direct way," Eldanore said, motioning toward a nearby woodling with a stubby body and legs so long they looked like stilts. "Go in peace."

Patton looked back at Seth and the others. "Follow me."

Yimo started walking fast enough that the horses needed to trot to keep up. Seth stole several backward glances at the mob of woodlings and the colossal oak. None of the wooden figures followed them.

As when they had followed the giant, their way through the wood did not seem like a path. The horses stayed at a trot, meaning they made more noise than earlier. They traveled a long distance in silence before Knox spoke. "I don't see any more woodlings."

"There's Yimo," Seth pointed out.

"Besides Yimo," Knox said.

"Maybe they're all back with the hamadryad," Kendra said.

"Or working in a different part of the forest," Seth guessed.

"The trees are louder here," Tanu said. "Might be a reflection of us."

Seth looked and listened. The trees did sound creakier. He noticed a particular banyan with many aerial roots drooping down from convoluted branches, where shadows seemed to gather thicker than elsewhere. He felt malevolence as he studied it, and it took an effort to look away.

"A little quieter here," Seth said, glancing periodically at the ominous tree until it was out of view.

After some time, Yimo came to a halt and indicated the way ahead. Beyond where he stopped, there was under-growth, and the trees were not so evenly spaced. The difference was remarkable. It was clear that Yimo intended to go no farther.

"End of the line," Patton said, dismounting. "We need to talk."

CHAPTER TWENTY-THREE

The Bewilderness

Kendra climbed down from Glory, patting the mare in appreciation. There had been a tense feeling while they were moving through the Sentient Wood, but Glory had performed beautifully.

"Yimo," Patton said, accompanying his words with hand motions, "we appreciate your help."

The woodling gave a little bow and strode away on his long legs. Everyone huddled around Patton, including the mounts.

"Our next step is tricky," Patton said. "The Bewilderness is not directly protected from dragons."

"No barriers?" Seth asked.

"Right," Patton said. "But dragons do not venture there."

"Why not?" Kendra asked.

"The Bewilderness is incredibly disorienting to many

animals and magical creatures," Patton said. "Dragons especially hate it. They get terribly dizzy and find the whole place deeply disturbing."

"Will we get dizzy?" Knox asked.

"We shouldn't get dizzy," Patton said. "But if we're not careful, we'll definitely get killed."

"What's the danger?" Seth asked.

"Risenmay dwells at the heart of the Bewilderness," Patton said. "I can get no more specific than that. I have found her before, but I do not believe I can do so as a stingbulb. Only one of us should try."

"Me," Seth said.

"Don't be too hasty," Patton said. "The person ought to be the one most likely to win Risenmay's aid. Kendra's fairy-kind status makes her the ideal candidate."

"Okay," Kendra said, though part of her would have been happy to let Seth volunteer. "Why just one of us?"

"The way to Risenmay will vary depending on the person," Patton said. "Think of it as if there are a thousand right ways to her, and a million wrong ways. Groups tend to argue and get killed."

"But don't we all need to get there?" Kendra asked.

"If she agrees to help you, Risenmay will summon the rest of us, and we'll get there easily," Patton said.

"If she doesn't agree to help?" Kendra asked.

"It gets scary in many ways," Patton said. "At this point, without her help, I'm not sure if we can reach Stormguard Castle in time."

"How do I find her?" Kendra asked.

"To those who don't know the secret, the Bewilderness is a death trap," Patton said. "The trick is simple, but not easy. Once you get inside the Bewilderness, you must always go in the direction that feels most wrong."

"The way that feels wrong?" Kendra checked.

"If you go the way that feels right, it will lead you into a fatal trap," Patton said. "I know of poisonous thorns, covered pits, monsters with limited domains—and those are just the dangers I have witnessed or heard about."

"What if I don't feel anything?" Kendra asked.

"Going in a neutral direction will also take you the wrong way and eventually kill you. Inside the Bewilderness, always go against your instincts."

"That sounds difficult," Lomo said.

"It can be," Patton said. "Take it slow. Beware of finding a way that feels wrong and deciding it must be right. Once it feels right, it will be wrong. Only keep going if it feels truly wrong."

"I'm terrible for this," Kendra said. "I overthink all the time."

"Truth," Seth said.

"That could be an advantage if you take it slow," Patton said. "Don't advance if it seems like the right way, or if you have reason to suspect you will get where you want to go. Don't head off in a random direction. Make sure it truly feels wrong. As hopeless as possible. And you will eventually make it."

"No horse?" Kendra asked.

"You don't want an animal in there," Patton said. "It's harder for them to work against strong instincts."

"The camel would rather be a bystander," Babak said.

"We're thinking horses," Charlemagne pointed out. "We can play the same mind games as you humans."

"You could succeed as an intelligent horse," Patton said. "You might be able to betray your instincts. But if a thinking horse goes with Kendra, your routes will not match, and you will confuse each other."

"I'll do it," Kendra said. "I should probably get going."

"Start promptly," Patton said. "But don't hurry. Take your time and get it right."

"Meaning get it wrong," Seth said. "Get every step wrong."

Kendra nodded. She had lived her life trying to get things right. Good grades mattered to her. So did pleasing her parents. She often earned perfect scores on tests. Couldn't she reverse the tendency? Get this perfectly wrong? She looked at the horses, the camel, the rabbit, her friends, and her brother. "See you soon."

She turned and marched away from the Sentient Wood. She told herself not to look back. There was no way returning to Patton and the others was the right direction.

She stopped.

If it felt like the guaranteed wrong way, didn't she have to go back?

She turned around.

Seth, Lomo, Tanu, Knox, Patton, Glory, Noble, Charlemagne, Rodolfo, Captain, Thistleton, and Babak all stood watching her. Calvin was too small to see at this distance. She wanted to return to them. That felt safe.

What felt worse was going onward.

And so she did.

Every step away from her brother and her friends took her closer to a point where she might not have the ability to find her way back. And that felt terrible.

She waded through undergrowth that sometimes snagged at her pant legs. The rising and falling terrain soon left her surrounded by trees large and small. Up ahead, two low hills came into view, with a natural path leading between them. It was the obvious way to proceed.

Kendra paused.

Less convenient would be climbing the hills, but she would get a good view at the top. It seemed like a smart idea, so she disregarded it. Heading back toward her brother still felt comforting. Going left or right showed no obvious advantage. As she considered both more carefully, she had a bad feeling about going left. It would lead into some thick trees that would take away her lines of sight. The more she thought about it, the worse it felt.

So she went left. As Kendra progressed, it continued to feel like a bad idea, until she was inside a dense grove of smallish trees. There was little undergrowth and no clear paths. Before long, she began to lose her sense of direction. Was she curving north? South? Back toward where she had entered? There was a sameness among these trees that left her disoriented.

She figured she would just keep going as straight as she could. That seemed the most reasonable choice under the circumstances.

And Kendra stopped.

What felt worst? Doubling back.

She reversed direction. As she walked, she felt unease about veering left, so she did. It kept feeling bad, and she kept going. Something in her gut warned her to go back the way she had come. She ignored it. Every step felt like a bad idea. So bad that it had to be the right way.

Kendra stopped. What really felt unsettling was going right. The realization that it felt bad did not make it feel good.

She turned right and tried to keep going straight. There were several other adjustments before she emerged from the trees, uncertain what direction she was facing. The sun remained too high for her to get oriented.

Onward she traveled, meticulously aware of whatever direction felt the worst. She shoved through denser under-brush instead of choosing easier ways. She traversed fore-boding thickets and clambered up awkward slopes. She waded through gooey mud when drier paths were available. Part of Kendra worried she was taking the advice too far, making her path unnecessarily difficult, but if Patton was right, she always needed to pursue the way that seemed worst to her. And that was sometimes very inconvenient.

Time passed, the sun slowly sliding across the sky. She felt lost, and she was certain she was only getting more lost, killing time when she needed to hurry.

Kendra reached a place where all directions were more or less open. Any direction seemed as good as any other, including doubling back. What could she do when all ways felt equal? She tried setting off in one direction or another, but kept halting because it felt fine.

Then she noticed the hole.

It barely looked large enough for a person to squeeze inside. Maybe a burrow for a badger or some other medium-sized animal. Did badgers have burrows?

Climbing into the hole undeniably seemed like a really foolish way to proceed. It clearly would not go anywhere—just a few feet down to an unseen dead end.

All other ways seemed much better. This would be a complete waste of time.

Sighing, Kendra got down on her hands and knees and peered into the dark hole. It went down at an angle, curving out of sight. She could see no end.

It truly seemed like a horrible idea.

Looking around, she hoped some direction would feel worse. Nothing came close.

Lying down flat, Kendra squirmed into the hole. It was uncomfortably snug. She had to worm forward on her elbows, swiveling her shoulders, pushing with her feet. Every inch forward felt like a bad idea. Would she be able to back up if the tunnel came to an end? The thought made her claustrophobic. Spindly roots tickled her head and the back of her neck. She could taste the soil in the air.

What if the roof caved in? What if it got so narrow she became fully stuck, unable to proceed or retreat? The little tunnel went deeper, the angle of descent steepening. Inching forward became easier, but she wondered if backing up the incline would even be possible.

The tunnel finally ended at another hole. The only way in was headfirst. Even with her fairykind sight, she could not perceive the ground in the dimness; maybe because it was dark soil like in the tunnel. She reached into the hole but could not feel the ground. How far was the drop? Five feet? Ten? A hundred?

Dropping into the hole seemed like a horrible idea. Trying to squirm out backward felt much more sensible, even though it would be difficult. Where was she supposed to draw the line with bad ideas? If the worst way to proceed was jumping off a cliff onto jagged rocks, would she do it? Wasn't that going beyond choosing the worst direction to travel? Wasn't that just being absurdly reckless?

Scooting into the hole in a tunnel with an uncertain drop seemed suicidal. It struck her as a likely way to break her neck.

But in order to find Risenmay, she was supposed to always disobey her instincts.

Perhaps if she disobeyed too well, it would kill her. Was she taking the idea too far? Disobeying all common sense?

Kendra scooted into the hole, trying to brace herself against the sides to keep from sliding fast. And suddenly there were no sides. And she was falling.

Kendra shrieked and slowly spun in the air, deliberately trying to land on her feet. During a period of rapid acceleration she was able to think about the fall and fear for her life. It was a long drop.

The impact of the water shocked her. She hit feetfirst, sinking deep but not touching the bottom. She stroked upward, reached the surface, and gulped air. The water was still, the room dim. She could not see walls in any direction.

Treading water, her clothes billowing as she moved, she thought about which direction felt worse. Seeing only more water in all directions, she had almost no sensory input to go by, but one way gave her an uncomfortable feeling. The feeling persisted and even grew as she stroked in that direction.

She tried to stay calm. Kendra had never been entirely comfortable with swimming, and being weighed down by her clothes was an odd sensation. She wondered if she should try to take off her shoes, but thought the effort might make her sink, and for now she was staying afloat.

In time, the shore came dimly into view. Heading to the lakeshore felt inexplicably like a bad idea, so she went there. Kendra emerged dripping wet, shivering in the cool air of the cavern. She spent a moment wringing her clothes out as best she could.

Now she could see the wall of the cavern, including the opening to what might be a tunnel or a cave. She also had room to proceed along the lakeshore in either direction. Something about the tunnel gave her an uncomfortable feeling. It seemed like it must be the lair of some animal or monster.

The more she thought about going into the tunnel, the worse the idea sounded, so she went. It ran for a long distance, and every step seemed to bring her closer to doom. At length she reached a junction of five passages, and Kendra paused.

None of the ways stood out as bad. None felt terribly good, either. After some searching, she found a smaller tunnel slanting upward. It seemed too narrow, and she suspected it would lead to trouble.

So in she went. The passage constricted and widened again and again. She scooted through the snug places, hoping not to get stuck. At length daylight came into view, and she crawled out of a crack near the base of a large boulder.

Kendra resumed traveling aboveground. She felt bad about a wooded area, went there, and became completely turned around. Time and again, Kendra ignored the routes that looked promising in deference to her most uncertain and disquieted instincts. She pushed through dense vegetation, climbed unwelcoming slopes, avoided pleasant meadows, abandoned inviting streams, and generally made the way difficult for herself.

Eventually her clothes dried.

She kept an eye on the sun as it got lower. Once it vanished, Midsummer Eve would start. Kendra did not want to get caught out in the open when that happened. She picked up her pace, hurrying wherever she felt she should not go, stopping to reassess when she seemed to be heading in a good direction.

As she emerged from a thick stand of young trees, a pond came into view. A series of stepping-stones led to an island in the center of the pond. Soothing music came from the island, though Kendra couldn't be sure whether instruments or voices generated the sound. There was also a glow from an unseen source on the island, bright enough to register despite the daylight.

Could this be it? Had she finally made it?

Kendra paused and looked around. On the far side of the pond rose a low bluff. She noticed a dark cleft in the rock.

Kendra tore her eyes away.

No!

She did not want to go back underground. That had been scary. She was lucky she hadn't died. The cavity in the rock seemed like a terrible idea, especially now that she had found the probable location of the fairy.

Kendra closed her eyes and thought hard, searching her feelings. The cleft seemed like a huge mistake.

She opened her eyes, walked around the pond to the cavity, and went inside. She did not have to duck, but the way forward was twisty. After several turns, she saw light up ahead. She realized it probably meant danger. A tribe of goblins could inhabit this cave. Or worse.

Kendra took a few more turns and emerged into a bright, sparkling cavern. Glossy white walls of calcite bristled with glittering quartz crystals. A tall, beautiful brunette wearing a shimmering white gown, framed by a pair of elaborate wings, stood awaiting her.

"Congratulations, mortal!" the fairy said with a smile that conveyed pure, welcoming joy. "You have found me."

"Risenmay?" Kendra asked.

The fairy's smile became less an expression of joy and more a shape her mouth was making. "You know my name," she said. "Someone helped you find me?"

"A stingbulb of Patton Burgess," Kendra said. "I knew to work against my instincts."

The smile warmed a bit. "Patton was a charming man. Still no small feat that you arrived."

"He warned me to follow the way that felt worst to me," Kendra said.

"Had you entered the Bewilderness unawares, following your best instincts would have led you to a clue. It would have suggested the same advice Patton offered, though a touch more poetically, I suppose. There are many such warnings around the perimeter of this realm, each with an attractor spell. After the warning, you would then have to follow the least welcoming route to survive. You skipped my personal warning due to the tip Patton gave you." Her smile faltered. "Amazing how many people fail to reach me. More than nine out of ten die instead."

"So many!" Kendra exclaimed.

"I can't offer something for nothing," Risenmay said. "It is interesting to watch how many individuals cannot obey simple instructions."

"Is it worth killing them?" Kendra asked.

"I don't kill them," Risenmay said. "Their choices do that."

"But you let them walk through a dangerous place, knowing they might die," Kendra said.

"Dying is what mortals do best," Risenmay said. "It's your inheritance. You are visitors in this world. From the moment you are born, the end looms. The question is not if, rather when and how."

"We get to live before we die," Kendra said. "That matters to us. We want it to last."

"I don't mind any life lasting a little longer," Risenmay said. "I'm not against you living. I don't cheer for death. I'm just aware that none of you endure for very long, no matter how desperately you cling to life."

"It matters to my friends and family how long I live," Kendra said. "And to me."

"Did you come all this way to lecture me, dear one?" Risenmay asked. "To teach me lessons from your finite experience that I have not learned in thousands of years?"

"I might know things about being a mortal that you don't," Kendra said.

"Does that somehow obligate me to think like a mortal?" Risenmay asked. "Are you required to learn to think like a dog? Or a mosquito? Can you not appreciate a dog but think like a human?"

"I didn't come here to lecture you," Kendra said, not wanting to argue.

Risenmay gave a relieved smile. "That moves us in a better direction. Why have you come to me?"

"I need your help," Kendra said.

"I see," Risenmay replied. "Something you cannot do for yourself."

"Yes," Kendra said. "My friends need help too. All of Wyrmroost needs help. The whole world, really. I'm the caretaker here."

"Now, child, I am a fairy, and not a mortal, but if I needed help, I might not approach my benefactor with a lecture on empathy for lesser beings, but rather pleading, begging, on my knees, perhaps."

Kendra got down on her knees. "Please."

Risenmay shook her head, lovely tresses bouncing. "Nay, child, rise. Begging loses all effect once the petitioner has been invited to grovel."

Kendra stayed on her knees. "I mean it. I'm sorry if I was rude. It was hard getting here and I'm worried about my friends. Please help me."

"I see you are trying," Risenmay said. "Arise, dear one, I insist. I detect your sincerity. You are fairykind. A gift from the Fairy Queen?"

"Yes," Kendra said, getting to her feet.

"Are you aware the current Fairy Queen is not a fairy?" Risenmay asked.

"She's a unicorn," Kendra said.

"Do you know who was Fairy Queen before her?" Risenmay asked.

"I didn't know there was another," Kendra said.

"*Queen* is a position, not an individual," Risenmay said. "Just as Horus was Dragon King before Celebrant."

"I don't know who preceded this Fairy Queen," Kendra said.

"She was actually a fairy," Risenmay said. "They were all fairies, in fact, before our current queen. True fairies, like me."

"You seem different from other fairies," Kendra said.

Risenmay laughed richly. "You mean the tiny ones who flit about plagued with insecurity. Yes, child, I am a great fairy. We have various designations. Some mortals have taken to calling us fairy godmothers."

"You're a fairy godmother?" Kendra asked.

"A quaint title, but yes, it helps make the proper distinction," Risenmay said. "We watch over the little ones. And one of us has always been queen. Until now."

"Does that upset you?" Kendra asked tentatively.

"No more than it would upset you if a lovely, intelligent swan were queen of all humans," Risenmay said.

Kendra scrunched her brow. "That would be weird."

"But not completely undesirable," Risenmay said. "Lovely in some ways. And peculiar that the ruler of humans would not be a human."

"The Fairy Queen can look like a fairy," Kendra said.

"Then imagine instead a swan with a human avatar," Risenmay said. "But first and foremost, a swan."

"I have seen other large fairies," Kendra said. "Were they great fairies?"

"More likely small fairies made large," Risenmay said. "The great fairies were never small. Our powers and comprehension exceed theirs. We can do far more and can be generous benefactors when the mood strikes us. How may I help you?"

"We need transportation," Kendra said.

"Patton suggested you come to me for transportation?" Risenmay asked.

"We all brought mounts," Kendra said. "We have to get to Stormguard Castle an hour after the festival night begins."

Risenmay narrowed her gaze. "Did this stingbulb tell you what I can do?"

"He couldn't," Kendra said.

"That at least is a relief," Risenmay said. "I thought perhaps his temporary reincarnation might have bypassed his pledge to silence. He hinted and then made sure you came prepared."

"Can you help us?" Kendra asked.

"I can," Risenmay said. "But will I?"

Kendra got down on her knees again. "Please, Risenmay, most beautiful of fairies. My friends need help getting here before the festival night begins. And we must reach the castle at the right time, or Wyrmroost might fall to the dragons. All dragon sanctuaries might fall."

Risenmay stifled a little yawn. "You don't know why great fairies take an interest in mortals, do you?"

"I'm not sure," Kendra said.

"You are fairykind," Risenmay said. "I can't read your mind. The wishes of your heart are hidden from me. Hints to what might motivate me survive in some of your stories."

"Cinderella had a fairy godmother," Kendra said.

"Did she?" Risenmay asked innocently.

Kendra thought. What might pique her interest? "The boy I like is in danger."

Risenmay brightened. "You like a boy?"

"I do," Kendra said. "He's older than me, so he's resistant. But he doesn't seem old."

"That sounds thrilling. Do you love him?"

"So much."

Risenmay clapped. "Your love is the important part! I

see that you mean it. Sometimes love is better when not fully returned. Juicier. More interesting."

"I'm so worried about him," Kendra said.

"Is he handsome?" Risenmay asked.

"Insanely handsome," Kendra said. "It's not just me who thinks so—naiads, fairies, everyone!"

Risenmay seemed delighted. "He is mortal?"

"He's a unicorn."

"Wait, really? Does he have a name?"

"Bracken."

Risenmay covered her giggle. "Of course you love Bracken! Who doesn't love Bracken? Sadly, this weakens your case a little. Makes your love a bit more generic. He is so aloof, and admired by all. I'm sorry, my dear."

"He likes me back," Kendra said.

Risenmay looked at her skeptically. "Can you be sure? The youth has a kind and jovial nature often mistaken for affection."

"He gave me his first horn," Kendra said, touching it.

Risenmay's eyes widened. "Did he indeed? Goodness, child. Why didn't you say so? Getting to Stormguard Castle will help your relationship?"

"He's been captured," Kendra said. "Getting to the castle could save him."

Risenmay laughed with delight. "Children!" she called in a singsong tone. "To me, my children! Mummy has an errand for you!"

CHAPTER TWENTY-FOUR

Winging It

"The sun is getting lower," Calvin said.

"That's how it works," Babak said. "After midday. As time passes."

"Right, but when the sun sets, the festival night starts," Calvin said. "And we all die."

"Makes the position of the sun an important topic," Patton said. "We have maybe half an hour left."

"Can we make it back to the Zowali place in half an hour?" Knox asked.

"Maybe," Captain replied, "if we leave now. And we run. And the trees don't mind."

"Are those fairies?" Seth asked, pointing into the Bewilderness.

Patton looked where Seth was pointing and then let

out a whoop. "Kendra did it, friends! Risenmay sent escorts! Mount up!"

As Seth climbed onto Noble, eleven fairies arrived. None looked like the rugged Wyrmroost fairies Seth had seen. These were colorful and delicate.

"Mistress Risenmay requests your presence," one of the fairies announced in her high voice. "We were sent to guide you."

"Lead on," Patton said. "We were hoping you would come."

"Stay with us," the fairy said. "The way ahead is fraught with peril."

Patton took the lead, and Seth rode up beside him. The others fell in line behind. "Kendra made it?" Seth asked. "She's safe? For sure?"

"No doubt," Patton said. "It's the only reason these fairies would come for us. Follow them closely."

The game of follow-the-fairies seemed a little absurd, the route unnecessarily circuitous over uncomfortable terrain. No roads. No paths. Lots of winding.

The talking mounts did not complain and maintained a brisk pace. Seth kept glancing as the sun slipped toward the horizon. Every time they made ridiculous turns that assured an indirect route, Seth clenched his teeth, reminding himself that they were steering around unseen death traps. But the setting sun was a death trap too! Being exposed on Midsummer Eve at Wyrmroost would kill them as surely as anything else.

A little space remained between the sun and the

mountaintops when a promising pond came into view. An island at the center emitted a suspicious glow, and ethereal music chimed in the air. The fairies led them past the pond to an opening in the bluff beyond.

Patton dismounted, and the others followed his lead. The fairies led them into the cavity in the bluff. Despite the close confines, the horses and the camel followed. The way wound back and forth around sharp bends.

Seth emerged into a crystal cavern, where a radiant, human-sized fairy stood in a dazzling white gown. Kendra waved to him. He waved back, relieved to see that his sister was actually all right.

"This is Risenmay," Kendra said.

The fairy was gorgeous. Seth was not sure if he had ever seen a more beautiful woman, even among the Fair Folk.

"Welcome," Risenmay said. "Come inside—there is room for all, horses too. Oh, and a camel and a rabbit! Quite a menagerie! I met you back when you actually existed, Patton Burgess."

"I remember," Patton said. "You look as enchanting as ever."

"Oh, stop," she said, color coming into her cheeks as she brushed a hand across one shimmery hip. "I wasn't expecting company."

Seth rolled his eyes. The fairy looked like she was about to walk the red carpet at the Academy Awards.

"Sun is getting low," Patton said.

"You'll be safe here," Risenmay said. "I would give you shelter for the night, but I understand you hope to make it to Stormguard Castle an hour after the festival night begins."

"That's right," Patton said.

"What's with the island out there?" Seth asked. "It had music."

Risenmay laughed lightly. "I suppose that is terrible of me. It's the last little trick on the way to my abode. A ferocious predator dwells in that pond. More visitors have succumbed to that trap than any others, the poor dears. For some reason, they decide the end of the road is when they should stop following instructions."

"They get eaten?" Seth asked.

"Well, injected with toxins and left to ferment underwater in a gelatinous cocoon," Risenmay said. "But yes, eventually devoured, bones and all."

"How will we get to the castle?" Knox asked.

"Don't be too hasty," Risenmay said. "To time this correctly, you want to wait several minutes before departure. And you must all make a solemn promise."

"What promise?" Seth asked.

"To keep my abilities a secret," Risenmay said.

"It's a generous offer for the aid we will receive," Patton said.

Risenmay extended her hand. "Lay your hands on mine."

"All of us?" Patton asked.

"Yes, well, all of you with hands," Risenmay said.

Seth approached with Patton and the others, including Kendra, and they huddled around Risenmay, arms extended, hands piled on hers.

"Two-four-six-eight, who do we appreciate?" Knox chanted. "Feels like a cheer after a game."

Seth snickered. It kind of did feel like that.

"The little one too," Risenmay prompted.

"I sometimes get forgotten at times like these," Calvin said. Seth helped the nipsie from his pocket and put him on the top hand, which belonged to Lomo. Calvin knelt and placed his hand down.

"Repeat after me," Risenmay said. "I solemnly swear to keep what happens here a secret."

They repeated.

"And I grant Risenmay permission to bind my tongue and hold me to this oath."

They repeated again.

Smiling, Risenmay withdrew her hand. "Marvelous. Now the animals, rabbit included."

Risenmay repeated the exercise surrounded by the animals, each of them touching her with hoof or muzzle. The animals who could talk spoke the words.

"Thank you for being so compliant," Risenmay said. "I felt agreement even from the silent ones. I hope Kendra will be able to recover her true love, and perhaps the high and mighty Bracken will finally succumb to Cupid's arrows."

"Is this about Bracken?" Seth asked.

"Eventually," Kendra said. "We can't save him if we lose the war."

"True," Seth said. He wanted to help Bracken too, but he was unsure why it was suddenly the top concern. His focus was on surviving the night and foiling the dragons.

"What are you going to do?" Knox asked.

"I have many abilities," Risenmay said. "Perhaps my signature talent is the power to bestow wings."

"You're going to give us wings?" Seth asked.

"I prefer not to bestow them upon humanoids," Risenmay said. "I don't want common beings mistaken for fairies. But your mounts are another matter."

"This must be where Mickette got her wings," Charlemagne said.

"What?" Kendra asked.

"Mickette was a mare who showed up with wings one day," Captain said. "Like a Pegasus. She refused to explain the origin."

"She died at a ripe old age," Charlemagne said. "A legend among the Luvians."

Patton was trying to say something.

Risenmay waved a hand at him. "Go ahead, in this company."

"Mickette was my horse," Patton said. "For a time, at least. I brought her here and helped her get wings."

"And you brought us for the same purpose," Seth said.

"Each with a mount," Patton said.

"I'm going to have a flying rabbit!" Calvin exclaimed. "Thistleton, do you want wings?"

"Yeah," Thistleton said. "My family won't believe it."

"Does this hold true for all of you?" Risenmay asked. "Will you accept my gift of wings? I must have confirmation to proceed."

"With these wings we'll be able to fly?" Charlemagne asked. "Like Mickette? Like a Pegasus?"

"The wings would be rather absurd if they didn't enable you to fly," Risenmay said. "These wings will not only let you fly—you'll be able to maneuver really well."

"And we'll always have the wings?" Babak asked.

"Always," Risenmay said. "Though you will not pass them to offspring. And you, sir, would be the first camel I have ever enhanced."

"I might be the first flying camel in history," Babak said. "I know of no others."

"I need confirmation first," Risenmay said.

The five horses, the camel, and the rabbit all assented.

"You're just going to make them sprout wings?" Knox asked incredulously.

"You be the judge," Risenmay said. She spread her arms, and suddenly she gleamed with an intense white light that reflected off the calcite and refracted in the crystals. Vivid rainbows quivered in the intense glare. Risenmay chanted unintelligible words that filled Seth with buoyant excitement.

When she lowered her arms, the radiance dimmed, and Seth was left blinking in an attempt to regulate his eyesight. As his vision adjusted, Seth saw the horses, the camel, and the rabbit all investigating their new wings, experimentally stretching one, or flexing the other, or tentatively flapping both. The rabbit leaped into the air and started darting around the cavern like a bat.

"Looking good, Thistleton," Calvin said.

"I suggest the larger creatures resist the urge to fly until they get outside," Risenmay said. "Looks like the enchantment was successful for all."

Seth crossed to Noble. "You look great," he said.

His horse stamped and tossed his head.

Kendra stroked Glory as the horse nuzzled her. "Won't it be really dangerous riding to Stormguard Castle on a festival night?" Kendra asked.

"Risenmay?" Patton asked.

"I can help there, too," Risenmay said, extending her arms again. A golden light infused the cavern, less intense than the previous glare. When the light faded, a golden glow lingered about the animals, particularly illuminating their wings. "I gave you my blessing. It will ward you from harm for a time, especially from the undead, and it will serve as a powerful distracter spell. As Kendra may have noticed on her way here, diverse attractor and distracter spells are a strength of mine."

Patton clapped his hands and raised both fists in the air. "That was what we needed. Thank you, Risenmay! We're all in your debt."

The beautiful fairy smiled and gave a gracious nod. "You owe me nothing, except to keep the nature of my abilities a secret. Do rain and sunlight ask repayment for the nourishment they provide? Do flowers require recompense from those gazing at their blooms? I help living things to blossom. I am a giver of gifts."

"Unless people die trying to make it here," Seth mumbled.

Risenmay glanced at him archly. "That nourishes the flowers too."

"What's the timing?" Tanu asked.

"We want to get there an hour after the sun goes down,"

Patton said. "Not sooner. Preferably not much later."

"Depart in a few more minutes," Risenmay said. "As the camel flies."

Babak fluttered his wings and hovered a foot or two above the ground for a moment. "Sorry," the camel said. "I know—not inside. It's hard to resist."

"What is the plan when we get there?" Lomo asked.

"I will not be admitted to the castle," Patton said. "Calvin might be denied as well, unless his small size allows admittance. Entering the castle will strip away all magic while you are inside. Potions won't work and magical items will lose their power. Kendra will no longer be fairykind and Seth will not be a shadow charmer. Lomo will lose whatever abilities are part of his nature."

"Not permanently?" Kendra asked.

"Only while inside the castle," Patton said.

"What do you know of conditions inside the castle?" Tanu asked.

Patton gave a weak smile. "Very little. I backed out before fully entering. I crossed the drawbridge to the gate and found a message embossed in a plaque on the wall: 'Conquer or Withdraw.' It was a festival night, but my instincts warned me the castle would be worse. I withdrew."

"Why did you go in the first place?" Lomo wondered.

"Nobody had achieved access to Stormguard Castle," Patton said. "I knew boundaries come down on festival nights, so I gave it a try. Lost two friends that night. Had a hard time making it back to a roadhouse, but I survived."

"So we don't know much," Knox said.

"We know Celebrant will be heading for the castle as well," Seth said. "Or sending other dragons."

"And once they step onto the drawbridge, they will be vulnerable," Patton said. "Mortal."

"I don't mind losing my potions if the dragons lose their powers," Tanu said. "That trade benefits us."

"It does," Patton said. "The problem will be for any of you to survive the cursed castle. The prize is great. Finding the Wizenstone would win the war for whoever claims it. But the obstacles will be significant as well."

"We don't know what to expect from the curse?" Knox asked.

"No idea," Patton said. "Except that none have ever left Stormguard Castle since the curse began, and none who explored in depth ever returned."

"Except you," Seth clarified.

"Well, I stood on the welcome mat and then ran away," Patton said. "I had no compelling reason to risk everything by going inside. Circumstances have changed. You have an excellent reason."

"I recommend leaving now," Risenmay said.

"I wish I could join you inside," Patton said. "Instead, I'll wrangle the mounts, help them get to the nearest road-house after dropping you off."

"Let me fly ahead," Calvin offered. "Thistleton is small. We can scout, see if the dragons are there."

"That could be wise," Patton said with a nod. "Thanks, Calvin."

"Work for you, Seth?" Calvin asked.

"Sure," Seth replied. "Don't get caught."

"I'll keep him safe," Thistleton said. "Climb aboard."

The rabbit landed beside Seth, who took Calvin and placed him on the furry back. Calvin withdrew a tiny sword and waved it in the air. Thistleton took flight and shot out of the cavern.

"The switchbacks on the way out are tight," Patton said. "But we should mount up anyhow. We want to get airborne as soon as we exit. It will be safer in the sky."

"Fly swift and true," Risenmay said. "Nowhere is safe at Wyrmroost tonight."

"Least of all the destination," Patton said. "We may not get to speak again before you enter the castle. Keep your wits about you."

"We'll do our best," Kendra said, relieved to be following what felt right again after having had to fight her true instincts in the Bewilderness.

When Knox climbed onto Babak, Seth longed for a camera as never before. They all had cool flying horses, and Knox had the winged camel. He wanted to preserve the image for future generations.

Seth mounted Noble and patted the horse. "Ready to fly?"

"He can't wait," Captain answered. "None of us can."

"Follow us," Patton said, urging Captain forward.

Seth ducked down as he wound his way out of the cavern atop Noble. When they exited the little cave, Noble sprang into the sky, following Captain, and the ground fell away. Seth observed figures roaming the woods but failed to get a clear view of them. Glancing back, he saw Kendra and the others rising behind him.

Not all light had bled from the horizon yet. The late evening was alive with sounds—drums pounded, beasts roared, victims screamed. Strange music infiltrated the night: unnameable instruments grinding out upsetting chords, foreign words chanted atonally. Chilling groans bespoke misery and longing. Disquieting screeches and bellows originated from unguessable sources.

As Seth scanned the landscape, off to the left he saw an entire tree burst into flame. To the right, a blaze of lightning blasted a natural column of stone. Shadowy giants roamed the wilds below, and winged behemoths created fearsome silhouettes in the sky.

Ephemeral shapes drew toward Seth, forcing Noble to climb and fall and swerve to avoid contact. The ghostly forms had large, grasping hands, wispy as smoke, but the air grew colder when they were near, and Seth could faintly discern their prolonged yearnings of hunger and thirst.

"Stay with me," Patton called, still gaining altitude.

Behind him, Seth saw the others still climbing into the fearful night. Certain sounds grew distant as they flew higher, but some of the most mournful moanings became more distinct.

Most of the ghostly forms moved slowly, drifting more than flying, but one dark shape drew even with Seth; as Noble tried to veer away, the entity stayed near them. More clearly delineated than the other spectral beings, it

looked like a gargoyle made from concentrated darkness.

A dangerous night to fly, shadow charmer.

The icy words entered Seth's mind as distinctly as if he had heard them.

"Leave me alone," Seth said, deliberately not staring at the speaker, but keeping him in his peripheral vision.

I could tear you from the sky, the voice said. *I could gorge myself on your warmth, quench your fragile spark.*

"I'd rather you didn't," Seth said.

You have much to learn, and little time, the chilling voice said. *Let me teach you.*

"I'm on a mission tonight," Seth said.

You could defeat the dragons, the voice said. *Leave their shattered husks in your wake. You could explore a night like this without fear. You could save those you love. You could thrive. Let me teach you.*

"No deals," Seth said, unsure if rejection would make the tenebrous gargoyle attack. "I do things my way."

You soar toward the castle, the voice said. *Your doom awaits. Without my help you will fall.*

"I'm sorry," Seth said. "I don't want help from flying shadow people."

What I now offer cannot be bought, the voice said. *In your hour of need you may regret denying my proposal.*

"I've regretted lots of things," Seth said. "Especially making deals with darkness."

Very well, the voice said. The dark figure swerved away, almost immediately becoming indistinguishable from the rest of the night.

Seth was left with an unsettled feeling.

As if the howls and shrieks and groans and geysers of distant dragon fire weren't scary enough. Now he got to wonder what exactly had approached him.

Stormguard Castle came into view in the distance because it was illuminated. At first Seth thought it might have electricity. A series of swooping dives brought them nearer to the castle. As they approached, Seth recognized magical light globes providing the luminance.

Patton pulled up into a slow glide, and Seth realized Calvin was reporting, astride his rabbit. Seth leaned in their direction, and Noble glided closer. Kendra, Tanu, Lomo, and Knox tightened into formation around Patton as well.

"Three people just entered the castle," said Calvin. "Two wore light armor—the third had a full suit of it. A woman and two men. The guy in the full suit had a dragon on his shield. Might have been Celebrant, but I'm not sure. I assume they were dragons in human form. I got as close as I could, but neither Thistleton nor I could get above the drawbridge. The knight in full armor noticed me and came to take a swipe at me. As I flew away, they entered the castle."

"This was just a minute ago?" Patton asked.

"If that," Calvin said.

"All right," Patton said, glancing over at Seth and the others. "Ready to follow some dragons into Stormguard Castle?"

"I finally get to spend real time with dragons, and

they look like people?" Knox complained.

"You just rode a flying camel through a sky full of ghosts," Seth said. "Be grateful."

Patton urged Captain forward. The others followed.

CHAPTER TWENTY-FIVE

Silver and Gold

Kendra felt relieved to have her feet back on the ground, even if she was standing near the drawbridge of a cursed castle. Being chased through the sky by shadowy phantoms with a horror soundtrack in the background had negated the fun of riding a flying horse.

"Thank you, Glory," Kendra said, petting her mount. "Stay safe."

"Good luck," Patton said. "I'll get our trusty steeds to a roadhouse and come for you after sunrise."

"Let me try to enter one more time," Calvin said, dismounting Thistleton and sprinting toward the castle. Once he reached the drawbridge, he collided with an unseen barrier and stumbled backward.

"Don't try to force it, Calvin," Patton said. "It could kill you."

"Wraiths," Lomo warned.

Kendra turned and found six dark forms striding toward them, having emerged from the nearest grove of trees. Lomo drew his sword and placed himself between the wraiths and the group.

"Get to the drawbridge," Patton said from astride Captain. "Horses, camel, rabbit—with me!"

Captain took flight, and the other mounts followed. Calvin had climbed back onto Thistleton, and the rabbit took to the air as well.

Kendra hurried toward the drawbridge. The moment her feet were on the wood, the boisterous noise of the festival night ceased. Sword held ready, still facing the oncoming wraiths, Lomo was the last to back onto the drawbridge.

The wraiths hesitated at the edge of the drawbridge. One tried to move forward and was hurled back with a sizzling flash, falling to the ground. Kendra felt some relief. At least she might not die in the icy clutches of a wraith tonight. The fallen wraith arose. The other wraiths milled about for a moment before withdrawing some distance. They huddled together, seeming to watch.

"Why is it so quiet?" Knox asked.

"Because you aren't talking," Seth said.

"The defensive barrier of the castle seems to filter everything," Tanu said. "Even sound."

"Unusually powerful," Lomo said.

Drawing his sword, Seth led the way across the drawbridge. At the far side of the bridge, a raised portcullis granted access to the castle.

"Not so fast," Tanu said. "Give the dragons a moment. We don't want to enter right behind them."

"Think we could catch them by surprise?" Lomo asked.

"It would be nice if they don't know we're here for a time," Tanu said. "Celebrant in full armor could be more of a fight than any of us are prepared to handle."

"It might not be Celebrant," Kendra said.

"I suspect it is," Lomo said. "The Wizenstone is too powerful. He would not trust his underlings enough to send any of them unsupervised. He undoubtedly wants the Wizenstone for himself."

"We have to break the curse by sunrise, don't we?" Seth asked. "At least that's when the festival night ends. How long do we wait?"

"Not long," Tanu said.

"Think they have alligators?" Knox asked, peering off the edge of the drawbridge into the murky water of the moat.

"Probably worse," Seth said. "We're at a dragon sanctuary. Think monsters."

Knox backed away from the edge.

Kendra looked up at the castle. Though enormous, even at night, it did not look terribly sinister. Walls of gray stone topped with battlements stretched from one rounded tower to another. Beyond the outer wall, a mounting series of towers, balconies, terraces, walkways, chimneys, and rooftops piled in an artful jumble up to the highest pinnacles.

"All right," Tanu said softly. "Stay quiet. We want to keep the element of surprise."

"This must be where Patton turned back," Seth said, pointing to the wall just beyond the portcullis.

CONQUER OR WITHDRAW

Kendra looked behind her and saw the wraiths waiting at the other end of the drawbridge. "I'm not sure retreat is an option now," she said.

"In we go," Tanu whispered.

As Seth stepped off the drawbridge into the tunnel through the gate, the splash of a gong reverberated from deep within the castle. Kendra flinched at the loud noise, then winced as it sounded again when Lomo entered the tunnel.

"Let's enter together," Tanu whispered. He, Kendra, and Knox stepped into the tunnel at the same time and were greeted by three rapid crashes of the gong. After a moment the metallic shimmer faded into silence.

"So much for surprise," Kendra murmured.

"Will there be monsters?" Knox asked.

"There could be anything," Lomo said. "Stay loose."

At the far side of the tunnel through the wall, they found a wide courtyard dominated by a large fountain in the center. Water gushed from several spouts to tumble from one level to another before reaching the large basin at the bottom. Life-sized human statues, each composed of silver or gold, stood around the courtyard seemingly at random, most positioned as if running. A few gold statues were locked in frozen combat with silver ones. One pair wrestled on the ground.

"Those look expensive," Knox said.

Seth crouched down at the far end of the tunnel, where he found large words emblazoned on the floor. Kendra and the others huddled near him.

SHED NO BLOOD
BREAK NO BONE
STOP NO HEART

"Think the dragons will play by the castle rules?" Kendra asked.

"Depends on what they think they can get away with," Tanu said.

"This warning is likely connected to the curse," Lomo said. "Whatever the dragons decide to do, we should heed the command."

Seth sheathed his sword. Lomo did likewise.

"Are those statues pure gold?" Knox asked, crossing to the nearest one.

"Don't touch it," Tanu said. "We don't understand what is going on here yet."

"The poses are strange," Kendra said. "Running and fighting."

"I don't see any living people," Seth said.

Kendra scanned the quiet courtyard and the still castle. "Neither do I."

Lomo leaned in close to the statue beside Knox. "That's real gold. At least the exterior. Probably not solid gold all the way through." He glanced around at some of the other statues. "Nobody has that much wealth."

"Can we still exit?" Seth asked.

"Good question," Tanu said, trotting back to the tunnel through the wall. He banged against an invisible barrier at the mouth of the tunnel and stumbled backward, then turned and gave a sheepish grin. "Looks like we're trapped here."

"So much detail on these statues," Knox said, reaching a hand toward a golden face.

"No touching," Tanu reminded him.

"Exquisite," Lomo agreed. "Each a true individual."

"They could be real people," Kendra said. "Turned into gold and silver."

"The thought crossed my mind," Tanu said.

"The silver ones should be tarnished," Lomo said, investigating a silver woman running with a sword in her hand. "But they look brand-new."

"Magic," Seth said.

"Greetings," a voice boomed.

They all turned.

A large, bearded man had exited one of the nearest castle doors. Broad-shouldered and large-bellied, he walked toward them. He wore princely attire and had a silver glove on one hand. "I would say welcome, but there is little to recommend this ill-fated place."

"Greetings," Lomo said, placing himself between the

newcomer and the others. "May I ask whom we have the pleasure of meeting?"

The man gave a light chuckle. "That question is mine, being master of this castle."

"King Hollorix?" Lomo asked.

"The king is . . . unavailable," the man said. "I am his eldest son, Tregain, regent of Stormguard Castle."

Seth put a hand on his sword. "Tregain?"

"Draw the sword, boy," Tregain encouraged.

Seth drew it and held it up.

"Bless my soul," Tregain said. "My boyhood weapon. How did you come by that?"

"The armory at Blackwell Keep," Seth said.

"Then you are friends of the caretaker," Tregain said. "Hold." He held up a hand, looking at Kendra. "I see the medallion? Has one so young truly taken charge of Wyrmroost?"

"We're both caretakers," Seth said. "It's her turn to wear it."

"I can't help noticing your glove," Tanu said.

Tregain gave a charming smile. "You have a good eye."

"Might it have anything to do with the silver figures?" Tanu asked.

"A worthy inquiry," Tregain said. "I'll not blame you for keeping some distance. Come with me. We must talk. The night is never long enough."

"Are you the only person here?" Lomo asked.

Tregain's expression became grave. "There is another. A very dangerous man. He nabbed the attention of the three who came before you." Tregain turned away from them. "This way."

Kendra looked at Tanu, who shrugged. They fell into step behind Tregain. He led them through a door, down a hall, up some stairs, and down another hall. Globes of light brightened the hallways much as they illuminated the castle's exterior. Lomo moved to walk nearest to Tregain.

She almost cried out when a hand tugged on her sleeve. Kendra whirled to find a skinny young boy of perhaps eight or nine, with tousled black hair and ragged clothes. He held one finger over his lips, dark eyes pleading for silence.

Pausing, Kendra watched the others proceed down the hall. Nobody was looking back. The kid motioned her toward a square hole low in a nearby wall.

Kendra pointed to Seth and her friends.

The boy scowled and shook his head, ducking nimbly into the hole and gesturing for her to follow. Kendra crouched and looked inside. It led into an extremely narrow passage behind the wall.

She felt torn. Seth and the others would be panicked if she vanished. But this boy might know things! He was waving her toward him. Could it be a trick? He seemed eager and nervous.

Kendra crawled into the hole, and the boy slid a panel to cover it, leaving them in darkness.

Real darkness.

Actual darkness.

It had been a long time since Kendra had experienced

real darkness. Since she had become fairykind, no darkness had been complete. At least not while she was awake.

"Don't be scared," the boy whispered.

"Who are you?" Kendra asked.

"Augie," he said. "None of them know about me. Everyone forgot me. Just a servant. No fancy connections. I've been hiding."

"All these years?" Kendra asked.

"All these years," he said. "We don't get older here."

"We?"

"Me and the brothers, King Hollorix's sons," Augie said. "We're the only ones not turned to gold or silver."

"Three brothers?" Kendra asked.

"Well, two," Augie said. "One disappeared."

"Hiding?" Kendra asked. "Like you?"

"Maybe," he said. "If so, he's good. I haven't found him."

"Why did you grab me?" Kendra asked.

"You're a kid," Augie said. "I figured I should help you. The other two were too far forward. Too close to Tregain."

"Will my friends be safe?" Kendra asked.

"Nothing here is safe," the boy whispered. "Nobody is safe."

"Will Tregain turn them to silver?" Kendra asked.

"You figured that out already?" he asked. "Good job."

"Do I need to warn them?" Kendra asked.

"We don't get many visitors here," Augie said. "Almost never. Before he makes a move to change them, he'll try to recruit them."

"For what?"

"For help," Augie whispered. "Winning the contest." He took her hand. "This way."

A pair of silver guards flanked the tall silver doors that Tregain opened. Seth had noticed several silver blocks among the stones composing the walls of the hallway. And now he noticed something even more important. "Where's Kendra?"

Seth, Knox, Lomo, and Tanu exchanged worried looks. Kendra was nowhere in view.

Lomo ran back the way they had come, passing out of sight around a corner. Tanu confronted Tregain. "Did you do something?"

"Of course not, friend. Your eyes were on me the whole time," Tregain replied.

They could hear Lomo calling for Kendra. The tone of his voice suggested that he was searching, not that he had seen her.

"An accomplice?" Seth asked.

"My accomplices are frozen in silver, lad," Tregain said, holding up the glove and flexing his fingers. "My aim right now is to talk."

"What could have happened to her?" Tanu asked.

Tregain shrugged. "The dangerous man is occupied with the three other strangers. He does not haunt the halls in this wing."

"Then what happened?" Seth asked.

"There is nobody else here," Tregain said. "She must have wandered off. Which is odd, because I was trying to keep my eyes on you."

"Should we spread out and search?" Knox asked.

"We need to talk first," Tregain said. "There are things you must know and matters we must settle."

"We need to make sure Kendra is all right," Seth said.

Lomo ran back into view. "I retraced our steps to the courtyard," he reported. "No sign of her. No answer to my calls."

"Talk to me before you search," Tregain said, walking through the silver doors.

"I'll keep looking," Lomo said.

"I'll help," Knox offered.

"Try not to disappear," Tanu said.

"We'll meet you back here," Lomo promised.

Seth and Tanu followed Tregain into a posh room where all the furniture was made of polished silver. Many of the floor tiles and blocks in the wall were silver as well.

"You turn things to silver?" Seth asked.

"With this glove, yes," Tregain said, sitting down on a silver chair. "Sit if you wish."

"We'll stand," Tanu said.

"It isn't contagious," Tregain said. "You won't turn to silver by sitting on the furniture."

"Why turn things to silver?" Seth asked.

"Why indeed?" Tregain asked. "The blasted contest."

"What contest?" Tanu asked.

"After all this time, word has never spread?" Tregain asked.

"Word doesn't get out," Tanu replied.

"A vile dwarf named Humbuggle tempted my father," Tregain said. "He established a contest, to be won by one of the king's three sons. Until the contest ends, the castle remains cursed."

"What is the contest?" Seth asked.

"More about that later," Tregain said. "For now, let it suffice that my glove can turn people and objects to silver. My brother Heath can similarly change objects to gold. Gold and silver help establish allegiance."

"You turned all of those people to silver?" Seth asked.

"They are not dead," Tregain said. "Just preserved that way for now. Which is partly why you interest me. I could use some fleshy partners. Swear to serve me in helping me win the contest, swear to help me win the prize, and we can work together."

"What is the prize?" Tanu asked.

"A bauble, really," Tregain said casually. "A stone that serves as the trophy. What I most want is to break the curse and free my parents."

"Where are your parents?" Seth asked.

"Trapped in the highest room of the castle until the contest ends," Tregain said. "I must claim the stone to free them."

"Why not work with your brother?" Seth asked.

"Because it is a contest," Tregain said. "And he cannot be trusted."

Seth glanced at Tanu. Tregain was obviously not being honest about the Wizenstone. Was it possible he didn't know?

"How do we win the contest?" Tanu asked.

"I may tell you after you pledge," Tregain said. "You would be wise to work with me. None of us can leave the castle until the contest is won."

"And it has been going for a long time," Seth said.

Tregain seemed to gaze into the distance. "A great while, yes. Years upon years."

"Any chance we solve it tonight?" Seth asked.

Tregain gave a hearty laugh. "Not unless you work with me and work quickly."

"Why not be content if we win the contest and break the curse?" Tanu asked. "Why must we work for you?"

"I want the stone," Tregain said. "I want the prize. It is a matter of pride. I have been after it for centuries. I will have the stone, sooner or later. If you help me, we will all gain our freedom sooner."

"Why don't we just agree to work together?" Tanu asked. "Must there be pledges?"

Tregain's eyes hardened. "There must. I am lord of this castle. I have labored here a long time. I have the know-how. You work either for me or against me."

"And if we work against you?" Tanu asked.

Tregain raised his gloved hand, waggling his fingers. "There are other means of persuasion."

"You'll turn us to silver," Tanu said.

"I'll claim you for my side," Tregain said. "But let's keep this pleasant."

"Threats are not pleasant," Tanu said. "Seth, run."

"But—" Seth began.

"Now," Tanu said, his stern tone allowing no argument. "Warn the others."

Tregain leaped from his chair, grabbing for Tanu. The potion master avoided the gloved hand as Seth backed toward the open doors. When Tregain changed course for Seth, the potion master tackled him from behind.

The last thing Seth saw before he fled the room was the gloved hand on Tanu's shoulder. From that point of contact, silver spread quickly across Tanu until he was a solid silver statue.

CHAPTER TWENTY-SIX

Contest

"Kendra! Kendra?"

She heard Lomo calling her name. "Can I answer?" Kendra whispered.

"Not if you want my help," Augie said, halting in the darkness.

"You can trust my friends," Kendra said.

"I can't trust you," Augie said. "I'm not going to show you the best secrets. I just can't. I survived this long by staying out of the contest. Because you're a kid, I wanted to give you a chance."

"Kendra?" Lomo called again, his voice more distant. "Make a noise if you can hear me."

"I don't want them to worry about me," Kendra whispered.

"It won't kill them," Augie said. "If they're looking for

you, it might help keep Tregain from entrapping them. At least for a little while."

"You told me he would recruit them," Kendra said.

"Probably at first," Augie said. "Tregain is as paranoid as Heath. They both have recruited live people from time to time. We've had a few visitors over the years. They all get turned to silver or gold. No truce lasts long. The brothers don't trust anybody. Once the people have been changed, the brothers know what side they're on."

"What is the contest?" Kendra asked.

"The dwarf set it up," the boy said.

"What dwarf?"

"Humbuggle," the boy said. "A magical trickster. Do you know about the prize?"

"I think so," Kendra said. "Do you?"

"Of course I know," Augie said. "A legendary magical object. You tell me."

"The Wizenstone," Kendra whispered.

"Yes, that's right," Augie said. "Not everyone knows this."

"The dragons know," Kendra said.

"Are dragons with you?" Augie asked apprehensively.

"They came before us," Kendra said.

"The three warriors," Augie said. "I saw them. They look tough. Heavy armor. Big weapons."

"If the dragons get the Wizenstone, they'll use it to destroy all dragon sanctuaries and take over the world."

"What would you use it for?" Augie asked.

"To stop them," Kendra said. "To keep the world safe."

"What else?" Augie asked. "It's supposed to be incredibly powerful."

"To do good," Kendra said. "And I'd try to keep it out of evil hands. I've already helped do the same with other magical items of great power."

"What items?" Augie asked.

"The keys to the demon prison," Kendra said. "You've probably never heard of the Chronometer or the Sands of Sanctity."

"I know more about stuff here at the castle," Augie said.

"So, what is the contest?" Kendra repeated.

"Tregain and Heath would never tell you the whole story," Augie said. "The dwarf recited a poem at the start of the contest all those years ago."

"Do you know it?" Kendra asked.

"Sure," he said, and proceeded to recite the poem:

> *"To find your way to treasure untold*
> *A coin of platinum, silver, and gold*
> *Must each be placed in the fountain clear*
> *All together or they disappear*
> *The golden touch can hold but one*
> *Another for silver and platinum*
> *Elusive though these coins may be*
> *Go pay the price of liberty."*

"What coins?" Kendra asked.

"That part has been solved," Augie said. "At least partially. From time to time the brothers have found a silver coin imprinted with the face of Humbuggle, a gold coin with the dwarf's profile, and a platinum coin that shows his full body. They have found them and lost them time and again over all these years."

"All they have to do is throw the coins in the fountain?" Kendra asked.

"Apparently," Augie said. "I stay out of it."

"Don't you want the contest to end?" Kendra asked.

"I want to survive it," Augie said. "Everyone who gets involved ends up silver or gold."

"Stay away from Tregain!" Seth shouted from a distance. "He turned Tanu silver! Can you hear me? Watch out for Tregain!"

"We have to help him," Kendra said.

"Wait here," Augie said. She heard him moving away in the darkness.

"Tregain turned Tanu silver!" Seth called, his voice closer. "Can anybody hear me?"

"I hear you!" Knox called from a distance.

"Me too!" Lomo cried faintly.

Several paces away, a panel slid aside, letting light into the dark space between walls. Augie leaned out through the opening, then came back in. Seth followed. He looked Kendra's way, and she waved. The panel slid, and darkness resumed.

Just outside the dark passage, heavy footfalls approached and paused. Was Tregain crouching to slide open the panel? Was he just listening? The footfalls resumed and moved away.

"No noise," Augie whispered after a quiet moment. "Follow me."

He took Kendra's hand, and she took Seth's. Augie led them forward, down a ladder, and around a couple of corners.

"Are you all right?" Kendra whispered to her brother.

"I'm fine," he said. "Tanu is silver."

"I heard," Kendra said. "That's terrible." She could hardly believe the potion master was now a statue. There had to be a way to turn him back.

"Hush," Augie cautioned. "If Tregain finds us, we'll all be silver."

Augie ducked down, and Kendra followed him, crawling along a cramped little tunnel. Eventually he helped her to her feet again. Seth emerged behind her.

Augie opened a panel, and they ducked into a bedroom.

"I leave you here," Augie said.

"Wait," Kendra said. "Tell us more."

"I told you enough," Augie said.

"You didn't tell me anything," Seth complained. "I'm Seth."

"This is Augie," Kendra said.

"Going around with you would be the end of me," Augie said. "I don't think you're going to make it."

"Why not?" Kendra asked.

"You want to win the contest," Augie said.

Kendra looked at Seth.

"We want to win it tonight," Seth said.

Augie smiled as if embarrassed for him. "Good luck."

"What was the rhyme again?" Kendra asked. "The one from Humbuggle?"

Augie repeated the rhyme for Seth.

"It's the contest rules," Kendra said. "Three coins have to go into the fountain at the same time."

"Be careful of the statues," Augie said. "If you touch them, you will also get turned to the same material. The statues change only living things. The gloves change almost everything."

"Thanks for the advice," Kendra said.

"Good-bye," Augie said, sliding aside a panel to enter the wall.

"Wait," Kendra said. "What if we want to go inside the walls too?"

"No way," Augie said. "It's how I stay alive. I don't want you two blundering around. If you draw attention to these passages, I'll end up silver or gold."

"What if we go into the passages anyway?" Seth asked.

"You might get caught in one of my traps," Augie said. "Or I might give you away. I helped you this time. I told you what I know. Don't make me sorry I reached out. Let me go. And leave me alone."

"Let him leave," Kendra said.

"But he could help us win," Seth said.

"He doesn't want to help," Kendra said.

"I'd help if I thought it would do any good," Augie said. "I'd rather survive. Please don't tell anyone about me."

"We'll try to keep your secrets," Kendra said.

"Good luck," Augie said, nimbly ducking into the hole in the wall and sliding the panel to conceal it.

Seth crouched and stared. "That's a good secret passage. I know it's there but can barely see it."

"Tanu is silver?" Kendra checked.

Seth nodded. "And Tregain is after us. Probably Heath too, before long. His is the gold team. Don't forget the dragons roaming around. And we need to find coins. I keep wanting to talk to Calvin and then remembering he's not here."

"Let's try to find Knox and Lomo," Kendra said.

"And avoid getting tagged," Seth said.

"Think we can change Tanu back?" Kendra asked, trying to hold her emotions in check.

"Hopefully, if we break the curse," Seth said.

They crept quietly from the room and into the hall.

Knox lay behind the bed in the room where Lomo had told him to wait, trying to stay calm. He had heard Seth calling out that Tanu had been turned to silver. Lomo had gone after Seth and suggested Knox hide so they could find him if they escaped Tregain.

But what if Tregain found him first? What if he came into the room? What if he looked behind the bed? Knox knew he would be cornered. He would spend the rest of his days as a silver statue.

Knox closed his eyes and rubbed them, trying to banish the worries. He had volunteered for this! What was the matter with him? He had come to Wyrmroost on purpose! What had he been thinking?

It had seemed magical and cool. He had wanted to help

Seth and Kendra, but did he really have anything to contribute? He had reasoned that anything Seth could do, he could do, no problem.

Wasn't that true? Wasn't he just as good as Seth? Or better?

Knox wasn't so sure anymore.

Seth could ride a flying horse through skies full of ghosts like it was normal. Seth stared down wraiths and entered cursed castles and didn't crack under enormous pressure.

Knox resolved that he wouldn't crack either. Even if he should. Even if he was in way over his head.

If Tregain entered the room, Knox would dodge him. But Tregain was in a hurry. If he came this way, he would probably peek in the room and keep moving down the hall.

Knox waited. And listened.

He heard some footfalls a couple of times. Thankfully, they did not come right by his room, and they eventually dwindled into silence.

Knox jumped and gasped when Lomo peeked around the bed. Lomo raised a finger to his lips with one hand and held up his boots with another. "Lose your footwear," he whispered.

Knox tugged his shoes off without untying the laces. "For quietness," he whispered back.

Lomo nodded. "Seth got away. I followed Tregain long enough to see that he is wandering blind, hoping to get lucky. I wonder how long it has been since he chased somebody. He did not seem terribly good at it."

"What now?" Knox asked.

"We try to find Kendra and Seth," Lomo said. "We stay away from guys with gold or silver gloves. We try not to get killed by the dragons who preceded us. And we try to learn what is going on here and how to break the curse."

"We're in big trouble, aren't we?" Knox asked.

"I'm not sure it gets much bigger," Lomo replied. "Come on."

❧ ❧ ❧

"Do you ever get bored inside of cursed castles?" Seth asked, moving carefully along a hallway with his sister, straining to hear footsteps.

"No," Kendra answered.

"I do, apparently," Seth said. "Are we just going to wander the night away?"

"I don't know," Kendra said. "I kind of agree with Augie that if we don't get turned to statues, we're doing pretty well."

They rounded a corner and both jumped. Only a few feet away, a silver figure was positioned as if running toward them, a determined look on his face.

"This is a person," Seth said. "Not a statue."

"Yes," Kendra said. "Doesn't look like a soldier. Maybe a servant?"

"Do you think somebody will find us like this someday?" Seth asked.

"Not if we avoid getting turned to silver or gold," Kendra said.

"Do you think this guy feels like he got second place?"

Seth asked. "With all the gold statues around?"

"Platinum is more valuable than gold," Kendra said.

"Ouch," Seth said. "Third."

"I haven't seen any platinum, though," Kendra said.

"Wait, doesn't platinum look like silver?" Seth asked. "Maybe this guy is platinum?"

"I'm not sure how to tell," Kendra said. "Augie told me the third brother disappeared."

"Does that mean no third glove?" Seth asked. "Wasn't there supposed to be one of each?"

"I think so," Kendra said.

"You need to talk more quietly," Lomo said, coming around the corner behind them. Seth jumped and turned, his sword halfway out of the sheath before he realized he didn't need it.

"I guess we stopped whispering," Seth said.

"Let's start again," Lomo said.

"We were looking for you," Kendra whispered.

"We were looking for you, too," Knox said. "I'm glad you don't look like the top of a trophy."

"Why are you carrying your shoes?" Seth asked. "Wait— same reason we're whispering. But my boots are magically stealthy . . . oh, not in here, I guess." Kendra and Seth crouched and removed their footwear.

"How did you elude him?" Lomo asked.

"Tanu bought me some time," Seth said. "Then a secret person helped me."

"Seth," Kendra admonished.

"I won't say too much," Seth said. "But he's a secret kid

who has hidden well enough to avoid becoming silver or gold all these years."

"Really?" Lomo asked.

"All he asked was that we keep him a secret," Kendra said.

"But you need to know what he told us," Seth said.

Kendra proceeded to explain what they had learned about the brothers and the poem. Seth thought that together they remembered the lines pretty well.

"We're hunting coins," Lomo whispered. "At least that gives us an objective." He held up a hand. Faintly they heard hurried footsteps.

Lomo motioned the three of them down the hall, around a corner, and into a room. "I'll go investigate," he whispered.

"We shouldn't all wait in the same room," Seth whispered.

Lomo gave a nod. Leaving Kendra and Knox behind, Seth tiptoed across the hall to a different room while Lomo crept away.

Seth decided the best hiding place was behind a wardrobe, because behind the bed was the more obvious spot. He carefully slid his sword out of the sheath. At the entrance they had been warned not to shed blood. Would that warning stop the dragons? What kind of penalty would there be?

He waited tensely until Lomo returned. The warrior beckoned to Seth, and they went into the room with Kendra and Knox.

"One of the dragons," Lomo whispered, "a woman—

green hair, dressed for battle—is moving quickly and search-ing. I worried she might have sensed me, but I hurried away without her following."

"Lots of people are looking for us," Knox said.

"She might be looking for us specifically," Lomo whis-pered. "Or she might primarily be helping the gold brother find coins. Hard to be sure."

"Heath," Kendra said.

"There are too many people working against us," Seth said.

"Can the dragons kill us?" Kendra asked. "The sign at the entrance said to shed no blood."

"I wondered about that," Seth said. "I hope the dragons obey the sign."

"What should we do?" Knox asked.

"Every option is risky," Lomo whispered. "I don't think we win this if we behave like the hunted. We need to search too."

CHAPTER TWENTY-SEVEN

Quiet

Kendra padded down the hall, wearing only socks on her feet and making almost no sound. She, Knox, and Seth had stashed their shoes under the bed before leaving the room. Currently out of view, Lomo was scouting ahead, returning periodically to help them avoid any of the others searching the castle. Seth and Knox walked with Kendra, peeking into every room they passed.

They encountered many silver and gold statues, sometimes solitary, sometimes in small groups. Most were posed as if in motion, walking or running. Kendra could not help wondering who each golden or silver figure had been and how long they had been incarcerated as a precious metal.

Lomo trotted back into sight with a finger over his lips. He pointed in one direction, then another, and then waved them forward. As Kendra followed him at a quickened pace, she heard footsteps from the left and the right.

Lomo paused at a heavy door bound in iron and eased it open, motioning for them to pass through the doorway and head down the stairs. Seth and Knox led the way down, Kendra followed, and Lomo came last, easing the door shut with barely a click.

The stairs descended a good distance to a small room with an iron door. Lomo did not look hopeful when he tried it, but the door opened. More stairs beyond led down into gloomier lighting.

"The dungeon?" Seth whispered.

"Might be as good a place as any for us to look," Lomo said.

"What are the chances of finding a coin in such a big castle?" Knox asked. "We're looking around like we expect them to be in plain sight. What if they're in a drawer? Or inside a mattress? Or hidden away in a silver pocket?"

"If we look too closely, we may not cover much ground," Kendra said.

"Covering lots of ground doesn't help unless we find something," Knox said.

"Supposedly the coins have been found before," Kendra said. "That means we have a chance. The coins do keep getting lost, though."

Lomo started leading the way down the stairs. The glowing globes were becoming less bright and less frequent.

"The poem talked about the coins disappearing if not placed in the fountain together," Seth said.

"And the golden touch can hold only one," Kendra said.

"Do they disappear forever?" Knox said. "Or do they just get transported somewhere? It doesn't make sense. This whole contest seems impossible."

Kendra quietly agreed.

"It's been going for a long time for a reason," Seth said. "Finding the coins is the only way out of this cursed castle. What else are we supposed to do?"

The stairs ended, and now they could see rows of cell doors, each with a peephole. "No statues down here," Kendra said.

Lomo peeked into a cell. "Empty." He tried the door and it opened.

Knox pulled a different door open. Lomo leaped in his direction and pushed it shut. "Look first," Lomo warned.

"Sorry, right," Knox said. "I didn't see anybody."

Lomo tried the peephole. "Neither do I."

"I can usually sense the undead," Seth said, "but the curse inside this castle is blocking any feeling one way or another. At least no one is paralyzed by fear."

Kendra moved along the aisle of cells, spying first, then opening doors. "The dungeon is deserted."

"Only one hall so far," Seth observed. "Easy place to get cornered if anyone follows us."

"Maybe a good place to hide a coin," Knox said.

"As good as any," Kendra said.

After the hall turned a corner, it forked. Both passages looked similar—gloomy stone hallways lined with cell doors.

"Stay together?" Seth asked.

"I think so," Lomo said.

They veered right and moved down the hall, checking all the doors. A big iron door awaited at the end of the hall. After opening it a crack and peering inside, Lomo hauled it open.

Beyond they found a large room. A golden statue stood in there, facing a tall cabinet of the sort a stage magician might invite an assistant to enter.

"Quiet Box," Kendra said.

"I believe so," Lomo agreed.

"What's a Quiet Box?" Knox asked.

"It holds one prisoner," Seth said. "Always one prisoner. The only way to get the prisoner out is to put a new prisoner inside. Whoever is trapped inside gets sort of frozen in time."

"Who would be inside the Quiet Box of a cursed castle?" Kendra wondered. "Could it be an ally? Or a terrible enemy?"

"Hard to guess," Lomo said. "They are usually used for the most deplorable criminals. The kind who might tend to escape from lesser confinement."

"Could be a demon," Seth said. "Nagi Luna was in a Quiet Box."

"Somebody got turned to gold down here," Kendra said. "She was looking at the box." She leaned close to the figure, staring into the young woman's gilded eyes. They were more detailed and lifelike than most statues.

"Maybe she was trying to get somebody out of the Quiet Box," Seth said.

"Or maybe she had just put somebody inside," Kendra guessed.

They stood together in front of the golden woman, staring at the Quiet Box.

"Could they hide a coin in there?" Knox asked.

"If somebody had it on their person," Lomo said. "It would be a clever place to conceal one."

"I guess we can't peek inside?" Knox asked.

"If we open the box, it will look empty," Kendra explained. "One of us would have to get inside and close the door. It will turn halfway around, and when you open the box again, the prisoner will be there."

"And will be free to leave," Lomo said. "The occupant could be incredibly dangerous."

"Isn't the whole situation incredibly dangerous?" Seth asked. "Maybe whoever is inside can stir things up."

"Or eat us up," Kendra said.

"It's a risk," Lomo said.

"Somebody good might have gotten placed in there," Seth said. "Or might have even hidden in there."

"Ah!" Knox cried, leaping forward and shaking one hand. "I brushed against the statue!"

"Where?" Kendra asked, surprised to see they were standing so near to the woman. "Was her arm reaching out like that before?"

"My thumb," Knox said. "The tip is gold. Oh no, it's spreading!" He held up his hand, and Kendra watched his thumb turn gold down to the base. Then the gold started to advance across his palm.

"She's moving," Lomo said. "Look at her hand."

Kendra watched the golden figure for a moment, and

she saw the hand moving ever so slowly toward her, the fingers slightly changing position, slower than the second hand on a clock. "She snuck up on us!"

"My whole hand is gold," Knox cried, on the verge of hysterics. "It's creeping up my wrist. It's not stopping."

"We'll fix it," Kendra promised, hoping they could deliver.

"It took Tanu only a couple of seconds to change," Seth said. "It was faster, but the glove had a hold of him."

"I barely got touched," Knox said. "Slower fuse. Same result, though." He turned to the golden woman. "Thanks a lot, lady!"

"It's getting your shirt, too," Kendra said. His sleeve was turning gold, the transformation trickling up his forearm.

"I can barely feel my fingers," Knox said.

"But you can feel them?" Lomo asked.

"A little," Knox said.

"Interesting, since it looks like pure gold," Lomo said.

"Almost to my elbow," Knox said, panic in his tone. He looked urgently at Kendra. "This is it. You guys were right. I shouldn't have come."

"You've done great," Kendra said, trying to be brave and sound calm. "We'll find a way to undo this."

"Oh man," Knox said, stomping in place. "Good-bye, elbow. Guys, tell my parents I love them. And Tess."

"We'll save you," Seth said.

Knox gave a terrified laugh. "Right. Find that magic lotion that turns statues back into people. Good luck." He looked to Kendra. "If you can, tell my family. I love you guys, too." He looked to Seth. "Sorry for calling you Seth Breath so much. Sorry for all of this. I meant to help."

"Get into the Quiet Box," Seth said.

"What?" Knox replied.

"It should stop the change," Seth said.

"He's right," Lomo said. "The transformation will halt while you're inside."

"That will be fun to think about for hours," Knox said. "Or days. Or years."

"It'll be like a dream," Seth said. "You won't really notice the time going by. We'll try to leave you in there until we have a solution."

"What if putting me inside frees a demon?" Knox asked.

"Let us worry about that," Seth said.

"If we're going to free the prisoner, now is the time," Kendra said. "It costs one of us to get the prisoner out."

Seth opened the Quiet Box. "If we change our minds and have to put the prisoner back inside, sorry in advance."

"Hurry," Kendra said. "It's to your shoulder."

"I guess some chance is better than none," Knox said, gold spreading toward his neck and chest and down his side. He stepped into the empty cabinet. "Good luck."

Seth closed the door.

The box rotated 180 degrees.

Seth opened the door on the opposite side.

Within the space Knox should have occupied stood a handsome young man, lean and tall, with fairly large hands and feet, and brown stubble on his chin. He wore a bright, silvery glove on one hand.

"Is it over?" the young man asked.

"Glove!" Kendra called, backing away from him.

The young man glanced at the golden figure. "No. Still going." He held up his gloved hand. "Don't worry, I'm not going to touch you. Unless you mean me harm. Who are you people?"

"We came here today," Seth said. "We're trying to break the curse."

"What is the year?" the young man asked.

Kendra told him the date.

The young man frowned. "I was in there for a long time. It was impossible to discern how long. It feels like I could have entered a few minutes ago instead of centuries. Mind if I come out?"

Lomo had his sword in hand. "Just keep your distance."

"Sure," the young man said. "I'm sorry, I take it you've met my brothers?"

"We met Tregain," Seth said. "He turned our friend to silver."

"Tregain and Heath transformed everyone," the young man said. "I'm sorry about your friend."

"You're Lockland," Kendra guessed.

The young man gave a small bow. "Unfortunately, yes." He held up his hand. "Platinum glove."

"Seth, the golden girl is slowly coming your way," Kendra said.

Seth moved a couple of steps away.

"We didn't know they could move," Seth said.

"Only on festival nights," Lockland replied. "They speed up over the course of the night."

"At first they weren't moving?" Lomo asked.

"Infinitesimally," Lockland said. "By the end of the night they will be almost as fast as a normal person."

"Not comforting," Kendra said.

"Nothing here is comforting," Lockland said. "I went into the box for a reason."

"You went inside on purpose?" Seth asked.

"Absolutely," Lockland said. "You can only play a rigged game for so long."

"Rigged?" Seth asked.

"You know about the coins?" Lockland asked.

"Yes," Kendra said.

"I played differently than my brothers," Lockland said. "I didn't try to build an army of platinum slaves."

"Are they slaves?" Lomo asked.

"Once transformed, they obey the will of whoever wears the corresponding glove," Lockland said. "Don't blame Bethany for touching your friend." He nodded toward the golden statue. "The order to attack came from Heath."

"Does he know we're here?" Seth asked.

"No," Lockland said. "It's a general order to attack. The statues obey simple commands. They can hunt for coins. They can try to change people."

"Who did you let out of the box when you went inside?" Kendra asked.

"A criminal named Jasmine Oxgard," Lockland said. "One of the Fair Folk. She stole something precious to my grandfather. I expect my brothers changed her after her release."

"You haven't explained how the game is rigged," Seth said.

"Humbuggle is clever," Lockland said. "I almost had two coins. I had the gold, and I found the platinum. But the moment I took hold of the platinum coin, the gold one vanished."

"Did anyone find it?" Seth asked.

"It was found again," Lockland said. "But none of us can hold more than one coin."

"Why not work together?" Kendra asked.

Lockland laughed, loud and bitter. "I tried so hard to persuade them. I told them cooperation was the only way. Humbuggle was smart. He created a trial that can be won only by cooperation, with contestants who will never work together."

"Don't the others want to break the curse?" Seth asked.

"Sure," Lockland said. "But mostly they want the prize. You know about the prize?"

"The Wizenstone," Kendra said.

"Exactly," Lockland said. "I suppose you three want it as well."

"We want to stop the dragons from getting it," Kendra said.

"Dragons have joined the hunt?" Lockland asked.

"Celebrant," Kendra said. "We think. And others."

"In human form, of course," Lockland said.

"Yes," Kendra said.

Lockland sighed. "The Wizenstone in the hands of dragons would be truly terrifying. Good thing nobody can win the contest."

"Somebody will win eventually," Kendra said.

"Will they?" Lockland asked. "From what I saw, despite the futility, my brothers were becoming more determined to win alone, not less. More set in their ways. What's going to change?"

"We'll change things," Kendra said.

"You'll try," Lockland said. "Then shortly you will be turned to gold or silver. The dragons too. And the same old conflict will drag on."

"If winning requires cooperation, how will they win without you?" Seth asked.

"If they ever decide to cooperate, my brothers will find me," Lockland said. "Until then, I'd rather skip the drama."

"Can we hold coins?" Kendra asked. "Those of us not turned to metal?"

"I'm not sure," Lockland said. "Everyone in the castle already had a glove or had been turned to gold, silver, or platinum before the first coin was found."

Kendra realized that not everyone in the castle had been transformed, but she decided not to mention Augie. He deserved to have his secret protected.

"Wait, some were turned to platinum?" Seth asked. "I thought you didn't change people."

"Not on purpose," Lockland said. "I transformed two accidentally. All it takes is careless contact."

"Do you know where any of the coins are?" Kendra asked.

"I know where I hid the platinum one before entering the Quiet Box," Lockland said. "It was a great spot, but they've had a long time to look."

"Help us retrieve it," Kendra said.

"Pointless," Lockland replied.

"Not necessarily," Lomo said. "You have people here to help you. Don't you want the contest to end?"

"I don't know," Lockland said.

"You'd rather stay trapped in this castle?" Seth asked.

"If either one of my brothers gets the Wizenstone, it could be really bad for the rest of the world," Lockland said. "Neither is fit to wield so much power. I'm not sure if anyone is, including myself. Keeping this contest going might protect the world much better than anyone winning it."

"Dragons are after the Wizenstone," Kendra said. "I'd be more worried about them than about your brothers."

"The dragons are ancient, cunning, and wise," Lomo said. "Even in human form, they stand a good chance of eventually solving this puzzle."

"You're of the Fair Folk?" Lockland asked.

Lomo gave a small bow. "At your service."

"Why not focus on stopping the dragons?" Lockland asked. "Rather than on winning the Wizenstone?"

"The dragons are in the midst of a worldwide rebellion," Lomo said. "Dragon sanctuaries are starting to fall. Great power may be needed to protect the world. Besides, if you stop these dragons, others will come. The secret is out."

Lockland folded his arms. "I see the argument. Even my brothers would be better custodians of the Wizenstone than dragons." He glanced at Seth and Kendra, then turned to Lomo again. "You are aiding these mortals? What about neutrality?"

"I don't subscribe to neutrality in times of real crisis," Lomo said.

"You believe in these two?" Lockland asked.

"None can know how they would wield the Wizenstone," Lomo said. "But the girl is fairykind, and I believe in her sincerity. The boy is a shadow charmer but avoids dark influences. I believe they have more chance than most to deal with the Wizenstone without becoming corrupted."

"The only way to avoid corruption by the Wizenstone's power would be not to use it," Lockland said. "That's part of the reason I have stayed out of the pursuit."

"We can't let the dragons get it," Seth said. "What if we promise to only use the Wizenstone to stop the dragon rebellion, and then to store it away after?"

"Such a promise might not be so easily kept with the power of the stone in hand," Lockland said.

"Do you trust us less than the dragons?" Kendra asked. "Than your brothers?"

"The dragons and my brothers are known," Lockland said. "I would trust nobody with the Wizenstone, but I trust you more than myself, and I trust my brothers and any dragon much less. The presence of the dragons could shake things up here. Until the dragons are claimed to gold, silver, or platinum, or until you are all claimed or destroyed, I will help you."

"Thank you," Seth said.

"My own risk is small," Lockland said, holding up the platinum glove. "I can't be changed to gold or silver while wearing this. As for you three and the dragons—you will probably not last the night. Once the gold and silver figures get to a faster speed, you will find avoiding them extremely difficult. You mean to store your friend in the Quiet Box for now?"

"He is turning to gold," Seth said. "Outside of the box, he will quickly transform into another golden enemy."

"Very well," Lockland said. "Follow me."

CHAPTER TWENTY-EIGHT

Coins

Climbing the stairs out of the dungeon, Seth stayed a few paces behind Lockland. He didn't expect the prince to try to turn them all to platinum, but he considered it best to be cautious. The lack of platinum statues seemed to support Lockland's story of being the peaceful brother, but he could also be the incompetent brother who got shut in the Quiet Box by the others at the start of the competition.

Lomo led the way out of the dungeon. He held a finger to his lips before opening the door at the top of the stairs. After stepping out for a moment and looking to the left and to the right, he waved for the others to proceed.

Seth exited last, just as a woman stepped around a corner down the hall. Tall and lithe, with long green hair and dramatic eyes, she wore light armor and carried a shield and sword. The shield looked to be made of pure gold.

Seth turned to find a man coming around the corner in the other direction. With long hair down past his shoulders and a full beard, he wore a heavy breastplate and greaves and carried a golden ax.

"We thought it might be you, Kendra, when we heard the gongs," the woman said. "And your brother, Seth. Lomo, the Fair Folk will pay dearly for your involvement. I see you have found the platinum brother. Does he have the platinum coin?"

"Should we retreat?" Lomo murmured, glancing at the stairs they had just climbed.

"Dead end that way," Lockland whispered.

"Don't try to flee," the woman said.

"Who are you?" Kendra asked.

The woman smiled without warmth, emerald eyes glittering. "How could you forget me? Were you not comfortable? Your taste still lingers on my tongue."

"Jaleesa," Kendra said.

"And you?" Seth asked the man in the other direction.

"As a dragon I was Obregon," the man said in a gruff voice.

"Didn't Raxtus replace you?" Seth asked.

"He filled my position for a season," Obregon said.

"Celebrant trusts Obregon more than anyone in his guard," Jaleesa said. "That's why he could count on him to temporarily step down."

"Hand over the coin and we will spare your lives," Obregon said.

"We have no coin," Lockland replied. "And you are in no position to threaten."

Growling, Obregon charged forward. Jaleesa dashed at them as well. Sword ready, Lomo stepped forward to confront Obregon. Heading the other way, Seth drew his sword to face Jaleesa.

She was taller than him, emerald hair blowing behind her as she ran. Her long sword had a slight curve at the end. She looked eager.

"Don't resist them!" Lockland shouted, having made no move to defend himself.

Sidestepping away from her charge, Seth deflected Jaleesa's first swing, feeling the shock of impact in his wrists and elbows. Her next swing was too quick, the blade hissing through the air until it bit into the side of his neck.

The instant the blade parted his skin, the entire sword turned to smoke, along with the arm wielding it. Surprised to be alive, blinking at the dissipating particles, Seth reached up to where the blade had kissed his neck. His fingertips came away red from the small cut there. The blade had disintegrated before it could bite deep.

Shocked, Jaleesa staggered back, eyes roving the empty space where her arm should have been. No blood issued from her shoulder—skin had grown over the remaining nub as if it had been that way for a long time. Seth stared at the one-armed woman, deciding not to attack with his sword.

Lomo had avoided several swings of the ax. After seeing Jaleesa, Obregon stepped away and let the weapon hang at his side, leaving himself open to an attack.

"Don't strike him!" Lockland called, lunging toward Jaleesa, who cowered away, cupping her armless shoulder with her remaining hand. He chased her until his gloved hand closed around her neck, and Seth watched platinum spread quickly across her from the point of contact.

Obregon fled.

"Should we chase him?" Lomo asked.

"Not now," Lockland said.

"What happened to her arm?" Seth asked.

"Shed no blood," Lockland said. "Break no bones. Stop no heart. The warning is serious. The moment her blade drew blood it vanished, along with the arm wielding it."

"We should move," Kendra said. "Obregon knows our location."

"This way," Lockland said.

"We're going after the coin?" Seth whispered.

"Just in case it remains where I left it," Lockland said.

"What are the chances?" Seth asked.

"It's possible," Lockland said. "I was in the Quiet Box for a very long time. And the metallic people can move quickly only at the end of festival nights. Over an entire year, they move roughly as much as they would at normal speed in a single day. My brothers are free to search every day, and I'm sure they do. But I hid it well."

They started up some stairs.

"Where did you originally find the gold coin?" Seth asked.

"Cunningly hidden inside a tapestry," Lockland said. "The image depicted a dragon with a treasure hoard. The coin was woven into the scene. Touching the coin caused it to detach from the image and materialize."

"That must have taken a long time to find," Seth said.

"A very long time," Lockland said. "I found the platinum coin in the crypt. We place coins over the eyes of our dead. The platinum coin covered one of the eyes of my great-grandmother."

"And you lost the gold one when you grabbed it?" Seth asked.

"The gold coin vanished and became concealed in a new spot," Lockland said. "Whether I hold the coins or my platinum statues carry them in my behalf, it all works the same. They are direct extensions of my will, so together we can only hold one coin. Same for gold or silver."

"That means we really could help you," Kendra said. "If we can each hold our own coin, working together, we could throw in all three."

"It's worth a try," Lockland said. "Assuming you can hold a coin. And if we can keep you from being transformed."

"Should we hunt down the dragons?" Seth asked. "Turn them to platinum?"

"It may not be easy," Lockland said. "Now that they understand they really can't shed blood, break bones, or stop hearts, they'll fight smarter." He raised his gloved hand, flexing his fingers. "If they come our way, I'll do my best to transform them."

"You accidentally touched some people?" Seth checked.

"It happens," Lockland said. "If I were you, I'd stay away from me, especially the side of me with the glove. If you get touched, I can't reverse it."

"What about our friends who were changed?" Kendra asked.

"It could be permanent," Lockland said. "Only Humbuggle knows the whole story."

Seth didn't like the news, but he was far from giving up on Tanu and Knox. Hopefully the dwarf would know a way to undo what happened. Or perhaps the power of the Wizenstone could help?

Lockland opened a door to a covered walkway connecting two towers. They were up quite high. Though Seth could see beyond the castle walls, all seemed shrouded in darkness, perhaps because the light globes around the castle were ruining his night vision.

"Somebody will probably see us up here," Lockland said. "Can't be helped." He stepped onto the railing of the walkway and swung up onto the roof. After a moment, Seth heard a crunch, and then Lockland came down holding a single shingle. "Come on."

Seth, Kendra, and Lomo followed Lockland back indoors. They hurried down some stairs and then along a corridor.

"These roof tiles are ceramic," Lockland said. "Not only do they last a long time, but the spell on the castle seems to preserve the physical structure without maintenance. I learned how to make the roof tiles when I was younger, so I baked the platinum coin into one and swapped it with a tile on the walkway roof in the middle of the night. Stand back."

Seth stepped well away from Lockland, who raised the ceramic shingle high, then hurled it to the stone floor. The roof tile broke into three pieces. Part of the platinum coin projected from one of the fragments. Lockland grabbed the fragment with the coin and banged it against the floor until he had the coin free. After wiping the dust off as best he could, he held it up for inspection. Still dusty, the coin featured a bearded dwarf standing on the front and what looked like the back of the same dwarf on the opposite side.

"Who wants to carry it?" Lockland asked.

"Why not you?" Kendra asked.

Lockland set the coin on the floor and raised both hands. "I chose to drop out of this contest. That decision stands. I'll help you try to end it, but I'm not looking to win it."

"We've got company," Lomo said as Tregain stalked into view.

Seth drew his sword as Kendra retrieved the coin from the floor. Lomo took up a position between them and Tregain.

"Lockland," Tregain said, stopping several paces from Lomo. "You're back in the hunt."

"I want this over," Lockland said, striding past Lomo so he stood closest to his brother.

"At any cost?" Tregain asked. "I had the gold coin. Intruders seized it."

"The dragons?" Lockland asked.

Tregain gave a nod. "I suspected they might be powerful creatures in human form."

"They could hold it?" Lockland asked.

"Aye," Tregain said. "They filched it from my room when I was away."

"You didn't keep it on you?" Lockland asked.

"I was hoping to find another," Tregain said through gritted teeth.

"And you can't possess two at once," Lockland said. "I turned one of the dragons to platinum. Only two left. They can't win the contest with two."

Tregain glanced past Lockland to Lomo, Seth, and Kendra. "I see three people with you."

"Yes," Lockland said. "Two mortals and one of the Folk."

"The girl has the platinum coin," Tregain said.

"I fail to see the problem," Lockland said.

A wild look came into Tregain's eyes. "Don't you? This is slipping away! Whatever happens, we have to keep it in the family, Lock."

"The family hasn't gotten much done for several centuries, Treg," Lockland said.

"And so you would hand the prize over to strangers?" Tregain asked, spittle flying from his lips.

"No offense, Tregain, but I *know* I can't trust you," Lockland said. "At least with the girl there is a chance."

Tregain grabbed at his hair and pulled, raising his voice even more. "Here I stand, betrayed by my own kin. You would rather dragons take the prize? Or children?"

"I want the curse broken," Lockland said. "We cursed ourselves by entering the contest. I want it finished."

"At what cost?" Tregain blurted. "The world will pay if the dragons win it! Or fools! Turn and help your brother. Let us purify these interlopers into silver and platinum. All platinum, if you prefer. Or all silver. And then the dragons.

Then we can sort out the rest among family."

Lockland laughed. "You'll use me, and then you'll do the same as you've always done. Nothing will get sorted out."

Tregain started shouting. "*Now* is the time to teach me a lesson? *Now* is the hour to mistrust your own blood? By delivering power to strangers?"

"They know it is the Wizenstone," Lockland said.

"Is that supposed to comfort me?" Tregain cried.

"So do the dragons," Lockland said. "They will keep coming. We must deliver the Wizenstone to the safest option."

"How is that not the rightful heir?" Tregain asked.

"Because you care only about yourself," Lockland said. "Heath too. We could have obtained the Wizenstone long ago had we worked together."

"You care about nothing!" Tregain spat, waving an arm. "You're an anarchist! You prefer strangers over family!"

"I prefer sanity over madness," Lockland said.

Growling, Tregain charged forward, and Lockland wrapped both arms around him, tackling him to the ground. Grunting and straining, they wrestled until Tregain ended up on top, holding Lockland down.

"Shall I help?" Lomo offered.

"Avoid his glove," Lockland said. "And mine. Hold him still, and I can remove it."

"You would strip me of what is rightfully mine?" Tregain bellowed.

"It's a contest," Lockland said.

As Lomo moved to get behind Tregain, the angry prince

pushed away from Lockland and returned to his feet. Rather than attack Lomo, he backed away. Lockland stood, positioning himself in front of Lomo.

"Look at you," Tregain said derisively. "So smug. We'll see how satisfied you are when the world falls to ruins."

After a final digusted look at his brother, he turned and fled.

"And I thought *my* family didn't get along," Seth said.

Lockland gave a rueful chuckle. "Neither of my brothers listens to reason. They are both so intent on claiming the prize for themselves that they are willing to keep the possibility of winning it forever out of reach."

"That is about to change," spoke a clear, authoritative voice.

Seth whirled. From the other end of the walkway, a man approached. He had regal features, with steel-gray hair and a closely trimmed beard, and he wore a chain-mail shirt that hung well past his waist and heavy trousers. Seth knew the voice, but usually it sounded like many voices speaking in unison and was magnified. In this form, Celebrant sounded human.

Behind him came Obregon, no longer holding his golden ax. Seth noticed that neither man had a visible weapon. But Celebrant wore a golden glove on one hand.

"That's close enough," Lomo said.

Celebrant and Obregon halted. "Very well. We overheard enough to grasp the situation. You have the platinum coin."

"Maybe we were bluffing," Seth said.

"We possess the other two," Celebrant said. "Gold and silver."

"Along with Heath's glove," Lockland said.

"My glove now," Celebrant replied, spreading his gloved fingers wide. "A fairly remarkable item. Please thank Tregain for the uproarious conversation. It simplified the matter of locating you."

"Heath?" Lockland asked.

"As golden as his former minions," Celebrant said. "We partnered with him at first. After we acquired the gold coin from Tregain, our relationship with Heath soured."

"You pinned him down and took the glove?" Kendra asked.

"We did," Celebrant said. "I started turning gold when I removed it, but putting it on reversed the process. Everything is so tedious in these pathetic human bodies, but using the glove is amusing." He touched the railing of the walkway and smiled as a portion of it turned to gold.

Seth and Kendra shared a glance. He suspected she was thinking along the same lines as he was. They should be able to save their cousin by putting a glove on him. Maybe Lockland would lend them his? Could they save Tanu that way, too? Would it work on a fully transformed person?

"Heath was liberal with his glove," Lockland said.

"I observed," Celebrant replied. "His entire room was gilded. Every item, every block, every tile. Now he matches."

"What is your offer?" Kendra asked.

"Isn't it obvious?" Celebrant asked. "We lost Jaleesa. To move forward, we need one more person to hold a coin. I could wait for more dragons to come in three months on the next festival night, but I would rather settle this now. Wouldn't you?"

"You want to throw the coins in the fountain together?" Seth asked.

"Naturally," Celebrant said. "Keep things progressing."

"What about the prize?" Kendra asked.

Celebrant shrugged. "May the best treasure hunter win."

"Can we have a minute to talk about this in privacy?" Kendra asked.

"I fail to see the need," Celebrant said. "You will not succeed in taking the coins from us. But I could turn you to gold in short order."

"Or we could turn you to platinum," Seth replied.

"Or I could steal the platinum glove," Celebrant countered. "Instead I offer a full truce until we toss in the coins. If the Wizenstone materializes, we will all do our best to get it. Or if there are more steps to win the prize, we will take them as they come."

"If we wish to move the contest forward, it's a reasonable offer," Lomo said.

"We don't want to wait for more dragons," Seth said.

"All right," Kendra said. "Truce."

Celebrant turned away briskly. "Shall we, then? The night is not getting any younger."

He and Obregon started walking. Seth, Kendra, Lomo, and Lockland followed.

"I expected to see you in heavy armor," Seth called ahead.

"You expected correctly," Celebrant replied without looking back. "Cumbersome armor did not match the circumstances. I don't require protection from blows, and it was slowing me down."

"And normally a dragon in human form has magically reinforced strength," Lockland murmured. "Without inhuman strength and endurance, a full suit of armor quickly becomes ponderous."

As they descended toward the courtyard, Seth tried to devise a strategy. How could they gain advantage in this situation? Dealing with the dragons probably made sense for now, but what would stop them from turning everyone to gold once the coins had been thrown? Or what if the Wizenstone appeared? Would it just be a matter of who was first to pick it up? No matter what, they could not let it fall into Celebrant's hands. Was there a realistic way to stop him?

Seth moved over to Lomo. "We'll have to be ready for anything," Seth muttered quietly.

Lomo gave a nod. "A lot is riding on the next few moments."

They exited to the courtyard and crossed to the fountain. Water splashed from seven spouts across multiple shelves into the wide basin. Celebrant produced the gold coin, and Obregon held up the silver.

"Give us the silver coin," Kendra said.

"That was not the arrangement I offered," Celebrant said.

"You need help putting the coins in the fountain, give

us the silver," Kendra said. "We throw two, you throw one."

"I'll have help in three months," Celebrant said. "I can wait."

"Are you sure you'll have help?" Kendra asked. "I can't imagine you trusting many dragons with this information."

"Not many," Celebrant replied, his gaze hard. "Is it easier to imagine me without contingency plans?"

Seth thought Celebrant looked like he was telling the truth. He could just be a good bluffer.

"Who cares who throws the coins?" Kendra said. "It saves you three months at least. Let us throw two."

"I care," Celebrant said. "I offered a truce under the condition that you would throw your coin with us. Would you prefer to break the truce?"

Seth knew Kendra had moved onto shaky ground. Trouble could start any second.

Kendra took the platinum coin from her pocket. "I'll play along."

Lockland stepped near to Seth and whispered, "If this goes bad, run and hide."

Seth got ready. He would run either to the Wizenstone or away from Celebrant if he started trying to tag them with his glove.

"I will count three, two, one, toss," Celebrant said. "Ready?"

"Yes," Kendra said.

"Three," Celebrant said.

Seth clenched his fists and bent his knees slightly. A quick reaction could be the key to grabbing the Wizenstone.

"Two," Celebrant said.

Seth glanced at Lomo, who stood ready as well.

"One," Celebrant said. "Toss."

Three arms swung forward, and three coins took flight, each plopping into the basin.

CHAPTER TWENTY-NINE

Banishment

Water stopped spouting into the fountain, and the liquid in the wide, circular basin grew dark and still. Surprisingly dark and suddenly still as glass. Kendra had positioned herself a quarter of the way around the fountain from Celebrant. Leaning over the water, she could see her reflection. She also saw the reflection of a dwarf. He looked to be in his autumn years, with playfully expressive features and a forked beard, reddish brown streaked with gray.

The compact man waved at her with just his fingers and spoke. "Hello."

Kendra looked sideways to where he would have been standing. After a moment looking around, she realized he was visible only in the water.

"This is a surprise," the dwarf said, looking from Kendra

to Celebrant to Obregon. "None of you three were present at the start of the contest."

"Are you Humbuggle?" Kendra asked.

Looking bewildered, the dwarf patted his vest as if feeling his pockets. "I'm afraid so. And I should have a poem ready for the next phase of the challenge, but I have waited a very long time. You wouldn't believe how long. Some people just can't seem to collaborate."

"What is the next phase?" Celebrant asked.

The dwarf wagged a finger at him. "This contestant is all business. Accustomed to command. You're a participant like everyone else tonight."

Celebrant sneered. "You have a poem?"

"I *had* a poem," Humbuggle said. "A good one. And that is no small matter in English. But I've misplaced it."

"Don't you have it memorized?" Celebrant asked.

"I did last time I checked," Humbuggle said. "But that was more than six hundred years ago."

"Can you just tell us the rules?" Kendra said.

"I suppose," Humbuggle said. "I could also eat plain oatmeal every day to stay alive. An explanation is more pleasant when it rhymes. And a tad more official."

"Make up a rhyme?" Kendra proposed.

"I'm not speaking Silvian," Humbuggle said. "This is English. I suppose I can give it a go." He laced his fingers, cracked his knuckles, cleared his throat, and recited:

> *"To tread where mystic waters roll*
> *You must be one who paid the toll*

Reclaim the token you have tossed
Or lose all hope to pay the cost
Then in the end if you reflect
The rod you surely shall detect
With pow'r to banish friend or foe
To realms above or depths below."

"We're looking for a rod?" Kendra asked.

"No more hints, young lady," Humbuggle said. "That poem was already far too plain." The dwarf clapped his hands and vanished.

Immediately the floor of the basin began to recede, sinking deeper and deeper, leaving behind one step at a time until a helix of stairs descended into darkness. As the water in the basin flowed down the newly forming stairway, the spouts began to gush again, keeping a steady stream of water tumbling down into the humid depths.

Celebrant glared at Kendra, pointing at her with his gloved hand. "If you want to survive this night, do not follow us."

Celebrant entered the basin at the top step and began going down the stairway. Obregon followed. The footing looked treacherous, with water swirling around their shins, but they sloshed out of sight without falling.

Kendra turned to the others. "I have to go, don't I?"

"Let me go first," Lomo said, trying to step into the basin and getting thrust back roughly as an unseen barrier flashed.

"The poem warned that only those who threw coins could go down," Lockland said.

"It's me or nobody," Kendra said. "We can't let them get

the rod. What if that means they will win the Wizenstone?"

"Don't go without this," Lockland said, removing his platinum glove. He set it on the ground and stepped away.

"Your glove?" Kendra asked.

"If you're wearing it, Celebrant can't turn you to gold," Lockland said. "All our hopes are on you right now. Take it."

Kendra crouched, picked up the glove, and put it on. Though it looked too big at first, the glove shrank to neatly fit her hand.

"Be careful what you touch with the glove," Lockland reminded her. "It can take time to get used to the consequences of wearing it. Your own clothes are safe, though."

"I can control the platinum statues?" Kendra asked.

"There are only a couple," Lockland said. "It's easiest to instruct them if you're touching them. But you can also send out commands mentally. I just have them trying to touch Obregon at the moment, since the glove makes Celebrant immune."

"I don't see them," Seth said.

"They're coming," Lockland replied.

Kendra looked at the other statues in the courtyard. All were gradually moving toward them, so slowly that the motion was only just becoming noticeable from a distance. "They're speeding up."

"By the end of the night they will be dangerous," Lockland said.

"I better hurry," Kendra said, stepping over the side of the basin onto the top stair.

"Celebrant could try to take your glove," Lockland said.

"Don't let them corner you. Touch Obregon if necessary."

"Be sneaky," Seth recommended. "They don't need to know you're behind them."

Water splashed around her ankles, soaking her socks. The top step was not as wet as the others—water from only one spout of the fountain drained onto it. As she made her first full downward circle, all the spouts would contribute to the cascade.

Kendra stared at the water slurping downward. Was she crazy? If she slipped, the fall itself could be lethal. Let alone the pair of dragons in human form who wanted to turn her to gold, and probably a bunch of traps created by the dwarf.

"Wish me luck," Kendra said.

"You can do it," Seth assured her. "See you soon."

Kendra looked at her brother. "I don't have my fairykind powers. It looks so dark."

"You should get going," Lomo said. "You don't want Celebrant and Obregon to get too far ahead."

"Hopefully you'll stumble across their dead bodies," Seth said.

"A girl can dream," Kendra replied, starting down the stairs. She kept a hand on the wall to help steady herself. The water gushing over the stone steps made the descent quite slippery. After another full downward circle, her friends passed out of view, and the darkness increased.

The misty air smelled of moss, stone, and water. The darkness increased the deeper she went, and the wall became mushy or slimy sometimes. The squishy textures made Kendra squeamish, but she was more scared of falling, so she kept her hand sliding across the unsettling surface.

Soon Kendra was descending in complete darkness, unseen water sluicing past her calves. She firmly planted each step before taking the next, winding down to unguessable depths. The water rushing ahead of her and behind her filled the stairway with white noise. The stone wall grew cooler, alternating between being gooey, mossy, and slick.

After some time, faint blue radiance appeared up ahead. The light grew brighter as Kendra kept going. She found a glowing crystal anchored to the wall just beyond where the spiraling stairs finally ended in a pool. At the bottom of the pool, Kendra noticed the glint of a coin.

Wading into the pool brought the water just above her knees, but her pants were already drenched anyway from water splashing up while she descended the stairs. Kendra crouched and fished out the platinum coin. The poem had made it sound like she might need it, so she tucked it into her pocket. Perhaps the light source had been placed here to give her a fair chance to find it.

Water overflowing from the pool at the base of the stairs continued down a gently slanted corridor. Some distance down the hall, Kendra saw the blue radiance of another crystal. There was no sign of either Celebrant or Obregon. A hurried search of the pool revealed no more coins, so Kendra assumed they must have collected theirs. Had they missed hers, or had they been unable to claim it? Perhaps the rule of one coin per person remained in effect.

The corridor looked ancient, the eroding masonry glossy with dampness and slime. The hall was wider than the stairway had been, meaning the water was not as deep, but it still covered her ankles. Kendra crept forward, wondering how she would respond if Celebrant and Obregon attacked her.

The corridor ran long and straight, with blue crystals placed far enough apart to allow for extended shadowy stretches between them, although light ahead or behind never fully passed out of view. At length Kendra reached a place where the water flowed down a short flight of stairs into a black river.

Kendra paused at the top of those stairs. She could not see the far side of the river, but the water was clearly flowing left to right, with the water from the fountain serving only as a small tributary. Unlike the water on the stairs, the water of the river seemed black as ink and only barely reflected the light from the nearest crystal.

Beyond the bottom of the stairs, a few steps led up to a wooden quay projecting a short distance out into the river. A single raft awaited at the end of the quay, with a single cowled occupant, who stood facing away from Kendra.

Nothing about what she saw enticed her to approach.

But there was nowhere else to go unless she simply dove into the tenebrous water of the river. Or turned back.

Could the occupant of the raft be Celebrant or Obregon? Perhaps, if they had found a hooded robe. If not, where were they? Had there been other options earlier?

Kendra descended the last stairs, water sloshing around her, then waded over and climbed the steps to the quay. The rotted wood looked thin and splintery, with so many gaps it would be more like walking on shutters than on a solid surface. The wood crunched beneath her first step, and she even felt it sag slightly. If she broke through, she would end up in the black river. The sides of the quay seemed better reinforced than the center, so she moved along the right side, wood creaking with each step.

At the end of the dock, she reached the raft. The robed figure turned, revealing a skull inside the hood.

Kendra gasped and tried not to stumble into the river. At least the skeletal figure made no harsh movements. A hand made of bones reached out, fleshless palm upward. The figure held that pose.

Kendra pulled the coin from her pocket and placed it in the skeleton's hand. The fingers closed and the figure stepped back, allowing Kendra access to the raft. Though wooden like the quay, the raft looked much sturdier. Kendra stepped aboard.

The robed skeleton gripped a pole leaning against the quay and pushed off. Slowly rotating, the raft drifted out onto the mysterious water. A jumbled mixture of faint whispers and sighs arose from the dark liquid, prompting Kendra to move to the center of the craft.

Though the skeleton dipped his pole into the water, Kendra did not think it looked like the pole was reaching the ground and pushing off, and the skeleton did not appear to put much real effort into the motion. Nevertheless, the raft traveled against the current at a slow, steady rate. The sound of the water splashing down the stairs to join the river gradually faded, leaving Kendra alone with the tangled susurrations of the black river.

As the darkness increased to impenetrable perfection, Kendra desperately missed her ability to see without light. What if the skeleton had set down the pole and was coming toward her, fleshless hands reaching? She would have no warning before those bony fingers closed around her neck.

Kendra tried not to fixate on the whispering water, but it was the only sound besides the gentle sloshing of the pole. She was glad that she could not make out individual words. The collective feel was unsavory.

A spectral light became visible up ahead, on the opposite side of the river from where she had embarked. They were still traveling upstream. In the ghostly light, Kendra saw two other rafts drawn up against a stone jetty. A skeletal boatman stood on each. She assumed this meant the dragons in human form had come this way ahead of her, but they were not within view.

The raft glided to a stop against the jetty. Kendra stepped off and glanced back at the skeleton, who seemed indifferent to her. She walked across the jetty to the shore before looking back at the three rafts, wondering if the coin provided a round-trip journey or if she might have to find another way to pay in order to return.

A path led from the jetty to an archway. Kendra could not discern where the light was originating—it seemed to somehow distill out of the air without a source, which perhaps was what made the glow feel ghostly.

The shore beside the dark river extended only a short distance in either direction. To follow the river would force her either to swim or to climb rock walls. The archway seemed the obvious destination.

She left the path and approached the archway from the side, hoping to take Celebrant and Obregon by surprise. Treading carefully, she peeked around the corner and saw a large, rectangular room. If the room was twenty yards wide, it must have been sixty yards long. Similar to outside by the river, the light in the room had no observable source. At the far end of the chamber, a smooth wooden rod stood vertically atop a tall pedestal. A rectangular reflecting pool filled most of the room, with aisles down the sides granting access to the opposite end. On the left side of the pool, Celebrant strode purposefully toward the pedestal. On the right side, Obregon hurried toward the same destination. Mysteriously, no matter how many steps they took, neither man seemed to make any progress.

Kendra crept into the room. If Celebrant or Obregon looked back, they would easily see her. The room was not very large, and both of them were only a third of the way toward the far end. Kendra crossed to the center of the base of the reflecting pool, directly opposite the rod, which was mirrored clearly in the still water. She heard forlorn whispers and sighs emanating from the dark pool, just like in the river. It was impossible to guess how deep the water might be.

Moving carefully, Kendra snuck over to the side of the pool behind Obregon. He was only about fifteen paces down the aisle from her, still walking briskly without advancing. If she could creep up behind him and turn him to platinum, that might even the odds quite a bit!

Her first step toward Obregon caused her to pause. With that step, the entire room seemed to elongate. The far end of the reflecting pool looked almost twice as far away, and it would now take more than twenty paces to reach Obregon.

Kendra took a couple more steps and watched the room telescope even more. Obregon had to be thirty or maybe even forty paces away now. And the far end of the room was getting truly distant. Kendra walked forward more, watching as the room continued to elongate until Obregon was barely in view and the rod was out of sight. The reflecting pool seemed to stretch ahead forever.

Looking back, Kendra found that the start of the reflecting pool looked much more distant than the number of steps she had taken. Walking back in the direction she had come, Kendra found that her progress was as slow as it looked like it should be. Evidently, her return steps neither stretched nor shrank the room, but steps toward the far side quickly increased the journey.

Kendra paused, considering her predicament. Celebrant and Obregon had a huge head start. No wonder they didn't see her—they had probably gone so far that the near end of the room was long out of view from their present perspective. They had also gone so far that they probably had an impossible lead.

Curious, Kendra jogged back toward the entrance. The ground she had covered in about twenty paces now required a five-minute jog. When Kendra got back to the near end of the pool, she found the room had returned to its original shape—Obregon once again looked perhaps fifteen paces away and was still only a third of the way to the far end.

The farther Celebrant and Obregon went, the longer

the room became for them. When Kendra followed, the room stretched for her as well. Was there a better way? Or was the dwarf requiring an epic journey that appeared short at the outset?

Kendra wondered whether Celebrant and Obregon understood how slowly they were progressing. Once both ends of the pool were beyond sight, it was probably difficult to perceive how much ground they had covered and how much remained. If her current vantage of their infinitesimal progress was accurate, it looked like Celebrant and Obregon would be traveling for a very long time.

Studying the room, Kendra wondered if there might be a shortcut. The rod looked tantalizingly close! Besides walking alongside the reflecting pool, the only other obvious option was attempting to swim. If the room didn't stretch when she was in the water, it would be a relatively short distance to cover. If it did elongate, she might, without going very far, get stranded and drown. Or maybe she could always swim sideways and get out? Perhaps only the length of the room could increase, not the width?

Kendra crouched at the edge of the water. The faint, overlapping whispers made the liquid seem sinister. She had a bad feeling about getting in. Was it just cowardice?

She was no longer trying to find Risenmay. Her instincts were probably there for a reason. Jumping into that water might be the end of her.

It was frustrating. It looked like she could walk to the rod in less than a minute! But as soon as she started to approach, she knew it would stretch out of reach again.

How could it be so near and so far? Squatting low like this, at the edge of the water, it almost looked like she could reach out and touch the reflection of the rod. As she considered the reflection, something about the perspective seemed off. Shouldn't the reflected rod be a little farther away? After she dropped her head even lower, the reflection appeared reachable.

Part of the poem came back to her:

> *In the end if you reflect*
> *The rod you will detect*

That wasn't exactly right. But it was close. Could it be so simple? There was no way. Her idea was absurd. Kendra did not want to touch the whispery water to test her theory. What if it gave cooties to her soul?

But the reflection seemed nearer than it should be. And the way to the rod was so far and difficult. And the dwarf seemed to like tricks.

Keeping her head low, Kendra reached out into the pool and grabbed the reflection of the rod. Feeling tangible wood in her grasp, she removed it from the pool. And the rod at the far end of the pool was no longer there.

CHAPTER THIRTY

Forgotten

You made that one look easy," Humbuggle said from off to one side.

Kendra jumped, nearly dropping the staff, and turned to face the dwarf. "Where did you come from?"

"I'm never far," Humbuggle said. "What's the fun of a contest unless you watch the competition?"

"You made this contest?" Kendra asked.

He gave a little bow. "Guilty as charged."

"Why?" Kendra asked.

He looked at her as if puzzled. "My dear girl, everything in this life is a contest. Finding food, shelter, the basic necessities. Endeavoring to thrive. Winning the positions and prestige you desire. Acquiring your needs and wants. Pleasing friends and besting enemies. At least my contest is fair."

"What's fair about everyone getting turned to gold or silver or platinum?" Kendra asked.

"Most contests get won by the strongest or the fastest or the wisest," Humbuggle said. "I get tired of the biggest sword or the sharpest fangs prevailing in every fight! Who wants the most powerful wizard to always take the spoils? I created a space without magic, a competition where the best fighter won't necessarily win. Other virtues are just as important here, like cooperation, and cleverness, and courage, and sacrifice. The biggest prize I know of is on the line, and anyone has a chance to win."

"Not everyone had the same advantage," Kendra said. "Seems like the no-magic condition doesn't apply to you. And the three brothers had the gloves and got to hear the rules."

"The contest was originally designed for them," Humbuggle said. "The gloves were indeed an advantage. And yet those three remained stuck on the first phase of the trial for centuries. I'm flattered when my challenges are difficult, but even I was getting a touch impatient. As for the rules, everyone gets to hear them."

"We didn't get to hear," Kendra said. "We had to talk to, um . . ." She didn't want to tell him about Augie.

Humbuggle jumped and spun. When he landed, he looked exactly like Augie. "I gave you the first poem, didn't I?" He sounded just like Augie too.

"That was you?" Kendra exclaimed.

Augie leaped and spun. When he landed again, he was a thin old woman. "The dragons met me. I went by the name of Elouise and told them the basics and the poem." The old woman jumped and twirled, becoming Humbuggle again. "Everyone got a fair chance."

"You're sneaky," Kendra said.

"Young one, you have no idea," Humbuggle replied.

Kendra looked to Celebrant and Obregon. They were still moving away from her, still about a third of the way to the far end of the pool. "They may not be able to see that the rod is missing for a long time."

"It would already be a long way back for them indeed," Humbuggle said. "However, the Banishment Rod is what powers this room. Once the rod leaves the room, this chamber will begin to collapse to its actual dimensions for everyone still inside."

"How long would it have taken them to make it to the rod the way they are going?" Kendra asked.

"At their present speed?" Humbuggle asked. "More than eight thousand years. And there is nothing to eat on the way."

"How long would it take them to get back if I were to leave the rod here?" Kendra asked, wondering if she could buy time to solve the next challenge, then return for the rod later.

Humbuggle gave her a sly grin. "That I cannot reveal, as it could give you an advantage. I will share that you cannot move to the next phase of the contest unless you take the rod with you."

"What does the rod do?" Kendra asked.

"That, I'm willing to explain," Humbuggle said. "The

Banishment Rod can send a single target extremely far away. It is rigged to do so only once. Take care how you use it—I do not believe the contest can be won without it. To keep the game fair, I will confess that the Wizenstone is jealously guarded by a powerful demon. Any who seek to claim the stone would have to ward off the demon before long."

"How do I use the rod?" Kendra asked.

"Simple," Humbuggle said. "Just extend the rod toward the target and cry 'Begone!'"

"And the target will be sent away," Kendra said.

"Use it carefully," Humbuggle said. "Remember, the rod will work only once for a single contestant. Are you ready to go?"

"Sure," Kendra said.

Humbuggle clapped his hands, and a secret door opened in the wall. Kendra saw stairs beyond.

"The others will be able to follow me?" she asked.

"In due time," Humbuggle replied. "As I said, once you leave with the rod, the room will start to return to normal."

"Can you give me any hints?" Kendra asked.

"Once you reach the top, I can bestow the next poem," Humbuggle said. "Off you go."

After a final glance at Celebrant and Obregon still striding without progress toward the far side of the room, Kendra went out the doorway and started up the stairs. To her relief, they were well lit and completely dry.

Seth backed away from a trio of silver statues who were getting near. It was easy to see them moving now, but they were still quite slow. Enough statues had converged on the courtyard that he, Lockland, and Lomo needed to stay alert.

"Behind you, Lockland," Seth said.

The prince glanced over his shoulder and moved a few paces sideways. "I haven't been vulnerable since this game began. Tregain chose first and got the silver glove. Heath chose next and it turned out to be gold. Platinum fell to me. All the gloves looked the same at the start."

"It's getting hard to stay near the fountain," Lomo said. "They might be slow, but the numbers keep increasing."

Seth estimated there were sixty gold statues in the courtyard now, and maybe fifty silver ones. More were gradually emerging from the castle.

"Don't let them form a ring around you," Lockland said. "And don't forget that they keep moving faster. Unless of course you want to end the suspense and rest. Getting turned to gold might serve just as well as the Quiet Box."

"Don't talk like that," Seth said. "We have to keep the Wizenstone away from the dragons. It's going to be tough. We need all the help we can get."

"Seth is right," Lomo said. "You could make a big difference."

"I'll try," Lockland said. "At least the challenge is moving forward. I had lost hope that the day would come when the three coins would enter the fountain together."

"Guys!" Kendra called, emerging from the castle holding

a rod slightly taller than her. "I got the Banishment Rod."

"Where'd you come from?" Seth called, running toward her with Lockland and Lomo, leaving the fountain and the majority of the statues behind.

"I came up a different stairway," Kendra said. "It led to a secret door in the throne room."

"What comes next?" Seth wondered.

"So glad you asked," Humbuggle said, appearing between Kendra and the three males. "I have a poem that might shed some light on the next phase."

"Let's hear it," Kendra said. "The dragons may not be far behind."

> *"To reach the storied stone of yore*
> *You shortly must unlock a door*
> *Those who dare may seek the key*
> *Without the aid of memory*
> *Plant the staff where five halls join*
> *All can proceed without a coin*
> *Those who advance may soon regret*
> *The many things they will forget."*

"Happy hunting," Humbuggle said, jumping with a clap and disappearing before his feet returned to the ground.

"We have to hurry," Kendra said. "The dragons are coming."

"Follow me," Lockland said. "There is only one place in the castle where five halls join."

Seth raced behind Lockland through a door into the castle. As they ran, Kendra explained about the Banishment

Rod and the demon that would try to reclaim the Wizenstone after someone took possession of it. When they found statues in a hall, they ran by them, but not casually. Seth knew a single touch would turn him to silver or gold, and, though still slow, the statues were gradually picking up their pace.

"How many things do you think we have to collect?" Seth asked.

"What do you mean?" Kendra replied.

"First coins, then the rod, now a key," Seth said.

"Sounds like the stone is behind a locked door," Kendra said. "Maybe the key is the last item."

Lockland stopped when they reached a small atrium on a high level of the castle, the ceiling open to the sky. Five corridors intersected around a curbed area of soil where several shrubs were growing. In the center of the shrubs was a flagpole supporting a blue flag emblazoned with a white lion.

"Here we are," Lockland said.

Seth checked down the branching hallways but saw no statues yet. "Where do we plant the staff?"

"Maybe in place of the flag," Lomo suggested. "See if it fits."

Lockland removed the flagpole, and Kendra plunged the Banishment Rod into the vacant socket. With a gentle rumble, a section of a wall slid aside, revealing a black door.

"Good guess," Kendra told Lomo.

"What now?" Lockland asked.

"I can go in," Kendra offered.

Seth looked at the black door. Kendra had already risked her life once. It was time for him to step up. "No. It's my turn. I'm the youngest. I have the fewest memories to lose."

"We all want our memories," Kendra said.

"I've got this one," Seth said. "With or without memories, I have great instincts."

"We could all try it," Lomo suggested. "The poem set no limit."

"But we can't all lose our memories," Seth argued. "Somebody has to stay out here in case those who go in forget what is going on."

"Good point," Kendra said.

"Let me go," Seth said. "Once I'm inside, replace the flagpole and take the staff someplace safe. Maybe that will keep the dragons from catching up and following me."

"Sounds like a plan," Lomo said. "I'll go with Seth. Lockland, can you protect Kendra?"

"I'll try," Lockland said.

The noisy splash of a gong reverberated from elsewhere in the castle. Seth looked at Kendra with wide eyes.

"Somebody new has arrived," Lockland said. "This is quite a night. Nobody in decades, and suddenly the arrivals keep coming."

"Sounds like just one," Seth said as the shimmering of the gong faded.

"We should hurry," Lomo said. "We may have even more company soon."

"Could it be a friend?" Seth asked.

"I doubt it," Kendra said. "I don't know of anybody else

on our side who knew about this. Maybe another dragon. Emergency backup."

Lomo patted Seth's shoulder and trotted toward the door. Seth followed.

"Be careful, Seth," Kendra said.

"I'll try to remember that," Seth replied with a smile. "Hopefully when I get the key I'll still know to bring it back here."

"Maybe you won't forget too much," Kendra said.

"Does it seem like that kind of castle?" Seth asked.

Lomo opened the door, but nothing was visible beyond the threshold. The light from the atrium could not penetrate the darkness.

"Not comforting," Seth said.

"In we go," Lomo replied, stepping forward and vanishing into the blackness.

Embarrassed that he had let Lomo go first, Seth quickly followed. A slight tingle sparkled across his body as he stepped through the veil of blackness. On the far side he found himself in a fairly large room illuminated by glowing globes. A black rectangle in the wall marked where he had come from, though strangely Seth could not recall what lay on the other side. An enormous pair of bronze doors was centered in the opposite wall, each embossed with a large, bearded face.

Two men already stood in the room. A handsome man with a dark complexion and an artistically sculpted goatee glanced back at Seth from only a couple of paces away. A wiry, older man, shirtless, with protruding ribs, waited over by the bronze doors. He faced Seth and the goateed stranger with excitement.

"Tell me what you remember," the man asked. "Why did you come here?"

Seth opened his mouth to answer before realizing that he wasn't sure. He glanced at the man with the goatee, who was scowling in thought.

"I have no idea," the goateed man said.

"Me neither," Seth replied.

"You came in together," the old man prompted. "Seconds apart. Any memory of one another?"

Seth studied the man with the goatee. Nothing about him seemed remotely familiar.

"Should I know you?" the man asked.

"I don't think we've met," Seth said.

"I'm Lomo," the man said. "Of the Fair Folk."

"Seth Sorenson," Seth said. "Of the Sorensons."

"And I'm Pietro," the old man said. "I'm also unsure why I'm here."

"YOU ARE HERE TO COMPETE FOR THE TROPHY," the face in the left door thundered.

"WE WILL AWAIT ANY OTHER PARTICIPANTS AND BEGIN MOMENTARILY," the face in the other door said.

"I'm here for a trophy?" Seth asked. The idea didn't sound familiar. Then again, nothing else seemed familiar either. He knew who he was. But he couldn't remember much of his past, any of the people he knew, or what he might be doing here today. Was he alone in the world? As he pondered, he could almost bring up memories of some people. He felt sure he had a family. But faces and names refused to come into focus.

"Remarkable," Lomo said. "I feel certain I have a life, but I'm at a loss for specifics."

"I get your meaning," Pietro said. "Same for me. What about you, Seth Sorenson?"

"Same," Seth said. "My whole life feels like it's on the tip of my tongue, but I can't remember details."

"I'd be tempted to scoff except I feel the same way," Lomo said.

A newcomer emerged from the black rectangle in the wall—a stocky man, well dressed and with a silver glove on one hand. He looked perplexed.

"Quick," Lomo said. "Why are you here?"

The man looked from Lomo to Seth to Pietro. "What happened to me?"

"You remember yourself," Seth prompted.

"I'm Tregain," the man said. "Otherwise . . . I'm at a loss."

Seth, Lomo, and Pietro made their introductions and explained they were apparently about to compete for a trophy. The faces on the doors remained silent.

Seth tried to gauge the unremembered men. Was it possible he knew all of them? None of them? They seemed pleasant enough, but if they were all trying to win the same trophy, they were his competition. Maybe even enemies? Or was it a friendly contest? How could his memory be gone?

Another man burst through the black rectangle, then doubled over, hands on his knees, panting. He had a beard and long hair and wore some armor, but he carried no weapon. It seemed like he had been running.

"What's your name?" Seth asked.

The man straightened and looked around. "Obregon," he said in a strong voice.

"Why are you here?" Lomo asked.

Obregon folded his arms and brooded before answering. "I have no idea."

Once again, introductions were made. Seth kept an eye on the black rectangle, wondering who might come through next. He tried to guess at the stories of the people already in the room. Seth wore a sword, and Lomo was the only other person with a visible weapon; a sword as well. Lomo was so well groomed that he looked less like a real adventurer and more like a guy who played an adventurer in a show. Pietro could have been an old marooned guy from a desert island. Obregon seemed like a warrior, with a face that had probably absorbed a punch or two. Tregain came across as a lord.

Seth could not guess how he had ended up competing against these men for a trophy. He seemed out of place with a bunch of adults. He didn't think he was related to any of them, but it was hard to be sure with his memories so unfocused.

"THE COMPETITION WILL NOW BEGIN," the face on the left door uttered.

"THE FIRST THROUGH THE GAUNTLET TO THE TROPHY IS THE VICTOR," the face on the right door pronounced.

"ENTER THE GAUNTLET AT YOUR OWN RISK," the face on the left door warned.

"SELECT ANY WEAPON OF YOUR CHOOSING," the face on the right door encouraged.

"ONLY ONE CAN TAKE HOME THE PRIZE," the face on the left door intoned.

"WHEN THE DOORS OPEN, ALL MAY PROCEED," the face on the right said.

The bronze doors swung outward.

CHAPTER THIRTY-ONE

Identity

S eth went through the bronze doors behind Tregain and Obregon. A foyer awaited beyond, the walls lined with weapons and shields; then a wide hallway proceeded onward, ramping steadily upward. Tregain grabbed a shield and a sword, as did Obregon. Lomo drew his sword, and Seth did as well. Pietro selected a knife.

From the back of the hall marched a group of clay figures, armed with spears, axes, clubs, and swords. A few carried shields. There must have been twenty in all.

"For glory!" Tregain called, sword held high as he charged up the incline.

Obregon followed him closely, then Lomo next. Seth brought up the rear beside Pietro. Seth wanted to be first into the gauntlet, but hoped hanging back while the others fought might provide an opportunity to slip ahead.

Either Tregain, Obregon, and Lomo fought well, or the clay figures fought poorly. The clay warriors proved brittle, shattering when contact was made. Obregon soon discovered that bashing them with his shield was perhaps more effective than hitting them with his sword, and Tregain copied the technique.

Two of the clay warriors slipped by Tregain, Obregon, and Lomo. One focused on Seth while the other came for Pietro. Seth ducked a clumsy swing from a scimitar and, while down low, slashed his sword through two clay legs, shattering them into fragments. The torso burst apart when it hit the floor. Glancing over, Seth found that Pietro had demolished his clay warrior as well.

The three men in the lead finished off the clay warriors and advanced to where the hallway leveled out. Most of the clay figures had broken apart so completely, they might have been smashed pottery. Seth and Pietro followed the others, but Seth worried that he was lagging behind too much.

Holes riddled the floor, ceiling, and walls of the hallway in this level section. Spikes thrust out from and retracted into the holes at random, threatening to stab anyone attempting to pass. Seth quickly realized the trick was to never line up your body with holes, which was a challenge, with opposing walls to consider as well as the ceiling and floor. There were some resting areas without as many holes, and also some areas so perforated that anyone hoping to pass had to trust a little bit to luck.

Seth paused where the holes began, watching the other men dodging, ducking, and jumping. A spike from the wall grazed Obregon's shoulder. One from the floor tore Tregain's pants.

Pietro sprang nimbly forward, moving with more grace and control than the younger men, dancing from one foot to the other, twisting, hopping, and sliding. Seth did not relish being in last place, so he rushed forward as well. He soon discovered there was a quick hiss of air right before a spike emerged, and he tried to use that as insurance against getting skewered.

Seth followed the route Pietro was taking, a student imitating the master. He checked the holes himself as well, but he consistently found the old man's path to be about as good as the patterns of holes allowed. Though Seth had a few close calls, he made it to the far side of the many holes untouched.

The hall elbowed, and Seth found Tregain, Obregon, and Lomo once again battling clay soldiers, even more than before. With a rumble, the walls of the corridor began closing together.

Seth and Pietro charged forward. Seth dodged the downswing of an ax and pulverized the attacker with a blow to the chest. Obregon, Tregain, and Lomo fought their way past where the walls were closing, leaving six clay soldiers behind. By retreating strategically, Seth tried to isolate them and take them one at a time. The clay fighters seemed to reach back before every swing, giving him time to anticipate and either counter or dodge. With weapons whistling nearby, Seth dispatched one after another, smashing four of the six. Pietro dodged and slashed, taking care of the other two, but receiving a lance through his thigh.

The hallway was now less than half the width than it had been when Seth had started, and it kept getting narrower every moment. Seth still had a good way to go before passing the closing walls, and a quick glance back showed him that Pietro was on the floor. The old man tugged the weapon out of his thigh and tried to stand, but his leg buckled and he collapsed. Pietro tried to rise again but fell once more, slipping on his own blood.

Seth paused, the walls grinding ever closer together. A big squish was coming for anything caught between them.

Tregain and Lomo looked back from beyond the moving walls. Obregon was already running ahead. After a moment, both men turned and chased Obregon.

Seth ran to Pietro.

"Go," Pietro said. "It's too late for me. There is serious damage to the muscles and tendons."

Seth regarded the walls. They would collide shortly. He couldn't let the old man get mashed. "I'll drag you."

"We won't make it," Pietro said.

He was right. Seth was sure he could still sprint past the moving walls, but not while dragging somebody. But he might be able to get Pietro clear if he went back toward the start, which was closer.

Speed would be everything. Seth doubted he could carry the older man fast enough, so he hooked him under his arms and started pulling, dragging the injured man behind him, the lean, shirtless body inadvertently sweeping up clay fragments. With the hallway tightening, Seth saw he had a chance but knew it would be close. The only sure thing would be leaving Pietro behind, but Seth refused to let that be an option.

Legs churning, muscles burning, Seth watched the walls close in until he could have reached out and touched them in either direction. With a final burst of effort, Seth made it past the narrowing hall, and a few steps later had dragged Pietro clear. The walls ground together with a crunch of clay fragments and then became still. Since the moving walls stretched from the floor to the ceiling, there was now no way to proceed.

"Thank you," Pietro said, panting.

"You're welcome," Seth replied, gasping for air.

"You won't win the trophy," Pietro said.

"I couldn't leave you," Seth said.

"Why not?" Pietro asked.

"There was a chance I could save you."

Pietro reached into the pocket of his pants and produced a jade key. "And I saved this for you. There is indeed a trophy at the end of the gauntlet, but it doesn't matter. The Key of Forgetting is the reason you all came here. Go, I'll be all right."

"Are you sure?"

Pietro stood, smirked, took a spinning jump into the air, and landed as a dwarf. He winked, clapped his hands, and vanished.

Seth was baffled by what he had just seen. The old man was clearly magical. Some kind of shape-shifter? Holding the key tightly, Seth turned back toward the start of the gauntlet.

He found that no spikes issued from the holes anymore, but he kept a wary eye on them until he had crossed that area. He ran down the incline and out through the bronze doors, then charged into the black rectangle in the wall.

Kendra withdrew down a hall beside Lockland, about a dozen golden figures coming their way at the speed an ordinary person would walk. The movements of the statues were not fast, but they were no longer terribly slow, either. Kendra knew there was no way to dodge forward through so many.

She held the Banishment Rod, having taken it from the atrium. She and Lockland had retreated farther away as the golden statues began to show up. Unfortunately, removing the rod from the socket had not hidden the black door.

"This way," Lockland said, guiding her around a corner. Kendra suspected that without his knowledge of the castle's twists and turns, the golden figures would have already apprehended her.

They rounded another corner to find eight golden statues coming down the hall. "They're getting faster," Kendra said.

"From now until sunrise, it only gets worse," Lockland said. "Change of plans. Follow me."

She stayed right behind him, but before long another group of golden statues cut them off. They doubled back to find yet another group closing in.

"We're in trouble," Lockland said. "I didn't want to get too far from the atrium. I wanted to work around them and keep a way back open. And now we might be sunk."

"What do you mean?" Kendra asked.

"They're making a coordinated effort to cut off all escape routes," Lockland said. "Earlier we might have tried splitting up. That will no longer help much. One last chance."

He went through a door into an empty room. It connected to another vacant room. And another. They came out into a hall with a dead end in one direction and a bunch of golden statues coming from the other way. Doubling back, they found golden statues striding through the rooms they had just crossed.

"What do we do?" Kendra asked, trying not to let panic take over.

"Create what space we can," Lockland said. He led Kendra back out into the hall, and they ran to the dead end. At least twenty golden statues advanced toward them.

"They can't change you while you wear the glove," Lockland said. "But they can grab you. Turn me to platinum."

"No," Kendra said.

"Hurry, or they'll turn me to gold and I'll be working against you," Lockland said. "Turn me to platinum, tell me to protect you, then follow me. Once I make an opening, move as fast as you can. Don't let them take hold of you. There is still a chance you can slip through without getting apprehended."

With the nearest of the golden statues less than ten

paces away, Kendra took Lockland by the hand with her gloved hand. Platinum spread quickly down his arm and across him until he was entirely transformed.

"Protect me," she said, feeling terrible for changing him and worried that it would all be for nothing.

The platinum statue of Lockland walked toward the golden statues, moving no quicker than they did. He locked hands with the first statue he met, twisting her aside, and jostled into some others. Kendra dashed into the narrow gap he made. The golden figures crowded together, hemming her in. The Banishment Rod was wrested from her grip. And then metallic hands closed around her wrists and ankles, holding her firmly.

Key of Forgetting in hand, Seth stepped into the atrium to find Celebrant waiting with at least forty golden statues. Down one hallway, golden statues were fending off silver ones. A couple of the golden figures held Kendra between them. She still wore the platinum glove. Celebrant held the Banishment Rod.

Seth's memories returned in a flood. He recalled not just what had happened inside the gauntlet but all his old memories as well. He tried to subtly slip the key into a pocket.

Humbuggle appeared just a few feet in front of him. "Well done, lad," the dwarf said. "I'm surprised you have come so far so fast. One last rhyme before the end."

"Do not interfere with my advantage, dwarf," Celebrant said.

Humbuggle raised both hands. "I don't play favorites. I'm here with information. You should want it as much as they do."

"Go on," Celebrant said.

Humbuggle cleared his throat and straightened his vest, then recited:

> *"The power of the Wizenstone*
> *Was never meant for man to own*
> *A single door impedes your way*
> *Where golden crest shines in the day*
> *The prize beyond compare is near*
> *You still have reason left to fear*
> *If you should choose to turn the key*
> *The price is your identity."*

"My identity?" Seth asked.

"Key of Forgetting," Humbuggle said. "Steep price for a big prize. Good luck!" The dwarf clapped his hands and vanished.

"You have the key," Celebrant said, glowering at Seth.

"Maybe not," Seth replied.

"I saw you put it in your pocket," Celebrant said.

"Maybe that was a candy bar," Seth tried.

"It was a key made of jade," Celebrant said. "And Humbuggle congratulated you."

Seth removed it from his pocket.

Celebrant smiled. "Well done. This has been quite a game."

"If you say so," Seth said.

"What if I gave you and your sister a sporting chance?" Celebrant said.

"I'd be incredibly suspicious," Seth said.

"Taking the glove from Kendra and turning her to gold would be no problem," Celebrant said. "Same with changing you to gold. But that would end our game, and dragons love a good hunt. I haven't had such sport in ages. And wouldn't you prefer a small chance over none?"

"I'm listening," Seth said.

"Do you know where the golden crest shines in the day?" Celebrant asked.

Seth glanced at Kendra. She shrugged. "Not really," Seth said.

"The second-highest tower of this castle has a golden crest on the outside," Celebrant said. "The tallest tower does not. There are only two locked doors in this entire castle. Have you noticed all the doors are unlocked? Even in the dungeon."

"Now that you mention it, yes," Seth said.

"The room atop the tallest tower is locked and holds the king and queen," Celebrant said. "The second-highest tower is also locked. And the room has no windows."

"Sounds like a candidate," Seth said.

"You get there by taking that hall," Celebrant said, pointing. "Turn left at the first intersection. After the turn, the hall leads into a room with a big chandelier. At the rear of the room are two staircases. Take the right one. Go down the hall and up the stairs at the end."

"This seems like a lot of help," Seth said.

"I am giving you a head start," Celebrant said. "Use it how you prefer." He turned toward Kendra. "Release the girl."

The golden statues holding Kendra let go of her.

"Clear the way," Celebrant said, and the golden statues opened a path to the hall he had first indicated. He repeated his instructions.

"Can we have the rod?" Kendra asked.

Celebrant grinned. "I can't make this too easy. Go, if you choose. I won't be far behind."

Seth glanced at Kendra. She gave a nod. They started running.

"You know this is a trick," Seth said. "He just wants us to open the door."

"And it's the one chance we have," Kendra said. "Better than getting turned to gold."

"I agree," Seth said. "Celebrant had us. Now we have some room to move. Where is Lockland?"

"We got cornered, so I turned him to platinum," Kendra said. "It was to keep him from getting changed to gold."

They reached an intersection. To the right, Seth saw golden statues approaching at a quick walk. He and Kendra turned left.

"Obregon and Tregain joined Lomo and me in the gauntlet," Seth said. "If they all live, they'll come out before long."

"Nobody else?" Kendra asked.

"The dwarf was there in disguise," Seth said. He noticed more golden statues coming their way down a side hall.

"We still don't know who made the gong ring," Kendra said. "The late arrival."

"Stay ready for anything," Seth said.

They arrived at the room with the large chandelier.

"Do we go to the tower?" Kendra asked.

Seth slowed, walking toward the stairs at the back of the room. "What if we run off and hide? Could that work?"

"I don't think so," Kendra said, wishing she could say otherwise. "We can't leave the castle, and wherever we hide, they will eventually find us."

Seth nodded. "Plus I think the statues are corralling us. Or maybe just still after us. They won't slow until sunrise."

"But to risk your identity?" Kendra asked. "To forget yourself?"

"It's obvious Celebrant wants somebody else to unlock the door," Seth said. "Enough that he's letting us do it unsupervised." They reached the right-hand stairs at the rear of the room.

"Do you think turning the key has to be voluntary?" Kendra asked.

"Looks like Celebrant thinks so," Seth said. "The poem talks about choosing."

"Do we keep going?" Kendra asked.

Golden statues entered the far side of the room. Seth started up the stairs.

"If we're too slow, Celebrant may catch up," Seth said. "Getting to the door first is better than getting caught again."

"Lomo will get mobbed when he comes out of the black door," Kendra said. "We're out of allies."

"This door is the last obstacle," Seth said. "We can do this. I'm going to open it. Once I do, I'll probably forget a lot. When I went for the key, I lost so many memories, but I kept a sense of who I was. Losing my identity sounds more extreme. Hopefully, when you get the Wizenstone and end the game, my memories will return like they did when I left the gauntlet."

They rushed down a hall to a winding stairway. No golden statues were currently in view.

"I don't have the Banishment Rod," Kendra said.

"If the Wizenstone is so powerful, you can use that to fight off the demon," Seth said.

"I don't know how the Wizenstone works," Kendra said. "The poem warned it's not for people to own."

"We can't let Celebrant get it," Seth said. "We have to flip this on them somehow."

"We could try to ditch the key," Kendra said.

They were passing doors as they climbed the stairs. "They have our escape routes cut off," Seth said. "If we chuck the key out a window, they'll find it before long. We're cornered. We have nowhere to hide."

"It seems clear that Celebrant *wants* us to open the door!" Kendra said. "Isn't that the last thing we should do?"

"It's going to happen either way," Seth said, panting with the exertion of running up the stairs. "If we wait, he'll have somebody else do it. If we unlock the door quickly, maybe you'll have a chance to do something before Celebrant arrives. Lock him out? Destroy the stone? Use it?"

"I'm not sure anything will work," Kendra said. "I think we blew it. I think we lost."

"At least I won't remember," Seth said.

"That isn't funny," Kendra said.

"Hopefully you can undo the forgetting somehow," Seth said. "If not, I'll still be me. I just won't know it. I'll get back to myself eventually. I'll relearn."

"I can't think of anything worse to lose than knowing who I am," Kendra said.

"I don't *want* to," Seth said, feeling tears sting his eyes and clenching his fists, determined not to cry. "We're trying to save the world. Small price if it helps."

They reached the top of the stairs and found themselves facing an ornate door made of silver-gray metal and set with gems. "There it is," Kendra said. "Are you sure about this?"

They approached the door together. Seth held up the key. "It wasn't too bad in that room when I lost memories," he said, trying to console her. "You don't really know what you're missing."

"That's sort of the most tragic part," Kendra said. "This is brave of you, Seth. Maybe too brave."

He shrugged. "I need to leave you time to try to do something." He pushed the key into the keyhole. "Sorry to check out. Good luck. Tell everybody I love them. Even Knox. Especially you."

Seth turned the jade key.

And swooned, staggering a little.

He stared at the door, perplexed.

He did not know where he was. He held up his hands, but they were unfamiliar. He seemed to be a kid. A young teen? He did not know his own name.

How did he know nothing about himself or where he was? Wasn't he somebody? What could possibly have happened?

"Seth, are you all right?"

He turned to face the girl who had spoken. She looked at him with concern, but nothing about her was familiar. Could his name be Seth? Did this young woman know him? She looked a little older than him.

Who was she?

And who was the man approaching behind her?

CHAPTER THIRTY-TWO

Wizenstone

Kendra held her breath as Seth turned the Key of Forgetting. He stood still for a moment, staring at the ornate door.

"Seth, are you all right?" she asked.

He turned and looked at her without recognition. Her heart sank—she could only assume that his mind had been wiped. Her brother no longer knew her. Or himself.

Then he looked over her shoulder with interest.

Before Kendra could turn, strong arms wrapped around her from behind, pinning her arms to her sides. "Don't struggle," a voice spoke in her ear. "We have little time."

She knew that voice!

"Ronodin?" Kendra asked.

"Celebrant is coming," Ronodin said. "We need to get into that room."

"What's going on?" Seth asked.

"This girl has a dangerous glove," Ronodin said. "It turns people to platinum. I can't risk her using it on us."

Kendra tried to twist her wrist to touch Ronodin, but he squeezed her too tightly, keeping a firm hand on her forearm just behind the glove. "Seth, attack him," she cried.

"She's trying to fool you," Ronodin said. "I'm your brother. Don't fall for her tricks."

"It's not a trick," Kendra said. "I'm your sister."

"She's a liar," Ronodin said. "Look who is attacking who. I didn't draw a weapon. I'm not trying to kill her. I just don't want her using the glove on us."

"Does the glove turn people to platinum?" Seth asked.

"Yes," Kendra said. "I'm using it to protect us. This is Ronodin, the dark unicorn."

Seth scrunched his brow. "He doesn't look like a unicorn."

"Kendra," Ronodin said, "we have no time. They will be here in a moment. Take off the glove. You can keep it. Put it back on when Celebrant arrives. I just need insurance you won't use it on us."

"What is this?" Seth asked. "What happened to me? What's going on?"

Kendra could hear footsteps climbing the stairs. Ronodin let her use her ungloved hand to remove the glove.

"Turning the key to that door erased your memory," Ronodin said. "For now, just watch."

Ronodin released Kendra but stayed near. She considered putting the glove back on and trying to touch him, but the dark unicorn was right—she had no time. If he went for the Wizenstone, she would put on the glove and tag him.

Kendra grabbed the knob and pushed the door open. They entered a windowless room with glowing globes of light and a pedestal at the center. Atop the pedestal sat a cut gemstone the size of a baseball. Geometrically complex, the crystalline jewel contained faint, scintillating hints of all colors in existence.

"The Wizenstone," Kendra said.

Ronodin closed the door and briefly examined the knob. "Can't lock it from the inside," he said.

Seth stood off to one side. "That looks expensive," he said.

"It's magical," Kendra replied. "What do I do?"

"Be smart," Ronodin said. "You don't have the rod, and Celebrant let you come here."

"We can't let him get it," Kendra said.

"No," Ronodin said. "We can't."

"Whose side are you on?" Kendra asked.

Ronodin laughed as if she were ridiculous. "Mine." He glanced at Seth. "And my brother's."

"You're not his brother," Kendra corrected. "I'm his sister."

"Who is Celebrant?" Seth asked.

"Bad guy," Kendra said. "King of the dragons."

"What she said," Ronodin agreed. "Kendra, Humbuggle is the greatest trickster the world has seen. He has guarded the Wizenstone for ages—long before coming here. Claiming the Wizenstone is bound to be more complicated than this appears."

"So I should do nothing?" Kendra asked.

Ronodin gave her a measuring stare. "With Celebrant coming, if I thought I could just take the Wizenstone, what do you suppose I would be doing right now?"

Kendra frowned. "It might not be the real stone? Or it might be booby-trapped?"

"You're starting to think like a survivor," Ronodin said.

"But Celebrant is coming with the Banishment Rod," Kendra said.

"Isn't it exciting?" Ronodin asked. "Such high stakes, and all we can really do is improvise. We may not make it. We're too close to the action on this one, but we can't let him have the Wizenstone."

"I can't let you have it either," Kendra said.

"The feeling is mutual," Ronodin replied with a grin.

The door opened. Celebrant entered, the Banishment Rod in his hand. Obregon followed. Behind them, Kendra caught a glimpse of gold and silver statues fighting before Obregon closed the door.

"Nobody has endeavored to claim the jewel?" Celebrant asked.

Kendra tugged on her glove. "I will if you loan me the Banishment Rod."

"Such a generous offer," Celebrant said. "Thank you for granting us access and then stepping aside. I'll make your endings swift." His eyes shifted to Ronodin. "What are you doing here?"

"Wouldn't have missed it," Ronodin said.

"You were listening when we spoke outside the black door," Celebrant said.

"I'm a good listener," Ronodin said.

"You got here just ahead of us," Kendra realized.

"I hid in the room below as you went by," Ronodin said. "What matters is we are here."

Celebrant narrowed his eyes at Ronodin. "Do you mean to stop me?"

"I just like to be in the know," Ronodin said.

"I don't trust you," Celebrant said.

"If you did, you would be the first in a long time," Ronodin said.

Celebrant held out the Banishment Rod to Obregon. "Swear to me once more," he said.

"My king," Obregon replied, dropping to one knee. "You have always had my complete loyalty. May you reign forever. If you grant me the honor of retrieving the stone, I will stand in your place, claiming it in your name. I swear on my honor as a dragon, and on my ancestors and on my descendants, the stone is yours if I retrieve it."

"Take the rod," Celebrant said.

Obregon rose and accepted the Banishment Rod.

"Quickly, now," Celebrant said.

With the rod in one hand, Obregon strode to the pedestal, paused to examine the surrounding area for a moment, and then reached out to pick up the Wizenstone with his free hand. As soon as his fingers touched the surface of the jewel, he froze. For a moment, his body began to jerk and then to vibrate intensely. With a flash of light, he changed to ash: clothes, breastplate, and all. The Banishment Rod clattered to the floor as the particles of ash spread out, percolating downward.

"Whoa," Seth said. "That guy turned into confetti."

Kendra swallowed drily, relieved she had not tried to grab the jewel. She glanced at Ronodin, who watched Celebrant.

The Dragon King glared at the Wizenstone, his body tense but still, fury held in restraint. After a moment he relaxed and folded his arms.

"Your turn to try, your majesty?" Ronodin ventured.

"Not yet," Celebrant growled.

"I take it your golden minions cannot enter?" Ronodin asked.

"Only those in possession of themselves may cross the threshold," Celebrant said, enraged eyes never leaving the Wizenstone.

The door burst open, and Tregain stumbled into the room. "I'm not too late!" he exclaimed. Lunging at Seth, Tregain grabbed his hand with the silver glove. Seth yanked his hand away and did not turn to silver.

"Interesting," Ronodin said. "Not in here."

Tregain glanced at Celebrant, then at the rod on the floor near the pedestal. Tregain charged for the rod. Celebrant took a step to intercept him, then stopped. Tregain scooped up the rod and grabbed the Wizenstone. He did not move after taking hold of the jewel, nor did the gemstone. Tregain's body began to tremble and spasm until he vanished in a burst of ash. The rod clattered to the floor again.

Kendra stared in amazement and horror. How was anyone supposed to claim the stone if it turned whoever touched it to ashes? Having the rod seemed irrelevant. No need to drive away a demon if your body evaporated.

Celebrant turned to Ronodin. "How do I claim it?" the Dragon King asked.

"I'm not sure," Ronodin said.

Kendra looked at Seth. He watched from off to the side, clearly bewildered, trying to make sense of what he was seeing.

The Banishment Rod lay unattended on the floor. Should she try it? Wouldn't she just turn to ash as well? Did the person have to be worthy? Might she be worthy? Her intentions were good. What if she waited? Celebrant did not seem to be in a hurry to take the risk of grabbing the stone. But he didn't have to rush. More dragons would probably come. He had the luxury of time.

Kendra knew her opportunity to do something might not last for long. But what could she do? She most needed to prevent Celebrant from obtaining the Wizenstone. Or Ronodin. Given enough time, Celebrant would probably succeed. Kendra looked at the rod on the ground.

And suddenly an idea occurred.

She dashed forward.

"Kendra, are you sure?" Ronodin asked.

Celebrant hushed him.

She was not sure. But she was sure enough. It was worth a try. Celebrant would not be kind to her as a prisoner. She was mildly surprised to still be alive. Seth was currently defenseless. She might not get another chance to affect the outcome.

Kendra picked up the Banishment Rod, pointed it at the Wizenstone, and shouted, "Begone!"

The rod thrummed in her grasp. In a blink, the Wizenstone vanished.

Only the empty pedestal remained.

Relief flooded through Kendra as she glanced over to find Ronodin smirking and Celebrant shouting. The Dragon King glowered at her, veins protruding in his neck.

Humbuggle the dwarf appeared between them. "Interesting choice," he said. "I'm afraid we'll have to call this contest a draw."

"Where is the stone?" Celebrant bellowed.

Humbuggle waved a dismissive hand. "Far away. Banished. None of your affair anymore. If you're angry, think about poor Tregain—he waited hundreds of years, only to get obliterated at the end."

"The Wizenstone is not meant to be owned," Ronodin said.

"I provided that hint in the poem," Humbuggle said. "Some people don't trust plain language."

"So you never own it," Ronodin went on. "You just set up contests for others to try to win it. Meanwhile, it is in your custody, and you use its powers to create your games."

"Enough out of you," Humbuggle said. With a clap of his hands, the Banishment Rod disappeared from Kendra's grasp and went to him.

"It must be possible to win the contest, or else the magic wouldn't hold up," Ronodin said. "But you rig the game so the best a contestant can do is send the Wizenstone away, ending the contest and letting you start another."

"Nobody likes a heckler," Humbuggle said.

"You're the demon guarding the Wizenstone," Ronodin said. "The only hope of winning the contest is replacing you—"

Humbuggle leveled the rod at Ronodin and called out, "Return!"

Ronodin vanished.

"What a bore," Humbuggle said. "Much too chatty. Some might say the curse of Stormguard Castle has ended. Some might call Kendra a heroine. I just say the contest is over, ending in a draw. The gloves have lost all power, and those who became gold, silver, or platinum are freed. The added passages I created are undone."

Kendra felt enormous relief to hear that Tanu and the others who had been turned to precious metals would be all right. She would need to go get Knox from the Quiet Box.

"What about Jaleesa's arm?" Celebrant asked.

"She chose to attack after knowing the rules," Humbuggle said. "Lost limbs are lost limbs. Personal injuries are personal injuries."

"Obregon?" Celebrant asked.

"He chose to claim the unclaimable," Humbuggle said. "He and Tregain are as dead as they could be."

"What about Seth?" Kendra asked, hoping for good news.

"There have to be some consequences," Humbuggle said. "The boy made his choice with knowledge of the outcome. Access to the Wizenstone comes at a price."

"Can't you undo it?" Kendra asked. "Can't I do something?"

"Rules are rules," Humbuggle said.

"Rules?" Kendra asked, sick with worry for her brother, hoping there might be some loophole. "We were playing for the Wizenstone and we don't have it. Doesn't that violate the rules? Shouldn't you take away the punishments?"

"You chose to send the Wizenstone away," Humbuggle said. "You terminated the contest. The king and queen are freed. Life at Stormguard Castle can be much as it was before. I'll send you home, then I'll go elsewhere too. I salute you brave contestants. To have survived and ended this contest is an outcome only you have achieved."

"What if I don't want to go just yet?" Kendra asked.

"Not really your choice," Humbuggle said. He swung the rod and cried, "Return!"

CHAPTER THIRTY-THREE

Taken

Kendra stood in her bedroom at Blackwell Keep in her socks. Though it was dark, she could see. She had her abilities back! Somewhere beyond her room, unsettling sounds flavored the night—forlorn howls, desperate shrieks, and ominous drums. The noises of Midsummer Eve were no longer screened out.

Was it really still the same night? So much had happened.

Was she truly safe? Back with her grandparents? Behind protective barriers?

It was disorienting to go from a cursed castle surrounded by enemies to her very own bedroom at the keep. But if she was disoriented, Seth must be utterly confused.

Kendra went out her door to visit his room and saw Mendigo racing down the hall holding Seth, who was squirming. They disappeared around a corner before she could really register what she was seeing.

"Mendigo?" Kendra called, running after the man-sized puppet. "Come here!"

Outside, the night remained tumultuous. Maybe the limberjack couldn't hear her. Maybe Seth was scared and had asked Mendigo to take him someplace.

But why had he been squirming?

Kendra dashed around the corner, down some steps, and out a door into a courtyard. Some clouds faintly brightening on the horizon hinted at the approaching dawn. The night remained as boisterous as ever. Mendigo raced across the courtyard, still clutching Seth. Rain began to fall, and lightning forked across the sky, the glare sharply illuminating her brother and the sprinting limberjack. Thunder growled.

"Stop Mendigo!" Kendra shouted to anyone who might hear. "Something is wrong!"

She raced after them, feeling sick with worry. The rain fell harder. She should have known something was wrong when Mendigo had refused to accompany her to Skyhold. What was Seth thinking right now?

The minotaur Brunwin jumped down half a stairway to join the chase. A dwarf was running after Mendigo as well. The limberjack exited the courtyard through a door to the storerooms.

Kendra ran through the rain as fast as she could. Lightning flashed again, brighter than before, loud thunder following promptly. Where was Mendigo going? Would the puppet try to hurt Seth?

She burst through the door in time to see Mendigo entering a storeroom down the hall. Seth bucked and slapped the puppet, trying to wrench himself free. They both passed out of view again.

Kendra kept running. Was this really happening? After they had survived all the danger at Stormguard Castle?

Brunwin caught up to Kendra at the storeroom door. The dwarf was a few paces behind them. Mendigo had cast aside several crates and barrels. Kendra no longer saw Seth. As she and the minotaur approached, Mendigo jumped into an open barrel and crouched out of sight.

By the time they looked inside the barrel, the limberjack was gone.

"Seth!" Kendra cried, looking around. "Seth?"

Her eyes returned to the barrel.

She remembered Knox telling her how the barrel had gone missing after he and Tess had come to Wyrmroost. The goblin guard had been murdered.

Everyone had assumed the killer must have come through the barrel.

What if the killer had been Mendigo?

What if the puppet had then stashed the barrel in a storeroom?

And had waited.

And now Seth was gone.

"Seth!" Kendra screamed once again, more for herself this time.

Wherever her brother was, she knew he couldn't hear her.

CHAPTER THIRTY-FOUR

Apprentice

Seth stood in a dim room lit by a single torch. The space smelled like ancient books and rotting ingredients. The strange puppet that had brought him here waited against a shadowy wall, upright but otherwise inert.

"I was worried they would steal you away from me," Ronodin said. "I had to act fast."

"Seemed like your wooden friend stole me," Seth said. "Where are we? You're the guy from the castle."

"Mendigo *rescued* you," Ronodin corrected. "You're quite powerful, Seth. Those people wiped your memory and wanted to recruit you to their side."

"Kendra told me she is my sister," Seth said.

"Maybe in a sense, once, long ago," Ronodin said. "As a child, you sometimes fought on the same side as she did. I was like that too, trying to please everyone, a lifetime ago.

Then you began to learn about your dark powers. You are my top apprentice. You are a shadow charmer, Seth."

"We're on the bad side?" Seth asked.

Ronodin laughed lightly. "We're on our own side."

Seth stared at him, unsure what to believe. Ever since he had found himself standing outside the fancy door, Seth had gone from one tense, nonsensical situation to the next. People had argued, and some had gotten turned to powder. A magical dwarf had appeared. Seth had been teleported to a dark room and carried through the rain by a giant wooden puppet. Then getting stuffed in a barrel and lifted out had somehow brought him here.

"How does the barrel work?" Seth asked.

"That barrel connects to the barrel at Blackwell Keep," Ronodin said. "Technically, it is a separate manifestation of the same barrel. In effect, having separate barrels that are also the same can allow a person to move from one place to another. I have my own ways of traveling. Helps if you know the Underking."

"Why would you have a barrel that connects to where Kendra lives?" Seth asked.

"A friend owed me a favor," Ronodin said. "He is called the Sphinx. Sooner or later I will introduce you. The barrel was delivered to him by a pair of goblins who escaped their dungeon. He gave it to me. A friend of his, Vernaz, helped reconstruct Mendigo, the puppet who assisted in your rescue. A feature he added lets the puppet receive overriding commands from afar."

"What now?" Seth asked.

"We start rebuilding you," Ronodin said. "Do you remember your powers?"

"I don't think I have powers," Seth said.

"You understand many languages," Ronodin said. "You can communicate with the undead, and often you can persuade them. You are nearly invisible when moving in faint light. And some abilities are just beginning to surface."

"Like what?" Seth asked.

"Like extinguishing light," Ronodin said. "Quenching fire. That torch, for example. You see it with your eyes."

"Of course."

"Feel it with your mind," Ronodin said. "I know you can. Feel the hot center, where the fuel is combusting."

"Weird," Seth said. "I can feel it."

"You're a shadow charmer," Ronodin said. "You're sensitive to light and heat. Some of the undead are not far from us. Seek their coldness as you sought the heat."

"Yes," Seth said, noticing the whispery presences. "Three of them. That way." He pointed.

"Very good," Ronodin said. "Can you sense how frigid they are?"

Seth shivered. "Yes."

"Borrow that coldness. There are other ways to find coldness, but this is the surest, easiest way."

"Borrow it how?" Seth asked. He could feel the cold presences with his mind, just as he could feel the core of the flaming torch.

"Bring the cold to the hot place on the torch," Ronodin said.

"How do I do that?"

"Think of it going there. Realize that by feeling it you can also influence it. Invite the cold of the undead to the hottest part of the torch."

Seth tried.

The torch sputtered.

"Not gently," Ronodin said. "All at once. Force their coldness to the torch."

Gritting his teeth, Seth pulled the cold to the torch. He felt the cold smother the heat.

And the torch went out.

Seth blinked in the darkness, surprised that the mental effort had worked.

"Very well done," Ronodin said, unseen but nearby.

"I guess I do have powers," Seth said.

"You're only beginning to scratch the surface," Ronodin said. "Seth, my brother, we are going to make beautiful music together."

Acknowledgments

I'm excited to have book two of Dragonwatch complete. The story is kicking into gear, and there is a lot more to tell in the final three books. Thank you for reading this one. If you are enjoying the story, please spread the word.

I write my books alone, but getting them into print is definitely a group effort. I'd like to thank my Dragonwatch publishers, Shadow Mountain and Simon & Schuster, for their ongoing patience and support. I don't release my books until I feel they are done right, and that can take lots of time and effort.

Many thanks go out to those who helped with the editing, including Emily Watts, Chris Schoebinger, and Liesa Abrams. Their insightful feedback has helped improve this story in numerous ways. My agent, Simon Lipskar, is always an invaluable resource. I also received useful thoughts from friends like Jason Conforto, Amy Frandsen, and Erlyn Madsen. Other friends who helped read for problems include Rosalyn Mull, Natalie Conforto, Cherie Mull, Tucker Davis, Pamela Mull, and Mary Mull.

Once again Brandon Dorman provided awesome illustrations for the story, with direction from Richard Erickson. Others at the publisher who assisted in the project include

Rachael Ward, Jill Schaugaard, Dave Brown, John Rose, and Ilise Levine.

As always, I owe thanks to my family for their love and support. My kids put up with Daddy working odd hours and disappearing for book tours at times. I love you, Sadie, Chase, Rose, and Calvin, and always will.

I'm so behind on responding to emails, but if anyone wants to get in touch with me, I have an author page on Facebook that you can follow, on Instagram I am writerbrandon, and on Twitter I am at @brandonmull. I am honored that you have taken the time to read this book, and will try to keep good ones coming. If you like Fablehaven and Dragonwatch, take a peek at some of my other stuff, like the Five Kingdoms series.

Reading Group Guide

1. At the start of this book, Kendra was worried the dragons would retaliate for how she and Seth had defied them. In what ways was she right? What trouble did she not anticipate?

2. In what ways does Seth like dragons? In what ways does he dislike dragons? If you could go to Wyrmroost, would you want to see dragons or keep away from them? Explain your answer.

3. Why did Knox want to go to Wyrmroost? Did his reasons for being there change as he spent time at the sanctuary? If so, in what ways?

4. What trouble was caused by the way Knox came to Wyrmroost? What might he have done differently if he had been able to anticipate the consequences of his actions? Share an experience when you made a choice that you later regretted.

4. Raxtus found himself torn between loyalty to his friends and loyalty to his family. Why do you think he made the choices that he did? When you make a hard choice, what helps you know whether you made the right one?

6. Some dragons began to challenge Celebrant after

Kendra stood up to him. Why do you think that happened? Do you expect it will continue to happen? Why or why not?

7. Why do you think Tanu took some risks to get potion ingredients from a dead dragon? What would you have done in his position?

8. Ronodin tried to help the dragons win their war against the caretakers. Why do you imagine he was helping them? Does Ronodin have any likable qualities? If so, what are they? Does he have unlikable qualities? If so, what are they? Do you think he would make a good ally? Why or why not?

9. Why do you think Kendra and Seth decided to visit Stormguard Castle? Was it a good choice? Support your opinion.

10. Why did the three sons of Hollorix get stuck in a stalemate for so long? What did Tregain and Heath seem to want most? What did Lockland seem to want most? Do you agree with Lockland's choice to stay out of the conflict? Why or why not?

11. The contest created by Humbuggle caused the curse that fell upon Stormguard Castle. Why do you think the dwarf created the contest? Do you see him as a good guy, a bad guy, or something in between? Explain.

12. This book ends with new trouble forming for some of the main characters. Are you glad to know there are more books coming in the series? How would you feel if the story ended now?

As a bonus in this paperback edition, I thought it would be interesting to show a scene from Eve's point of view, to let you know what happened to her after she was left behind at Terrabelle, and perhaps reveal a little more about the Fair Folk in the process.

Eve

Eve used her elbows to scoot along the crawl space. Sometimes being young was an advantage—most adults would not fit into the snug confines between the floor of her bedroom and the ceiling of the level below. Even at her size, it was a tight squeeze, and she had to be willing to push through spiderwebs and ignore the squeaks of scurrying rodents.

Her father would be furious if he knew she sometimes used the hole she had carved in the floor of her closet to squirm to a place where she could hear conversations in the Red Room. Only his top advisers were invited inside that secret chamber. Most of the people he worked with didn't even know the Red Room existed.

Fortunately for her father, Eve was not working against him. The information she overheard was never shared. And fortunately for her, she had never been caught listening.

And if he caught her today? She was already in enormous trouble for running off to help Seth after the Feast of Welcome. How much worse could it get? During her initial scolding, Eve had begged her father to throw her in the dungeon so she could join Seth and the others, but he had not wanted to reward her with company. As usual, she had been confined to her room.

Though Eve had been punished for sneaking out before, getting caught was a rarity. She doubted whether the designers of the city knew as many secret ways as she did, and she could also use her powers to disguise herself. When she had lost privileges in the past, Eve had preserved her independence by continuing to sneak out.

An *X* scratched into the floor marked the spot to place her ear. At dinner her father had told a servant that he must not be disturbed after the meal. For Lord Dalgorel, that usually meant a meeting, and the most important meetings happened in the Red Room, so with hopeful anticipation, Eve pressed her ear against the floor.

The first voice she heard belonged to her mother.

"Her desire to help is natural. This is not wickedness that needs to be purged, but rather a virtue she must learn to manage."

Eve smiled. They were talking about her! And her mother was defending her. This was ideal. Father was never more candid than when speaking to her mother. If Eve could learn what they were saying behind her back, she could better know how to disarm their frustration.

"I never called it wicked," Father said. "But I believe her behavior has grown dangerous. We could have lost her."

Eve felt her face flushing. It was nice to know her father cared.

"Living is dangerous," Mother said.

"Reckless living is unnecessarily dangerous," Father said. "We're lucky she is alive. Running off to help those young caretakers was careless. It jeopardized her safety, as well as our neutrality status."

Eve scrunched her face. Father seemed to worry about nothing so much as keeping the Fair Folk neutral.

"Have you grown fond of our neutrality?"

"You know I hate it," Father said.

Eve let out a little gasp—she never heard her father disparage neutrality, even in private.

"Can you blame her for disliking it as well?" Mother asked.

"I don't find fault with her convictions," Father insisted. "She needs to master her emotions. We all live in reality. She is our daughter and has a responsibility to protect her people. I must do my duty, and so must she."

Eve closed her eyes for a moment in disappointment. This was the familiar version of her father.

"The sanctuary is in real jeopardy," Mother fretted. "Could the hour have come to leave neutrality behind?"

"Don't tempt me," Father said. "We help where we

can, and within reason. I do not set policy for the Fair Folk. I execute the orders of the supreme authority. That is my role. Abandoning neutrality could end us. It is not my decision to make."

Eve heard a sharp knock and tried to cover her surprised gasp. She looked back over her shoulder, unsure where the knock had come from.

After a brief pause, her father called, "No interruptions, please."

Eve exhaled in relief. Apparently, it had been a knock on the door to his chamber. Nobody disturbed her father when he was in a meeting unless the matter was extremely urgent.

The knock came again.

Only a true emergency could have prompted a second knock.

"Come," her father said.

She heard the door open. "Apologies for the disruption, Lord Dalgorel," a voice reported, clearly nervous. "Most of the prisoners have fled the dungeon."

"A warranted intrusion," her father approved. "Which prisoners?"

"Seth Sorenson; the nipsie known as Calvin; the potion master Tanu; Knox, the cousin of Seth . . ." The voice faltered for a moment. "And Lomo."

"Lomo?" her father asked. "After all this time?"

"Indeed" came the reply.

"And the satyrs?" her father asked. "Tess, the cousin of Kendra?"

"They remain," the voice responded.

"How did the escapees depart?" her father asked.

"We believe they were carried in miniature by Creya the eagle," the voice answered. "Unless it was a diversion."

"Thank you for the news," her father said. "Summon my advisers. We will convene after I finish this discussion with my wife."

"Very well," the voice said.

Eve heard a door close.

"Lomo's departure is a surprise!" Mother exclaimed.

"Somewhat," Father said. "We knew he would leave sooner or later. What surprises me is that anyone thinks our guest facility is a legitimate dungeon."

"Having a dungeon allows us to host dignitaries longer than normal etiquette would dictate," Mother said. "And the security is lax enough to allow them to leave when they desire."

"By comfortably hosting our prisoners, we keep to neutrality by not formally offering anyone sanctuary," Father said. "A prisoner is not a guest. I'm glad Lomo took the opportunity to depart. These are stormy times. At least one of our number will be helping the cause."

"Even if we cannot officially approve," Mother said.

Eve felt hope kindling inside. She had been unaware her parents were so deliberately trying to help.

"We can't ever encourage the behavior," Father said. "But every society has outlaws. Frankly, I wish we had a few more like Lomo. We'll make efforts to retrieve him.

And we will quietly hope he eludes capture long enough to do some good."

Eve was unaccustomed to hearing positive words about Lomo from her father. She tended to assume her father was out of touch, but there was clearly much she didn't know. An increase of respect for him filled her chest. But why couldn't he speak admiringly about *her* behind closed doors?

"Tell me about your interview with Dromadus," Mother said.

"The dragon does not foresee an end to the war," Father said.

Eve's jaw dropped. She had never imagined her father would visit the former dragon king.

"What insights did the conversation yield?" Mother asked.

"He is fond of the young caretakers," Father said. "It is hard not to sympathize with them—they are brave and committed, but woefully inexperienced. I could see that Dromadus felt tempted to aid them. I never would have expected such an inclination from him."

"He has a peaceful nature," Mother said. "He sympathizes with the weak."

"He is also a realist," Father said. "The young caretakers have true hearts, but they are drastically outmatched against Celebrant. He knows it is only a matter of time before the dragons seize control of Wyrmroost."

"What will become of Terrabelle? And the other protected territories?"

"Dromadus believes the dragons have their sights set on world domination," Father said. "Celebrant and his cronies will probably move on from Wyrmroost once the barriers are down. But they will return after they have crushed Selona."

"If that day comes, we will be isolated, without allies," Mother said. "Our defenses will not hold indefinitely against the onslaught."

"At present, our hopes lie in the hands of others," Father said. "Perhaps Dromadus is wrong. The young caretakers have performed better than anyone expected. If Kendra and Seth take the proper precautions, they could last a good while."

"Celebrant will be making moves of his own," Mother said.

"Eventually he will succeed," Father said. "Our options are bleak. Could we help stabilize Wyrmroost if we break neutrality? Undoubtedly. But the cost! We might undo the protections for Fair Folk everywhere. The last time the Fair Folk went to war, all who participated were annihilated. We could usher in the destruction of those who remain. We could leave Selona vulnerable. If our mother country falls, it could create a permanent imbalance, an unending age of dragons. The world might never recover."

"Do you really believe the world can't get along without the Fair Folk?" Mother asked.

"We're the original source of all magic," Father said.

"The fairies say the same," Mother said. "And the demons."

"We're at least one of the original sources," Father said. "And we've been the only consistent enforcers of balance. Enough that we were granted incredible power for pledging to remain neutral in disputes among the other magical races."

"But I fear our neutrality has removed us from our roles as enforcers of balance," Mother said. "What do we enforce by doing nothing?"

"At Selona, our people maintain checks and balances to prevent any race from becoming dominant," Father said.

"Unless some group becomes powerful enough to destroy us," Mother said. "We are talking about rampaging dragons. If *we* fall, everything could fall. It hurts to do nothing. I fear it is eroding the character of our people."

"Deliberate neutrality is far from nothing," Father said. "It requires restraint and patience."

"I envy Lomo," Mother said.

"As do I," Father replied.

"How can we help without breaking neutrality?" Mother asked.

"It's a hazardous game," Father said. "One I can't play directly. With my leadership role, I have to follow the decrees from Selona. Whatever my personal convictions, I must keep the promises and disavow those who break them."

"Poor Eve," Mother said. "She only wants to help."

Eve found herself silently nodding. She wanted to

make a difference. If rebel Fair Folk were needed, why not her?

"I wish more of our warriors had her drive," Father said. "Not only is she too young and untrained, but she is our child. Until she reaches adulthood, we are responsible for her actions. Her rebellions carry too much weight."

Eve scowled. It wasn't fair! Her choices were her own. Why should anyone else get blamed for her behavior?

"Her rebellions are the adventures of a child," Mother said.

"I fear for her," Father said. "We're not talking about swiping a neighbor's pumpkin. Or letting a stray cat follow her home. These times are perilous. Under present conditions, the adventures of a child could prove fatal."

"What do we do?" Mother asked.

"We manage one crisis at a time," Father said. "I believe Dromadus knows more than he is telling. I learned all I could. If Kendra and Seth could reach him again, he might have more to share."

"And our daughter?" Mother asked.

"We train her," Father said. "Until she learns, we treat her like a prisoner."

Eve lifted her ear from the floor, the muscles in her legs tense and quivering. It was hard to express outrage silently. She started scooting back toward her room. It was clear the conversation was ending, and her mother might visit her room afterward. The next knock could be on her door.

Eve had heard enough. Her father wanted to treat her like a prisoner instead of like a daughter? She hoped he remembered how easily prisoners of the Fair Folk tended to escape.

Adventure awaits in the Five Kingdoms—

by the *New York Times* bestselling author Brandon Mull.

"*Keeper of the Lost Cities* is a little bit *Alice's Adventures in Wonderland*, a little bit *Lord of the Rings*, and a little bit *Harry Potter*. And it's all fun!"

—MICHAEL BUCKLEY,
New York Times bestselling author of the Sisters Grimm and NERDS series

NEW YORK TIMES AND USA TODAY BESTSELLING SERIES

"A delightful and dangerous adventure with complex characters and relationships you'll root for to the end of time."

—LISA McMANN,
New York Times bestselling author of *The Unwanteds*, on *Keeper of the Lost Cities*

EBOOK EDITIONS ALSO AVAILABLE

ALADDIN
SIMONANDSCHUSTER.COM/KIDS